D0810042

THE LONDON BOROUGH
www.bromley.gov.uk

Please return/renew this item
by the last date shown.
Books may also be renewed by
phone and Internet.

to hear fro
her websi

30128 80355 418 0

Trish Morey is an Australian who's also spent time living and working in New Zealand and England. Now she's settled with her husband and four young daughters in a special part of South Australia, surrounded by orchards and bushland and visited by the occasional koala and kangaroo. With a life-long love of reading, she penned her first book at age eleven, after which life, career and a growing family kept her busy until once again she could indulge her desire to create characters and stories, this time in romance. Having her work published is a dream come true. Visit Trish at her website www.trishmorey.com.

Jessica Steele lives in the county of Worcestershire, with her super husband, Peter, and their gorgeous Staffordshire bull terrier, Florence. Any spare time is spent enjoying her three main hobbies: reading espionage novels, gardening (she has a great love of flowers), and playing golf. Any time left over is celebrated with her fourth hobby: shopping. Jessica has a sister and two brothers, and they all, with their spouses, often go on golfing holidays together. Having travelled to various places on the globe, researching backgrounds for her stories, there are many countries that she would like to revisit. Her most recent trip abroad was to Portugal, where she stayed in a lovely hotel, close to her all-time favourite golf course. Jessica had no idea of being a writer until one day Peter suggested she write a book. So she did. She has now written over eighty novels.

Rebecca Winters, whose family of four children has now swelled to include three beautiful grandchildren, lives in Salt Lake City, Utah, in the land of the Rocky Mountains. With canyons and high Alpine meadows full of wildflowers, she never runs out of places to explore. They, plus her favourite vacation spots in Europe, often end up as backgrounds for her Mills & Boon Romance novels—because writing is her passion, along with her family and her church. Rebecca loves to hear from her readers. If you wish to e-mail her, please visit her website at: www.cleanromances.com.

Affairs of the Heart

TRISH MOREY
JESSICA STEELE
REBECCA WINTERS

MILLS & BOON

First Published in Great Britain 2018
by Mills & Boon, an imprint of HarperCollins*Publishers*
1 London Bridge Street, London, SE1 9GF

AFFAIRS OF THE HEART © 2018 Harlequin Books S. A.

The Italian Boss's Secret Child © 2005 Trish Morey
Falling for her Convenient Husband © 2009 Jessica Steele
The Brooding Frenchman's Proposal © 2009 Rebecca Winters

ISBN: 978-0-263-26876-8

0818

MIX
Paper from
responsible sources
FSC™ C007454

This book is produced from independently certified FSC™
paper to ensure responsible forest management.

For more information visit: www.harpercollins.co.uk/green

Printed and bound in Spain
by CPI, Barcelona

THE ITALIAN
BOSS'S SECRET CHILD

TRISH MOREY

CHAPTER ONE

WHAT a day! So far he'd chewed out two suppliers who'd let him down, put the fear of God into his IT guru for delivering late—again—on the new system and had a stand up fight with the HR manager, who seemed to think it was a good idea to pay every single employee a Christmas bonus generous enough to rival the gross national product of any number of tiny Third World nations.

Not yet eleven o'clock and already he'd been through the wars.

Not yet eleven o'clock and already it was shaping up to be the perfect day.

He pushed back in his leather recliner chair until he was almost horizontal, hands clinched behind his neck, legs stretched out with feet on the desk, and breathed deeply. Closing his eyes against the Melbourne skyline shown to full advantage from the floor to ceiling glass windows of his Collins Street office tower, he relived the turbulence of the morning's altercations.

Ruthless, difficult and a man to be feared, Damien DeLuca's reputation as the toughest CEO south of the equator wasn't likely to come under threat today.

Which suited him just fine. He was proud of his reputation—after all, it had taken him long enough to build. As a first generation Australian, the youngest son of Italian parents who'd left everything they'd known to make a new life in Australia over thirty-

5

five years ago, he'd worked hard to get where he was. From humble beginnings helping out in the family's former market garden, he'd made the most of a scholarship to a top college, then followed it up with a successful stint at university. Seven years later he'd walked away with a double degree plus a masters in business and a raft of eager employment offers to select from.

It had given him the start he'd needed. Within two years he'd set up his own financial sector software company and begun making inroads into the same competition that had been so desperate to snap him up.

A few more years on and he'd taken over two of his rivals and was an acknowledged innovator in the industry. Other companies now looked to his for an example of how to succeed. It was hardly a secret. He hadn't built Delucatek by being soft. He'd got where he was by being tough, by expecting a lot from himself and from his staff.

And he'd done it on his own. He had no time for partnerships, no time for sharing control. He was the boss, pure and simple. That was the way he ran his life, in the boardroom as well as in the bedroom. The women that flitted in and out of the scene were soon made aware of it too, even if they sometimes thought they could change him. They were wrong. He didn't need them.

Damien DeLuca didn't need anyone.

He pulled an arm out from behind his head, flashed a look at his TAG Heuer watch and frowned. Enid Crowley, his PA, should be returning from her break with his coffee any minute. Meanwhile his marketing manager, Sam Morgan, was late for his meeting to present the international marketing proposal to launch Delucatek's newest software package.

Very late!

He swung his legs down off the desk, irritated that someone who needed his approval to splash hundreds of thousands of the firm's dollars on what he understood was a radically different campaign hadn't even bothered to show up yet. It didn't augur well for the proposal.

It augured even less well for Sam.

What a day! She didn't need this. Not today.

Philly Summers hugged the file containing the proposal to her chest, her eyes still itching with the threat of tears, her throat tight and constricted, and knowing that all too soon she'd be deposited at the executive level of the DeLuca Tower whether she liked it or not.

Of all the days for Sam to go down with flu!

In normal circumstances she'd be celebrating being called in at the last minute to present the marketing plan to the famous if feared head of Delucatek. After three months working as Sam's deputy, it was clear to her that he was a man more than happy to take a disproportionate amount of credit for the work of others.

In normal circumstances she'd consider it a real coup, having the chance to present what was ninety-nine per cent her very own proposal to the man who could make or break her career in a moment.

In normal circumstances...

But these weren't normal circumstances.

Today she had more important things to worry

about than where her career might be headed or in seizing opportunities when they came knocking.

She sucked in a deep breath, seeking fortification, but the oxygen charged air was no match for the memory of the words that played over and over again in her mind. "I'm sorry but legally we can't help you. If you were married…"

If she was married! Now there was a joke. Bryce had well and truly put paid to any chance of that when he walked out two months ago, barely one week before their wedding. Besides which, if she'd been married she wouldn't have had to seek the help of the IVF clinic in the first place—she might already be pregnant.

But she wasn't married.

No man. No prospects. Not a chance of conception unless she considered trawling the late night bars and clubs for a stud. Her teeth dragged a path through her lip-gloss. Would she dare? Was a promise made to a dying woman worth stooping to such levels?

Her mother's pain-racked face flashed in her mind's eye, her once soft features twisted and hardened with both the progress of her disease and the anguish of deep, unbearable loss. She thought she'd do anything to assuage her mother's pain, to give her hope, but could she resort to picking up some no-name one-night stand in order to fulfil her promise?

'No,' she whispered on a shiver, her voice cracking in the empty lift. No question. She might be desperate but reckless wasn't her style. She lifted a hand and swiped at the sudden moisture on her cheek, recognising that maybe it meant there was no way she'd be able to fulfil the promise she'd made.

Maybe she'd just have to accept that she wasn't

going to be able to give her mother the grandchild she craved more than anything—the grandchild she needed to make her smile again. It wasn't fair but maybe it just wasn't going to happen.

The button marked forty-five lit up with a ding, breaking into her thoughts as the door slid open on to the plush foyer of the executive level. She stepped out, fingers white-knuckled on the file as she tried to turn her thoughts back to the proposal. This meeting needn't take long. She could focus on the proposal for the few minutes it would take. She knew it by heart after all, given she'd written just about every word of it.

Then she'd go back to her office and think this whole thing through again. She couldn't give up now—not while there was still time. Based on her mother's prognosis, she still had three months to conceive. Three chances to fulfil her promise. She would come up with something. There had to be another way.

There had to be.

'Sam! You're late. Come right through.'

The voice, deep and edged with impatience, emanated from the open office door adjacent to the unmanned workstation to her left. Dazzling light from the windows beyond illuminated the door, bright and radiant, before splashing into the corridor and bouncing along the walls.

'Sam!'

It had to be him. She'd only spoken to him once and that had been very early on in her three months with the company when she'd answered Sam's unattended phone, but if she wasn't mistaken that was the voice of Delucatek's esteemed and highly feared leader, Damien DeLuca. Admittedly it had been a very brief conversation as Sam had just about wrenched the phone from her ear when he'd discovered who was calling, but she'd lay money on those strident and demanding tones originating from the man everyone quietly and reverently called *Numero Uno*.

She tugged at the hem of her sensible tweed jacket, steeling herself for her meeting with a man coffee room chatter insisted was more to be feared than the Godfather.

'*Sam!*'

Philly jumped in irritation. Godfather indeed! Just where did this guy get off? He might be her boss and admittedly he might even be a genius where his business was concerned, but she just wasn't in the mood to put up with some egomaniac today. Especially not some shouting egomaniac.

She sucked some air into her lungs and pushed herself down the corridor in the direction of the open office door. The voice beat her to it.

'Well?' the voice rang out again impatiently before someone suddenly dimmed the lights. She blinked and opened her eyes to see the body that owned the voice filling much of the doorway. At least that accounted for the diminution of light—as his broad-shouldered body effectively blocked the dazzling rays. She stopped dead, just paces away, as his backlit form loomed tall and dark over her, his outline glowing like an aura, features indiscernible as her eyes tried to adjust to the sudden shift in the light.

She knew what he looked like, the marketing department had a filing cabinet full of photos of the boss in various poses—working at his desk, leaning over an employee at his computer, standing in the forefront of the building named after him.

She knew what he looked like, from the calculating, sharp eyes topped with thick, dark brows to his rugged, square jaw and the cleft in the centre of his chin. Dark hair backswept to control the strong natural wave and generous classic bow lips. He had features that film stars would envy. Some would have to spend a fortune on cosmetic surgery in an effort to attain the same brooding good looks.

Yes, she knew exactly what he looked like—yet still she felt a *frisson* of sensation shimmy down her spine. None of the photos hinted at what she now felt, at what his shadowed face spoke to her.

Danger.

Excitement.

And maybe, just maybe, something more…

CHAPTER TWO

'WHO are you?'

The woman in the mousy-brown suit seemed to stiffen, her jaw open as if in shock as her eyes searched his face. She clung on to the folder in front of her as if it was body armour and, given the size of her, she could do with it. There was so little to her it looked as though the folder was the only thing anchoring her to the earth.

'You're not Sam,' he accused.

Her mouth snapped shut and her chin kicked up. The action added only millimetres to her tiny frame but by the sudden spark in her eye he got the impression she imagined she was looking straight into his. Then her eyebrows arched and her lips curved into a smile.

Momentarily he relaxed. She wasn't completely mousy, now that she was smiling. In fact, in a way, she was quite pretty—in a homely sort of way. Of course, the tortoiseshell glasses and shapeless brown suit didn't do her any favours.

'Mr DeLuca,' she said, tilting her head to one side, her surprisingly husky voice edged with honey as she relaxed her grip on the folder enough to hold out a hand to him. 'They told me you were a genius. Obviously they were right.'

The way her hazel eyes glinted told him she hadn't just paid him a compliment.

12

He sucked in a breath, desperate to replace the lungful that had just been knocked out of him, as she kept right on smiling and holding her hand out in the air between them as if she hadn't meant a thing with her last comment.

'I'm Philly Summers, from Marketing. Pleased to meet you.'

He looked at her hand, hanging there, then crossed to the fake smile she was brandishing, and knew she was lying. She was no more pleased to meet him than he was to find Miss Brown Mouse lurking outside his office. What on earth was Sam Morgan thinking to send her? He gave her hand a brief shake, momentarily annoyed that someone so diminutive could have such a firm grip, before he swivelled around and stalked across the floor of his office.

'Where's Sam?' he asked once he'd deposited himself back in his deep leather chair, elbows on arm rests, a Mont Blanc fountain pen spinning between his fingers.

She hesitated for a moment by the door before apparently assuming he'd invited her to follow him, taking a few tentative steps towards the desk.

'Hopefully home by now. He's got the flu. He just about collapsed at his desk half an hour ago. We sent him home in a taxi.'

'And no one thought to inform me?'

Her head tilted to one side again and her eyes narrowed to slits, almost as though she thought he had a nerve asking the question.

'I was led to believe you were informed.'

'I wasn't.'

She considered him for a second, looked for a moment as if she would argue, but then thought better of it.

'In any event I assume it is more important that your presentation goes ahead as planned. I understand you have a very tight schedule and who knows when Sam will be back on deck? And we really need your go-ahead on this proposal today if we're to meet our timelines for the new product launch.'

And her taking the initiative was meant to impress him?

Dammit but it did. Everything she said made sense. So why did he still feel so aggrieved?

Because he should have been told!

He grunted in response, waving to a seat. 'So long as you have some idea of what the proposal is. I don't want to waste my time here.'

The muscles tightened around her mouth as if she'd just had to button it, but she kept on standing. 'I'll do my best not to waste a moment. However, I'll need to access your computer, if you don't mind. I've put a PowerPoint presentation on the share drive we can go through. This hard copy…' she indicated the file in her hands '…is for your records.'

He shrugged and gestured to the laptop on his desk. 'Be my guest,' he said, without moving an inch.

A blink was her only response. *Good.* Did she really expect him to make this easy for her after the lip she'd given him? If she wanted his computer, she could come and get it.

'I'm all ears,' he invited, a smile finally finding its way to his face. At last it looked as if he'd turned the tables on Miss Mouse. He wouldn't be surprised if any moment now she scampered back to her hole in the wall.

He watched her swallow, following the movement in her throat to her chest, which rose on a deep breath, considerably further than he would have expected. But then, with her jacket buttoned up to her neckline, there was no way of saying what lay beneath the uninspiring cut of her suit.

'All right,' she said, rounding the desk until she was on his side. She surveyed his legs, currently providing a very effective barrier between her and easy access to the computer, and almost as if she'd determined they were an immovable object reached over them to the laptop on the far side of his desk. A faint hint of something fruity and sweet stirred his senses as she stretched across him.

He prided himself on knowing the names of all the top perfumes and he had a talent for picking them for his dates. A different perfume for a different skin, a different personality, a different woman. To Carmel, sleek and elegant, he'd given the classic Chanel No.5. Warm and lush, Kandy had adored the heady tones of Opium, while for Belinda, fair and dreamlike, he'd chosen Romance.

But this perfume was something new, totally unlike anything else he'd come across. Something tantalisingly unsophisticated.

It suited her. She sure looked innocent enough. Though the way her skirt hugged her as she stretched over his legs—there was shape hidden away under that skirt after all. She straightened and his nostrils caught a second subtle whiff. *Apricot?* Yeah, she smelled like apricots. That *was* different.

*   *   *

Where did this guy get off? Didn't he realise she was doing him a favour? Next time he could wait for Sam to get back from sick leave. She didn't need this kind of aggravation in her life right now.

She swivelled the laptop around and drew it closer to where she stood so that she didn't have to keep bending over the boss's legs. She could almost feel his eyes boring into her back, searing her skin through her wool mix suit until it prickled, just knowing he was there, a bare metre behind her, scrutinising her every step of the way.

Knowing he was her boss in no way suppressed the sensations she was experiencing right now. *Raw sexuality.* It emanated from him in waves. Even the way he casually sprawled in his chair couldn't hide the latent power contained in those long limbs. She was used to dealing with bosses on equal terms—not one had ever made her so aware of his inherent sexuality.

Not one had made her so aware that he was a man. *That she was a woman.*

She shifted, comfortable with neither where her thoughts were going nor how her body was suddenly tingling. He sure wasn't making this easy. But then, no one had ever described Damien DeLuca as easy.

Impossible; arrogant; genius—she'd heard all those words used in conjunction with his name. But easy? Ha! Not a one. The sooner she got through with this meeting and got out of here the better. If only she could focus on her presentation!

Naturally his sudden appearance at the door had thrown her. Just for a moment there had seemed something more to Damien than she'd heard, another angle, another dimension.

She'd been kidding herself. Now that his face was out of the shadows he was just another good-looking, over-achieving workaholic who had no people skills whatsoever.

She turned her head a fraction and caught a glimpse of his smug-looking face out of the corner of her eye as she manoeuvred her way through explorer to the share drive.

Okay, maybe that wasn't quite fair. Make that drop-dead gorgeous, over-achieving workaholic who lacked people skills but exuded testosterone by the bucketload. *That* might be closer to the mark.

The photos in the marketing files certainly didn't do him justice. No doubt the current photographer had been in place since the year dot. First thing she'd do when she got back to her office would be to organise a new photographer who knew how to use great material rather than take it for granted. Because whatever his personality faults, the guy sure had great genes. No doubt that with his looks and IQ his kids were bound to be intelligent and great looking, just like their dad.

Maybe what she needed was a guy like him?

Her fingers stopped dead over the mouse, her mouth suddenly, inexplicably dry.

Why would that occur to her? Clearly her other problem was starting to affect her brain. Now she was having fantasies about the men at work. Or, at least, fantasies about this one.

And having fantasies about Damien DeLuca was pointless. He was so far out of her league it wasn't funny. Even if he wasn't, from what she'd heard, the guy was a confirmed bachelor—a one man band all the way and probably just as well the way he treated people. You'd have to be mad to get tangled up with someone like him.

Not that getting tangled up with Damien was on the cards.

'Is something wrong?'

She jumped as if she'd been stung. 'Oh, no.' She shook her head, shielding from him what she had no doubt would be a give-away red face. 'Not at all. Um, here's the file…'

She took a couple of steadying breaths before finally turning. With the opening slide on the screen that she hoped would pull attention from her sudden colour, she gave a weak smile. 'Okay, all set?' she asked before launching into her presentation.

'What do you know about her? That *Filly* woman. Though I have to say she looks more like a mouse than any horse I've seen.'

Without looking up from her computer screen or mis-hitting a key on her one hundred words per minute typing speed, Enid responded drily, 'And I should know?'

'You know everything about everyone in this office, Enid, and you know it.'

She still didn't look up, but he did notice the tiniest tweak at the corner of her line-rimmed lips.

'Then it's Philly, with a P-H, short for Philadelphia. Her parents had a travel urge at one time apparently, though never got farther than the maternity unit at Melbourne General.'

'Family?'

'Lives with her mother. A widow. There was a

brother, though he died in tragic circumstances, I believe.'

He raised his eyebrows. 'Anything else?'

'Twenty-seven years old, single—was about to be married a month or two ago but something happened. Could be a left at the altar story.'

Left at the altar? Yeah, that would do it. He'd got the distinct impression that despite her professional presentation she had a real thing against men.

'By the way,' she said, 'now that you've finished early you might like to tackle your messages.' She swivelled around on her chair to pick up a stack of papers she handed over to him. 'Don't worry about the top one; Sam left a brief message on my voicemail while I was out that he was unable to do the presentation. No doubt you got that message anyway.'

He looked briefly at the stack before pocketing them. So Philly had been right. Someone had tried to let him know. So now he couldn't even hold that against her. He wasn't entirely sure he liked that.

'Snippy little thing,' he said as he rested a hip on her desk, putting down his now tepid coffee and replacing it with a card from her in-tray, spinning it between his fingers. 'Did a good job, though—really knows her stuff. Sam would have taken three times as long. But I don't think she likes me.'

'*No one* at Delucatek likes you. You're the original boss from hell and you love it.'

'But you like me, Enid.'

Enid's fingers stopped dead on the keyboard, her index finger hovering pointedly over the ''I''. She looked up at him over her reading glasses, her eyes narrowed to slits, and she let her head tip to the side in a bare nod. 'I have a great deal of respect for you—yes, that's true. In addition to which I have to admit you do wonderful things for my cash flow. But like you?' The movement of her head now looked less of a nod and more of a shake.

He held up his hand before she could say any more. 'Okay.' He laughed, rich and loud. Of course she was kidding. She was crazy about him. 'Why is it you're the only person in this building who doesn't take me seriously?'

'Somebody has to do it,' she replied, adding a wink for good measure before she turned back to her keyboard.

He stopped flipping the card in his hands long enough to read it.

'Damn. Whoever decided on a masked fancy dress theme for this year's Christmas party?'

'*You* did,' came the terse response. 'You said it would help break down barriers between the staff—get them warmed up and mixing without copious quantities of alcohol. And I think it's a great idea.'

'What are you going as, Enid? Little Bo Peep?'

The look she gave him was pure ice and the lines around her pursed lips condensed to form canyons.

'And there I was thinking Xena, Warrior Princess was more my style. Besides,' she continued, 'I'm not telling. You'll have to work it out on the night. Masks only come off at midnight.'

He shrugged. It was a good idea to break the ice. Break down the barriers he could already see developing between his managers and their staff. Barriers were the last thing he wanted and it was clear, if Sam and the Marketing Department were any example, that those barriers were already being put up. He'd had no idea there was someone in that area with the skills Philly possessed—Sam had certainly never mentioned her.

And it would be interesting to see what his staff came up with for their disguises. Some people wouldn't need much help of course. Already he could see Miss Brown Mouse—with the addition of a couple of little pink ears and a tail she'd be utterly convincing.

CHAPTER THREE

'YOU look like a princess!'

Philly smiled and did a twirl as she entered her mother's room, the ends of her black wig flicking out as she spun. 'You don't think it's too much? The woman in the costume shop said it was fine.'

'Too much? No, dear, it's just perfect. You'll be the belle of the ball.'

'I don't know about that.'

'Oh, but I've got some lovely perfume I never wear any more that would be perfect with that outfit.' She pointed the way to the cabinet and Philly followed her directions, giving a spray to her neckline and wrists. It was nice, rich and exotic, and quite a change from her usual apricot scent. Well, tonight was the night for change, or so it seemed.

She plumped the pillows behind her mother's frail back, making sure she was comfortable before fetching her a cup of tea. Then she sat down on the bed alongside and held out a small saucer holding several brightly coloured pills.

'I still don't know why I'm going, really. If you'd prefer, I'm quite happy to stay home.'

'You don't get out enough as it is,' said her mother, her fingers hunting down a fat capsule. 'You should enjoy it when you get the chance.' She dropped the pill on her tongue, washing it down with a swig of tea as she foraged for another.

'I guess going out just doesn't bother me all that much,' she said with a shrug.

'Then it should. It's not natural for a young woman to shut herself away from the world when she should be out there enjoying it and meeting people.'

'I've got a job. I meet plenty of people.'

Her mother took another sip of tea, picking up the last few pills.

'You're not still pining over that Bryce, are you?'

Philly pulled a face in response, putting the now empty dish over on the bedside table. Of course it had hurt, being dumped for another woman like that just before their wedding—another woman she'd discovered he'd been seeing for a year, another woman he'd made pregnant. She'd felt stupid, naïve and desperately hurt. Most of all she'd felt cheated of the child she was so desperate to have, a child he'd so freely given someone else, and for a while she'd longed to have him back. For a while.

'No,' she said on a sigh, knowing it was true. Abandoning her one week before their wedding had come as a huge shock. He'd let her down badly and knocked her confidence for a six but she wasn't exactly without blame over the failure of the relationship herself.

She'd fallen in with his plans for marriage, indeed his plans for everything, because it had suited her to do so. And while she'd believed she loved him, she knew now that she'd talked herself into it because she'd so desperately wanted it to be right, to make forming a family with him and having his child right.

But it hadn't been right. She would have been marrying him for all the wrong reasons.

'Marriage to Bryce would have been a mistake; I

know that now,' she said, squeezing her mother's hand. 'He did us both a favour by walking away when he did.'

Her mother nodded. 'He just wasn't the one for you. But the right man *is* out there, you mark my words. Look at Monty; he took out dozens of girls before he found that one special woman. Annelise was so sweet. They were so happy together.'

Her mother sighed wistfully, and together their gazes drifted to the framed photo standing in pride of place on her dressing table. The smiling couple, beaming their happiness and their pride as together they held up their newborn son for the camera.

It was happiness that had been tragically short-lived. The very next day, on their way to show off the new arrival to his grandmother, all three lives had been wiped out, victims of foul weather conditions and a horrendous light plane crash.

Philly drew in a breath and turned to her mother, still transfixed by the photo and clearly thinking, re-membering, as two tears slid a crooked path down her hollow cheeks. Then her mother sniffed, still looking at the photo.

'I'd just love to see you settled, dear, bef...' Her words trailed off mid-sentence but she didn't have to finish them. Philly knew what she'd been going to say—the unspoken words hung fat and heavy in the air, weighed down with the inevitability of what was to come.

Before I die.

Something squeezed tight in her chest.

Less than twelve months to live. Her mother de-served some happiness, something to look forward to. Something that promised a future that would take her mind and thoughts beyond the doctors' sad prognosis. Something to help her—not forget, she could never forget—but maybe just ease the pain she was feeling at the premature deaths of a young family who'd had everything to live for.

Instead she was giving herself up to the disease, accepting her fate almost as if she was looking forward to being reunited with her late husband and especially Monty, his beautiful wife and the grandchild she knew by this one lone photograph.

The doctors had been sympathetic when the drugs just didn't seem to work any more in arresting the disease. 'She has to want to live,' they'd said. 'People often need something to live for, a reason to survive.'

Philly had failed her. She'd promised to give her mother a grandchild but now, with a failed relationship, an aborted marriage behind her and not even eligible for IVF, she'd run out of options. Sure, there was a chance she might find a boyfriend in that time, but there was no way she was likely to settle down and form a family within the next twelve months— no way she was going to be able to brighten her mother's last few months with the promise of a child.

But then, what real chance did she have of even finding a boyfriend? Every time she'd thought about men or dating lately only one man had sprung to mind. Every guy she met paled in comparison. He was better looking, better built, more intelligent and had a charisma that reeled her in.

She shook her head. Work must really be getting to her if Damien DeLuca kept crowding her thoughts. Sure, he had great genes but if she kept comparing every guy she met with him she was never going to find anyone who made the grade. And she couldn't even say that she liked him—he was far too arrogant and autocratic—though he sure had plenty going for him besides.

What would he be dressed as tonight? Probably a pirate with his looks. A buccaneer, swashbuckling and dangerous, in a soft shirt, ruffled at the sleeves and open over his chest, the stark white a contrast against his dark hair and tanned olive skin, and tucked into tight black breeches...

Her mother tugged a tissue from the box on her bedside table, pulling Philly out of her thoughts with a jolt. Her nervousness at attending this costume ball must be getting to her. Now she was imagining all sorts of strange things.

'Oh dear, I am getting maudlin,' her mother said, blotting away her tears and then blowing her nose. 'Don't listen to me. I'm just tired.'

'You get some sleep then,' Philly said, squeezing the older woman's hand gently and kissing her softly on the cheek before she picked up the empty cup. 'I won't be late.'

She shouldn't have come.

From behind her sequinned mask she took one look inside the door, saw the myriad of characters in the lavishly decorated auditorium, the mirror balls spinning crazy colours against the bizarre outfits of the crowd dancing to the loud music, and knew she should have stayed at home.

What was she doing here anyway?

Standing in the lobby, tossing up whether or not to enter the party, she didn't know. Yes, it had been nice to dress up, to put on something pretty rather than shrug into her sensible work wardrobe for a change—

Lord knows it had been long enough since she'd taken so much care with her appearance. But what did she hope to achieve by it?

Who did she think she was trying to impress—Damien? Fat chance. In terms of being a woman, he didn't know she was alive and he probably didn't even care. The way he'd tried to make her feel so inconsequential when she'd given that presentation… It was pure fantasy to think that she might make an impression on him tonight.

As if he cared.

She wouldn't go in. There was no point at all. Even if she didn't harbour a tiny desire to turn the tables on the one guy who'd made her feel as insignificant as a gnat, she was just no good at this sort of thing. No good at mixing with near strangers. Sure, she'd met plenty of pleasant people in the few short months she'd been at Delucatek, but no one she knew well enough yet to term a friend. Though admittedly that was nobody's fault but her own. She'd been the one to turn down the Friday after work drinks invitations, always too anxious to go home and see to her mother.

And, of course, after Bryce and the fiasco of their wedding, trusting people enough to get close to them hadn't been high on her list of priorities. Just because he'd made the right decision in calling off the wedding didn't mean she'd forgotten the pain of cancelling the church and reception and explaining to the invited guests that the wedding was now off.

The external doors behind her swung open as a new party of guests arrived and the summer night air rushed inside, clashing with the air conditioning in a gust that swirled across her bare shoulders and under her slim-fitting gown. She hugged her arms to her, fighting the unfamiliar sensations as she sidled as inconspicuously as possible out of their path, using a potted palm as a screen.

She must be crazy!

As soon as this group extinguished their cigarettes and entered the party the coast would be clear and she'd make her escape.

'Hello? Who have we here? Don't tell me—Cleopatra. Am I right?'

She looked up at the gruff voice, startled to see a large nun, complete with moustache and cigar, bearing down on her, the eyes of the rest of his group all turned in her direction. The most disturbing thing was that the nun sounded exactly like Sam Morgan.

'Don't you look something! Aren't you Sylvia from Accounts?' He took hold of her hand in his own meaty paw and pulled her out from behind the pot plant where she'd sought refuge.

She looked at them all, speechless. A fluffy grey koala, Tin Man and Humpty Dumpty all stared back.

'Sylvia?' the nun prompted. 'Is that you under that sexy get-up?'

She shook her head, unwilling to give away her identity. If she was going to go home, the last thing she wanted was for Sam to question her on Monday as to her sudden disappearance. She'd rather people thought she'd never bothered to attend. 'Um. Marie,' she murmured, trying to add a different note to her voice. 'From—the Sydney office.'

'Welcome, Marie!' said the nun. 'No wonder you're shy. Why don't you come in with us? We'll take good care of you. Won't we, Tin Man?'

Tin Man rattled as he tried to nod enthusiastically, earning himself a quick dig in the ribs from the koala.

Before she could protest and extricate her hand from Sam's, Humpty grabbed her other one and together they steered her towards the doors. 'Don't worry about Tin Man and Koala,' Humpty said conspiratorially. 'Newlyweds. And I know we're not supposed to take off our masks till midnight, but I'm Julia. If you get lost or need any help, look for Sister Sam—' she nodded her big egg head in the direction of the nun '—or me. Now, let's join the party, shall we?'

Before Philly could protest, she'd been swept into the throng inside the large room and her plan altered. She'd slip away in a few minutes, while everyone was otherwise occupied. They'd assume she'd just met up with some other people in this crowd and wouldn't give it a second thought.

Someone put a glass in her hand. Tin Man took Koala off to dance to make up for his gaffe and Humpty and Sister Sam found a group of colleagues and were busy comparing outfits and guessing identities.

Philly stood on the fringe of the group, planning her escape. Just her luck to run into Sam! At least he hadn't recognised her. Father Time stood, scythe in hand, just across from her, a large fob watch conveniently around his neck. Already after nine.

She'd give it just a few minutes and then she'd steal away and go home.

She was a goddess!

He was wending his way through the crowded room, enjoying the anonymity lent by his disguise, dropping in to catch snatches of conversation with this group and that, when he saw her. Even in this sea of costumes and colour she stood out like a beacon. How could she not, looking like an Egyptian queen?

She wasn't tall yet her legs had to be sensational under the sleek gown that looked as sheer and fine as gossamer, accentuating the feminine curves apparent beneath. Golden sandals peeped out below.

The gown ended at her breasts with some sort of twist of the fabric in a strapless arrangement that hugged her form and had him immediately calculating how difficult it would be to get off. Her lips were a splash of red, vibrant and lush and a contrast against the jet-black hair swishing over her bare shoulders. Coiled bracelets adorned her arms.

Her costume was unmistakeable. She was Cleopatra, Queen of the Nile. Little wonder emperors had fallen under her spell.

He drank in every detail and his prolonged scrutiny confirmed what he'd known immediately.

He wanted her.

Who was she? With her mask covering her eyes there was no way he could pin down her identity. Did she work for him or was she someone's partner?

He scoured the group she was standing in, but no one guarded her possessively, no one fielded admirers. She had to be alone. No one in their right mind would let her fly solo in such an outfit. If she was his date he wouldn't let her out of his sight.

Who was he trying to kid? If she was his date he wouldn't let her out of his bed.

He had to have her.

Two minutes. Just two minutes more and she'd excuse herself. They wouldn't miss her now. Sister Sam and Humpty were both deep in conversation with Noddy and Big Ears. She'd leave, make the excuse of a headache if anyone asked her, but chances were no one would even notice in this crowd.

Escape was at hand.

She placed her barely touched glass of champagne on the tray of a passing waiter and slid into the crowd, heading for the door. The sudden hand around her arm told her she hadn't made the clean escape she was hoping for.

'You're not leaving?'

She stopped dead as the tremor passed through her, but there was no mistake.

It was him!

She'd know Damien DeLuca's autocratic voice anywhere. But now his tone held something else— interest?—*desire?* She turned and gasped. Relieved her mask would hide the shock in her eyes—the admiration in her eyes—she drank him in. He looked sensational, from the overlapping metal plates at his shoulders to the carved breastplate and the slatted leather tunic ending above his knees. His arms were bare, olive-skinned and gleaming, except for some sort of wide band at his wrist. He held a helmet under one arm, a sword hung at his side.

A Roman gladiator or an emperor going off to lead his army to war? Whatever, he looked magnificent. He fitted the part, with his Italian colouring, hair lazily windswept, curling at his collar and with his chiselled cheekbones accentuated by the simple mask tied over his eyes.

If she'd thought he'd exuded masculine sex appeal in a suit, that was nothing to the sheer testosterone surge he gave off in this outfit.

She swallowed and looked back towards the door. His hand still held her arm and the heat from his grip weakened her resolve to leave.

'Stay, Cleopatra,' he said intently, almost reverently. 'I've been waiting over two thousand years to find you again.'

She shuddered, his words going straight through her in a flush of heat that seemed to touch and awaken every last extremity of her and then bounce back, settling at her core, warm and heavy. He reached across and took her hand.

'Surely you recognise me? Mark Antony?'

He inclined his head and for the first time she allowed herself to smile. It was Damien—*really Damien*—and he'd noticed her, amongst all these people. And not only had he noticed her; if she wasn't mistaken he was coming on to her.

Her head dipped in response; she couldn't allow herself to speak. Her brain had too much information to process to cope with making small conversation. Besides, why spoil this magic? He thought he'd found Cleopatra. Why let on just yet that she was Philly from marketing? He wouldn't hang around two minutes if he knew. Tonight she might just stick to being Cleopatra.

'Come,' he said, tugging on her hand so that she came closer to his body, closer to the source of that heat, as he gestured to the dimly lit dance floor beyond. 'Dance with me.'

She didn't have to think about whether or not she should; her feet drifted after him of their own accord, her plan to exit all but forgotten. He led her to the dance floor and drew her into his arms, his hand at her back anchoring her close, his other hand wrapped around hers, securing it close to his shoulder, his wide shoulder, the armour enhancing his masculine form.

'You're beautiful,' he said, his voice low and husky.

His words tripped her heartbeat. *Beautiful.* No one had told her that for a very long time. She had to remember to breathe and when she did it was with a gasp that immediately rewarded her with the scent of him—masculine, clean and enriched with the smell of leather. But not just his scent. She was sure she could just about taste him.

He started swaying to the song, taking her with him, their bodies moving in unison as the music took them away.

Heaven. This must be what heaven was like. Sheer bliss. She closed her eyes, allowing herself to be carried along by the music and by the man who held her in his arms with such strength, yet such tenderness.

Suddenly he stopped. She blinked her eyes open, the music still playing, and saw Damien's head swivelled to the side. He was talking to someone; it looked like a geisha but the voice was unmistakably Enid's. She caught a snatch of her words here and there— *London—crisis*—and Damien rattled off something in response and the geisha disappeared.

He turned his face back to hers, the line of his mouth grim, tension replacing the liquid heat she'd felt within his grasp.

'I have to take a phone call.'

His arms continued to surround her and he stared at her as if he was wavering between the phone call and the woman in his arms. 'I'll be back. Ten minutes max.' He hesitated. 'Maybe twenty.'

She looked up at him, his face so close to her own,

and she knew she would wait forever if it meant feeling like this again. Then he dipped his head and his lips brushed hers, so gently that his breath was as much a part of the kiss, as much a part of the sensation, as his lips.

'So beautiful,' he whispered, his voice suddenly rougher. 'Wait for me.' He smiled and let her go.

And then he was gone.

It was like being in a vacuum. Damien had gone, all too quickly, and she felt cold, suddenly bereft of his heat. *But he'd be back.* He'd promised he'd be back. And that knowledge started the warmth pooling inside her all over again.

For a moment longer she stood, all by herself, in the centre of the crowded dance floor, couples jostling for space all around until she realised she had to move.

Ten minutes, he'd said. Maybe twenty. Where should she wait for him? How would he find her?

She made her way to the bar, ordered a mineral water and held the iced glass to her cheeks, trying to think about the time, trying not to think about the time. How many minutes now—five?—ten? She wanted to be back in his arms and every minute he was away felt like for ever.

The band finished its set and the dancers dispersed as someone took over the microphone. A stand-up comic. Good. At least that might take her mind off the time.

Damien cursed, loud and emphatic, before turning the microphone on the speaker telephone back up. It was worse than he'd thought. Enid sat nearby, armed with pen and paper and tactfully ignoring his comments, her delicately made-up white face giving nothing away.

He raked a hand through his hair, waiting for someone to pick up, snagging it on the mask. He tore it off, flinging it down on the desk of the makeshift office. It was actually a storeroom but with her usual efficient style Enid had already organised a couple of chairs, a phone and a fax machine. He didn't need a computer—this was no time for email. He wanted action.

Of all the times for Delucatek's United Kingdom agent to collapse. The news had been splashed in London's Saturday papers and now there were a hundred clients all screaming for help. Okay, these things happened in business. He'd dealt with worse before and no doubt there'd be worse to come, but why did it have to be tonight? Why now? Already he'd been here forty minutes but he wasn't going anywhere until he'd cornered his agent's CEO. There were plenty of questions he wanted to ask him.

He picked up a pencil, tapping it furiously on the table as he waited.

Strains of laughter drifted in from the nearby auditorium and his mind wandered back to the ball and the woman he'd left behind. She was waiting for him. Or at least he hoped she was.

He could still feel her in his arms, the magic way her body floated into his, matching his moves and the music so that her sweet body flowed, her curves swaying to the rhythm. How he'd like to feel that body sway to a different rhythm, how he'd like to feel her body dance to a different music, a music they would make together. His body ached just thinking about it. He was a normal man; he liked sex. But it had been a long time since he'd wanted anyone as much as he wanted her.

There was something about her. Something special. That body, those lush lips. The way she'd come as Cleopatra, Mark Antony's seductress. That had to be fate.

He glanced again at his watch. What if she'd found someone else? The thought of her with another man— holding her, dancing with her, maybe even... His teeth ground together. She'd tasted so sweet, so ripe. The mere idea that someone else was sampling her mouth or even something more...

The pencil in his hand snapped in two.

At the other end of the line the phone rang out. Damien slammed down the receiver and checked his notes for the next number. He'd track this guy down and get him to take responsibility for this mess if it killed him.

He wasn't coming back. The sad truth hit her like a blow to the gut. Almost two hours now. The comedian had finished, the band had done another two brackets, leaving taped music in its wake, and it was clear there was no way Damien was coming back. Either whatever had called him away was taking more time than he'd anticipated or he'd found someone else and changed his mind.

There was no question as to which scenario was the most likely. She'd been kidding herself to think she was that special.

It was getting late. She should go home. Staying here longer just increased the feeling of bitterness, the sense of overwhelming loss that gradually but irrevocably gnawed away at her earlier euphoria.

He wasn't coming back.

She had one last look around the ballroom. The party was in full swing and laughter and music filled the air. Her evening hadn't been a total loss. She'd chatted with a few people, sticking to safe topics like costumes and the party. She'd enjoyed the comedian. Even the lavishly spread tables, covered with all manner of finger food and nibbles, had proved a diversion, at least for her eyes, helping for a little while to take her mind off the time and its passing.

But now it was time to go home. There was no point staying. She put her glass down and turned towards the exit.

'Would you care to dance with me?'

She smiled her thanks at the six foot tall kangaroo looking down at her and shook her head. 'I was just leaving but thank you.'

'Just one dance before you go? Come on, it'll be fun. You ever danced with a kangaroo before?'

'Um, no actually.'

'Then now's your chance.' The kangaroo held out its paw.

She laughed a little and slipped her arm through his furry one. 'Well, if you put it like that.' One dance wouldn't hurt. It would be nothing like dancing with Damien had been, but it might be fun, and it would be something to tell her mother in the morning. She'd certainly enjoy a story like this.

Kanga made it to the dance floor in a combination of skips and hops that had Philly laughing before they'd even begun. When he started to move to the music she couldn't stop. She was either being buffeted by the huge hind legs of his costume or he'd swing around and collect her with his tail. It was impossible not to have fun.

She was still here.

For a while he'd been unable to find her, scared beyond belief that she'd already left when he didn't even know who she was. But then his eyes had been drawn to the dance floor and there she was.

My God, she was even more beautiful than he remembered. Her smile was so wide her whole face lit up and she moved so well to the fast rock and roll number, her body picking up the beat and making it her own.

He checked out her partner and discounted him in the same glance. He could deal with Skippy. He'd dealt with much stronger adversaries, like the CEO he'd finally caught up with. He was history in the business community from here on in.

He moved closer, sensing the music track was nearing its end, preparing to cut in before anyone else had a chance to get anywhere near her. He'd wasted enough time tonight. Now he was going to make her his.

What made her look around? There was no way she could have heard a thing over the loud music, but something made her turn. Something made her look.

Not something.

Someone.

Her steps faltered in time with the skip of her heartbeat.

Damien. He was back and he was heading straight towards her. He'd come back for her. She sucked in a breath, watching his approach. He looked like a triumphant general returning from war. She was un-aware she'd stopped dancing until Kanga tapped her on the shoulder with his paw.

'You tired? It's like an oven inside here. I'm getting a drink. Want one?'

She was aware her head was shaking but only just. Every other part of her concentrated on Damien's purposeful approach, her body tingling in mounting anticipation with each step he took closer. His eyes were still masked but she could tell his focus didn't leave her. It was empowering knowing that he could no more take his eyes off her than she could from him.

'Okay, then. Thanks for the dance.' Kanga bounded off to find refreshments as Damien reached her side. He took one of her hands, lifted it to his mouth and held it there, pressed to his lips.

Finally he removed his mouth. 'Now,' he said, 'where were we?'

His grip was firm, his hand warm and strong. The fast rock and roll number came to an end as, without letting go of her hand, he drew her closer. For a few seconds he just stood, looking at her, ignoring the jostling of the crowd around him, waiting for the new track to cut in.

She couldn't move. Even if he hadn't had a grip on her hand, she wasn't going anywhere. From under his mask the heat from his gaze pulled her like a magnet. Her body responded, breasts swelling, nipples tightening, as his sheer presence touched her in places his eyes couldn't.

When the gentle strains of guitar playing signalled the start of a slow Robbie Williams ballad Damien pulled her gently into his arms and suddenly he was all around her. His chest, solid and warm, pressing against hers, his thighs firm, his arms encasing her, modelling her like clay to his form while he swayed to the music.

She gave in to the pressure and let her head fall against his chest to rest upon the plates that covered it. It wasn't exactly comfortable but she didn't care. When she breathed in it was his scent, natural and masculine, that intoxicated her senses.

His large hands held her close, one cradling her shoulder, the other firm at the small of her back, and his head rested over hers as they moved together to the music, their bodies as close as they could be with clothes on.

He breathed deep, unable to get a hold on her scent—frustrating for someone who prided himself on knowing them backwards. She was wearing a wig—that didn't help—but there was some kind of rich perfume, something exotic, just like she was. Something else lurked below too, but the signals were blurry and he couldn't quite make it out. Whatever it was, she smelt all woman. He liked that.

The rest of her he could make out just fine. She fitted him perfectly. Something told him she'd fit him *everywhere* perfectly. She moulded to his body as if she was made for it. The jut of her breasts, soft but firm against his chest, the dip to her waist and the flare of her hips. She was perfect.

His hands moved slowly over her back, exploring, taking inventory. He liked what he felt as she followed his swaying rhythm, her body curvy and sensual and just the way he liked them.

The only thing he hated was the mask she wore. He'd do away with that the first chance he got.

Besides, he wanted to see her eyes when she came.

He stiffened at the thought and the reality of his situation hit him like a brick. He wasn't sure how the Romans had coped, but the thought of his costume betraying his desire on the dance floor in front of five hundred employees and their partners wasn't appealing. He had to get them both out of here, now, while he could still think straight.

The music track had reached its climax. He was vaguely envious as it wound down to a slow refrain. There was no way he was winding down any time soon—unless this woman had something to do with it. And if he had any say she'd have everything to do with it!

'Let's get out of here,' he whispered, nibbling on her ear.

She felt too weak to respond, lost in the multitude of new and wonderful sensations she was being bombarded with.

Was this how seduction felt? Never before had she felt such liquid heat pooling inside her. This total absence of real thought, all mind function replaced by body function and totally concentrated on one thing, the fruition of one act. One utterly irresistible, inevitable act.

She wanted more of what he was doing to her, more of what he was making her feel. She wanted him.

This was new—to feel such intense longing and desire for any one man! Passion like she'd never before experienced. Bryce had never once made her feel like this in their entire two-year relationship. He'd always made her feel that lovemaking was an obligation.

What was happening now with Damien couldn't be

more different. Right now making love with Damien felt like her destiny. A destiny she felt powerless to deny.

With his hand at her back steering her towards an exit, she allowed him to propel her towards that destiny.

He swooped and opened a side door in her path, his other hand encouraging her through to the dimly lit hallway beyond. He pulled the door shut behind them and spun her against the wall in the same rapid-fire action.

Her back met the wall at the same instant his mouth meshed with hers.

Frantic.

Hungry.

His lips slanted over hers and a moment later he was inside, his tongue seeking hers. He tasted rich and real, of masculine heat and warm brandy, and she let herself go with the sensation, the ecstasy of him filling her mouth.

One hand found her breast and she gasped as his fingers grazed her nipple, searing through the light fabric.

The other dropped to her skirt and he filled his hand with the round of one perfect cheek. Her muscles tightened in response and he was rewarded by the push of her belly into his growing hardness.

He growled, long and low, at the building tension, the anticipation of its relief, and she squirmed under his hands.

His touch was a brand on her, exploring, pushing, urgent and hot. Need radiated inside her like a fire front, the flames spreading wider until every part of her was alight. The oxygen delivered by her rapid breaths fuelled the flames.

The door alongside swung open. Someone looked around, mumbling a quick apology before diving back into the auditorium. Damien pulled his mouth away giving a low soft curse. He grabbed her hand again. 'Come on,' he said.

She followed behind him down the corridor, senses reeling as he tugged her insistently along, then round a corner, up a flight of stairs and over a parquet floor. He stopped outside a pair of solid doors flanked with impressive brass framing. The boardroom. He pulled something from a pocket somewhere—a keycard— and shoved it through the slot. In the wooden surrounds and over the muted sounds of the revelry below the click echoed loud and long. *And final.*

She swallowed as logic fought for precedence in her mind. Once inside there was no turning back. No chance to change her mind.

But she had no intention of changing her mind. There was no way she didn't want to follow this scene through to its logical conclusion. She'd come too far.

He pulled her into the room, though she hardly needed persuading. The door closed behind them and he turned the lock. They were alone, the room unlit but for the venetian blind dressed window sending slices of moonlight cascading across the sleek boardroom table.

Her eyes adjusted and in the gloom it was as if the years had peeled away and history itself was replaying.

Right now she was Cleopatra and he was her Mark Antony.

He reached out a hand to her face, touching her mask.

She flinched from his grasp and shook her head. 'No!' she whispered. She wouldn't kid herself. He wouldn't be doing this if he knew who she was. Only after, when it was too late for him to change his mind, only then would she let him take off her mask.

He would be angry, no doubt. Even worse, he would be disappointed. His fantasy would end right then and there. But she would have this memory to treasure for ever. And, no doubt, she would.

In the pale moonlight she saw the corner of his mouth lift. 'All right, let's do it your way. I have more urgent business first.'

His hands went to her waist and he lifted her easily to the table, pushing away the chairs to each side. He eased down the bodice of her gown, releasing her breasts to the air and his gaze. Her skin tightened, her nipples achingly firm.

He growled low and rough, and dropped his mouth to one pert peak. Her swift intake of breath pushed her breast further towards him; he filled his mouth with the flesh as his tongue traced the tip. He left that breast, focused on the second, delivering the same languid pleasure strokes with his tongue, his hands now at her legs, running her gown up her bare legs, spreading them as he forced himself between.

She clung to his head, her fingers raking through his hair, down his neck, exploring his wide shoulders, drinking in the width and strength of his back.

One hand rounded her thigh and against the fabric of her thong. The damp fabric of her thong. 'Oh, God,' he muttered as her head fell back, his fingers continuing their gentle exploration, the fabric no barrier to flesh already inflamed and exquisitely sensitised. She clawed at his costume, attempting to fill her own hands with the touch of his skin, frustrated that she could find no way in.

Suddenly he wheeled away, impatiently pulling at his garments, shucking off the shoulder gear and chest plate with a clatter and tearing off his tunic. He returned to her, naked but for his black underwear and his sandals, his skin gleaming in the soft moonlight.

She pulled him into her arms and relished the feel of the skin at his back, hot and slick with expectation and desire, as he continued his exploration, driving her crazy with need as he teased her with his fingers.

'So beautiful,' he murmured against her nipple. 'And so wet.' Those last words sounded as if they had been wrung from him. He lifted her slightly and removed her thong and with both hands he pulled her closer to the edge of the table. His underwear was no barrier to the hard bulge of his erection butting against her.

He was so big.

Anticipation kicked up a notch. She wanted him inside her. All of him. He pulled himself away fractionally, wrenching down his own underwear. And then he was free. Even in the dim light he looked magnificent, all pulsing energy with its own special rhythm. She reached down a hand, wanting to feel the power, to guide him to her, to share the dance.

She touched him, her fingers cupping him, entranced by the weight, the contrasts in the feel of him, rock-hard yet with skin like silk, so rigid yet pulsing, filled with life.

She closed her fingers around him and he gasped. This fantasy woman would not escape him tonight.

He had to have her. Had to feel her wrapped around him, hugging him tight inside, her muscles clamping around him in spasms when she came.

Her hand moved the length of him, her thumb flicking over his sensitive tip.

Oh, God!

Exit rational thought.

He grabbed her wrist, pulling her hand away as he scooped her yet closer, directing himself at the same time that he dropped his mouth on hers. His rapid action took her by surprise—her lips already open and forming a surprised 'o' even as he plundered her mouth with his. And then he brought her closer still, until her legs wrapped around behind him and her slick wetness welcomed him, urging him to drive himself home.

He didn't need further invitation. With one smooth thrust he entered her, wrapping himself in liquid velvet. She cried out something indiscernible, but even muffled by his mouth over hers he recognised the same note of victory and ecstasy he'd felt in joining her.

She felt magnificent.

Slowly he withdrew, only to slam into her again, leaning into her and forcing her lower. Her hands went back to support herself and she threw her head back, gasping for air, her shiny fake hair falling back from her pale skin like the tide receding.

He loved the way it moved.

He loved the way she moved, especially when he was inside her.

He planted his mouth over her throat in the spot where her pulse flickered and jumped as he pumped into her again. She felt so good, so damned good, and as she squeezed her muscles around him and the pressure built inside he knew that though he wanted this feeling to last longer, for ever, there was no way he was going to be able to make it last.

No way on earth.

There was nothing he could do. Control ceased to exist. Then she bucked under him, her muscles tight and urgent, inflaming, drawing him deeper and deeper inside and he was lost.

He cried out, something harsh and guttural and triumphant as he emptied himself into her shuddering body, collecting her up and pulling her down on to him in a broad conference chair.

Oh, wow!

She hadn't known what to expect but it sure hadn't been such an all-consuming experience. Her body still hummed from their union, her pulse and breathing slowly settling back into a more normal routine.

He sprawled below her, cradling her, as her brain tried to kick back in.

But what had she done?

She took a few deep breaths, feeling her pulse quieten and trying to make sense of what had just happened.

She'd just made love with the boss. And not just any boss. She'd made love with Damien DeLuca.

What was more, they'd not used protection. Nothing. Hadn't even stopped to think about it.

She must be mad. She'd thought she wasn't the reckless type but one feeling of desire, one whiff of Damien being attracted to her, and logic had vanished from her mind. Completely and utterly.

She must be crazy.

And now she was cradled on top of him, Damien's

hand at her breast, caressing her, his naked body below already showing signs of recovery.

The languid feel of her muscles and limbs vanished as cold, hard truth replaced it. Without trying to touch him too much, she tried to angle herself off, tried to edge away. How was she going to explain what had happened? How could she ever face him again? Guilt and shame settled upon her like a shroud.

She had to get out of here. Before he discovered who she was. There was even a chance she might even lose her job over this—who knew how he might react?—and she couldn't afford that, not with the prospect of expensive hospice care for her mother coming up some time soon.

She had to get out of here. *Now.*

'What's wrong?'

She glanced at the door and her pulse went into overdrive as an idea formed in her mind. With Damien naked, at least she had a running start. Her hand patted her throat. 'Th…thirsty.'

'I think I can fix that,' he said easily, easing her from his lap gently.

She pulled up the bodice on her dress and reached down to retrieve her underwear.

'Don't bother putting that back on,' he said, leaning over to kiss her on her already swollen lips. 'We haven't finished with each other yet. Not by a long shot.'

Still she clung to the scrap of material as if it was life-support while his words turned to a desire that curled deep within her.

He wanted her again.

She wished he hadn't told her that. She didn't want any regrets from this night—she had enough of those already. But the last thing she wanted was to lie by herself in bed during the long lonely nights ahead thinking about what pleasures she might have missed out on.

Naked, he turned and padded his way to a built-in cabinet along the narrowest wall. She watched him go in the pale light even as she edged closer to the door, his skin deliciously firm, his legs long and powerful, unwilling to tear her eyes away. He pulled open a door, exposing a bar fridge behind and hunkered down to look inside.

This was her chance!

She hit the door running, doing battle with the lock and finally wrenching it open. Behind her he shouted for her to stop but she couldn't stop, couldn't turn.

She raced over the parquet floor to the stairs as fast as she could, the heels on her sandals clattering and echoing in the dark-filled space, blood pumping so loudly it drowned out the curses ringing in her ears.

She was down the steps and halfway to the exit before she calmed to a brisk walk, heading purposefully for the safety of the night, ears straining over the music for anything that would signal less than a clean getaway. But behind her came no sound of pursuit, no hint of a chase.

She was going to make it. Euphoria replaced panic.

She was safe.

CHAPTER FOUR

SHE was a mess of nerves.

On Monday morning Philly sat at her desk, responding to emails and organising herself for the day and the week ahead. Walking into the office had been hairy—everyone had been talking about the ball, laughing about the costumes and the night's revelries.

She'd purposely avoided talk of the ball, hinting at a quiet night at home with her mother—and had waited with breath frozen in her lungs for someone to out her. If anyone had recognised her, this was it. But her colleagues just expressed their sympathies that she'd missed the event of the year and drifted away to talk amongst themselves. Even Sam just grunted and headed off for a meeting with Damien.

Thank heavens Sam had recovered from the flu—she didn't fancy running into Damien DeLuca right now. She wasn't at all sure how she would ever face him again.

At least now Sam was back from sick leave and holding the reins again and she could keep a low profile. Sam would certainly make sure of it.

She was mid-sentence in a response to a lengthy email when the phone rang. She propped the phone up to her ear, still typing, with her train of thought still focused on her detailed reply.

'Ms Summers?' Damien's voice belted down the line faster than she could make her own greeting. Her body tensed on a shiver and the phone dropped from her shoulder, landing on the desk with a loud thunk. The noise snapped her out of her temporary paralysis and she grappled for the receiver. Why was Damien calling her?

Did he know? Had Sam recognised her after all and informed Damien of her identity?

'What the— Ms Summers, is that you?'

'S-sorry,' she stammered. 'The phone slipped.'

She heard something like an exasperated sigh and could imagine the rolling of eyes going on at the other end of the line.

'Ms Summers, I need you in my office. Now.'

Philly clutched the phone. She wasn't ready for this. How was she going to explain what had happened? How could she look him in the eye after what they'd done together, the intimacy they'd shared?

She was bound to get the sack over this. She didn't deserve anything less. How was she going to explain that to her next prospective employer?

'Are you still there?'

She swallowed. 'I'll be right up,' she croaked.

He slapped the phone down, regarding it critically. What was her problem? He hoped he wasn't making a big mistake over this.

He turned back to Sam, who was waiting anxiously in the chair opposite, scraping at his fingertips with his thumbnail and looking every inch a man insecure about his position in the world.

Right now Damien knew the feeling. He'd had it ever since the woman dressed as Cleopatra had abandoned him on Saturday night. No one had ever walked out on Damien DeLuca before—that was bad enough. But right now there was a woman out there who'd done even more than that—she'd run out on him and he didn't even have a clue who she was.

It had only taken him a few seconds to throw his costume back on but by the time he'd done that and raced downstairs there'd been no sign of her anywhere. She'd been swallowed up by the night.

What was her game?

Why had she run away like that? Why had she panicked? She'd had plenty of opportunity to change her mind if she'd so wanted—and she hadn't wanted—that much was patently clear. On the contrary, she'd been perfectly willing all the way—perfectly accommodating—perfectly inviting.

A perfect fit.

He'd been cheated of exploring that knowledge further. He'd been cheated of seeing how far they could take each other. He'd been cheated of seeing her eyes…

Could it be that she'd recognised him? Was that what had scared her off? Suddenly afraid of being with the company founder and CEO she'd fled? But she hadn't seemed that obtuse—surely she would have realised when he'd been called away suddenly by Enid, if not before, of his true identity? So why would she suddenly panic later on?

He didn't like it one bit—the prospect of her knowing his identity when he had no idea who she was or where to start looking for her. He studied the man sitting nervously opposite him.

But Sam might.

When the masks had come off he was sure he'd seen Sam dressed up as a nun. There'd been a nun in the group where he'd first seen the woman standing. He might know. And if Sam didn't someone else had to. She'd been there for hours waiting for him to return. Someone had to have spoken to her, someone had to know who she was.

'Sam,' he said, adding a smile for good measure. 'Did you have a good time on Saturday night?'

Sam chortled and sat up, eager to please. 'A great time. Wonderful party. Just wonderful. The staff are very grateful to you—'

Damien held up one hand. 'Good, that's fine. But I wonder if you can help me with something.'

'Anything—name it.'

'Only there's someone there I meant to catch up with before the end but I missed her. She was dressed up as Cleopatra. Dark hair, white gown—sound familiar at all?'

'Too right, she does,' said Sam enthusiastically before he suddenly frowned. 'Not sure where she got to, actually—one moment she was there and the next—poof—she was gone.'

Damien felt his pulse kick up. He was on the trail. Hot on the trail. She wouldn't stay out of his clutches for long. 'And her name,' he prompted. 'Can you tell me her name?'

Sam thought for a moment. 'She did tell me.' He looked ceilingwards and scratched his chin while Damien resisted the urge to slam his fist into it. If he thought it would jog his memory the fist would have won hands down.

'Oh, that's it. I remember now.' Sam looked triumphant. Damien tried to remain seated.

'And?'

'Marie, from the Sydney office I think she said. Didn't catch a surname. She was a little bit wary of going in—must have been off-putting, not knowing anybody at one of those things. Awkward when you hardly know a soul. She came in with us but then we lost contact with her.' He frowned, contemplating his nails. 'Wonder where she got to?'

Damien knew something of where she'd disappeared to. He'd asked her to dance and at first she'd seemed reluctant but then something had changed and she'd moved like warm chocolate in his arms—soft, luscious and ready to be consumed.

Very ready as it later turned out when he'd returned from his calls. She'd waited for him for way longer than what he'd promised. But she'd waited for him as if she could no sooner forsake the hope he'd return than he could abandon the absolute necessity to get back to her.

Then she'd fallen into his arms and the tension had built between them again. The trek to the boardroom had been an exercise in restraint but he'd made it and she was every bit a willing partner when they'd got there. More than willing, he recalled, as she'd practically invited him to enter her. And he had.

It had been like a dream. The sex had been everything he'd anticipated with the promise of more, even more mind-blowing. And then she'd gone and his evening had turned into a nightmare.

Sam continued to prattle on, openly contemplating where Marie might have gone. Damien ignored him, diving instead for his internal phone directory, scouring the lists. The Sydney office wasn't large and the name didn't ring any bells but the way this company was growing there was no way he could keep up with all the new staff.

He made one unsuccessful pass through. No luck.

Too fast, he decided, and set his eyes to something less than warp speed as he scanned the lists.

No Marie!

He picked up the phone, oblivious to the stream of consciousness coming from Sam's direction. 'Enid,' he snapped as soon as she answered, 'have we taken on anyone recently in the Sydney office called Marie? There's no one on the phone lists.'

He waited the few seconds while Enid responded in the negative before then throwing the phone down in disgust.

'Are you sure it was Marie?'

'What? Oh, er…' Sam thought for a moment before nodding his head. 'Pretty sure. I tend to take more notice of what people say when they're such stunners, if you get my drift.'

Damien sent him a look that would curdle milk and watched Sam shrink down in his chair with some satisfaction. He wasn't entirely comfortable with the thought that every other man in the room had felt the same powerful attraction to his mystery woman. 'No, I'm not sure I do.'

But what Sam had said bothered him. His mystery woman had chosen a fake name to go with her fake outfit. Now how was he going to find her?

It had to be someone who worked in the company. One of maybe three hundred women. Half of them he could write off as being too old, a good percentage of those left didn't have the same kind of head turning figure. There couldn't be more than one hundred who'd qualify. He'd find her, whatever it took. And when he found her…

A tap at the door shifted his attention from Sam.

'You wanted to see me?'

Miss Brown Mouse stood at the door, looking even more timid than her creature companion as her eyes scampered around the room, settling finally somewhere near Sam.

'Ms Summers,' Damien said, turning his mind back to business. 'I've been waiting for you. Come in.'

She took tentative mouse steps across the room, finally lowering herself into a vacant chair alongside Sam. She was wearing the same brown jacket as the first time he'd met her, but this time with matching trousers. They fitted her better than the skirt; at least they gave some sense that she had legs, decent ones by the look, under all that tweed.

For just a second his gaze narrowed, his thoughts scrambling for sense. Surely she couldn't be one of the one hundred most likely? He looked to her face, pink and shy, her lips tight and her eyes skittering from side to side.

No, no chance. But she might know who his Cleopatra was. 'Were you at the ball on the weekend?'

She jumped as if she'd been shot but it was Sam who responded. 'Philly wasn't there.'

Damien looked from Sam to Philly. 'Why was that?'

'Well, you see,' she said, licking her lips, not wanting to add lying to her list of transgressions, 'my mother isn't well…'

He seemed to think about it for a while and then he nodded.

Philly couldn't wait to get out of there. She wasn't sure what had just happened here, but it looked as if she'd managed to survive, her secret identity intact.

'So,' she said. 'If that's all?' Her hands were already pushing her up out of the chair.

'No, that's not all. Sit down.'

She obeyed him, not because she wanted to, but more to do with the fact that her knees had turned to jelly, the exhilaration at her near escape evaporating.

'I asked you in here because I need someone to work closely on a new project with me. After that presentation you delivered the other week, I figure you're just the person for the job so I asked Sam if he could do without you for a few days.'

She looked desperately at the man next to her. Surely he wouldn't let anyone else get an opportunity this good? 'And Sam said?'

'Sam said he couldn't spare you.'

She let go of a breath she'd been holding. Good old gatekeeper Sam—never let someone else get an opportunity you might want yourself. Maybe he wasn't such a bad supervisor after all.

'But I told him he had no choice.'

His words were like a punch to her lungs and she scrambled for air in the wake of his announcement.

'So it's all settled.' He turned to Sam and gave him a brief nod and a look that had him dismissed and heading for the door before Damien turned his focus back on her. 'Enid will arrange to have your work station things moved up here—there's a spare office just down the hall. We've got three days before we have to be in Queensland for meetings at the Gold Coast. We have to move fast on this. It's an opportunity too good to miss. Palmcorp is a rapidly growing business whose needs have outstripped their current systems. If we get on the ground floor with this company, it will be worth millions to us.'

'The Gold Coast,' she muttered. *With Damien.* She gulped. No, that was the last thing she needed. 'But I can't...'

He looked up sharply. 'Can't what?'

'I can't go with you.'

'What do you mean?'

I don't want to go with you!

'Well, for one thing I can't just up and leave my mother. I told you. She's ill.'

'So who looks after her now, while you're at work?'

'No one.' She noticed the victorious look in his eyes, as if he'd just scored a winning goal in the dying minutes of the Aussie Rules football grand final, and she longed to vanquish it, longed to have the umpire declare it a no goal. 'But I don't like to leave her alone at night, just the same.'

'I don't want anyone else for this presentation. I want you.'

'Well, you're just going to have to find someone else. I can't go. I won't go.'

'I see.'

The grinding of his teeth told her he didn't see at all.

'And what's the other reason?'

She looked up, confused. 'Other reason?'

'You said before, *for one thing* you had to look after your mother. What's the other reason you don't want to come to Brisbane with me?'

'Oh.' She shrugged as she felt the colour and heat flood back to her face. 'It's just a... a figure of speech.'

His piercing eyes continued to assess her, as if weighing up her words, stripping right through the layers of her deceit. But he couldn't see that far. He didn't know. He couldn't know.

She shrugged. 'What other reason could there be?'

'Are you worried I might seduce you? Is that what this is about?'

Her lungs sucked in air like a drowning woman coming up for oxygen.

'Because, let me assure you, there is no chance of that. *Absolutely no chance.* This is a business deal. I need your professional help, so if that's what's worrying you, forget it. Right now.'

Philly battled to regain her mental balance. There he was trying to put her mind at rest. If only he knew! She could ignore the implication that she wasn't worth seducing if she didn't have to explain her real reasons for not wanting to go with him.

'Of course. That's what I'd expect.'

'Good. Now that we've established that, once I arrange for round-the-clock nursing for your mother, I take it you'll have no objections to accompanying me?'

His words were framed as a question but the tone he used made them more like a challenge. She opened her mouth to talk but nothing came out.

'Fine,' he said. 'That looks like it's settled then.'

He picked up the phone and started issuing instructions to Enid regarding moving Philly's office upstairs, arranging their flight bookings and organising a round-the-clock nursing service. She sat there, looking across at him, her blood heating at his complete disrespect of her wishes, not to mention her desires.

She still hadn't agreed to go with him. How was her mother going to react to having a stranger in the house, even if there was the bonus that she'd have someone to look after her twenty-four hours a day? He hadn't even given Philly the chance to ask her.

'How dare you?' she said, rising to her feet as finally he returned the phone to the cradle. 'How dare you make arrangements for my family to suit yourself? How would you like it if I went around organising your family, so you could fall in with whatever my plans were?'

He looked up at her, his eyes for once strangely empty.

'If that pleases you, go right ahead. But you might have some trouble. My whole family was wiped out when I was nine years old.'

CHAPTER FIVE

THE words hung between them like lead weights in the still air of the climate-controlled office, the hum of his laptop the only sound.

'I'm sorry,' she said, standing there awkwardly, unsure whether to stay or leave.

'Don't be,' he said without looking up. 'It wasn't your fault.'

'No, I mean…' Her hands found each other, together they wrestled for the right words. 'I mean—'

'Forget it,' he said with a sweep of his hand, as if it meant nothing to him. 'We've got a lot to get through today so I suggest you get yourself organised. I want you back here in half an hour so we can get started.'

Fine, she thought, *whatever you say*, her compassion evaporating at his dry tone. She nodded though she was sure he didn't notice; his head was already focused on the papers in front of him. She turned to leave.

'Oh, and Ms Summers—'

'Yes?'

'Do you have anything to wear that's not brown?'

Philly looked down at her jacket and trousers. Okay, so what was wrong with her clothes? Maybe the suit didn't have an expensive label, but it was a good name brand and it had been an absolute bargain, even if the jacket was a size too large.

61

'You have a problem with brown?' She could, of course, tell him she had a little Egyptian number stashed away at home waiting to be returned that was a real crowd pleaser, but somehow she didn't think that was what he had in mind.

'This deal's worth a lot to Delucatek. The people we'll be dealing with are real high-flyers. We should look the part. Do you have anything suitable?'

Meaning *she* should look the part. His suit smacked of designer while hers screamed bargain basement. She mentally flicked through her wardrobe's contents, more spartan than ever after a pre-wedding economy drive. Bryce had been keen to get a property portfolio established between them as soon as possible and she'd been on a strict budget. Of course, she hadn't realised that at the same time that she was budgeting, he was out splashing everything he could on the other woman, Miss Hot-Property.

All her scrimping hadn't left much in the way of spending money though, especially for new clothes. Three suits, one tan, one summer-weight beige and the tweed she had on, plus black trousers, assorted blouses and a winter jacket was all that quickly came to mind if she didn't count one pristine wedding dress still in its cellophane wrapping. She really ought to think about returning that some time. She wouldn't be using it now.

She could have used her savings to buy new clothes since then, of course. But there was every possibility she'd need all of that and more once her mother got too sick to stay at home.

She was no fool. As much as she wanted to be able to care for her mother, there would come a time when it just wouldn't work. She wouldn't be able to be there twenty-four hours a day and she'd need to move somewhere with better care options. And from the enquiries she'd already made, good hospice care didn't come cheap.

'I don't know,' she said honestly. 'What will I need?'

He barely looked up. 'See Enid later. She'll have the schedule and you can work out what you have to get and go shopping this afternoon after we've worked out a strategy. I'll arrange an allowance.'

'Fine,' she said, feeling totally aggrieved, ramming her glasses up her nose defiantly as she turned on her heel. 'I just hope it's enough.'

It was more than enough. Philly surveyed the figure on the letter of authority Enid handed her with shock. Surely someone had made a mistake?

'I think there's one too many zeroes,' she suggested.

Enid glanced over, eyes peering through her bifocals. 'No, that's right. Now there are three boutiques listed where this authority is valid. They should be able to supply everything you need. If you have to go elsewhere, keep the receipts and you'll be reimbursed.'

'But this is a fortune.'

Enid smiled at the younger woman. 'He just wants you to look nice. It's important to him.'

'It's important to the deal, more like it,' she said, certain that nothing Damien thought about her would be personal. It would all relate to business.

The older woman's head tilted to one side.

'I think you'll find he's right. This deal's very important to the company and we have to do everything we can to ensure it comes off. I'm quite sure you'll feel more confident and more professional with a couple of new outfits and much more capable of holding your own. And I know Damien can seem a little tactless at times. But you mustn't take it too seriously. He simply hasn't had the same start most of us have had.'

If Philly hadn't heard his comment about losing his family earlier, she'd think Enid was mad. The guy was a multimillionaire, for goodness' sake, and here was someone practically feeling sorry for him.

Could Enid be right? The question plagued Philly's mind as she spent the next two hours searching for outfits suitable for meetings, possible cocktail parties and flash dinners in boutiques she'd only ever dreamed about entering before.

Was the early tragedy in his life the reason why he was so driven to succeed? So demanding of everyone around him? Was he trying to show the world he could make it on his own? Was that why he rode roughshod over everyone else's feelings—because his own had been so desperately and critically shattered at such a tender age?

Whoa! Next thing *she'd* be feeling sorry for him too. She didn't need that—not with the secret of last Saturday night playing on her mind.

And she couldn't afford to feel anything for Damien. If he'd thought he was easing her mind by declaring there was no way he'd be tempted to seduce her, he had another think coming.

He'd no doubt thought he was being considerate,

allaying a sweet innocent nobody's fears of seduction at the hands of her boss. When it was already too late for that. Much too late.

All he'd done was insult her. Making love with Cleopatra was one thing but making love with Philly Summers was never going to happen.

How reassuring! He'd made it clear that the man she couldn't stop fantasising about had her pegged around at the level of the woman least likely. How flattering—and yet here she was, supposed to feel relieved.

And all he'd done was to reinforce her resolve not to reveal her secret. Given his attitude he would be less impressed with the revelation. Clearly he would be embarrassed at the thought—probably even humiliated. Well, she would save them both that. She would forget it had ever happened. He need never know.

But if she became pregnant?

She shivered. She didn't want to go down that path. It was altogether too exciting and yet too terrifying. And the chances were so slim. How many couples got pregnant the first time they had unprotected sex anyway? It was hardly likely to be a consideration.

She sighed, fed up with both shopping and with the direction her thoughts were going. Spending two days in Damien's company would be bad enough. But to spend one night away—that could only be worse. She would have to do her best to remain cool, aloof and totally professional and with any luck he'd treat her with his usual professional disregard. Then in two weeks she'd have her period and there'd never be a reason she'd have to reveal a thing to him.

And in time she might even forget about what had happened in the boardroom, might stop thinking about the way his body had rippled in the slatted moonlight as he'd driven into her, the way he'd felt inside, possessing her.

Forget that night?

That was a laugh. There was no way she was ever going to be able to forget that.

She was late. The plane was due to take off in less than half an hour and she was nowhere to be seen. She couldn't have changed her mind—he'd arranged everything. The last time he'd spoken to her she'd even admitted that the live-in nurse Enid had organised was wonderful and that her mother was totally relaxed about the whole arrangement.

Not so Ms Summers. He could still see the nervous pinch to her lips, the strain in her face so evident whenever they'd discussed the upcoming trip. What was really bothering her? She couldn't be worried about him coming on to her. Hadn't he assured her this was purely a business trip? She wasn't his type for a start. Sure, she was great at her job but he had no more intention of seducing her than he would ask someone to marry him. It just wasn't going to happen.

In any event, he preferred his women lush, sexy and temporary, like that woman on Saturday night— her outfit accommodating, her attitude willing.

Though she'd proved far too temporary for his liking.

Who the hell was she anyway? Two days of scouring staff lists and making discreet enquiries had got him absolutely nowhere. His mystery woman remained that, a mystery. All he had was the memory of her, her fingers clutched behind his head, her tight breasts spilling out and her body open to him. His body responded to the images in his mind and he cursed low and rough as he helped himself to a cup of espresso.

He hadn't had enough of her, not by a long shot, but thinking about her now wasn't going to help him.

He lifted his head, scouring the airline club lounge once more as he emptied a stick of sugar into his cup but there was no sign of a sandy-coloured ponytail, no thick tortoiseshell glasses in evidence anywhere.

Damn, where the hell could she be?

A blonde in a pale green trouser suit approached the coffee station and he moved away to make room for her.

'I was wondering when you were going to get here.'

He swung back, coffee sloshing over the side of his cup. He steadied it with his other hand. His brain wasn't so easy to get a handle on. *Ms Summers?*

Sure enough it was her hazel eyes staring up at him, but they looked different. *She looked different.* He blinked.

'I booked one of the offices so we could go over the paperwork—just this way.'

He followed her into the small office, wondering just what had happened to his little brown mouse. She still smelled the same, the now familiar apricot scent wafting freshly in her wake. It was her looks that had changed. The long-line jacket sat over a fitted white shell top and seemingly floated behind her as she walked in matching trousers that weren't tight yet still hinted at womanly curves below.

Her hair, uncharacteristically worn down, was shoulder-length and feathered at the ends and it didn't look the colour of sand any more. It looked more like honey, honey sprinkled with crystals of sugar, the ends swishing and flicking with her motion. And what had she done with her glasses?

He was seated at the desk before he could talk. 'You look—different,' he said at last.

She smiled, almost as if self-conscious, as her gaze flicked over the outfit. 'I hope it's appropriate. I know business is a little more relaxed up in Queensland.'

He nodded his approval as his eyes slowly moved up her body. She fingered the ends of her hair and caught him looking. 'Oh, that. I was due for a cut so I let them talk me into something extra this time. But I didn't use your money. I paid for the hair myself.'

'What happened to your glasses?'

'Contact lenses. I lost one and had to get a new prescription made up. Still, I don't wear them as much as I should…' She hesitated. 'What's wrong?'

He realised he was staring. He coughed as he pulled his eyes away, lifting his laptop case to the table. 'Nothing,' he said with a shake of his head. 'We'll be boarding soon. We'd better get on with it.'

It was time well spent on the ground and in the air. By the time they'd arrived at Coolangatta Airport they'd thoroughly reviewed their potential client's specifications and finessed their plan of attack. Damien was feeling more and more confident even though he knew there was still a mountain of work ahead and a myriad of meetings with Palmcorp, their lawyers and financiers. But they could do it. He'd made the right choice in bringing her. They made a good team.

This was Damien at his best. In the large meeting room at Palmcorp's offices on the Gold Coast, Philly listened to his spiel, watched him charm, tease and manoeuvre the two directors and get them thinking his way. It was like watching a master at work.

No wonder he'd built his business to be the success it was. When he spoke he made you believe, the passion for his work and his products coming to the fore.

He held them in the palm of his hand.

It was a new side to Damien, one she hadn't witnessed before. Now his obsession with perfection, with driving his staff hard, made some sort of sense. He couldn't be that passionate about his business if the people who worked for him gave him less than their best.

His strong, deep voice flowed over the assembled group, his expressive hands adding gestures for emphasis where required, addressing them at their level, not preaching, not patronising, but taking every one of them with him. No one stopped him for questions or interrupted the flow. He was in his element. He was supreme.

It was impossible not to be impressed. And it wasn't just the way he spoke. The way he held himself and the way he looked had as much to do with it. He'd discarded his jacket and the fine white shirt only emphasised his olive skin and dark features.

He looked great in white. Even though his business shirt contrasted in a major way with the Roman armour he'd worn to the ball, both styles suited the man that he was.

She swallowed. He'd looked great in that outfit.

Then again, he'd looked great out of it. The way he'd discarded the armour, then the tunic, pulling it over his head and flinging it on the floor, the way his chest had expanded as her eyes had drunk him in, the way he'd stood next to her, waiting, anticipating…

Oh Lord, was she never going to get those pictures out of her head?

'Ms Summers?'

She came back to the meeting with a jolt to meet Damien's quizzical gaze. 'Is everything all right?'

She looked around in panic but the others all seemed busy helping themselves to the pots of filtered coffee and jugs of orange juice that had suddenly materialised from nowhere.

'You would like to handle the marketing perspective next up, I take it?'

'Oh yes, of course,' she said, her cheeks scorched and with confidence battling for dominance over visions of one gloriously near naked man. 'I was simply mentally preparing myself for the task. Excuse me, I think I'll get myself a juice.'

Her presentation sailed along, her earlier embarrassment soon forgotten as she got underway. She used the same basic format that she'd shown Damien at their meeting just a few weeks ago, expanding it to include additional detail for people less familiar with the company and the product. It seemed to go well and afterwards she fielded questions from the group before they all broke for a late lunch.

Damien sidled up alongside her as they were heading for the cars that would take them to the restaurant.

'Well done,' he said, bending down to whisper softly into her ear, his hand at her back. 'Excellent job.' He moved on, the curl of his breath against her skin rippling through her and tripping her heart-rate.

It took a deep breath to know how to respond as she battled to sort out the emotions vying for supremacy inside her. The employee side of her ego couldn't help but swell with pride that he considered she'd done her job well and his faith in her had been vindicated.

Yet another side of her that was already battered felt as if he had pressed hard on her most sensitive bruises. If only he had as much faith in her as a woman—if only he hadn't been so quick to write her off. Maybe there could have been a chance for something more to develop.

But what chance was there of that? They hadn't even shared a one-night stand. It had been more of a one shot wonder.

But by the time she'd realised that she should just smile and thank him he'd already turned away, thoroughly absorbed in a discussion of the finer points of European motor vehicle engineering.

She sighed. She'd missed her chance. Or she'd read much too much into his comments in the first place. Whatever, she really needed to relax more.

The afternoon didn't afford that. It was spent in more discussions and a tour of Palmcorp's offices before meetings with the finance and legal specialists that ran late. Again Damien steered the proceedings with skill and startling business acumen but did it in such a way that she could see the Palmcorp directors actually believing they were driving the process.

Businesswise, it was all proceeding very well. But with their early start it was a full-on day and all Philly wanted to do by the end was to go to her hotel room and enjoy a long hot soak. There was no time for that though, with a business dinner already arranged. At a pinch there'd be just enough time to shower and change.

Her room back at the hotel was spacious and elegant, luxury all the way, decorated in cool pastels with a wall of windows leading to a balcony, showcasing the brilliant blue of the ocean and the white sandy beach that stretched for miles to the north and south. A pity there was no time to enjoy it.

She had half an hour before she was to meet Damien in the lobby but she rang home before anything else. The nurse answered on the second ring, passing the phone over without hesitation. Her mother came on, her voice weak but with a bright note she hadn't heard for some time.

'How's it all going?' Philly asked her mother.

'I've been playing mah-jongg with Marjorie,' she said, 'and what's more I've been winning, so don't you worry about a thing. We're having a lovely time.'

She said goodbye and hung up on a smile, satisfied that she could at least relax on the domestic front. Tomorrow she'd be home and then, with any luck, she'd be able to relax on the Damien front too.

She'd done it again. Just like when she'd turned up in the airport lounge that morning, her appearance knocked him for a six. The dress she wore looked more like a coffee-coloured sheath, so hugging in the bodice that the tiny diamanté shoestring straps must be there purely for adornment, the floaty skirt constructed in separate panels wafting around her legs as she walked so that with every step the panels shifted slightly, revealing an ever changing and tantalising glimpse of flesh.

She'd put up her hair in a clasp but he could see the odd tendril floating free, bouncing as she moved towards him, and she'd done something with her face. Make-up? Whatever it was, her eyes looked bigger, her smile looked wider and her lips...

Red and lush, her lips looked like an invitation.

He swallowed. What had happened to his little brown mouse? Not that he didn't approve—she'd obviously made the most of the allowance he'd supplied for just that purpose—it was just that he hadn't been expecting such an amazing transformation.

Such an alluring transformation.

Dinner was fun. Stuart and Shayne Murchison, the directors of Palmcorp, were a dynamic pair in their late twenties, as attractive as they were successful. Both shared the same tanned good looks, with blue eyes and hair bleached by too much sun and surf from the regular iron-man competitions they took part in, competing as much against each other as the clock.

They were also very good hosts, treating their guests to a fabulous seafood dinner on a restaurant terrace overlooking the beach, entertaining them with anecdotes from their long history of competitions and all the while arguing incessantly as to who was the fastest swimmer or could catch the best waves.

'So why aren't either of you married?' she asked, partly for fun, partly curious that neither of the men had been snapped up.

'Ah, that's easy,' said Stuart.

'No one's ever been able to swim fast enough to catch us,' finished Shayne, and the brothers laughed as if it was an all too well practised line.

'But,' Stuart offered, his eyes glinting wickedly at Philly's, 'that doesn't mean we're not still looking.'

As she laughed her way with them Philly felt the tension of the last few days slipping away. She hadn't enjoyed herself so much for ages. Knowing her mother was being well taken care of, and in her new clothes under the sails of a sunny terrace just a stone's throw from the sparkling blue ocean, she felt a new woman. Certainly to be the only woman at a table of such good-looking men was a novelty. Maybe it wasn't such a bad idea coming on this trip after all.

All three men turned heads in the restaurant, making her the object of envy from the waitresses and plenty of the guests besides, but even though all were good-looking there was no argument in Philly's mind as to just which man dominated the proceedings. The brothers were ultrafit and no weaklings, yet Damien, all dark brooding looks and latent power inherent in his every move, dwarfed them with his sheer presence.

Her eyes settled on him now as he quietly allowed the brothers full rein at being hosts. Only the scowl between his dark brows betrayed him. No doubt he'd be thinking about the meetings to come, wheels spinning as he developed plans and devised tactics to close the deal.

He turned suddenly and snagged her eyes with a look that sparked and flared and she jerked her head away sharply, feeling caught out, not understanding the sudden aggression in his eyes and trying to focus back on the conversation with a face that bore the heat from his gaze.

'Tell me about your name.' Stuart Murchison leaned closer, clearly oblivious to her discomfiture, one arm at the back of her chair, his body turned to hers, his other hand swirling what was left of his glass of premium Hunter Valley shiraz. 'Philly. That's so unusual. There must be a story behind it.'

Damien bristled as he glared at Stuart's back. Okay, so the dinner had gone well, the whole day had gone well, and with a pinch of luck tomorrow Palmcorp would sign on the dotted line, but that didn't mean his assistant was up for grabs. She wasn't part of the deal. Sure, he'd wanted her to look presentable, had even supplied her with the funds to do so. But did she have to have done it quite so successfully?

He stirred his coffee longer than was absolutely necessary and discarded his spoon with a solid clink. The sooner this night ended the better.

Alongside him, Philly smiled in response to Stuart's question and took a sip of her mineral water.

'This is probably going to sound really silly…'

'Of course it won't,' said Stuart, stroking her shoulder, 'you can tell us.'

Damien resisted the urge to growl, instead focusing on Philly's response.

She cradled the glass between her two hands on the table and smiled. 'Okay then. My parents wanted to give their children names that were a bit different. They decided on the names of cities that they liked the sound of.' She looked from the face of one brother to the other. 'Oh, gosh, that does sound weird, doesn't it, especially seeing no one but my mother calls me Philadelphia anyway. It always gets shortened to Philly.'

'Not at all,' Shayne said, shaking his head. Stuart put down his glass. 'So they named you Philadelphia?' He nodded. 'Yeah, I like it. So what did your folks call the other kids—Melbourne—Paris—Constantinople?'

Even from where he was sitting Damien sensed the change in her as she ignored the light-hearted banter, her eyes focusing on the glass between her hands. 'There was only one other. My kid brother. They named him Montreal.'

'Montreal. That's unusual,' said Stuart.

'I know.' She smiled softly, letting her head fall to one side. 'He hated it so we call him—' She hesitated, suddenly biting down on her bottom lip. 'We used to call him Monty instead.'

There was a quiet resonance in her words that went way beyond what was spoken.

'What happened to him?' Damien asked softly, before he'd realised he'd even put voice to his question.

Her eyes were fixed on the glass, her thumbs stroking away the condensation forming and reforming on the outside.

'He was a pilot, flying home for the weekend with Annelise, his wife, to show off their new baby son. They'd named him after our father—he died ten years ago and mum was so proud that they'd named the baby after him. She couldn't wait to meet her first grandchild.' She took a breath, as if unwilling to give voice to what came next for fear it would be true.

'There was a storm *en route* and something went wrong; they think a lightning strike took out the electrical system.' She shrugged. 'Whatever. The plane crashed and they all...every one of them. They all died.' Her voice dropped to a whisper. 'Thomas was just ten days old.'

Forces shifted inside him as the silence that followed blanketed the table. The quiet emotion of her words betrayed a feeling he recognised, a feeling buried deep inside.

But it was a feeling he didn't want to be reminded of. He didn't want to pull it out and examine what it meant. It was better off left exactly where it was.

Philly looked up at the faces around the table. 'Oh, I'm sorry, you didn't want to hear all that. Please forgive me.'

Stuart was the first to react. His arm shifted from the chair back to around her shoulders and he gave her a squeeze, putting his wineglass down so he could cover her hands in his. 'Don't apologise,' he said softly. 'There's absolutely no need.'

She smiled up at him, her lashes moist, eyes glistening. 'Thank you, Stuart.'

'Call me Stu,' he said, his voice low and sympathetic. 'All my friends do.'

Her smile widened. 'Thank you, Stu.'

Damien pushed himself out of his chair. 'Time to call it a night. Thank you, gentlemen. We'll see ourselves back to the hotel.'

Philly looked up, surprised by his sudden action. 'Oh, right. Okay.'

She made a move to stand but Stuart placed an ironman fist over her arm, pinning her to the chair. 'It's still early,' he said, his eyes fixed on Philly but the tone of his words aimed directly at Damien. 'Maybe Philly would like to see a little more of the Gold Coast entertainment.'

His eyes softened. 'Would you like that, Philly? Do you like to dance?'

'Um, yes, actually,' she said, her voice wavering. 'I do.'

He turned to Damien triumphantly. 'So that's settled, then. Sorry you don't feel up to joining us, Damien, but we'll see you tomorrow morning at the office. And don't worry, we'll look after Philly for you.'

Damien battled with the urge to rearrange one smug face, but he wasn't about to undo all the goodwill they'd built up today. Then again, he wasn't about to be out-manoeuvred either.

He dredged up a laugh, as if he was enjoying the banter, and schooled his voice to sound civilised while inside him his heartbeat pounded like jungle drums. 'Another time, perhaps. Sorry to disappoint you, but Ms Summers and I have some important details to go over tonight. I'm sure you understand.'

With that he placed a firm hand under her elbow and levered her from her chair. Stuart was left with no choice but to remove his hand from her arm though he made no pretence that he was happy about it.

'Good night, gentlemen. I look forward to further-ing our discussions in the morning.'

He steered Philly out of the restaurant and into a waiting taxi without saying another word.

'What was that all about?'

She was sick of the silent treatment, sick of the brooding male who had sprawled over the taxi seat like a despot, arrogant limbs taking up space as if he owned it, sick of the way he'd frog-marched her to her door like a prisoner to be locked in for the night.

As his silence continued her anger grew and grew, simmering away, fuelled by the heat he was giving off with his black mood.

'What was what all about?'

'Don't give me that,' she said as she inserted her card key into the reader. 'You acted like some cave-man back there at the restaurant.'

Down the corridor the lift doors binged open, spill-ing a load of camera-wielding tourists into the hall-way.

The lock clicked open. Damien grabbed the handle and turned. 'Inside,' he said, half shoving her across the threshold, closing the door behind them.

'Excuse me,' she said, wheeling around to face him, hands on hips. 'What the hell do you think you're doing now?'

'Keeping our private business just that. Private. There's no need to share it with a busload of tourists.'

'Well, don't make yourself comfortable then be-cause what I have to say to you will only take a mo-ment. You had no right to come on like that back there.'

'I'm your boss. I had every right.'

'Is that so? Then where's this important work we need to go over then? You never said anything about it before. You made that up.'

'We have important meetings tomorrow and you know it.'

'Yes, with people you did your best to completely alienate tonight. What on earth were you thinking?'

'I was thinking I brought you up here to work with me, not to flirt with the customers.'

Her mouth fell open in disbelief. 'I wasn't flirting!'

'Come on. You had *Stu-baby* draped all over you like a gorilla.'

'He was being sympathetic, that's all.'

'Sympathetic? Is that what you call it when someone's angling to get into your pants?'

'How dare you?' The crack of her palm against his cheek was as loud as it was satisfying. Her victory was short-lived though as he snared her still open hand in one swift-moving fist. His other hand stroked the region, a red weal already brightening under his fingers.

'You deserved that.' She spat the words out over a gasping breath, refusing to give in to her first instinct to apologise.

He looked down at her, dark fire burning in his eyes, his breathing strangely calm under the circumstances. 'And this,' he said, pulling on her wrist so that she collided full length with him, 'is what you deserve.'

Still half off balance, she felt his arm surround her and haul her tightly against him as his head dipped lower. Panic, outrage and sheer bliss all welled within her as his lips meshed with hers; panic that he would somehow recognise her as the woman he'd made love to on Saturday night; outrage that he could treat her this way, and sheer unadulterated bliss that he had.

Since their encounter at the ball she'd dreamed of nothing else but to be in Damien's arms once more. Those dreams had ended in disappointed awakenings and frustrated tomorrows. But now he was here, really here, holding her, *kissing her* and it was no dream.

Her thin sand-washed satin dress might not have been there. She could feel all of him, the length of him, the heat of him, searing her through the fine fabric.

He let go of her wrist and his hand went behind her head, drawing her closer, holding her firm and somewhere his anger turned into something else. It was desire she could feel from him now, a hot, urgent thing that was as tangible as the flesh beneath her hands and it called to her, tempting her, insisting she give herself up to it.

Why shouldn't she?

It would be so easy.

She knew the pleasure she'd find. She'd only had a sample of what he had to offer, but there was no doubt there was so much more that she'd like to experience. Why should it matter if she did?

But how could she?

Things were complicated between them already. Already there were secrets. Already there was too much to explain. This wasn't going to help.

Besides, he didn't want her. He'd made that perfectly plain when he'd set the boundaries for this trip. What was happening now had more to do with his competitive nature and showing her who was boss than any real interest he had in Philly Summers. Because he'd made it perfectly clear that he had none.

And that was the killer punch. If she'd thought for a moment that he felt something for her other than pure animal lust, if she thought she had something else going for her in his eyes other than simply being available, then yes, she'd like nothing more than to give herself up to the pleasures he promised.

But this was no fancy dress ball where he had no idea of her identity. This was no masquerade. Here there was no avoidance of the truth. He'd never wanted her and, whatever his motives, he didn't really want her now.

This was simply wrong.

His hands slipped to her shoulders, sliding her thin straps away. She gasped as his hands followed the curve of her shoulders, around to the front, lower, capturing her breasts, thumbs hooking in her bodice top, easing it lower.

Her hands found his chest as she dragged her face away from his. She pushed but his hands caught her and pulled her back. She pushed again, harder, turning her face so that he couldn't kiss her.

'No,' she said, her breath choppy. 'Stop this.'

His mouth was at her neck, cajoling, insisting and panic gripped her.

'*No!*' she yelled. 'Just because you bought these clothes don't assume you own what's in them.'

'The clothes are yours,' he muttered, ignoring her jibe, his breath hot and persuasive against her skin. 'Keep them.'

She squeezed her eyes shut, praying for strength.

'You promised!'

His head lifted but he didn't let go. 'What did I promise?'

'Not to maul me. You promised me there was no chance you would seduce me on this trip. You made it perfectly clear there was not a snowball's chance in hell—remember? So let me go—now.'

He had promised, he remembered. Why the hell had he done that?

His arms slackened their grip around her and she eased herself away, hitching up her shoulder straps before flicking back her hair with her fingers. Her face was flushed, her lips bruised and swollen from his attention and he ached to take her back into his arms and finish what he'd begun.

He'd made that promise to someone else, though—someone else who wore ill-fitting brown suits and glasses that wouldn't be out of place on a welder. He hadn't made that guarantee to the woman standing in front of him. He would have been mad to have done that.

'I think you should leave,' she said, not moving, clutching her arms over her chest like a shield. 'Now.'

He took a deep breath. He would go. After all, he had promised.

But he definitely wouldn't make that mistake again.

CHAPTER SIX

CHRISTMAS came early to the Summers' household.

Five mornings before the big day, Philly clutched the white stick, hand shaking, eyes disbelieving, mind unable to comprehend. She looked again at the instructions, reading the last section twice over until she was sure she had it clear in her mind, then she looked back at the stick.

There was no mistake.

She had read it right.

She was pregnant.

Elation zipped through her. She'd done it! She was carrying a child. Having a baby was no longer just a dream, just a hope. It was now a reality. And in less than forty weeks, all going well, she would hold that baby in her arms. And her mother would hold her grandchild.

Please God it wouldn't be too late for it to make a difference.

But it couldn't be too late. It was a miracle. She was having a baby.

Her baby.

Elation suddenly gave way to another emotion.

Dread.

This wasn't just her baby. It was Damien's too.

Guilt gripped her heart, squeezing it as tight as the instructions now crumpled within her fist as her body swayed into the bathroom vanity unit, knocking the soap dish to the floor.

This was not some IVF pregnancy, where the sperm had been donated with the intention and hopes of furnishing someone with a child anonymously. This child's father was no phantom, no unnamed donor whose chosen part in conceiving a child was over.

This child's father was Damien DeLuca, about as far from a phantom as ice was from the sun. And he would have to be told.

Oh, he wouldn't like it. The self-confessed career bachelor and man about town was hardly likely to be excited at the prospect of discovering he was to be a father. But if he was angry about it he could hardly blame her. Neither of them had given a moment's thought to protection that night. Sure, she was the one who was pregnant, but he wasn't exactly the innocent party in all this.

Yet none of that really mattered. There was no question that she had to tell him. It wouldn't be right or fair to deny Damien the existence of his own child, just as it would be wrong to prevent that child from knowing the identity of its father.

She gazed unseeing into the mirror. And maybe, once he knew, just maybe there was a sliver of possibility that he might even care...

She shook her head, shaking out the wistful dreams and hopes. She was having a baby—wasn't that enough?

Damien would just have to deal with it, just as she would. First though, she had to tell him.

She hauled herself upright and away from the vanity. It was just as well the office was closing over Christmas. She had two weeks off to spend with her mother. She'd use the time well, see a doctor, get confirmation of her home pregnancy test result and obtain some advice about the best time to tell her mother.

'Philly?' Her mother's voice came muted from outside the door. 'Are you all right? I thought I heard something crash.'

She looked around her and saw the soap dish, now lying shattered in pieces on the floor. She hadn't even noticed. 'I'm fine,' she called back. 'Just clumsy today.'

Her mother would be delighted when she discovered why. She stooped to pick up the largest pieces and tried to quell a sudden pang of remorse. She wouldn't be judgmental—her mother wasn't like that—but she'd be curious all the same and maybe just a tiny bit sad that there was no boyfriend or husband on the scene. She'd wanted to see Philly settled down after all.

But she'd considered that same scenario when she'd applied to undergo IVF treatment. She'd known that it would still be worth it, that any disappointment would be short lived in the joy that a new baby brought, especially when that baby meant so much.

As for telling Damien? She had to tell him as soon as possible. It had been one thing to keep her secret to herself when there was no chance of him ever finding out. But now there was no way. The product of that secret would soon betray her anyway.

As soon as the doctors had confirmed the pregnancy. The first chance she had, she would tell him.

CHAPTER SEVEN

'ENID!' Where was that woman? *'Enid!'*

Enid appeared at his office doorway, pen and blue folder at the ready.

'You rang?' she asked, one eyebrow skewed north.

He gritted his teeth. He never liked it when she took that tone. Having a PA who knew too much about you was a positive drawback at times.

'Where the hell have you been?'

'Completing the papers you asked me to fax the last time you bellowed at me, not five minutes ago. Not to mention,' she added before he had a chance to respond, 'sorting out two weeks worth of mail you demanded barely five minutes before that. And answering the phone in between—you did ask me to take even your direct line calls for today. And thank you for asking, I had a wonderful Christmas holiday. At least, I imagine that's why you demanded my presence this time?'

For a moment he was speechless. 'Well, good for you,' he replied with a snarl, wondering just why the hell he had wanted to see her.

'And Switzerland?' she continued, her eyes narrowing as if she was peering right into his soul. 'How was the skiing this year? Normally you come back a little more relaxed after your break.'

'Fine,' he snapped, drumming his fingers on the table while he tried to forget all about his failure of a holiday and remember what he wanted Enid for. 'Switzerland was fine.'

'Wonderful,' said Enid in a tone that said pigs could fly. 'Then maybe you'd like to go over what's in your diary for today.'

His head snapped up. That was it. 'Only if you've finished discussing my social calendar,' he retorted. 'My diary *is* why I asked you here in the first place.'

'I see,' said Enid, clearly nonplussed. 'Only you never said.' She flipped open the folder in her hands. 'First up at nine, you have an hour long meeting with Philly about the roll out of the new campaign, after which…'

He jerked upright and out of his chair at the sound of that name, turning to the window as Enid's voice droned on in the background listing today's appointments.

Philly. What was it about her that made him so unsettled? How did she do that? He glanced down at his watch as Enid's unheeded dialogue tailed off. Eight-thirty. She'd be here in half an hour. Barely any time at all. So why did thirty minutes suddenly seem so long?

Philly wondered if this was how morning sickness felt. It was still only early in her pregnancy, but she'd been fine up until now, finding it difficult to believe she really was pregnant, even after her doctor's confirmation and referral to a specialist. She had felt so unchanged, so utterly well.

Until today. Her gut churned, her legs felt less solid than the rice pudding she'd made for her mother last night and it had nothing to do with the motion of the train wending its way closer to Melbourne's city centre, closer to making her announcement to Damien. She knew she couldn't put it off. She knew she'd have to tell him some time. But she just wasn't at all confident she could do this today.

But neither could she delay it. The longer she did that, the harder it would be.

The train stopped, mid station. Heads lifted from newspapers and novels, knitting needles stopped clacking and fifty heads swivelled around, searching for some explanation for the delay. The speakers crackled into life with the grim news. A minor derailment ahead and a delay of at least an hour. Fifty disgruntled passengers gave a collective groan, giving up any hopes of an early start, and pulled out mobile phones to relay the news before turning their attention resignedly back to their activities.

At least an hour. Another hour to think about what she had to do. Another hour for her insides to rebel. It was the last thing she needed today. She glanced at her watch, realising she wouldn't be at work anywhere close to being in time for her meeting with Damien and rummaged in her handbag for her own mobile phone. At least she could let him know she'd be late.

Damien knew the moment she arrived. Standing with his hands in pockets, gazing out over the view of the city, he'd heard the soft ping of the lift bell and the whoosh of the doors and he'd known instinctively that she was finally here. He was sure those were her hurried footsteps tearing along the plush careting, and already he could even imagine the scent of apricots drifting along the corridor.

Funny how he couldn't get that scent out of his

head. Even in the chalet in Klosters, surrounded by beautiful women, perfumed and perfectly made-up and offering the ultimate *après-ski* experience, it had been the faint scent of apricots that had haunted his dreams. For someone who'd almost made a career of studying the effects of different perfumes on women, enjoying the effects of perfume on them, suddenly they no longer appealed. They were all too heavy, too sickly, too cloying.

It hadn't been a good holiday. Instead of being relaxed he'd had too much time to think. And there were two women he couldn't get out of his mind. One was a woman who'd let him make sweet love to her and then disappeared off the face of the earth, a woman who defied every attempt of his to track her down.

The other was a paradox, a strange mixture of innocence but with a hidden core, a centre he was finding more beguiling as the layers came off. And when he'd wanted her, she'd turned him down flat.

No one had ever done that before.

Two women, two totally unsatisfactory experiences. No wonder he was having trouble sleeping.

And now one of them couldn't even make it into work on time. Things were going to have to change around here.

He heard her brief greeting to Enid and the older woman's reply, followed by a low, 'He's waiting for you. Better go straight in.' It sounded to Damien like a warning. *Damned right.*

He waited until he could hear her footfall near his door, her breath rapid but soft, as if she was trying not to let on she was worried. He turned.

'You're late!'

'I'm sorry, but—'

'Our meeting was for nine o'clock. It's now closer to ten.'

'I phoned you…Enid—'

'You don't work for Enid. You work for me. When you can be bothered to turn up.'

'That's not fair—'

Her protest was cut off with a violent slash of his hand through the air that ended with a slam of his open palm on the desk.

'Are these the sort of hours you expect to be paid for? Because there's no place for freeloaders in this organisation.'

'I can't help it if the trains are late.'

'It's your job to get to work on time. Period. If the trains can't get you here on time, find a reliable form of transport.'

'I'll work through lunch. I'll make it up.'

'Damned right you will.'

'Fine,' she said with a sniff, pulling herself upright that way she did as if it added inches. 'At least we agree on something.'

He stopped, the wind taken out of his sails as soon as she'd stopped defending herself. His pause gave him his first chance to really look at her. Her soft linen shift fitted her well without being tight, its pastel tones cool and perfect for summer. By contrast her hazel eyes were blazing but instead of her face glowing red she looked so pale, her skin almost translucent.

'Are you okay?'

Something flared, bright and potent in her eyes, before it was just as quickly extinguished. 'Perfectly well.'

'It's just that you look a bit…washed out.'

Could he tell? Was it that obvious?

'Er, I ran all the way from the station and…' She licked her lips. She'd been going to wait until after their discussion of the roll out of the new campaign, but maybe this was as good a time as any. It might serve to wipe that pompous look off his face.

He watched her. 'And?' he prompted.

'And I'm pregnant.'

Stunned silence met her announcement. But only for a few moments. Then all hell broke loose.

'You're *what?*'

'I'm pregnant.' Actually, now that she'd said it out loud, she felt pretty good. It was good to say it. It was good to tell someone who didn't have the title of doctor before their name. A smile made its way to her lips as her hand rested over her tummy. 'I'm having a baby.'

His eyes followed the movement of her hand but there was no accompanying smile. In fact the way his lip curled made him look positively hostile.

'How the hell did that happen?'

She shrugged, still unable to stop smiling. That smug look of his was nowhere to be seen. 'The usual way.' She thought about that for a second more, enjoying the experience of turning the tables on him. 'Or not so usual, I gather.'

He grunted, clearly unimpressed, his anger wrapped around him like a shroud. 'I didn't pick you for being careless. I certainly hope you're more responsible when you're at work.'

'*I* was careless? Oh, that's rich, coming from y—'

'If you don't mind,' his terse words interjected,

'we're supposed to be talking about the campaign—that is, if you're up to it.'

'Of course I'm up to it. But Damien, I need to tell you that—'

His body jerked up in his seat. 'That what? You're not thinking of leaving the company, are you? That would be damned inconvenient after promoting you. I'm relying on you to see this new campaign through.'

'No, nothing like that. Not unless you think I should.'

'Why would I think that?'

'Well, it's just that…'

She paused, aware of a disturbance down the hall which was rapidly escalating into a commotion—someone was arguing with Enid. A moment later the door was flung wide open.

Her mouth dropped open as her ex-fiancé, carrying a large bunch of stem roses and a bottle of champagne, burst in with Enid close on his heels.

'Excuse me, Mr Chalmers, you can't go in there.'

'Relax,' Bryce crooned as he lit up one of his dazzling smiles. 'I'm sure whoever this is—' he nodded dismissively towards Damien '—will excuse us. Philly and I have important business to discuss.'

'Mr Chalmers, would you please leave. This is not Ms Summers's office.'

'Don't worry, Enid.' Damien took a step back as he lowered himself into his chair, sensing an opportunity to learn more about the secret life of Philly. First pregnant, now this character, whom one could only assume to be the father. Was he the reason she'd knocked back Damien's advances at the Gold Coast?

He felt himself bristling at the thought.

Bryce completely disregarded everyone's presence

but Philly's, sitting himself down on the desk opposite her. She made an attempt to get up but he pushed her back down, thrusting the bunch of flowers into her lap. 'For you, sweetheart, and hey, you're looking better than ever.' He leaned over and pecked her on her still open lips before he began removing the foil from the top of the champagne bottle.

Philly stared blankly at the flowers but had finally found her voice. 'Bryce—what's going on? What are you doing here?'

'I was going to surprise you when you got home but I thought it would be much more fun to whisk you away from here to a nice romantic restaurant some place. You've moved up in the world. Last time I visited you in here you were on a lower floor. Sam—someone-or-other told me where to find you.'

Damien made a mental note to have a quiet word with Sam about company security while he thought about grinding Bryce's face into the carpet for stealing that kiss. But then why would she be so shocked about her child's father turning up—unless they'd broken up after the baby had been conceived? His little brown mouse had more layers than the DeLuca Tower.

'Bryce, why are you here? This doesn't make sense.'

The visitor ignored her protest and, despite the early hour, levered out the cork, setting it free with a loud pop, and pouring the wine into two glasses he'd extracted from his pocket. He handed her one and took a swig from the other.

Then he turned and locked his baby-blue eyes on her, a lock of his blonde hair escaping from under the designer sunglasses perched on his head.

'Then let's go make sense somewhere private,' he said. 'Away from all these cronies.'

Damien couldn't keep silent any more—whoever this guy was, there was no way he'd let Philly leave while he was paying her salary.

'She's not going anywhere with you.'

Bryce turned, obviously displeased to find the company he'd so readily dismissed hadn't instantaneously vaporised.

'Excuse me, this *is* a private conversation.'

Enid tut-tutted at the door and put her fists on her hips.

'Imagine that, and we all thought it was *you* interrupting a private conversation.'

Bryce smiled a false smile that got no further than his bared teeth. 'I appreciate your loyalty to Philly. It's very…touching. But she's safe with me. Aren't you, Philly?'

Philly took a long look at Bryce as she put her untouched glass on the desk. Even in the midst of her surprise, when he'd first walked in she had been blown away with how good-looking he was, with his tanned skin, blue eyes and blonde hair. For just a while there she'd felt this huge sense of loss—she'd loved and lost this perfect specimen.

But then she'd noticed the way he treated people, the way he rode roughshod over anyone who didn't serve a purpose to him, and the way he'd assumed she would fall into his arms without a thought to ask her what she wanted.

Why had she put up with him for all that time? She must have been so desperate to have a child it had completely blinkered her view. But the shutters were off now and there was no way he was barging his way back into her life.

'Philly?' Bryce prompted.

She looked around Bryce to where Damien was sitting poised, ready to pounce. With his face like thunder, he looked as if he was prepared to tear Bryce limb from limb. Standing behind her at the door, Enid looked more than ready to deputise.

It was empowering having them both here for moral support. And comforting. Only this was something she'd have to deal with herself. Besides which, if she was going to have to explain her pregnancy to Bryce it would be better not to have Damien around to complicate matters.

She exhaled on a long sigh before glancing up to Damien and Enid. 'I'm sorry, I don't know what's going on, but if you'd give me just a moment to sort this out? I appreciate your support but we need a little privacy. If you don't mind, we'll continue this in my office. It won't take long.'

Enid and Damien looked at each other, as if neither was prepared to be the first to leave.

'You're sure?' Damien asked.

'I'm sure.'

'Then you stay here. I'll be right outside if you need.'

She smiled. 'Thanks.' Their eyes met again and locked. *It'll be okay*, they seemed to be saying. Warmth spiralled through her, touching her in places only he seemed to be able to reach. It was a good feeling.

'Right!' Bryce announced, clapping his hands and jolting her out of her mood. 'You've both been a wonderful audience but the show's over. Allow me to show you the door.'

Damien stood, visibly bristling even as Enid made for a quick exit. Bryce stopped dead in his tracks. 'Come on,' he urged, sounding less cocky, 'you heard the lady. We'd appreciate a little privacy.'

From her chair Philly could tell Damien was itching to do something—she didn't know what, but he looked as tight as a drum. His dark eyes took on the character of petrified wood—the hardness of stone, polished and glinting.

The contrast between the men hit her then. There was Bryce, elegant as always in his superfine wool suit and with his charming good looks, but soft on the inside. And there was Damien, rock solid, staring him down, exuding more masculine power in those eyes than Bryce owned in his entire body.

A breath caught in her throat as a thrill descended her spine.

He was defending her!

Something warm and luxurious enveloped her just as effectively as if Damien had wrapped his arms around her. She had a champion. Damien would look after her. She knew it just as surely as she knew to draw her next breath and that knowledge gave her strength.

He must care for her—just a little, at least. Maybe one day he could care for them both…

A movement caught her eye and she realised it was Bryce's Adam's apple jerking up and down.

Damien raised his chin fractionally and repeated, 'I'll be right outside,' before he turned on his heel and left the room.

A moment later Bryce closed the door behind them.

He shrugged. 'Well, he's certainly uptight about something. Why don't we just clear out of this nuthouse altogether? Philly, grab your jacket and bag, we may as well hit the road and find that restaurant, even if it is still early.'

She leaned back in her chair. Already he was barking orders at her and he'd only reappeared in her life barely ten minutes ago. What would it be like if she took him back? Not that that was on the cards once he heard her news.

'We don't need a restaurant. We can talk here. What I have to say isn't going to be any more palatable when accompanied with fine food and wine.'

He came back around the desk and reached for her hands. 'Aww. Come on, Philly. Can't you let bygones be bygones? I made a mistake, pure and simple. Everyone does. But I'll make it up to you.'

She shook her head slowly. 'Bryce, I honestly don't think…'

'Listen, I would never have left you if Muriel hadn't told me she was pregnant. And she lied to me. It was never my baby! She tricked me into moving in with her. It's all her fault.'

'You were having an *affair* with her for at least a year before that happened. Or am I supposed to conveniently forget about that?'

Bryce shook his head, looking wounded. 'But this is what you wanted. When you rang and told me you'd do anything to get me back, you weren't worried about a meaningless little fling then.'

She bowed her head. It was true. In those first few days after Bryce had left she had wanted nothing more than for him to come back to her. She'd even been willing to overlook his straying ways if only he'd soothe the huge sense of rejection he'd left her with. And, after a great deal of hand-wringing, she'd swallowed what little pride she had left and called him on his mobile phone, pleading with him to come back to her.

Funny, but she couldn't remember him saying that he'd see how it went with Muriel and get back to her if it didn't work out. As far as she could recall, his parting words had been, '*Get a life*'.

She smiled inwardly at the words. How was Bryce going to feel when he found out she'd done just that?

'That was a long time ago. I don't think I could forget about it so easily now.'

'It's all in the past. Can't we move on?'

She looked at him for a moment. Muriel must have put him through the wringer. Now that she was over the shock of seeing him again, close up she could see the tell-tale signs of strain around his eyes. His face had a more pinched look than she remembered.

He was obviously hurting and he'd come to her. Once she might have fallen for his hangdog expression. But no longer.

'I have moved on. I don't want to go back.'

He looked up. 'You're seeing someone else then?'

Philly laughed. The way he'd so confidently just waltzed in and assumed she was available and waiting for him to come back into her life—and now he looked almost worried.

'Well, not exactly—'

Relief took over his features.

'So why can't you just give me one more chance?'

'Even if I did, what's to stop you having another affair?'

'No, not a chance. I've learnt my lesson. I'll stick with the tried and true.'

Raising her eyebrows, she could barely manage a response to that back-handed compliment. 'Gee, thanks, that makes me sound special.'

'You are special, Philly. I shouldn't need to tell you. You're sweet, you're clever and you love me. What more could I ask?'

Philly knew full well that whatever her supposed attributes he'd wandered before while he had her love. What would stop him now that he didn't?

'Look, it just won't work—not now.'

'Because you won't forgive me?'

For a moment the temptation to tell him she was pregnant was overwhelming. After all, this guy had featured large for over two years of her life. She was used to sharing secrets and life stories with him. Though that was before…

Now he was merely part of her history. There was really no reason to tell him about the baby at all. Sure he wouldn't want her once he found out about the baby, but she needed him to understand she didn't want him anyway.

'No. Because you were wrong. I don't love you any more. I'm not convinced I ever did. It's taken me a while, but I'm getting my life together. I want it to stay that way. There's no place in my life for you now.'

His face stilled momentarily before a slight tic started up under his right eye.

'You're joking, right?' He tried to smile, but the tic got in the way, jerking up the side of his lip.

'I'm joking, wrong.'

Putting his head down, he paced a few steps around

the office. Suddenly he stopped and looked up at her. 'Then what am I expected to do? I gave up my flat when I moved in with Muriel. I've got nowhere to go.'

Philly almost laughed, until she realised he was serious. 'Excuse me, but I don't think that's my problem.'

His face took a bitter twist as his tic worked overtime.

'Then think again, sweetheart. I'm moving in with you tonight.'

Suddenly she needed to get out of there—and fast. For someone who'd up until today had an enviable absence of morning sickness she felt pretty close to losing everything she'd managed to keep down in the last six weeks and more.

'Excuse me—' She rushed for the door and pulled it open, only to almost trip over the huddled form of Enid, who was trying to look inconspicuous watering the pot-plants just outside the door. Damien stopped his pacing in the waiting area beyond and looked up at her, the storm in his eyes giving way fractionally to concern. For a moment as their eyes met in the confusion she forgot her nausea completely. But only for a moment. Then she felt the surge inside her once more and she rushed past Enid into the rest-rooms beyond.

'What the hell's going on out there?' Bryce called. 'Philly, where are you?'

'I'll go see how she is,' Enid volunteered, following.

'The hell you will. I'll go!' asserted Bryce, pushing his way into the bathroom.

Almost immediately he wavered, turning back at the sounds of her distress, his face taking on a noticeably green tinge. 'Aah, I don't think she's very well.'

Enid scowled at him. 'A lot you seem to care.'

Damien joined them outside the door. 'You idiot. She's probably feeling sick enough with the baby coming without you upsetting her.'

'I've explained that,' Bryce stated. 'It wasn't my…'

There was silence for a few seconds until Philly wobbled to the door, looking washed out and holding a damp paper towel to her face. 'Phew, that was too close. Panic over.'

Damien held out his arm, questions in his eyes. 'Lean on me. Come and sit down.'

She took his arm, avoiding the questions and letting herself sink her weight gratefully against him as he led her down to the more comfortable chairs in the waiting room.

'You need a nice cup of tea,' suggested Enid, disappearing into the small kitchenette to put the kettle on.

Bryce trailed them down the hall, all the time his eyes dashing between Philly and Damien and back again before finally settling around the region of Philly's still flat abdomen as she reclined into an armchair. His tongue darted out and flicked around his lips nervously.

'Um. What's going on?'

She looked up at him, her eyes weary. 'Bryce, there's no place for you back in my life. I wasn't going to tell you because it's actually none of your business, but I'm pregnant.'

He looked around, panic evident in his eyes. 'But—you can't be. We haven't—I always used—It's been months!'

'Oh, don't worry,' she said, 'I never said it was yours.'

'Then who the hell have you been sleeping with?'

Damien couldn't stay quiet any longer. He didn't have any idea how this baby had been conceived, but he sure as hell was happy it had nothing to do with Bryce. 'You've got to be joking! Surely you don't expect Philly to answer that question,' he snapped.

'I want to know. The minute my back is turned, she goes and gets herself pregnant. Whose is it?'

'Philly told you, it's none of your business. Maybe it's about time you were thinking about leaving again—this time for good.'

Bryce looked around and threw Damien a hateful expression. 'Why don't you just stay out of this?' he snapped, before his eyes suddenly narrowed. 'Hang on…'

He looked from Philly's face to Damien's and back again. Damien glared right back.

'Damien's right,' she said. 'You should go.'

Bryce's searching gaze focused once more on Philly, his lip curling. 'It's his baby, isn't it? You probably couldn't wait for me to be out of the picture. In fact, it was probably going on before I left. That's what you're doing up on this swank floor. You earned your promotion on your back. Go on—deny it.'

Philly squeezed her eyes shut and wished she could do the same for her ears. This couldn't be happening.

'Why deny it?' said Damien, his voice heavy with anger, his hands curling into fists. 'It is my baby.'

Philly's heart missed a beat as her eyes snapped open.

'Damien…'

'So understand me when I say,' continued Damien as he forced Bryce to the lifts without touching him but by his sheer physical presence. 'You stay away from Philly. I never want you to contact her again. And I don't want to see your face around here either. Got that?'

The lift doors behind Bryce slid open. For a moment it looked as if he was trying to make a last-ditch attempt. His chest puffed out and his red cheeks swelled as if he was trying to come up with something cutting in response. It was a futile gesture.

Damien took one step towards him and with one hand shoved Bryce into the compartment. The low heel of Bryce's shoe caught in the gap and he sprawled backwards, crashing like a deck of cards into the corner.

Then the lift doors hummed closed.

Damien watched the doors for a few seconds, as if ensuring Bryce was truly gone, before turning back to her.

She lifted her face to meet his, saw his eyes soften and warm as they swept over her face, and his gaze rocked her soul. He was fantastic. Did he have any idea of just what he'd done for her? There was no way she could have faced a scene at home tonight with Bryce pushing his way into their house. Her mother just couldn't handle that sort of stress. But Damien's actions had meant that there was no likelihood of having Bryce crashing her home and upsetting her mother. Damien had saved them both.

And it hit her then, like a blow to the gut. What

she felt now towards Damien was much more than grateful thanks. She didn't just appreciate what he'd done.

She loved him.

She loved the father of her child.

And he knew. Somehow, by whatever means, he already knew the truth about the baby. Maybe that might pave the way for a future for them all together.

She smiled up at him. It felt weak and lopsided but she couldn't stop herself from smiling with the surge of these novel and profound emotions welling up inside.

'How long have you known?' she said.

Frown lines appeared at his brow and his eyes muddied. 'Known what?'

'You know. About the b—'

All at once she realised what he'd done. That in order to get rid of Bryce the simplest way had been to turn his accusations back on him and agree that the baby was his. And it had worked. So well that even she'd been convinced he believed it.

'Oh, my God,' she said.

He grabbed her then, his hands like iron bands on her arms, wrenching her up from the chair to face him, his eyes dark and menacing and searching for answers.

'How long have I known *what* exactly?'

His fingers bit into her flesh even as she tried to form the words. 'You're hurting me.'

He let go so suddenly her knees buckled beneath her and she swayed, battling to keep her balance. His large hands caught her before she hit the ground and he swung her up until she crashed against his chest, firm and strong, the clean, masculine smell of him the last thought in her head before everything went blank.

CHAPTER EIGHT

'WHERE am I?' She came to with a start on an unfamiliar bed in equally unfamiliar surroundings. Only the city skyline, outlined through the wall of windows to her side, looked vaguely familiar.

'Relax,' Damien said, easing her shoulders back down on the soft pillow. 'You're in my penthouse apartment. I thought it would be more comfortable than the sofa in my office. Here,' he said, indicating the tray on the side table next to her, 'have something to drink. I brought juice and water—your choice.'

Her gaze skidded half-heartedly over the tray. This was his apartment? Then that meant— Her eyes swung around the room, taking in the personal effects on the dresser, the silk robe hanging on a door, and she swallowed.

His bed.

She made a wobbly move to push herself up. 'I'm sorry. I should get back to work.'

'No.' His hand on her shoulder barred her rising. 'Not until you tell me what's going on.'

She looked up at him, the underlying menace in his soft words echoed in the shadows in his eyes.

'I want to know what you meant back then.'

Still she fought it. She'd thought he'd known—it could all have been so simple.

'I want to know. You made it sound as if your pregnancy had something to do with me.'

Her eyelids fell shut on a deep breath. 'Damien,'

she said, 'please let me up. I can't explain with you standing over me.'

With a sound of impatience he twisted his body up and away from the bed. She followed by slowly swinging her legs over the edge, sitting still for a second, testing whether her legs would give way again before she too pushed herself up and away, her hands smoothing her hair as she walked to the wall of windows on the far side of the room.

'Well?' he prompted, the decibels in his voice up a notch. 'Go ahead and explain then.'

She clutched her arms around her middle, staring at the floor and trying to find words that would make her news more palatable. It would be bad enough for him to realise that he'd slept with her without the double blow that she was pregnant with his child.

But there was no easy way to say it. No way to smooth the impact of the words.

'It's true,' she said at last. 'I'm carrying your child.'

'This is ridiculous,' he said. 'We've never even had sex.'

Her head dipped in a nod. 'Obviously we have.'

'Like when? The only time we came anywhere close was at the Gold Coast and you threw me out of your room before I had hardly a chance to kiss you. Remember? So if you're pregnant from that time, someone else must be the father.' He stopped for a second, surveying her critically as if he'd just latched on to something significant.

'What did you do? Go and find good old Stu the moment I left? Is that why you were so upset with me—you had to slink back to meet him? I wondered why he wasn't too upset the next day—you'd already smoothed his wounded ego. Well, don't expect a bonus from me for what you've done just because you were away on business. It doesn't work like that.'

She unwrapped her arms from around her and felt her hands ball into fists that pounded into her thighs. 'What is your problem? Stuart wasn't upset because he didn't give a damn. He'd only asked me to go dancing. Yes, you were unnecessarily, unbearably rude that night but it wasn't exactly as if he'd asked me to marry him.

'Besides which,' she continued before he had a chance to respond. 'You really must have a pretty low opinion of me if you think I'm capable of falling into bed with any guy who crosses my path.'

'Well—' he pointedly gazed at her lower abdomen '—given your condition, you've obviously fallen into bed with somebody.'

'Maybe not,' she said, a smile emerging on her lips for the first time in their conversation. 'Who said this baby had anything to do with bed?'

'What the hell is that supposed to mean? And if you're saying it didn't happen while we were at the Gold Coast, when else have we been together long enough for this amazing conception to have taken place?'

She looked right at him, desperate to take the smug look off his face. 'The office Christmas party.'

'You weren't even there. You said—'

'*Sam* said I wasn't there. I told you my mother was ill.'

He looked at her for a moment, his face a tangle of confused emotion. 'Can't you think of anything more original than that? Are you that desperate to pin this baby on me? Maybe I should have left you to

Bryce, after all. Seems to me you two are made for each other.'

His words stung her deeply but not half as deeply as the realisation that her fears were true. He simply couldn't abide the thought of having made love to her. Damien DeLuca would never have stooped to such a thing.

Well, damn him! It was the truth. He had to believe her.

'I didn't realise it would be so confusing for you. Tell me, exactly how many women *did* you make love to in the boardroom that night?'

Something in his eyes flared. Disbelief? Panic?

'No,' he said. 'It's not possible.'

'Oh, it's more than just possible,' she said with a smile that should have hinted at much more.

'Then tell me what you were wearing.'

She allowed the corners of her mouth to kick up another notch. Still he was fighting the inevitable. 'I was dressed as Cleopatra. You were Mark Antony.'

'And that proves exactly nothing. Other people would have seen us together. How do I know what you are saying is the truth?'

She sighed, remembering the words he'd greeted her with, the words that had warmed her soul deep and fixed her in his spell. 'You said you'd been waiting two thousand years for me,' she remembered, her voice barely more than a whisper as she recalled that special moment.

'You could have overheard that.'

'True,' she acknowledged, her good feelings evaporating in the harshness of his desert-dry tone. 'So maybe I should tell you about how you locked the door behind us and lifted me on to the boardroom table, the way you released my breasts into your hands and mouth. Or maybe I should tell you how you entered me, naked but for the leather on your feet...'

Watching his face, she caught the exact moment he realised there was no escape, caught his eyes darkening, the pupils dilating as if letting in the truth at last, the slideshow of emotions—surprise, shock and outrage moving fast over his features as he digested the news.

'That was *you*?'

He sounded appalled. She'd expected nothing less but the words sliced into her all the more deeply now, knowing how she felt about him.

'Hard to believe, I know.'

Hard to believe? He'd spent how many hours trying to track down the mysterious woman who'd plagued his hard, lonely nights and filled his dreams with unrelenting frequency since the ball and here she was, right under his nose the whole time. Yet still something didn't make sense.

'But your perfume—it wasn't the same.'

For a moment she looked shocked. 'No, it wasn't. I wore my mother's perfume that night. It seemed to go better with the outfit.'

So it was her. The woman in the filmy gown, with lush red lips and a body to die for, was none other than Philly, his little brown mouse—his little not-so-brown mouse—as it turned out. And she was here now.

In his bedroom.

Serendipity.

A very happy accident indeed, he considered, congratulating himself for preferring the privacy of his apartment to the sofa in his office when she'd collapsed. There was more than a little justice in the arrangement.

He moved closer. 'I'll need proof, of course.'

Her eyes darted up to his, uncertainty flickering in their hazel lights. 'What? You mean DNA testing?'

'Eventually, yes.' He took another step closer, angling himself so that he was between the door and any escape route. She edged back against the wall of windows and he smiled to himself. There was no escape that way. 'I was thinking of something much simpler for now.'

'What do you mean?' Now she'd just about plastered herself to the glass.

He came to a stop right in front of her. 'You were wearing a mask. Even though you seem to know the details, someone could have told you.'

She moved to make a sound—a protest—but he shushed her with a finger pressed to her lips.

'I just need to be sure you are who you say you are. If I'm to believe this story of a baby, I need to know it was you that I slept with.'

He looked down at her, noticed the kick of her chin as she swallowed, enjoying the play of emotions skitter across her eyes—perplexity, fear and something else.

Anticipation?

Oh yes, without a doubt if the outline of her peaked nipples through her summer dress was any indication.

'What did you have in mind?'

He lifted a hand and she flinched. 'Relax,' he urged, his voice set to reassurance. 'You were wearing a mask. I just wondered how you looked with your eyes covered—just to be sure.'

Her eyes blinked twice and she relaxed a fraction though her breathing was still tight. It wasn't the only thing, he reflected, shifting slightly as he lifted his arm, placing his hand palm down across her eyes. Her lashes moved against his skin, soft and like the touch of a feather before they fluttered closed.

'There,' he said, his voice little more than a whisper, 'that's more like it. Now, lift your head towards me so I can see you properly.'

His hand under her chin tilted her face higher. Her breathing was shallow, her breath warm and inviting and there was no way he was going to be able to resist.

'Are you convinced now?' Her voice was tremulous and soft, her breath sweet on his face.

'Almost,' he said. 'Just one more thing.'

He dipped his head and angled his mouth over hers, brushing her lips with his. Her startled response turned into a shudder and so he deepened his kiss, parting her lips and probing further inside. When her tongue meshed with his he removed the hand over her eyes and brought it behind, holding her away from the glass and closer to him.

He sensed her arms flailing momentarily until they settled around him and her hands tightened to fists bunching up his shirt and it was her turn to pull him closer.

It was her. There was no mistake. He could stop now and be satisfied that what she said was true, that she had been the woman in the boardroom. But why should he stop?

Redundant question, he realised as his lips trailed a line down her neck. He had no intention of stopping. Not when he'd been searching for this woman ever since that night. And he hadn't been searching for her all this time to let her go again.

Her breathing was coming fast, her chest rising and falling rapidly against his and making him painfully aware of her breasts and their inaccessibility in this straight dress. His hand released her head, slid lower until it found what he was looking for. He tugged on the tab gently and slid it down to where it ended low down on her back in one silky movement. Her head jerked back, as if suddenly aware of what he was doing, but his mouth took hers again, his tongue tracing the line of her teeth, his teeth nipping at her lips while his hands slid into the gap and up under the fabric across her skin. She gasped into his mouth at the same time that her whole body moved with tremors of promise and expectation.

With his hands he slipped the dress over her shoulders, gently easing her arms down so that it could fall to the floor.

She let it go reluctantly, as if she was doing battle with herself. So be it. Whatever the outcome of her own personal dilemma, however she resolved the battles raging inside, he was intending to win the war. He crushed her to him, feeling the press of her flesh hard up against him, nothing between him and her naked form but a fine lace bra and a tiny white matching thong that left her rounded cheeks exposed to his touch. He groaned as his hands cupped them, pushing her even closer to his aching hardness.

Before she had a chance to change her mind he lifted her, her skin smooth and cool yet at the same time on fire under his hands, and swivelled her around and across to the bed.

She was certifiably insane. She must be, to let

Damien do this to her. Five minutes ago he'd been accusing her of sleeping with someone else. She should be so offended she'd never think of giving him even the time of day.

And yet there was definitely something to be said for being insane. She sank into the soft down quilt and writhed under Damien's hot mouth, currently blazing a trail towards her breasts, relishing the sensations triggered in her flesh.

Because sanity had no place here. Logic had ceased to exist. Feelings took precedence and what she was feeling now, what Damien was making her feel, was extravagant and pervasive enough to block out every other rational thought.

Except one. He wanted her. She'd expected rejection to follow the disbelief; she'd been prepared for it. No way would he have expected her to turn out to be the woman he'd made love to in the boardroom. But it hadn't happened that way. He hadn't rejected her.

He wanted her!

His mouth moved lower, fingers tracing under the edge of her bra and hot breath met her lace-covered nipple, already exquisitely sensitive with her early pregnancy, setting off spears of sensation that pierced her deep inside. Her back arched and she shuddered into his mouth.

Nothing else existed, nothing else mattered, but what he was doing to her and the way he made her feel.

Special.

Beautiful.

Loved?

No. That was what she wanted, not what he was

giving. He wasn't the kind of guy to fall in love. And right now she'd settle for feeling special. Right now she'd settle for feeling beautiful.

A noise, half purr, half groan, escaped her. And right now she'd settle for more of what his magic hot mouth was doing to her breasts—and lower...

Her fingers curled in the quilt as his hands caressed her, his tongue possessing her, circling her navel and driving her crazy with want and need as he deftly discarded her lace underwear. He touched her on her now exposed flesh and her breath caught with the intensity of the feeling. Nerve-endings she'd never known existed all but screamed their presence, their effect expanding inwards, waves of pleasure rippling to her every extremity only to come crashing back again at her core.

What force magnified mere touch to make it so bold, so all-consuming that it carried her away on its tide? Whatever it was, it was beyond comprehension, beyond dispute. Instead she let herself go with it as his tongue dipped lower, unable to fight the onslaught of heat and sensation on her skin and deeper, much deeper, inside.

She wanted more of this. She wanted more of him. She wanted so much more...

Nothing would ease this delicious torture but having him deep inside her.

'Please...' she begged, the agony of her need rendering her powerless in his hands. And he gave something like a low growl and pulled away from her so abruptly that she felt his absence like a snapshot of grief. Her eyes fluttered open to see him looking down at her as his shoes and clothes came off, a flurry of leather and fabric until only air separated their naked skin. And then even the air was gone.

He lay down next to her, pulling her close, his smouldering eyes fixed on hers as he brushed a strand of hair from her cheek.

'You are so beautiful,' he said. 'I've dreamed of having you again ever since that night.'

And before her heart had a chance to swell he rolled her beneath him and entered her in one swift, deep movement.

And then it was his turn to cry out, something guttural and indiscernible, but which spoke of his hunger and need.

She clutched his shoulders, momentarily relishing the feeling of completion with him deep inside, pulsing with life and heat before he moved, easing back, teetering on the edge before stretching her full again.

She responded to him, meeting his rhythm, joining him in the dance as he repeated the movement, again and again, slowly, then faster, building the pace and her anticipation until he slowed again, driving her to the edge of need and desperation as her hips urged him home.

She felt his need peaking with hers and spurred him on, angling her hips to meet him as he drove himself deeper with every plunge, building her higher and higher with the magic of his rhythm until his whole body powered into hers with one final shuddering thrust. She went with him, her senses exploding in a thousand directions that started and ended at the place he now pulsed within.

For a while they lay there, bodies slick with limbs entwined as their breathing returned to something like normal and their bodies cooled, their craving and desire burned up in the fire of their passion—burned up yet far from extinguished. He shifted so his head was lying across her stomach and with his hand he traced circles over her abdomen, his light touch hypnotising her skin at the same time that it stirred her nerve endings.

'So somewhere inside here—there's a baby growing.'

His words took her by surprise. He'd hardly reacted to her news that she was pregnant to him—it certainly hadn't seemed to have had any impact—until now. Did he have no concept of what a child meant? Was the idea of family that foreign to him?

'What happened to your family?'

His hand stopped and dropped back to his side as he swung his gaze up to the ceiling.

For a while she didn't think he was going to answer, his steady breathing the only sound in the spare masculine room.

She touched her hand to his head, stroking his hair with her fingers.

'I'm sorry,' she said. 'I didn't mean to pry.'

He caught her hand in his, brought it to his mouth, and pressed her open palm against his lips with a half kiss, half sigh. 'It's okay. I don't think about it too much.'

'It must have been awful.' She knew loss. The death of her brother and his family had been bad enough. She didn't have to know the details to understand that losing his parents and possibly other members of his family too at such a young age must have been devastating.

'They had a market garden near Adelaide, where they'd settled after coming out from Italy. It was only small to start, but they built it up and when they could they did picking work as well—apples or pears—before the tomato season really kicked in. I was the youngest so I stayed home but they took my two older brothers—Santo and Jo. Before the tomato crop ripened they could make more in one day picking than the market garden could make in a week. It was my job to look after the garden.'

'How old were your brothers then?'

'Thirteen and fourteen. Santo was the image of Dad; he was so proud of him.'

'What happened?'

He made a sound, a sigh mixed with a note of despair, and she noticed his whole body tense. 'The orchard they were working on was up in the hills. They hitched a ride in the back of a pick-up truck with a bunch of others from the city. The access road was narrow, a steep dirt track with no safety rail. A car came round a bend the other way. The truck swerved to miss it but too far, too close to the edge. Once the front wheel went over there was no hope...'

Her breath caught as she imagined the horror of the accident and its impact on a young child. 'You lost everyone?'

'There were fourteen packed into the back of the truck. Only two survived. They didn't stand a chance when it rolled.'

He took a deep breath and raised a hand to rub his temple. 'I didn't know about it until the next day. It took the police that long to identify everyone.'

'You spent the night alone?'

He shrugged against her belly. 'You get used to it,' he said, his voice flat.

'That's so unfair,' she said. 'Did you have other family who could take you in?'

'No. Not in Australia and my two remaining grand-parents in Italy were too frail and I didn't want to go back. I'd grown up here. Even though my roots were Italian, I felt Australian, I belonged here. The market garden was sold—it barely covered the debts—and I ended up in foster care—' He gave a brief laugh. 'For a while, anyway. They didn't want me and I didn't need them. I worked as hard as I could at school and earned myself a scholarship and then escaped to Melbourne first chance I got.'

'So this child will be your only family,' she said, thinking aloud.

He lifted himself from the bed in one rapid move-ment and scooped up his clothes and she cursed her-self for provoking his change in mood. This was a guy who had made it in the world without family. He certainly wasn't going to be thrilled about having it thrust upon him.

'I have to get back to work. What do you plan to do?'

She laughed, low and brittle. 'I would have thought it's a bit late for planning. I'm going to have a baby. How's that for a plan?'

'You're keeping it then?'

Something congealed cold and hard in her heart.

He'd just made love to her.

She was carrying his child.

If she'd had any hopes that either one of those meant he'd consider her as something a trifle more special than plain old Philly-from-marketing, he'd just smashed those hopes to smithereens. 'I'm disap-pointed you could even ask.'

'Oh, don't feel so aggrieved. How am I expected to know what you intend to do? It's not like we really know each other.'

True, she thought, seeking the refuge of her own clothes. But that doesn't stop you wanting to make love to me. That doesn't stop me wanting you to.

And it certainly doesn't stop me loving you.

'So what do you expect from me?'

She looked up at him, her hazel eyes focused acutely on his, hoping they conveyed the sense of cold he'd just doused her with. Much as it would have been easier never to have let Damien know that he was the father, she'd done the right thing. He now knew about the baby. Her responsibility to him ended right there. If he wasn't prepared to have anything to do with this child, then she'd be more than happy to assume sole responsibility. It would sure save any complications.

'What do I expect from you? Absolutely nothing.'

His face starkly displayed his disbelief. But then, why would he believe her? No doubt he'd be expecting her to take full advantage of the benefits of a rich father for her child.

'It's true,' she said. 'I don't want anything from you.'

'You think you can do this all by yourself?'

'Of course I can.' *If I have to.* 'It's what I want.' *If that's what it takes.*

'What about what I want?'

'It's obvious you don't want to be involved. You've made that perfectly clear by even assuming I could do anything other than keep this child. You didn't ask for this to happen. You didn't ask for a child.'

'And you did?'

Her eyes dropped to the floor. He'd never under-stand if she told him. He'd never understand how much this baby meant, how much it would mean to her mother and how she'd dreamed so fervently of having a child. But those reasons had nothing to do with him. He didn't need to know.

'Of course it was a shock,' she said. 'But now that I've accepted it I'm going to do everything I can to make this child's life worthwhile. This baby's never going to feel like it's not wanted or that its life is the result of a mistake. I'm going to make it a home.'

'Very noble sentiments. And just how do you plan on doing all this by yourself?'

'I'll manage.'

'You'll manage,' he echoed hollowly, his voice dry and flat. 'A single mother, either unable to work or having to put the child into care all day and scraping by on a pittance if you can work. Is that how you intend to manage?'

She knew it wasn't going to be easy—she'd never thought that. But hearing him put it like that— She swallowed, attempting to bury her doubts and regain the confidence she'd felt when she'd worked out that this was what she should do. 'Lots of women do. They get by.'

'Not with my child they don't!'

The vehemence of his words took her by surprise. Was this really the man with the reputation of a con-firmed bachelor and dedicated non-family man?

'Then what are you suggesting? Some sort of fi-nancial support for the child?'

'Not just that,' he said as he looped his tie deftly into the perfect knot. 'Something much more appropriate for all of us. An arrangement that will mean you don't have to worry about balancing work with child-care. Something that will ensure your and the child's security for life.'

Her breath caught as a tingle of sensation bubbled inside. No, it wasn't possible. Surely he wasn't about to suggest marriage? But what else could offer the security the child needed, the solid foundation for a future life?

Maybe she'd underestimated him. Marriage didn't sound like something the commitment-averse Damien would suggest to anyone, least of all to her. Did the existence of a baby make so much difference, that now she was worthy of consideration as his bride, now she was considered marriage material?

Marriage.

Marriage to Damien.

How would it feel to be Damien's wife? To wake up alongside him every day, to feel his strong body holding her safe at night, to make a family with him.

To have his child and to have him too—dreams were made of lesser stuff.

So he didn't love her. She knew that. But they could still make it work. She loved him and she'd make it work if it meant pretending to be Cleopatra every night to do it. She'd do whatever it took.

It would be worth it.

She waited, almost too scared to breathe, unable to speak and ask what he could possibly mean. After what seemed an age he returned from the bathroom, his hair restored to its usual executive state, the tracks of her fingernails obliterated.

'I have a property, out of the city about one hundred kilometres or so. I can't get out there as much as I'd like but the house is in good condition and there's a full-time housekeeper and manager.

'It'll be a perfect place for you to bring the child up,' he continued. 'I'll pay all the household expenses and give you an allowance as well so you don't have to worry about working.'

A freezing dump of despair oozed over her and it was seconds before she could convince her jaw to thaw enough to let her speak.

'You'd set me up in a house of yours?'

He shrugged. 'It's the best option for both of us. I'll visit on weekends when I can get away.'

'And what of my mother? Who would look after her? No, Damien. There's no way.'

'She can come too. There's plenty of room. You can all be together.'

'Thanks so much for your kind offer, but I'm sorry, I'm not actually in the market for a new home. Maybe some other time...'

She pushed past him, trying to reach the bathroom and find a place where she could breathe again, a place where she could think, but he grabbed her arm, wheeling her around.

'Listen to me. I'm offering this child a home, security. I'll arrange the best doctors for your mother, the best paediatricians for the baby. The child will have everything it needs.' His fingers tightened on her arm. 'What are you waiting for—a better offer?'

'Lovely to know you're so concerned about this child. And what will my role be in this arrangement?'

'You'll bring up the child. I take it that's what you expect to do? And you won't have to do housework or the cooking and cleaning or worry about a day job. I'll even get private nursing for your mother, and on top of everything I'll pay you for the privilege. So maybe you could try to be a bit more grateful.'

'*Grateful!* And let me guess—will I also be expected to share your bed whenever you feel the urge? Is that how you expect me to show how grateful I am? Am I expected to extend my gratitude to you on my back?'

She wrenched her arm but his grip merely tightened, locked on, his fingers like steel manacles. She suppressed a gasp as his fingers bit into her flesh. He might be stronger than she was, but still she wasn't going to give him the satisfaction of knowing that he was hurting her.

He drew her closer, so close that she could see the white-hot fury in his eyes, feel his heated breath on her cheek. One side of his lips kicked up in a smile that went no further. 'You didn't seem to have a problem with being flat on your back ten minutes ago. Or have you forgotten already how good I made you feel, how you bucked under me until I blew your world apart?'

Her pulse hammered, her temple throbbed, as her heart cranked up the pressure through her veins as his dark eyes locked on hers. She could never forget how he made her feel, not in this life.

'Have you forgotten already how you begged me to take you?' His free hand cupped her breast. Her shocked intake of breath was fast and tremulous as he massaged the tender flesh, her nipple firming and reaching out into his palm.

He closed the gap between them, pushing himself against her. She felt his arousal with shock and awe, excitement building in her own deep places.

'Are you seriously telling me you wouldn't like to make love with me again?'

His hand left her breast and dipped down her back, pressing her into his hardness. 'Are you seriously trying to tell me you don't want me again?'

His words were seductive, hypnotising her, a mantra for her soul. His touch was persuasive, compulsive, like a mantra for her body.

He dropped a hand into her still open zipper, slipping his hand down until his warm fingers cupped the flesh of one cheek, squeezing, massaging, his fingers exploring more...

'There's no denying it, you realise that. You want me just as much as I want you.'

'Damien,' she half-pleaded, sensation blotting out rational thought once more, nerve-endings screaming for release. It was true. She could no more deny wanting him than she could deny the sun a place in the sky. But that didn't mean he could buy her like just one more part of his business.

'See,' he said, a tone of victory injected into his voice. 'There's no way you can deny me. Not now.'

'Damien,' she said, stronger this time, his arrogance fuelling her determination to fight back. 'I won't be your mistress.'

'You don't mean that,' he said. 'Let me show you what you really want.' His mouth dipped lower as if intending to claim hers but it never made its mark. Summoning strength she didn't know she possessed, she pushed and twisted at the same time, swivelling out of his arms and swaying across the room until dozens of cubic metres of super-charged air swirled between them.

'Believe me, Damien. I won't be your mistress. I

won't be *anyone's* mistress. Have you no idea what an insult that is?'

'Then what were you expecting? Marriage? Is that what you were hoping for? A white picket fence and a fairy-tale ending?'

She schooled her face blank, her chest heaving, not trusting her voice to hold steady if she uttered a word. Of course it sounded ridiculous when he put it like that. But what was wrong with wanting things to be right, wanting to bring up a child in a proper family? What was wrong with hoping love might have something to do with it?

But there was no way she'd tell Damien that.

'Don't be ridiculous,' she said, only when she was sure her voice wouldn't betray her. 'I told you, I don't want anything from you.'

Still, his eyes narrowed, focusing on something in her face. 'Ah, but that's what you were hoping for, wasn't it?'

His words cut uncomfortably close to the truth. Why had she had to go and fall in love with him? It had been so much easier in the beginning, before she'd seen beyond the arrogant businessman behind whom Damien existed, before she'd felt his lovemaking and experienced the sheer magic of his touch.

Until then she'd been happy to think about a life with her child—Damien didn't even have to figure. But she did love him. And now she couldn't imagine life with his child without him.

Her chin kicked up. 'You must really fancy yourself. I told you and I mean it. I don't want anything from you.'

He watched her for a few seconds more, cold emotion drizzling down over them. 'So be it. Because I don't do family. It's not going to happen.'

He walked to the slatted timber bifold doors separating the bedroom from the rest of the apartment. 'I'm going back to work. Let yourself out when you're ready.'

'I'll be down shortly,' she said, knowing it would take her a good ten minutes to get herself back together enough to appear in public.

'Don't bother,' he said. 'Go home.'

And then he was gone.

CHAPTER NINE

'How is she?' asked Enid on his return.

'Gone home,' he snapped back, 'and if she's got any sense, she'll stay there.'

Enid's eyes narrowed speculatively, her lips tight and puckered. 'I see.'

'You do? I sure wish the hell I did. Hold my calls, Enid. Tell everyone I'm in conference.'

'As you wish,' she said as he entered his office. He closed the door behind him but for once ignored the expansive desk to his right. Instead he strode to the wall of glass, his window to the outside world, and gazed out across the city, looking for answers amongst the columns of office towers, the low-rise buildings and homes at the city's fringe and the warehouses of the harbour near the port. The sea lay lifeless in the distance, flat and dull. He empathised. It matched his mood perfectly.

It had been one hell of a day. To finally find the woman who'd been haunting his thoughts and dreams for so long only to discover it had been Philly all along. What was more, to learn she was pregnant with his child.

He was going to be a father.

The concept was as exciting as it was terrifying. Yet he didn't want a child; he'd never wanted one. He'd survived without the whole family thing for this long. He didn't need it.

So why did some small part of him insist on feeling

proud? He'd spent his life avoiding such possibilities with a vengeance. So why didn't he break out in a cold sweat as he'd expect? Why did he feel such a sense of exhilaration at the idea?

He was going to be a father.

He was going to have a child.

And, no matter what Philly said, he would make sure that child was properly taken care of.

What was her problem, anyway? He'd just offered her a house, a housekeeper, nursing care for her mother and an income. She wouldn't have to lift a finger. It was a great deal.

So why wouldn't she accept? What did she want? He'd made her a reasonable offer. More than reasonable. And she'd turned him down flat.

He sighed deeply, his forehead and hands pressed against the glass as he looked down to the street below. It was a long way down. He'd been down there, at rock bottom and lower, not even within cooee of a rung to begin the long, lonely climb up the ladder.

And he'd made it. All the way to the top on his own. No one to help him, no one to turn to for support but a drunken foster mother who had drunk his foster money blind and the faded memory of a family tragedy that had taught him never to get close to anyone.

He lashed out with his foot, slamming his shoe into the reinforced glass and making the entire window shudder before he spun around and tracked a course round his desk.

What the hell was wrong with him? He hadn't thought so much about his family for years and yet today, in the feel-good hum of some of the best sex he'd had since their encounter in the boardroom—the *only* sex he'd had since that encounter in the boardroom—the mere suggestion of a honeyed voice had dredged it all up.

He paced the carpet, trying not to ignore the pictures that were surfacing in his mind's eye, the pictures like dusty film clips he'd been avoiding for years. His father, tall and straight, strong featured, with hair swept back much like his own, but greying already at the temples, the white shirt and dark trousers, his standard uniform; even when picking fruit or working in the garden he had always liked to look his best.

His brothers, loud and broad-shouldered like their father and always wrestling in the yard outside when they should have been doing homework.

And his mother, dark and handsome, with eyes that had sparkled with love and pride, scolding her two eldest sons only to toss her thick, dark hair and leave them, laughing as she'd turned back to her cooking.

He sucked in a jagged breath and closed his eyes but the pictures became even sharper and more distinct.

Unrelated snippets of memories exploded into his mind like the coloured contents of a party popper.

These were real people he was remembering, not some cardboard cut-outs that could be neatly filed away in a corner of his mind, buried deeper than the four wooden caskets that had lain side by side in the old church.

They'd been his family and now they were gone. And he'd done his best to leave them behind, moving cities, moving states. Burying them in his mind.

He shivered.

Suddenly he had to get out of there. Had to go somewhere—*anywhere*. He pulled open the door in time to see Philly placing some papers on Enid's desk. She jerked around guiltily at his appearance, her face pale but her eyes challenging. Then she frowned and her features softened into something closer to concern. She took a step towards him.

'Are you okay?' she asked.

'What are you doing here?' he demanded. 'I told you to go home.'

She stopped dead, her back stiffening. 'I've just had two weeks leave. I have work to catch up on.'

'You're not fit for work.'

'I'm pregnant,' she said, forcing herself taller as if that would convince him. 'I'm not ill.'

'What do you call what happened this morning then?'

Her chin kicked up even as she coloured.

'I think most people refer to it as sex.'

'Not that,' he snarled. 'When you fainted.'

'I'm over it. That won't happen again.'

'We'll see.' He looked around, settling his gaze on Enid's empty chair before striding to the lift. 'Tell Enid I'm going out.'

'When will you be back?'

'I don't know,' he said as he allowed himself to be swallowed up by the hungry cavern of the lift.

'I don't know.'

CHAPTER TEN

HE DIDN'T know where he was heading.

Anywhere.

Nowhere.

It didn't matter. He drove aimlessly with no sense of direction and less sense of time until something drew him towards the coast. It was sunny, the day was fine, the top of his black BMW convertible was down and his passing drew envious looks from the men in cars around him, wishful glances from the women.

Normally he'd get a buzz out of the experience, a fillip to his ego, the successful businessman out enjoying the spoils of his success.

Success.

How did you measure that? In dollars and cents, in bricks and buildings, corporate takeovers and fast cars? Sure, on that score he was as successful as they came, no question.

Or was success measured in more human terms—in connections built between people, in relationships, *in families*?

The human factor.

On that score, so far all he'd been successful at was avoiding that very thing. But now he was going to be a father and the one thing he'd evaded for so long was happening.

A father. Why did that change things so much?

Why should that suddenly make his business success ring so hollow?

Finally he left the highway and crossed the train lines before pulling alongside the kerb, opposite a battered brick veneer house in a post-war building boom suburb.

What was he doing here? He'd never been here before, he'd just snatched a glimpse of the address in some papers on Enid's desk one day. Amazing he'd even remembered it.

He studied the house. It had seen better days by the look of the shabby brickwork, the flaking window-frames and the tired garden, its leggy native plants wafting listlessly in the warm breeze. Once he was out of the car he could just smell the sea, the tang of seaweed and salt in the air, though the beach was nothing more than a dull promise across the train tracks and beyond the strip of kiosks and mid-rate hotels lining the highway.

He'd never asked her about her home. He'd never asked her how her mother was. It had never occurred to him. But now it seemed important. He wanted to know more about her, about the woman who was to be his child's mother, about her family.

He knocked on the door. And waited.

The clang of the crossing barriers started up, loud and insistent, as a train surged along the track, all electric whine and squealing metal before gradually the noise died down and quiet resumed. He thought about leaving but had no idea where he'd go. The train was probably already at the next station when he finally heard a sound inside the house, spotted a blurred shape moving through the panel of misted glass.

The door edged open, a security chain clamping in place. Through the gap he could see her wary gaze, in dark-ringed eyes that looked almost too big in her sunken face.

'Mrs Summers?'

'Yes,' came her voice, brittle and shaky and obviously unused to visitors during the day.

'My name is Damien DeLuca. Philly works—'

'Oh, my,' she said, panic swamping her eyes as she unlatched the door and shoved it open. 'Is she all right? Has something happened to her?'

He held up his hands. 'No, no. She's fine. Really.' He watched the panic recede and cursed himself for his stupidity. 'I didn't mean to alarm you. I was— just passing. I thought I'd drop in—for a chat.'

One of her hands went to the wispy dull fuzz of her hair, the other clutched a walking stick in a white knuckled grip.

Cancer. She had cancer and she'd lost her hair from the chemotherapy. She was tiny, a tinier version of Philly, and paper-thin under the buttoned up house-coat.

He bristled in irritation. Why hadn't Philly told him? He'd had no idea. How on earth was she managing a full-time job and caring for her mother?

'Well,' she said in a voice which was frail, yet years younger than she looked. 'I'm not really dressed for visitors, but it's lovely to meet you. And please call me Daphne. You know, I've heard such a lot about you.'

'You have?'

'Of course. You're a very talented young man by the sounds of it. Philadelphia's told me how you like to rule the roost. Would you like a cup of tea?'

He somehow managed to nod while digesting that brief and unexpected character sketch. 'Thank you.'

She shuffled her way into the small kitchen and made for the kettle. 'I'm sorry to take so long to answer the door. I'm not as fast as I used to be.'

He looked at her, struggling with the walking stick to move around, wincing with the effort every few steps and trying unsuccessfully to mask the pain.

'Please,' he said, sidestepping her. 'I'm the one interrupting you; let me get it. Why don't you sit down?'

She looked up at him, surprised, as if his offer of help was the last thing she'd expected—just what had Philly told her?—before a smile illuminated her gaunt face. 'Thank you. I could do with a sit down even though that seems to be all I do these days.' She showed him where everything was and with a sigh eased herself into an armchair while he made the tea.

'I must thank you for sending Marjorie while Philadelphia was away,' she said when Damien placed their tea on the table and sat down opposite. 'She was a wonderful companion.'

For a moment he scrabbled to get his head around who she was talking about. Then he realised. The trip to the Gold Coast—the nurse he'd had Enid organise. 'It was no trouble,' he said, casting his mind over the unwashed breakfast dishes in the sink, the picked over lunch tray waiting on the bench. It was clear Daphne could do with a little help every day.

'How do you manage here, by yourself, during the day?'

'Oh, we get by. Philadelphia gets me organised in the mornings and fixes me a tray for lunch.' She sipped at her tea. 'If I have a good day I try to start dinner to help her when she comes home from work, though sometimes it doesn't quite work that way.'

He nodded blankly, his mind working overtime. What the hell was Philly thinking? This was no way to live, leaving her mother alone all day out here in the suburbs, while she worked at least twenty kilometres away in the city. And yet she'd turned down his offer of a house with carers and laid on help, *and* she'd turned it down flat. Did she think she was managing here any better than he could provide for them? If so, she was kidding herself.

Would her mother have found his offer so unattractive? Casting an eye around the simply decorated room, neat and tidy but long overdue for repainting and renovation at the very least, he doubted it.

But this wasn't just about Philly and her mother now. If she thought for a moment he would let her bring up his child in such circumstances, then she could think again.

'You must find things very difficult.'

'It's harder for Philadelphia. She's my only child now.' She looked up, the pain of loss in her eyes unmistakable. 'Did you know about…?'

He nodded. 'Yes, I heard.' He could almost feel her loss reach out to encompass him, a thick, tangible thing. Or was it simply that his own loss was now so close to the surface that he could just about taste it?

Philly had done that. Had brought these feelings to the surface, feelings that were better off left to moulder deep down below.

He swallowed, as if that would bury these unwanted feelings deeper again. He knew loss just as surely as did the wasted woman sitting opposite him. *Loss.* Such a tiny word yet it was so big—larger and more encompassing than anything anyone could ever warn you about. And if you couldn't deal with it, tuck it away and bury it in the back of your mind, it could take over your life.

So he'd buried it. Deep down inside him, concealing the site under a ton of concrete will. Until today. He groaned inwardly.

Oh, hell, yes, he knew loss.

'That must have been terrible for you,' he said.

Her eyes misted, a silent affirmation. 'And of course that means that Philadelphia has to do it all, I'm afraid. She's stuck with me and she knows I want to stay at home as long as possible.'

'As long as possible?'

She put her cup down and sighed. 'I will have to move into a hospice in a few months the doctors say—there's nothing else for it. Philadelphia won't be able to look after me soon and I can't expect her to. So if you're worried about me getting in the way of her work...? I imagine that's why you're here?'

She was dying. It should have been clear from the moment she opened the door—her bird-like frame, her gaunt features and pained walk. It should have been clear. But then he'd had plenty of experience in ignoring death, shoving it aside in his quest to reach the top.

She was dying and she thought he was here to find out whether Philly would still make a good employee.

'No,' he said, bursting out of the chair. 'No, that's not why I'm here.'

He paced around the small room, trying to banish the nervous tension invading his senses. But why *was* he here? What did he hope to achieve? Certainly something more than this sense of hopelessness and despair, this struggle for an answer to questions he couldn't even frame—something that would answer this desperate need he couldn't even put words to.

He stopped beside a display of photographs assembled along the mantle. The history of a family, laid out before his eyes. A wedding photograph, fading with age, showing a young Daphne and her late husband on their wedding day, smiling for the camera, happy and hopeful for the future. A photograph of the young family with two children, a boy—just a toddler—and his older sister, maybe six or seven years old, with pigtails and wearing a frilly dress.

Philly.

Just a skinny kid then, but there was no mistaking her eyes and that chin, defiant and serious even back then.

And now she was a woman. Every part a woman, as this morning's heated passion had attested. What drove her then, to deny him? Three times she'd evaded his reach. Three times she'd slipped away from him. The Christmas party when she'd stolen away, that night at the Gold Coast when she'd pushed him from her room, and today, when he'd all but offered her luxury on a platter. Still she seemed to want no part of him.

But he would have her. He'd never failed at anything in his life. Anything he'd wanted he'd strived for and achieved. Philly would be no exception.

He dragged his eyes away to the graduation photographs, the two children all grown up and about to set the world aflame. Another wedding photograph, more recent, no doubt Monty with his new bride, smiling into each other's eyes, totally oblivious to the camera. And the last one, another young family, a tiny baby cradled in its proud parents' arms.

He swallowed as he continued to stare, feeling swamped by the history, the tragedy, but most of all by the sheer force of emotion contained in the photographs so lovingly arranged on the mantle. Those most wonderful moments in a family's history recorded—disparate images of a particular moment of time—together making up a snapshot of a family's history, a pictorial chronology.

For some reason the picture of the baby drew him, its doll-like quality, the sprinkling of downy hair on its head and its surprisingly long fingers poking out from beneath its blanket as it slept.

He didn't know the first thing about babies. He'd never wanted to know. But now there was this overwhelming sense of fascination. A door had been opened to him and there was a whole new world to explore. Philly had opened that door.

'That's little Thomas,' Daphne said, her voice soft and heavy with sorrow. 'He would have turned two just last week. I can't help but think what he'd be up to now if he were still alive. No doubt toddling about everywhere, getting into everything.'

He looked over his shoulder. She was so small and weak, her sadness so much a part of her. 'You must miss them very much.'

Her nod was no more than a tilt of her head, even her gaze still fixed on the floor in front of her. 'I do, but then there's something so special about babies,' she said, as he turned back to the photograph. 'I think that's almost what I miss most—the wonder of new life, the hope for the future. It's too late for me to experience that again now.'

She sighed and reached for a handkerchief to blot the dampness from her eyes. 'Oh, just listen to me,' she croaked, almost to herself, 'rambling on like a silly old woman.'

He put the photograph down and turned, barely noticing her words as what she'd said earlier slowly permeated his consciousness.

She didn't know.

Philly hadn't told her.

Why on earth wouldn't she tell her own mother about the baby? Couldn't she see how much it would mean to her?

He looked back at the mantle, mentally seeing one more photograph—a beaming Philly holding a tiny child—another chance at life and a future.

Didn't Philly want her mother to see that photograph already? Or was she more worried about the absence of another? His eyes flicked over the wedding photographs. He could almost see the space where Philly's wedding photo would slot in alongside her brother's. Was the prospect of an illegitimate child the reason why Philly was holding off sharing the news with her mother?

Was she trying to save her mother hurt by not telling her the truth?

Something shifted inside him, sliding away to reveal a solution which was on the one hand so unexpected, yet at the same time so logical. He could help. He *wanted* to help. And he would have Philly in the bargain.

'Maybe all hope isn't gone,' he said, taking Daphne's hand in his own before sitting down. 'Maybe there's still a chance for something good, something that could give us all hope.'

She peered up at him, her dark-ringed eyes curious and hopeful at the same time. 'Whatever do you mean? Why *are* you here, Mr DeLuca?'

'I have something to tell you,' he said, struck by the fragility of her bird-like hand, her thin bones covered by barely more than a paper-thin cover of dry skin. He covered her hand with his other as if to keep her warm. 'Actually, I have something to ask of you.'

He paused, momentarily wondering if he was doing the right thing, but one look into her eyes told him that for the first time in what seemed like for ever he was doing something that mattered, something that had a beneficial effect beyond just the bottom line. And yet it would still get him what he wanted.

He took a deep breath before he continued.

'Would you give me the honour of allowing me to marry your daughter?'

CHAPTER ELEVEN

THERE. He'd said it. And it didn't feel so bad. In fact, taking in her sudden gasp of delight, the following smile which lit up the older woman's face, it felt pretty damned good.

It was the most logical solution. Philly obviously couldn't cope here, with a sick mother, a full-time job and a baby coming. And marriage would mean the baby would carry his name while Philly would bear none of the stigma attached to being a single mother.

It solved everything. Sure, he'd never intended getting married; in fact, he'd done all he could to avoid it. And he'd spent most of his lifetime alone—it wasn't as if he needed anyone—but if it meant that his child would be brought up the way he wanted, then maybe it would be worth sacrificing his independence just this once.

Because he'd get to spend his nights with Philly. That would at least be some compensation. He would have settled for mistress, but he'd marry her if that was what it took.

A key grated in the front door lock and he glanced at his watch, surprised at the late hour and realising just how much time he'd spent aimlessly driving around today.

'I'm home,' came Philly's voice from the small entrance hall. She sounded tired. She should have come home when he'd told her. Except he wouldn't have been here now if she had.

He rose to his feet and swung around alongside Daphne, his hand resting on the back of her chair.

'What are you doing here?' Philly felt the hair on the back of her neck stand up as she took in the cameo, her mother and Damien together, empty tea cups on the table where they'd sat opposite each other, much too cosily.

She should have known something was up when she'd spotted the sleek black coupé across the road. A car like that in this street was as unlikely as Damien stopping by for a cup of tea. And yet he was here...

'What's going on?'

'Sweetheart,' her mother said, battling her way to her feet with Damien's help by way of his hand under her elbow. 'Congratulations. I had no idea.' Her mother pulled her close, so close she could feel her wasted ribcage pressing into her through the thin cotton housecoat.

She glared at Damien over her mother's shoulder. 'You told her?' she said.

'Of course he told me,' said her mother, resting both her hands on Philly's shoulders. 'How else could he ask for my permission? Oh, you've made me so happy, I can't quite believe it. How soon do you plan to be married?'

'*Married?*'

She blinked as her insides lurched crazily. She'd imagined he'd spilt the beans about the pregnancy, but this... This wasn't happening. This didn't make sense. She opened her mouth, about to deny it, about to say there'd been some kind of mistake, when her eyes jagged with Damien's and the denial she expected to find echoed within his was nowhere to be seen. Instead, their dark intense depths seemed aflame with victory even as they threw out a challenge.

'Oh, married,' she said, wanting to sound as rational as possible for her mother's sake while her mind reeled with insane possibilities. 'Well, Damien and I have to talk about that. Just like we have a lot of other issues to resolve. *Don't we, Damien?*'

He smiled in response, one eyebrow arched, and not looking half as uncomfortable as she would have preferred him to. What was he up to?

Her mother broke the impasse. 'Well, this is wonderful news but I'm afraid I need to lie down for a little while now before dinner. All this excitement has worn me out. But I'm sure you two have plenty to catch up on. So if you'll excuse me, I'll just have a nap.'

'Of course,' said Philly, kissing her mother on the cheek. 'I'll see you get comfortable. We can have a late dinner tonight.'

Daphne turned to Damien, who dropped a kiss on her cheek likewise. 'Oh,' she said in response, 'if I were twenty years younger, I think I'd fancy giving you a run for your money myself.'

'If you were twenty years younger, I'd be taking you up on that.'

Her mother laughed like she hadn't heard for ages and Philly was half tempted to enjoy the sound. It was just so good to hear her mother laughing, let alone flirting. But she knew how fragile her mother was. How devastating it would be for her to realise this was all just some game Damien was playing.

Why was he doing this? What on earth was he trying to prove? She wouldn't see her mother hurt for anything or anyone. And this bizarre idea about marriage wasn't going to help anyone. Damien had had his chance earlier today and he'd made it more than clear then that he simply wasn't interested. So what was he doing here, putting thoughts of weddings and goodness knew what else into her mother's head?

Had he really not said a word yet about her pregnancy as she'd first feared? It was far too early to tell her just yet. What the hell was he playing at?

She saw her mother settled on her day bed and returned to the living room, white-hot fury building within her with every step.

Damien was waiting for her, still standing, the look on his face like a cat that had just caught a mouse. Well, this mouse was about to fight back.

'Welcome home,' he drawled, one side of his mouth curving up mockingly. 'Hard day at the office?'

'Don't ''welcome home'' me. We need to talk,' she said, her voice a low snarl.

'Sure,' he said easily with a shrug, as if he hadn't the least idea what she would want to talk about. 'Shoot.'

'Not here. Outside.' She didn't want any chance of her mother overhearing this conversation. She stalked through the kitchen to the rear entrance, leading the way to the small timber deck without looking back. But she knew he was there. She could feel his smug expression laughing into her back as he shadowed her out the door. She'd wipe that smug look off his face if it killed her.

She turned and somehow the deck had shrunk. The small outdoor table and chairs still took up the same space but Damien consumed the rest as he leaned his length over, propping his arms on the railing and looking out over the sun-dried back lawn and the fringe of shrubs lining the fence.

How dared he look so relaxed and at peace with the world? How dared he turn her life upside-down with a click of his fingers? And how dared he fool with the emotions of a frail, sick woman?

The fury inside her only mounted as he continued to gaze out, ignoring her completely. She crossed her arms over her chest but the action only seemed to magnify the crazy thumping of her heart.

'What are you doing here?'

He turned slowly, almost lazily, towards her, as if her question and tone were no more than the buzzing of an annoying insect somewhere nearby.

'That doesn't sound like the kind of greeting I'd expect from the woman I've just become betrothed to.'

'I never said I was going to marry you. What the hell is this all about—some kind of warped payback because I said no to your earlier demands?'

'You're having my baby, aren't you?'

'And what's that got to do with it?'

'That's got everything to do with it.'

'I thought you said you didn't do family.'

'I don't. Normally. But you can't bring up my baby here and you wouldn't come as my mistress. I had no choice. Now you have no choice.'

She let his slur on her house and what she could provide for a child slide away. She couldn't tackle everything at once. 'Did you tell my mother about the baby?'

His hands left the railing as he turned fully to face her. 'No, but I was left to wonder why you wouldn't. So now you don't have to worry about having an illegitimate child. Now your child will have a name and your baby will have a father. You could thank me for taking care of your problem.'

'*Thank you? My problem?* Tell me, where does your particular brand of arrogance come from? Did you make it yourself or did you take it over, like just another one of your corporate acquisitions?'

It was his turn to bristle, she noted with considerable satisfaction as he shifted his stance. 'Do you seriously think I haven't told my mother yet because I'm worried that she'll be devastated about me being an unmarried mother?'

'What else? You don't seem to realise how much a baby would mean to your mother. How could you not tell her such news?'

'Don't you think I know what my own mother needs? You're the last person who needs to tell me how much she would love to see another grandchild.'

'So now it's not an issue. Now you have nothing to be ashamed of.'

'I *never* had anything to be ashamed of. For your information, I haven't told my mother yet because I'm little more than six weeks' pregnant. Do you understand that?'

'You mean,' he interrupted, his face a tight frown, 'there's a chance you could be wrong?'

'No. The pregnancy has been confirmed. But that doesn't mean things can't still happen. What if I lose the baby?'

'Is that likely?'

'Not likely. But not impossible either. This is still very early days in the pregnancy. The last thing I need is for my mother to get her hopes up and then have them dashed once more. That's why I haven't told her yet—not because of some stupid idea that she won't be happy unless I have someone's ring on my finger.'

His silence lasted for barely a second and then he shrugged. 'It's of no consequence. We're getting married anyway—it's all decided. You can hardly let your mother down now.'

'And if something happens to the baby?'

'We'll have another.'

She shook her head. 'Damien, you're not listening to me. I never said I'd marry you.'

'You don't want marriage? You surprise me. That seemed to be exactly what you wanted this morning. You weren't satisfied with just my house, my servants, my income. It was clear to me you wanted more.'

'You can't just waltz in here and take over this house and this family like it's one of your business deals. Those kind of tactics might work in the boardroom, but they certainly don't wash here.'

Immediately she'd mentioned it she wished she could take it back. There was no way she could think about boardrooms without thinking of that night, of the night that had started it all, and with the memories came the heat, heat that was all the more raw after their lovemaking of today. She didn't need to remember such things now, *especially not now*, when she was trying to put distance between them, when she was trying to make him see sense.

Her eyes sought his. *Damn.* They narrowed, a predatory gleam infusing them, and she saw that he'd made the connection. With two quick steps he'd forced her backwards until his arms dropped either side of her and she was trapped.

'I'm not the only one around here who engages in boardroom tactics—or have you forgotten that first little episode?'

She shook her head as she backed up hard against the railing, fighting the sheer magnetism of his body, the pull of his body increasing with his proximity. 'No. But it's not relevant. You can't just make people do what you want. You can't just decide for them their future without a thought for their own needs and desires. You can't—'

Her words were cut off as his arms crushed her to him and his mouth found her throat, sending bold heat suffusing her veins, washing through her on a torrid tide that threatened to blow her resolve, if not her sanity.

His head forced hers back, leaving her neck and throat exposed to his mouth, his lips and tongue working together immediately finding all of those special places—that spot on her neck just below her ear lobe, the line where her skin disappeared under the neckline of her dress. All of her skin, anywhere his mouth touched, came alive and it was impossible to stop her body responding to his assault.

'You see...' His head lifted just a fraction so his lips skidded over her skin, a dance of breathy heat and liquid movement. 'See how much you want me,' he said. 'I could take you here, on the deck, and you would be powerless to stop me.'

She tried to breathe, to clear her mind. Yes, she wanted him. No matter how much she wished she could refute his claims her body would not be denied. Her heart would not be denied. She wanted him body and soul. But that still didn't make what he was doing

right. It was one thing for her to give herself freely.
It was another for him to take it.

'But that's the way you always operate, Damien.
You take what you want.'

'You don't fool me. You want this too.'

'So why not take me then? Take me now, right
here, while my mother sleeps inside. And what exactly will that prove? Do you for one moment imagine I will be so blown away by your love-making that
I will be desperate enough to rush down the aisle for
more?'

The change in his breathing told her that her words
had hit their mark. His head twisted to rest on her
shoulder as his arms relaxed their grip. He surged
away towards the house without looking at her, one
hand on his hip, the other sweeping back through his
hair all the way down to his neck.

She was driving him crazy. He must be crazy, to
want to attack her on her own back step, her mother
sleeping inside the house.

But he wanted her—so much. Why did she continue to frustrate him? She'd fled from him that first
night, hidden her identity and kept it concealed. And
she still made out she was an innocent in all this when
she'd held all the cards right from the beginning.

'You seem to take a great deal of satisfaction in
pointing out my failings, but do you think your own
behaviour is beyond reproach?' She looked up at him,
startled, as if not expecting him to go on the attack
so soon.

'What do you mean?'

'You're the one who ran away the night of the
masquerade ball. You're the one who kept your identity a secret. If you hadn't told me today about the

baby—' He stopped, reeling back the hours to that time.

She hadn't told him.

He'd intervened in her dispute with that loser, Bryce, and Bryce hadn't been the only one who'd believed him. In her fragile state she'd thought he was telling the truth. She'd thought he really did know the baby was his.

He looked up at her, his eyes open for what seemed the first time as the layers of her deceit peeled away.

'You weren't going to tell me, were you.'

It wasn't a question, it was an accusation. 'You were never going to tell me.'

'No, Damien, that's not true.'

'You were going to keep this baby a secret. You never intended to let me in on it. If I hadn't come to your rescue and you hadn't taken me seriously, I never would have known.'

'No! I was going to tell you today.'

'But you didn't.'

'I didn't have a chance. I was about to tell you, in your office, but Bryce—'

'Bryce nothing. I don't believe you. You've hidden the truth from me all along. Why should today be any different?'

'Because it's the truth.'

'No. You were going to keep it your secret. Another little secret. Like making love to me that night. That was your secret. You didn't want me to know who you were—that's what that mask was all about—why you wouldn't take it off. You never wanted me to find out.'

'Damien, listen to me—'

'Why should I listen to you? You've hidden the

truth all along. You hid your face that night so I wouldn't know who you were. Then you let me believe you were never at that Christmas party. Why would you do that and then suddenly decide to tell me you're pregnant and it's my baby?'

'Because it is your baby. You have a right to know.'

'You care about my rights?' he scoffed. 'I very much doubt that. But this isn't about rights. I believe you never had any intention of admitting you were in that boardroom let alone advising me that I was the father of this baby. If it hadn't been for that blunder you made when I threw Bryce out, you would never have told me.'

'Damien, that's simply not true.'

'Isn't it? You can honestly say you never once considered hiding the truth about this baby from me? You never once considered the possibility of bringing this child up on your own?'

Her eyes slid sideways before they slowly meandered their way back to his. His own narrowed in response. *What did that mean if not an acknowledgement of his claims?* She'd planned to keep this baby secret from him. Blood rushed to his temples in a flush of heat and anger. Just as well she had no way out of this arrangement. She'd never escape him again.

'I…' she flailed. 'You see…'

'I don't see, Philly,' he barged in. 'I don't see at all. You had ample opportunity to tell me you were the woman behind that mask, and yet you said nothing. Then, when we were up at the Gold Coast, I tried to kiss you and you acted like I was mauling you— and yet we'd already made love. What was that all about unless you were wanting to keep that first night a secret?'

She gasped, her eyes wide open in protest. 'You didn't want me that night. It was one thing to make love to some fantasy woman at the ball, but you had no intention of making love to me then. You just didn't want anyone else to. You couldn't stand the thought that anyone else might be interested in me.'

No intention of making love with her? She had to be kidding. He'd burned that night, back in his room, pacing away the tension she'd provoked in his loins.

'No,' he said. 'That doesn't make sense. You wanted to keep your identity secret. That's why you pushed me away that night. So there would be no chance I might recognise my elusive boardroom lover.'

She was shaking her head. 'Things were already too complicated. You wouldn't have believed me.'

'And things are less complicated now? How do you work that out?'

He didn't wait for her answer. He took three strides, stopping at the top of the steps leading down to the thirsty lawn below. 'How do you expect me to believe you?'

'Because it's the truth.'

He sighed, long and deep, before he looked over his shoulder to where she was still standing against the railing. 'So then, explain it to me. Why did you keep that mask on? Why did you run away from me that night, unless it was to ensure I'd never find out who you were? Why didn't you tell me it was you?'

She didn't answer and a train rushed along the track, sounding its horn over the crossing. Then gradually the quiet resumed, leaving only the plaintive notes of the windchimes tinkling in the lame summer breeze.

'Have you forgotten what it was like back then? Forgotten how you were?'

She looked over to him and gave a wan smile. 'Remember the first day I came to your office? When Sam had gone home sick? Remember how you were then?'

'What do you mean?'

'I knew what you thought of me. You'd summed me up and written me off with one glance. I was so low on the food chain I didn't even register.'

'It wasn't like that.'

'Of course it was. There was no way you'd look twice at me. And yet, at the ball...'

'You looked so different that night.'

She gave a shrug, a small laugh. 'You never suspected it was *me*. You never had any plans to make love to plain old Philly Summers. And I didn't want you to find out. Because I knew you wouldn't want to know. It never would have happened if you'd known who I was.'

'That's not true.'

But he knew it was. He hadn't looked twice at her, not the way she was back then. He'd had no idea what was hidden away under that brown suit and those glasses.

'It was such a fantasy, that night,' she continued, her voice low and wistful in remembrance. 'And afterwards, afterwards I got so scared.'

'Scared of what?'

'I couldn't believe what I'd done—what we'd done. I just panicked. I knew you'd resent me for what had happened. I knew you'd be angry. And even if I kept my job, I didn't think I'd ever be able to face you again. I had to get out. So I ran.'

'You thought I'd fire you?'

'I didn't know what you'd do. I had no way of knowing. I just knew you wouldn't be happy to find out that the woman you'd seduced in the boardroom was only me.'

Only me. So she'd hardly been the type of woman that usually attracted him back then. Heck, did she have any idea about how many nights' sleep he'd lost since then thinking about his mystery lover?

And then there'd been the Gold Coast trip. That was when Philly had started to look different. Her clothes, her hair, even getting rid of her glasses. Ever since that trip she'd been a different woman. A sexier woman. And he'd made it plain he thought so in her room that night. And she'd been the one that night to turn him away.

He'd wanted two different women only to find out that they were the same person all along. Surely that counted for something? He wanted to reach out a hand to her then, to soothe her fears and assure her that he did want her, but he wasn't ready to do that. This whole discussion had left more than just a bitter taste in his mouth.

'How long will you wait until you tell your mother about the baby?'

She looked up at him, all hollow eyes and pale skin. 'I thought maybe another month, just to be sure. That should get me over the most critical time.'

'We'll schedule the wedding for a month's time, in that case. We can tell her together then.'

Her head jerked up. 'You still plan on going through with this? You still intend to marry me?'

'You have no choice. Your mother has been told and I certainly don't want to be the one to disappoint her. Do you?'

She dropped her eyes to the decking, her heart hammering in her chest. There was no way in the world she'd do anything to upset her mother—Damien knew that—she'd been effectively locked in this marriage deal from the moment she'd walked through that door.

But if he thought she was trapped, it was nothing to how he was going to feel when he found out the truth.

He was determined to marry her to have control over their child and its upbringing. He had no idea he had control over her heart.

CHAPTER TWELVE

SHE was married. No longer Miss Summers. Now she was Mrs DeLuca, wife to Damien. His ring on her hand, his name in place of hers.

Teringa Park, his country property, had made the perfect setting for their wedding vows. She'd imagined it was just another country home, another executive hobby farm, but she'd been wrong. The lush property dated back to early colonial times, the large home testament to the success and wealth of its first owner.

Just as this wedding was testament to the success and wealth of its current owner.

A large marquee had been set up on the expanse of lawns, which were green and lush in defiance of the dry summer heat. Filmy white fabric had been hung in drifts along the veranda of the old stone homestead and it billowed softly in the gentle breeze, while champagne-coloured helium-filled balloons jostled together in large urns bedecked with ribbons and bows, set about the gardens between bowls of fragrant apricot roses.

The service itself had been brief, though the guest list surprisingly large, considering how few family members there were between them. But obviously Damien wasn't the kind of man who would do anything by halves. The *Who's Who* of Melbourne society was in attendance along with a contingent of society page reporters, and everyone wanted to meet the woman lucky enough to snare Melbourne's most eligible bachelor.

By the end of the day Philly felt drained, emotionally and physically, the stresses and tension of the day overwhelming her. She turned her head to the man at her side, the man to whom her life was now linked, and the magnitude of what she'd done moved through her like an earthquake—a shudder of realisation, an instant of fear as her world shook under her.

She had the perfect husband—rich, intelligent, drop-dead gorgeous. She was the envy of every woman here, if the looks from the assembled guests were any indication. She had everything, or so they thought.

Strange, how empty you could feel, when you were supposed to have everything. Strange how those things everyone seemed to want did nothing to fill the hole deep inside her, the hole that could never be filled with mere luxury and a marriage built on control.

The one bright light was her mother. She sat on a shady terrace watching the proceedings, unable to erase the smile from her face. She looked serene today, even beautiful, in a silky soft aqua outfit Damien himself had personally selected for her and it complemented her pale skin and softly waved regrowing hair perfectly. Make up enhanced her features, already looking healthier than they had in months.

Damien had been right. While news of the baby was sure to delight her mother, knowing that Philly was married and that her grandchild would therefore be raised within a family unit with both parents, would make it all the more special. Already the bloom on her face made the hastily arranged marriage worthwhile.

But it wasn't just her appearance. It was also the apparent improvement in her health. Even the doctors were amazed by the sudden change in her well-being, the steadying of her condition and the indisputable easing of the pain. Quite simply, her mother seemed a different woman.

Philly hugged the thought to her chest. How much more so would her mother be when she discovered the whole truth? That she would have a grandchild again. And now, with her mother's progress, it seemed more certain every day that she would get to hold that grandchild.

She watched as Marjorie handed her mother a cool drink. Damien had even managed to track down the nurse and retain her as her full-time companion. She stole a glance up at the man at her side, still confused by the person he was. For someone who 'didn't do family', he'd done all he could to make Daphne's life more comfortable. That would have been enough for Philly, she couldn't have expected more. Yet beyond that the two seemed to share an easy relationship, a *genuine* relationship, and she could tell there was a warmth and sincerity from Damien that went further than mere obligation.

Had he changed? Was there a chance his warmth would extend to her too? In the past few weeks he'd been distant, focused on work, while wedding arrangements had been drawn up around him, almost as if now that she'd agreed to become his wife he had no further need of her. But was there a chance her love might one day be reciprocated? Was there a chance that this marriage might mean more to him than the means of controlling his child's upbringing?

Damien's hand brushed against hers, snaring it in his grip and interrupting her thoughts. She looked up at him.

'Did I tell you how beautiful you look today?'

She felt herself colour under his sudden scrutiny. The ivory silk gown was indeed a triumph of design and needlework, the line complementing her body as it moulded to her shape before spilling into an extravagantly full skirt. It was enough to wear it to feel beautiful. Having Damien tell her it was true was something else entirely.

He squeezed her hand and smiled down at her as the last of the guests drifted away. 'I have something for you,' he said. 'Come with me.'

Dusk was falling, the light changing by the minute as the night inexorably clawed out to claim the day. Marjorie had taken her mother indoors as the summer heat tempered into warm evening and the wind picked up, bringing dark clouds and the promise of a summer storm.

She smiled back at him as he tugged on her hand. 'Come on,' he said.

He led the way around the house, their steps crunching on the white gravel leading to the garage. She frowned. There was a champagne-coloured sports car parked alongside—someone had left their car here, though why anyone would leave a car like that... Hang on, there was something else— It was tied with a wide ribbon and bow.

She looked up at Damien, confused, but he only met her stare with an inscrutably questioning look of his own.

'Do you like it?'

'Do I like it?' He had to be kidding. 'You mean…?' She looked from Damien to the car and back again. 'You mean, it's mine?'

He dipped his head in the briefest affirmation. 'Consider it a wedding gift.'

She thought about her mother's ageing sedan that she used for the shopping and their infrequent trips, as different from this vehicle as a wooden dinghy to a top of the line ski boat. 'I'm not sure I'll be able to handle it.'

'I'll give you lessons. Starting tomorrow.'

He pulled something from his pocket—a loop of satin ribbon tied with a key. He lifted it over her head, placing it around her neck, his hands lingering at her shoulders.

She looked up at him, one hand cradling the key, stunned by his gesture and guilty that she hadn't thought to make him a gift.

'But I have nothing for you.'

He pulled her close, so that his fierce heartbeat was linked to her own but for fine layers of fabric in between. 'I will collect mine…' his head dipped and his mouth brushed over hers—a gentle touch that belied the heat and passion below, the heat she could feel in the look he gave her '…later tonight. But for now, it's time we said goodnight to your mother. It's time she learned our news.'

Daphne was resting in the large Victorian sitting room inside, sipping on a rare sherry. She beamed up at them as they entered the room, the delight on her face further reinforcing in Philly's mind that for her mother's sake at least she had done the right thing today.

'That was a perfect day,' she said as they both leaned down to kiss her. 'Just a beautiful wedding. Thank you for making me so happy.'

Damien smiled. 'We have more news if you're not too tired already.'

She shook her head. 'It's been a long day and I'll need to turn in soon but I don't want it to end just yet. Though I don't know what you could tell me that would top today's excitement.'

He looked across at Philly and nodded, letting her give the news. Philly sat down alongside her mother and took her hands in her own. 'Mum,' she said, watching her mother's face intently. 'This might come as a bit of a surprise, but we're going to have a baby. I'm pregnant.'

Daphne snatched her hands out from between Philly's and slapped them up against her open mouth, her eyes wide with shock.

'Oh!'

A second later tears welled up in those wide eyes until they brimmed over. 'But this is wonderful. Just wonderful.'

Damien leaned closer. 'You're not disappointed? We jumped the gun a bit on the wedding.'

She pulled her hands away, brushing away the tears which were still falling. 'How could I be disappointed? And don't you think I know what it's like to love someone so much you can't wait until the wedding? Remember I was young and in love myself once.'

He would have argued—he knew nothing of love, and love had nothing to do with how their baby had been conceived, but this was no time for argument. Besides, it wasn't as if he didn't feel something for Philly. He wanted her, in bed and out of it, and knowing he had her now, knowing she was tied to him, was more satisfying than he could have imagined.

But that was hardly the same as love...

He watched Daphne's eyes settle on her daughter, suddenly more alive and alight with possibilities than he had ever seen them, before she pulled her into an embrace, Philly laughing out loud with the reception to their news and the delight taken in it by her mother. Laughter merged with tears as they rocked together and, watching them, mother and daughter, his breath caught in his chest as if something had swung free, something hard-edged and heavy, that rammed against his lungs, winding him, before breaking off and plunging deep into his gut.

Philly's eyes landed on his and her smile broadened as their hazel lights shone warm and real into his, setting the space inside him strangely aglow.

He felt a deep satisfaction and a good deal of pride, together with a whole plethora of unfamiliar emotions he couldn't even begin to put a name to.

'I can't believe it,' Daphne said, releasing her daughter from her arms only enough to take her hands in hers. 'Remember that promise you made to me? That you even cared enough to make that promise meant so much but I never once thought it might actually happen.'

'Promise?' Damien shifted, noticing Philly's back stiffen. 'What are you talking about?'

'Oh, that,' Philly replied, shakily trying to laugh it off, her eyes evading his. 'It seems nothing now.'

'Nothing?' said her mother. 'How can it be nothing, when your daughter promises you something you think only a miracle can deliver and yet she makes it happen? It's truly a miracle.'

'What did she promise you?'

'Damien,' said Philly, grabbing his hand. 'Mum looks tired. I'll tell you later.'

'But Philly sounds such a wonderful daughter,' he said, ignoring her attempts to stop him. 'Tell me, Daphne, about how special my new bride is. What did she promise you?'

Daphne patted Damien on the hand, fresh tears pooling in the corners of her eyes.

'Well, it was after Monty, Annelise and baby Thomas died in that terrible accident. I was so upset about the family, and about my grandson. It was so unfair—he was just so young. And I felt cheated. I was a grandmother and yet I'd never had the chance to be one. I never even got to hold him or to kiss his soft cheek or feel his tiny hand cling to my finger...'

Damien reached for her hand then and squeezed it, even though dread was seeping inside him, settling into dank, stagnant pools that banished the sensations of contentment and goodwill he'd been feeling just moments earlier.

She stared ahead, her vacant eyes fixed on a point in the middle distance. 'Not a day goes by that I don't wonder what he would be doing now or how he would be growing. Not a day goes by that I don't feel the pain of his loss.'

She swallowed and turned her face back to Damien's. 'When they discovered my cancer was terminal I thought I'd never have the chance of holding a grandchild at all. But Philadelphia knew what it meant to me. She knew how much I yearned for another grandchild and she made me a promise.'

She blinked rapidly, clearing the tears from her eyes as she took a deep breath. He held his.

'It seems quite mad now yet it meant so much to me at the time—and now? Well, maybe it wasn't so mad, after all. I remember it was my birthday and I was feeling particularly sad and she promised me then that she would do anything she could to make me happy and that I wasn't going anywhere without holding her baby first.'

'She said she would do—*anything*?' He directed the half-statement half-question to Daphne but his eyes were searching for the answer on Philly's face, waiting for her to deny it but knowing by the fear in her swirling hazel eyes that she couldn't.

'Yes.' Daphne chuckled, oblivious to the sudden tension now crackling in the air between the newly-weds. 'I don't know what Philadelphia had in mind. I thought once the wedding with Bryce fell through that there was no chance but then, as luck would have it, you turned up.'

'As luck would have it.'

His voice was icy and flat, a slippery track she felt herself sliding along, further and further away from him.

'And I'm a very lucky woman because of it. But now I must rest. So, if you'll excuse me…'

'I'll see you to your room,' Philly offered, relishing the thought of a moment's respite from the heated accusations of his dark eyes, but Daphne would have none of it.

'No! Marjorie can look after me. It's your wedding night, after all.'

Daphne made her goodnights and disappeared with Marjorie in a whirl of excitement and congratulations. The second they'd left the room Philly turned, trying to take the offensive.

'Damien, it's not how it sounds. We have to talk.'

Without looking at her, he walked straight past and out of the room, leaving her to chase after him in his wake, a combination of his woody cologne, fury and a sense of betrayal wafting behind him. Lifting her full-length silk skirts she tripped down the hallway after him, barely able to keep up with his long, purposeful stride. He entered the room that was to have been theirs, the massive master suite, dominated by the large four-poster bed intended for the newlyweds to share tonight.

But the bed might not have been there for all the notice Damien took of it. He moved straight to the walk-in wardrobe, where he collected a leather overnight case and started flinging the few items he'd brought into it.

'What are you doing?' she asked.

'What does it look like? I'm leaving.'

'Damien, let me explain.'

'Explain what?'

'It's not how it sounds.'

'No? You mean you didn't make that promise to your mother?'

'Yes, I did, but that doesn't mean—'

'You didn't say you'd do anything you could?'

'Damien, that's not the point.'

'Isn't it? You promised to do anything you could to give your mother a grandchild. When it all went belly-up with Bryce you had to find some other way of doing what you'd promised, and quickly. And you found it in me.'

He strode across the room with long, purposeful strides into the large *en suite* bathroom. 'What did your mother say?' he continued, hurling toiletries into the bag. '"As luck would have it, you turned up"'.

'No, Damien, it wasn't like that. I explained all this to you before.'

'Did you? Seems you left out the best bit. You left out the bit about being determined to have a baby. Someone's baby. *Anyone's* baby. That night at the masquerade ball, you weren't there for my benefit. You were trawling for a sperm donor.'

His words cut her deep, so deep that she was unable to respond. It hadn't been like that...

'My God,' he continued, 'when I think that I almost believed you. I thought all you wanted to do was to keep this baby a secret. And, no doubt, you did. Until you worked out there was an even bigger prize. You could have the baby and the money too. Money and luxury for life. Not a bad return for one night's work.'

He lifted his head to look at her. 'Such a wonderful daughter.' He zipped up the bag, shaking his head. 'Such a lousy wife.'

'Damien, it's not true. You have to listen to me. Please.'

'Why should I listen to you? You've lied to me ever since we met. Every step of the way you've hidden the truth, pretending to be something you're not, the shy virgin, the dutiful daughter. Well, the truth is out. You're neither dutiful nor shy. You're manipulative and devious, out for what you can get.'

'I *never* pretended to be anything, least of all a shy virgin. I never said that.'

'No? You didn't have to. Those baggy suits. The big glasses. You looked like a shy little mouse but all the while you were planning with rat cunning.'

'What? Now you're blaming my wardrobe for what's happened? Listen to yourself, Damien. You're not making any sense.'

'Maybe not but at least now I'm seeing sense. I'm seeing things I should have seen a long time ago.'

He tossed the bag over his shoulder and stormed across the room to the door.

'Where are you going?'

'Anywhere you're not.'

'But you can't go, not yet.'

'Why not? You've got what you wanted—the baby, a husband, somewhere your mother will be comfortable and well looked after. You've fulfilled your promise. You have no more need of me.'

'That's not true. I do need you.'

He tossed her a look of disdain over his shoulder as he headed across the driveway to the detached triple garage. 'Why? Have you made more promises you haven't bothered to share with me?'

'No! But I need you, Damien. I… I love you.'

He stopped dead at the garage door, his hand on the automatic door opener and his head lowered as the metal door rolled up and away.

Her breath was fast and shallow, her heart hammering as she waited for his response, any response.

When the door had rolled high enough he stepped under and around to the side of his black BMW, tossed in the bag and finally turned, his features frozen, his eyes cold and hard.

'I'm disappointed, Philly. For a woman who's gone to the lengths you have to get pregnant, I would have expected something much more creative than that. Running out of ideas, are you?'

He lowered himself into the car and turned the key, kicking the black beast into life. She ran to the side of the car as he pulled his door shut, her voice rising to counter the engine.

'Damien, it's the truth. And no matter how much you don't want my love and don't need it, you've got it. And I don't even know why. But it's true. I love you.'

He gunned the motor, one hand on the steering wheel, the other tense over the gear stick as his window slid down in a hum. 'Don't bother, Philly. That's hardly likely to change things, even if I did believe you.'

The window slid up and the car jumped forward out of the garage. Philly sprang back as the sleek car roared out.

'Damien!' But he was gone, in a cloud of rich petrol fumes and the powerful roar of an engine being given its head.

He couldn't go—not like this! He had to believe her. She had to convince him. But how could she do that? She looked around, her eyes falling on the Mercedes coupé still parked just outside the garage, the large gold ribbon still tied around it. She touched the key at her throat, the key Damien had placed there earlier.

He must be heading for the penthouse, intending to spend the night alone there. If she could just talk to him—she needed time to explain, to put his fears to rest, and letting him stew on everything tonight was only going to cement his case against her.

She looked at the car. She hadn't driven it yet and

it was as different from her old sedan as satin was from serge, but it was still only a car. And right now it was her only hope.

She flipped the ribbon necklace over her head as she headed for the car. With two tugs the large bow came away and fluttered to the ground and, collecting her skirts in one hand, she slid behind the wheel, the soft leather seat wrapping itself around her. She took a few seconds to familiarise herself with the controls. Then she snapped on her seat belt and started the engine.

The sports car gave a throaty purr that spelt superb engineering and promised power. She wouldn't need too much of that—she was more interested in making it to the penthouse in one piece than in catching him *en route* after all. With a final deep breath she found the headlights and released the handbrake, easing the car along the driveway.

There was at least twenty kilometres of country road to negotiate before reaching the highway that would take her straight into the city. She couldn't wait to get there.

Thick clouds skudded across the sky, obliterating the moon until the night sky became dark and threatening. Gum leaves and bark danced across the road, whipped along by the rising wind which bowed the roadside trees in the car's powerful headlights.

While the car was smooth and powerful, it was enough to concentrate on the unaccustomed journey and the worsening conditions and she longed for the familiarity of her old sedan. At least on that one she knew which side to find the wipers and indicators in a hurry if she needed.

She missed two turns on the narrow bush roads and

had to backtrack to find the right route, but eventually the glow from the lights over the freeway on-ramp told her she was close. With a sigh of thanks she stretched back into the rich leather upholstery, knowing the worst was over and that the freeway would soon take her into the city and to Damien. The few first drops of rain splatted on to her windscreen. Slowly at first, before fast turning into a torrent.

She almost missed the car on the side of the road as she battled to find the wipers. For a second she thought it was Damien parked there and her heart leapt, but as she got closer she could see the dark colour belonged to a different, older make of car. The bonnet was up and a woman ran out in front of her, waving her arms in the rain. For a second she thought about driving on—it was dark and she wasn't entirely comfortable with the idea of stopping. But the conditions were awful and what if the woman had children in the car? If it was Philly herself who'd broken down the last thing she'd want would be people to just drive by.

If only she'd grabbed her bag before she'd rushed off. At least then she would have had her phone to alert the authorities. As it was, she had no choice…

She pulled up just behind the car and found the button for the window. Cold bullets of rain took advantage of the opening glass, crashing cold and hard on to her face and chest. The woman rushed alongside.

'Can I give you a lift?' Philly asked.

'You can do better than that,' said the woman, pulling open the door before ramming something cold and hard against Philly's cheek. 'You can give me the car.'

CHAPTER THIRTEEN

THE call came at three o'clock in the morning from the security desk downstairs. He hadn't really been sleeping, more like tossing and turning, running over words and conversations in his mind, trying to make sense of the tangle of his thoughts. So the call hadn't really woken him up, but the words the security officer had spoken snapped him immediately to attention.

Two officers. To see him.

He wasn't all that familiar with the workings of the police force but he knew enough to know that they didn't go making social calls at this time of night. He just had time to pull on jeans and a sweater when his doorbell buzzed.

'What's this about?' he said before the uniformed officers had cleared the entrance.

'Mr DeLuca, are you the registered owner of a Mercedes vehicle?' He rattled off a registration number Damien recognised instantly.

'That's my wife's car—yes. I bought it for her as a wedding present. Is there a problem?'

'Can you describe your wife for us, sir?'

'Well, yes. Five-sixish, slim figure, sandy-blonde hair. What's this about?'

The officers exchanged glances. 'You might like to sit down. The car was involved in an accident this evening. I'm afraid we have some bad news.'

His blood ran cold. 'What kind of bad news?'

'The car spun on a bend and went over an embankment. The driver wasn't wearing a seat belt. She was thrown from the car.'

Damien turned away, chilled to the core, trying to swallow though there was nothing to lubricate his throat as the ashes of his past choked him. *'Spun on a bend,' 'Over an embankment'*. Was he truly hearing this or were these images dredged up from another disaster, another tragedy over a lifetime ago?

Why did it seem that history was repeating itself?

'A woman was driving. Do you recognise this?'

The officer placed something in his palm and he tried to concentrate as he looked down on the loops of thin satin ribbon and a key—the same key he'd placed around Philly's neck just last night. His fingers curled tight around the cold metal. 'My wife… Is she badly hurt… Or…?'

'Mr DeLuca,' said one officer, his voice laden with compassion. 'It's more serious than that. The driver was killed. Under the circumstances we fear it may be your wife. We'd like you to come and assist with identifying the body.'

Philly!

They thought it was Philly. But he'd left her back at the house. It couldn't be her. He'd left the car out of the garage. Someone must have stolen it. But then why would they have the key?

There was one way to find out.

He explained and reached for the phone. She had to be at the house. Someone else must have taken the key and stolen the car. That had to be what had happened. He called up the number from the phone's memory, knowing he'd never key it in as quickly while in this state. Eventually his manager answered, businesslike but clearly half-asleep himself.

'It's Damien,' he said. 'I need to know if Mrs DeLuca is in the house. It's important. And check the garage too,' he added as an afterthought.

He found shoes while he waited, avoiding the pity-filled eyes of the policemen as they looked everywhere but at him. But it wasn't Philly. It couldn't be.

Eventually the manager came back, his worried manner immediately sending shivers down Damien's spine. The words only confirmed his tone. No sign of her. Hadn't slept in any of the rooms. And the car was gone.

He held on to the phone for a good minute longer, only half-aware of the concerned voice on the other end of the line. 'Phone me on my mobile immediately if you hear from her,' he said at last, hanging up.

He looked over to the officers, his mind blank, his gut cold and empty. 'Let's go,' he said.

She must have followed him. Why the hell hadn't he considered she might do that? She'd followed him and now she was dead. *Their child was dead.* Grief welled up within him with the force of a tidal wave.

And it was all his fault!

She'd wanted to talk and he'd run. She'd wanted him to stay and he'd fled. She'd told him she loved him and he'd turned his back on her.

And so she'd followed him. Why would she have done that? Why had she been so determined to make him see reason if she already had everything she wanted? Unless the baby and the house weren't enough. Had she really needed him too? Had she really loved him?

She'd crashed, gone over an embankment, had never stood a chance in a car she hadn't known how to handle. A car he'd given to her. He'd inflicted upon her the same fate that had met every other member of his family. He'd done that to her because he'd never once had the courage to accept what she'd said and faced up to what he really felt.

That he needed her. That she made him feel special and strong and protective. That he wanted to look after her.

That he loved her.

Anguish twisted him inside.

My God, but he did!

He loved her. And now it was too late.

He'd never wanted to love. Love only compounded pain, made it infinitely worse than it would otherwise be. But why had he thought he could deny love by simply ignoring its existence, by simply not thinking the thoughts or saying the words?

By not telling the woman he loved?

He was right not to want to love. Wouldn't the pain he was feeling right now be so much easier to bear if he hadn't loved her?

But he hadn't told her, and right now that made his pain worse. He'd denied what she'd meant to him and he'd rejected her love. How must she have felt following him along those roads in those conditions? She must have been desperate to catch up with him.

The police car pulled up outside the hospital, its lights making crazy patterns on the slick roads. The storm had long gone and a strange calm had descended. That was outside at least. His storm had only just begun.

He looked up at the horizontal concrete façade, the

windows lit with a dull glow and the occasional blip of colour from a machine.

He didn't want to go inside. He wanted to deny it now, even though he knew it must be the truth. It was going to be one of the hardest things he'd ever done. But there was something even harder to follow.

How was he going to tell Daphne?

They led him along the long corridors, the atmosphere antiseptic, their bright fluorescent lighting garish and cold in this late hour. Then they made him wait outside a room in the morgue, giving him even more time to think about how he should have done things differently, how he should have told her what she meant to him, how wrong he'd been.

He hadn't been fair to her. He'd bullied her at work, he'd bullied her at the Gold Coast, and he'd bullied her into this wedding. And now there was no chance to tell her he was sorry.

Now it was too late.

They called him inside, into a room where the clinical furniture and fittings faded into bland insignificance, where the cloaked trolley held centre stage. He walked slowly to one side, the policemen close behind, and stopped, wanting to know, not wanting to know, because until he knew for sure, there was always a chance they were wrong, however unlikely that seemed.

'Mr DeLuca?' The attendant's brow was furrowed with concern.

'She was pregnant, you know. Our first child.'

The man's eyes blinked slowly, as if he hadn't wanted to hear that. 'Are you all right, Mr DeLuca?'

He gave a brief nod. 'Ready,' he muttered on a breath that tasted of death and cold ash.

The attendant peeled back the sheet. Damien's heart stopped and he rocked on his heels as he scoured her face. Under the scratches and contusions her features still looked quite lovely considering she'd suffered such a sudden, savage end, her eyes closed, her lips slightly parted as if ready to draw her next soft breath. She looked at peace.

But she didn't look familiar.

'It's not Philly.' He sagged on a breath that brought relief, just as quickly replaced by a savage new fear. He turned to the officers behind him.

'So where's my wife?'

CHAPTER FOURTEEN

IT WAS so cold. Two minutes in the driving rain had been enough to soak her to the skin. Now she was out of the weather but there was no way she could warm up here. She'd found what had to be an old picnic rug that smelt as if it had seen more dogs' breakfasts than picnic lunches, but it was at least something to drag over her shoulders and it helped to break up the otherwise wall-to-wall motor oil smell.

She was cramped, uncomfortable, and had no idea of the time, only that it must be still dark and she was so tired but way too cold to sleep. It hurt to move. It hurt not to move. But what hurt more was that she wouldn't even be missed for hours. Damien was at the apartment, most likely, and at the house no one would question her absence before lunch time.

Every time she'd heard a car approach, she'd banged and yelled till she was hoarse. But no one had heard her and the cars had just kept on driving.

She was stuck here, shivering, until the sun rose. How long until sunrise? But how hot was it expected to be today? Right now the idea of warmth was attractive but how long would it take before she cooked inside here?

They had to find her first. *Damien* had to find her first. Before she died…

Before their baby died.

She hugged her abdomen gently, marginally relieved that right now the discomfort she was feeling down there had more to do with a pressing bladder than a sign that anything was wrong with her pregnancy, and she tried to rock in the cramped, airless space, crooning softly as if calming her tiny child.

How long could she hang on to both her bladder and her sanity? Hopefully long enough.

The police had said they'd contact him as soon as they found her, but if they thought there was any way he could sit and wait by a phone while his wife was missing they had him all wrong. Even if they had reason to wonder.

Tactfully they'd asked why it was that a man who'd just married had spent the night in his apartment in town, while his pregnant wife was left somewhere else.

It wasn't easy to explain—a stupid argument—a misunderstanding. In the light of what had ensued, it all seemed so pointless.

By the time he'd started his own search dawn was lightening the sky, tingeing the few remaining clouds pink in an otherwise grey-blue sky. He set out, confident that if she'd been on the highway someone would have found her by now. She had to be somewhere between the house and the highway.

How the woman had stolen the car, he was too scared to think. The only thing he could hang on to was that she was alive somewhere, alive and waiting to be found. She had to be.

He almost missed the car, only the perfect circles of its tail-lights looking too regular amongst the shrubs along the side of the road. Someone had tried to hide it—why else park it like that?

His heart raced as he pulled up nearby, watching

for any indication that anyone was about, but all he could hear was the morning cries of magpies and crows high up in the trees. Until something thumped and thumped again, dull and repetitive and totally at odds with the sounds of a bush morning and hope sprang wild and unfettered in his chest. He heard a cry, muffled and weak, but he heard it all the same and he rushed to the car.

It had to be.

'Philly,' he yelled, his face up close to the metal. 'Is that you? Can you hear me?'

He wasn't sure if it was a squeal of relief or of delight that he heard in response, but it sure was the best sound he'd ever heard.

She was alive.

He checked the boot but there was no external release mechanism. Without a key he'd need to break it open. Unless… The car was old but there was a chance. He pulled open the driver's side door and sent up a silent prayer of thanks when he saw the boot release lever. He flicked it up and heard the satisfying click as the catch was released.

A fraction of a second later he pulled open the boot lid and scooped her out of the small space, holding her in his arms and hugging her tightly to him.

Her gown was torn and grease-stained, an old rag hung off her shoulders; she smelled more of car and oil than her familiar apricot scent and tears had left tracks down her grimy face but she'd never looked more beautiful to him than right now.

'Philly.' He held her close, his lips brushing her brow as she sobbed gently against him.

'You found me,' she said, her voice shuddering on a sob.

'I was afraid I'd lost you for ever. Are you all right? Did they hurt you?'

'I'm stiff and sore and cold. But I think I'm okay. A woman took the car; she had a gun. She made me get in the boot and then drove it into the bushes.'

She'd had a gun.

Breath hissed through his teeth. What might have happened? What was he thinking, to lead her into danger like this?

He carried her to his car and sat inside with her cradled on his lap to pass on his warmth. He pulled the smelly rag from her shoulders and replaced it with the mohair rug from his car. She snuggled closer, enjoying the warmth both his body and the rug lent as he pulled out his mobile phone and made a quick call to the police.

'How did you find me?' she asked when he'd finished the call.

'The police found your car. You weren't in it.' He didn't tell her about the driver; there were some things that could wait. And some things that were more important and couldn't.

'I'm so sorry,' she said, her voice quivering. 'I didn't mean to cause you so much fuss.'

'Shh,' he said. 'It's not your fault. I shouldn't have left like that. You were following me, weren't you?'

'I had to talk to you. You wouldn't believe me. I couldn't let you go, thinking what you did.'

He smoothed her tangled hair with his fingers. 'I was wrong to think all those things. I was wrong.'

'But Damien—' she sniffed, rubbing her nose with her hand '—in a way you were right.'

'No,' he said, interrupting her. 'You don't have to do this now.'

'Please, I have to. I was crazy with wanting a baby; that much was right. I'd asked about IVF but they wouldn't take me on because I wasn't married. I'd even thought about picking someone up, a one-night stand.'

He stiffened, not sure he wanted to hear this.

She looked up at him, her eyes earnest. 'I thought about it but I couldn't do it. I'd all but given up hope of having a baby by the time the masquerade ball happened and it didn't even occur to me that night. Because of you. You made me feel so good, you felt so wonderful, that nothing else mattered. It was only afterwards that I realised what we'd done. I panicked.'

'You really thought I would have sacked you?'

'I didn't know and I was too scared to find out. But as soon as I discovered I was pregnant, I knew you had to be told. I couldn't keep it a secret any longer. I'm sorry now I even waited that long. It made it harder for you to believe me.'

He sighed and squeezed her tight against him. '*I* made it hard to believe you. I didn't want to be close to anyone. But I couldn't stop wanting you. Not believing you became my way of pushing you away. If I couldn't trust you, I couldn't feel anything for you.

'But I was mad,' he said, cocking his ear to the wail of an approaching siren. 'Mad to think I could shut you out. It was only when I thought I'd lost you that I realised just how much you meant to me.'

She looked up at him, her expression hopeful. 'I do?'

He raised her in his lap and brushed his lips against hers. 'Oh, you do.' His lips moved over hers and he felt the tremor that passed through her and the depth it added to her kiss. 'Did I tell you lately,' he said, raising his lips just a fraction, 'that I love you?'

This time she pulled her mouth away completely, her tired eyes blinking, bright and beautiful. 'You've never told me that.'

'Then it's time I did. I love you, Philly. It took almost losing you to realise that, but I do. I love you and I'm proud, even honoured, that you are now part of my family and you will be part of my family for ever, if you still want me after all I've done to you.'

Her eyes shone up at him, her teeth gripping her bottom lip. Tears welled in her bright eyes, as if she was afraid to believe what he was saying.

'Oh, Damien,' she managed to say when the bubble of happiness had cleared from her throat enough to speak. 'I love you so much. I can't imagine being anywhere else. You saved my life.'

'Fair payback,' he said. 'You've given me back mine.'

She opened her mouth as if to argue the point and he shushed her with a finger to her lips as the sirens screamed closer.

'Don't argue with me; any minute now we're going to be surrounded by emergency services and I have much more important things right now to be doing with my time.' And she smiled under his finger, her eyes sparkling as he slanted his mouth over hers, his lips warm and gentle, his breath and his final words moving her soul.

'Much more important…'

EPILOGUE

WHAT a day! Damien turned off the highway, loosening his tie as the hot air blew through the open top. He could have kept on the roof and the air conditioner—the temperature sure warranted it—but now that he was out of the city he wanted to feel the air around him, he wanted to smell the scents of the baking, crisp countryside, he wanted to feel a part of it.

It was a great day—two o'clock in the afternoon and he'd decided that being home was more important than being in the office.

He'd been making a habit of that lately, Enid had been quick to point out. Not that she minded; she'd scolded him half-heartedly as she'd set about rejigging his timetable. He'd spent much of the last two years taking the time to feel things and the novelty was yet to wear off. He'd never have believed he could have found satisfaction in a life outside the office, but then it was only just over two years ago that he'd met Philly and she'd changed everything.

He looked at the clock on the dashboard as he pulled into the driveway. Great, it was still early enough to see little Anna before she went down for her afternoon nap.

He found the women sitting out on the veranda, shaded from the sun and where the breeze cooled naturally as it filtered through the hanging wisteria covering the pergola alongside. A small paddling pool sat between them, a dark-haired toddler sitting within an inflatable safety seat inside, splashing at the shallow water with obvious delight.

She squealed as soon as she saw him round the corner of the home, raising her chubby arms high and calling 'da-da, da-da' in her sweet baby voice. She bounced up and down in the seat, her toothy smile stretching wide across her chubby cheeks.

He swept her up, naked and wet, and she shrieked with delight as he blew raspberries over her skin.

'You're home early,' said Philly, laughing as he reached down to kiss her, the giggling infant still in his arms and replying with raspberries of her own.

'How could I stay away, knowing how much fun the three most important women in my life are having?'

He ruffled the curly black locks of his daughter's hair as she yawned widely, her eyelids suddenly droopy. 'Is it sleep time for you, little lady?'

'I'll take her,' said Daphne, looking slim but healthy in a cool sundress. 'I could do with an afternoon siesta myself.'

She wrapped the infant in a fluffy towel and let her kiss both her parents and wave goodbye wearily before she turned into the house. Damien watched her go before he pulled Philly to her feet and walked with her to the veranda railing.

'It's remarkable, the change in your mother. She could never have been strong enough to lift a child before.'

'I know,' said Philly. 'The doctors are amazed. I know she's far from being out of the woods, but they say it's because she's had a change of attitude; she's allowing the drugs to work.'

Something in her tone twigged in his mind. 'And what do you say?'

She turned from the view to face him. 'I say it's a miracle and that miracle has a lot to do with you and what you've done for my family.'

'You're my family now,' he said, gently lifting her chin. 'Always and for ever. And I thank the stars for the day you walked into my life. I love you, Philly.'

His lips brushed over hers even as she said the words, 'I love you, too.' She caught his intake of air before his kiss deepened, as if powered by the words she'd spoken. When at last he pulled his mouth away, he smiled and reached a hand down to the firm swell of her abdomen.

'And what of our other miracle? How does my son progress?'

She laughed. 'You're so sure he's a boy. Well, maybe you're right, the way this baby is kicking. I think he's practising for when he's the boss. He's going to be just like his dad.'

He wrapped his arms more tightly around her, pulling her close. 'I hope you're not mocking me,' he warned. 'To think I once thought of you as a shy little mouse. You know I'll make you pay for any insubordination.'

'And just what did you have in mind for my punishment?'

His eyes twinkled down at her, the love within them aflame with desire.

'Slow, delicious torture,' he said, tugging her towards the house, his lips curled into a wicked smile. 'I'll have you screaming for release.'

And he did.

FALLING FOR HER CONVENIENT HUSBAND

JESSICA STEELE

CHAPTER ONE

PHELIX had not wanted to come. Oh, she loved Switzerland, but her previous visits had always been in winter when the skiing was good.

Yet now it was September and, apart from the remains of winter's snow on some of the highest peaks, there was no snow. In fact the weather was sunny and beautiful. And here she was in Davos Platz, having arrived last night—and still feeling very annoyed because, in her view, there was no earthly reason for her to be there.

It was 'business' her father said. What business? She was a corporate lawyer working for Edward Bradbury Systems, her father's company. But she could not for the life of her see why any lawyer, corporate of otherwise, would need to attend a week-long scientific, electronic, electrical and mechanical engineering conference!

'I can't see why I have to go,' she had protested when her father had informed her of the arrangements he had made.

'Because I say so!' Edward Bradbury had replied harshly.

At one time she would have accepted that. Would have had to accept it, she knew. But not any longer. Not blindly, and certainly not without question. In the past she had been forced to accept every edict her control-freak father uttered. But not now. So, 'Why?' she challenged. It had taken a long while for her to get where she was, to get to be the person she now was. There was nothing left now of the weak and pathetic creature she had been eight years ago. 'If it's work related, I could understand a need. But for me to spend a week in Switzerland with a load of scientists who—'

'Networking!' Edward Bradbury chopped her off, but unbent sufficiently to explain that there had been whispers for some while that JEPC Holdings, one of the biggest names in the industry, were about to outsource a vast amount of their engineering. He had now, personally, along with the top brass from other competing companies, been invited to make the same Swiss trip next week, when the top men from JEPC would be flying in for a round of exploratory talks, give a general outline, and chat with the various highest of executives. 'It will mean millions to whichever company gets the contract,' he stated, money signs flashing in his eyes. Phelix still did not see, since as yet there was not a sign of any contract, why she had to go. 'I'm sending Ward and Watson with you. I want you all to keep an ear to the ground; listen for anything else going on that I need to know about.'

Duncan Ward and Christopher Watson were both scientists and wizards when it came to electronics. But Phelix doubted that there would be anything going on apart from a load of boring old speeches. It made her feel a little better, though, that the two scientists, both men she liked, would be there too.

'I've booked you into one of the very best hotels,' her father stated—as if that was an inducement!

'Duncan Ward and Chris Watson too?' she asked.

'Of course,' he replied stiffly. And that, as far as he was concerned, was that.

It was not that, as far as Phelix was concerned. The very next day she went to see Henry Scott, her friend and mentor, and who was also the company's most senior corporate lawyer. Henry was nearing sixty and, through their various conversations over the years, she had learned he had been a very good friend to her mother.

He must have been an excellent friend, Phelix had long since realised. Because it had been Henry that her mother had called on the night she had died. The night she had taken all the cruelty she could take from her domineering husband and had attempted to run away from him.

Phelix's thoughts drifted back to that dreadful time. Back to that awful night. It had been a foul night when, pausing only to make that phone call and to throw some clothes on, Felicity Bradbury had fled her home. When she pieced everything together afterwards, Phelix thought that her mother must have seen car headlights coming towards her in the storm thrashing about overhead, and had run out into the road in the blinding rain. It had not been Henry, and the car driver had stood no chance of not hitting her. Henry had been held up by a tree that had crashed over in the storm and which had blocked the road. By the time he had found another route and reached her home, he had been acquainted with the news he had arrived too late. The police had waved him on.

But while he had not been in time to help Felicity, he had made sure that her daughter would not ask for his help in vain.

It had been Henry who, almost eight years ago now, had aided Phelix when she had decided that she wanted a career of some sort. He had taken her seriously to suggest, 'Being a corporate lawyer is really not as dull as it may sound.'

'You think I could become a lawyer?' she'd asked, for one of the few times in her listless life feeling a surge of excitement at the thought.

'I know you could—if that is what you want. You're bright,

Phelix. It will mean a tremendous amount of hard work, but we'll get you there, if indeed law is what you fancy doing.'

And she had rather thought she did fancy a career in law. She had recently—no thanks to her father—had quite a lot to do with lawyers. She had found them upright and trustworthy which, having discovered the duplicity of her father's nature at first hand, was more than she could say for him.

He, needless to say, had not cared for the idea of her taking up legal training—most probably because it was not his idea. But by then she'd been on the way to receiving ten percent of the very substantial sum of money her grandfather—the same type of hard nut as her father—had left her.

'I said *no*!' Edward Bradbury Junior had declared vociferously. 'I forbid it!'

She had still been in awe of her father in those days. But, having only a short while ago been party to the biggest untruth of all time, she had again felt the stirrings of breaking free from the chains of his life-long dictatorship over her.

'Actually, Father, I'm eighteen now, and no longer require your permission,' she had dared.

He had taken a step nearer and, purple with rage, had looked as though he might strike her. And it had taken every scrap of her courage not to cower back from him, but to stand her ground.

'I'm not paying for your years of training!' he had spat at her, enraged.

'You don't need to," she had answered, still watching out for his clenching and unclenching fists at his side. 'I've been to see Grandfather Bradbury's solicitors. They tell me—'

'You've done *what*?'

He had heard, she was not going to repeat it. 'They were most surprised to learn that the letters they had sent me had gone astray.' Not half as surprised as she had been to hear the full contents of her grandfather's bequests to her—nor the conditions imposed. 'But what happened to my private and confidential mail is no longer important. I now know I have sufficient money to fund my own studies.'

Edward Bradbury had thrown her an evil look. She'd always been aware that he had no love or liking for her, and in the days when it had mattered to her she had wondered if it would have been different had she been the son he had so desperately wanted. But his love and liking had never been there, and had he ever loved her mother that love had died stone cold dead when she had failed to produce the male heir he'd so badly wanted.

'Would you like me to leave home?' Phelix had been brave enough to volunteer, more than hoping he would say yes.

She supposed she had known in advance that he would say no—she was the buffer between him and their housekeeper, Grace Roberts. In actual fact Phelix knew that Grace had only stayed on after her mother, the gentle Felicity, had been killed, for her sake. Edward Bradbury was under no illusion that if his daughter left then Grace, who was only a few years away from retirement anyway, would leave too. He enjoyed Grace's cooking, enjoyed the fact that his shirts were laundered exactly as he liked them, enjoyed that his home was run on oiled wheels—he had not the smallest interest in spending his time trying to find a new housekeeper who would only measure halfway up to Grace's standards.

'No, I wouldn't!' he had reported bluntly, and stormed out of the room.

Phelix came out of her reverie and supposed she ought to make tracks for the Kongresszentrum. But she had little enthusiasm for the day's events: a general introduction and getting to know some of the people. 'Networking' as her father called it.

She was more than a little off him at the moment. Had she not made that phone call to Henry from the airport before she had left yesterday she would probably not have known until today exactly why her father was so insistent that she attend.

'Do I really have to go, Henry?' she had asked the senior lawyer.

'Your father will play hell if you don't,' he'd answered gently. 'Though…' He'd paused.

'What?' Phelix had asked quickly, sensing something was coming that she might not be too happy about.

'Um—you're coming back a week tomorrow, right?'

'I'll come back as soon as I can. Though I suppose I'd better stick it out until then. My father and all the big chiefs will be there from a week Wednesday—thank goodness I don't have to be!'

'Er—not all the bigwigs are leaving it until next week,' Henry informed her kindly—and suddenly her heart lurched.

There was a roaring in her ears. No, she definitely wasn't going! Though, hold on a minute, her father would never send her on this mission if he thought for a single moment that *he* would be there.

'Who?' she asked faintly, wanting confirmation and urgently.

'Ross Dawson,' Henry supplied, and a whole welter of relief surged through her.

To be followed a few seconds later by a spurt of annoyance at yet another sign of her father's underhandedness. Ross Dawson was a few years older that her own twenty-six years. He was the son of the chairman of Dawson and Cross and, it had to be said, had a 'thing' for her despite Phelix telling him frequently and often that he was wasting his time.

'Do me a favour, Henry?'

'I've already done it.' He laughed, and she laughed too. All too plainly Henry Scott had known that she would check in with him before she left London.

'Where am I staying?' she asked, loving Henry that, without waiting to ask, he had transferred her hotel booking.

'A lovely hotel half a mile or so from the conference centre,' he replied. 'You'll be more than comfortable there.'

'You've cancelled my other reservation?'

'Everything's taken care of,' Henry assured her.

She rang off a few minutes later, knowing that her father would go up the wall if he ever found out. But she did not care. It went without saying that Ross Dawson would be staying at the hotel she had previously been booked into—her father would have got that piece of information to him somehow.

Deciding she had better be going, Phelix checked her appearance in the full length mirror. She'd had her usual early-morning swim, in the hotel's swimming pool this time, and was glowing with health. She stared at the elegant and sophisticated unsmiling woman who looked back at her, with black shiny hair that curved inwards just below her dainty chin. She used little make-up, and did not need to. She wore an immaculate trouser suit of a shade of green that brought out to perfection the green of her eyes.

Phelix gave a small nod of approval to the female she had become. There was nothing about her now—outwardly, at any rate—of the shy, long hair all over the place, gauche apology for a woman she had been eight years ago. And she was glad of it—it had been a hard road.

Having hired a car in Zurich and driven to Davos, she opted to walk to the conference centre, and left her hotel quietly seething that her father so wanted an 'in' with Dawson and Cross that he was fully prepared to make full use of Ross Dawson's interest in, not to say pursuit of her to that end. He was obviously hoping that by spending a week in close proximity of each other, with limited chance of her avoiding Ross, something might come of it!

She wouldn't put it past her father to even have telephoned in the first instance on some business pretext, and then casually let Ross, a director of Dawson and Cross, know that his daughter would be in Davos for a whole week.

She felt hurt as well as angry that her father, having sold her once, cared so little for her he was fully prepared to do it again. Over her dead body!

But, thanks to Henry having got wind of what was going on, he had been able to forewarn her, and at least do a little something to limit the time she had to spend with Ross. Not that she didn't like Ross. She did. She just had an extreme aversion to being manipulated. And, in the light of past events, who could blame her?

She knew that her father had been having a liaison with his PA, Anna Fry, for years. She wished he would concentrate his attentions more on Anna, and leave his daughter out of his scheming.

As Phelix neared the Kongresszentrum she saw other smartly dressed representatives making their way towards the entrance. She would be glad to see Chris and Duncan, she realised, and hoped nobody else would wonder, as she had before Henry had tipped her off, what possible reason she could have for being there. At least she had been spared the surprise of seeing Ross Dawson unexpectedly.

She made her way inside the building, hoping there were no other unexpected surprises waiting for her on this trip.

'Where did you get to?' She turned to find that Duncan Ward and Chris Watson had spotted her coming in and had come over to her. 'We looked high and low for you last night. Reception said you hadn't checked in.'

It was gratifying to know that they had been concerned about her. 'I should have let you know,' she apologised. 'I'm sorry. I thought I'd prefer a hotel a bit further away.'

'As in I might have to put up with you two talking shop during the day, but I want some rest from it in the evenings?' Chris grinned.

'Not at all.' She laughed, and did not have a chance to say anything else because someone was calling her name.

'Phelix!' She looked over to where Ross Dawson was making his way over to her. 'Phelix Bradbury!' he exclaimed as he reached her.

'Hello, Ross,' she replied, and was about to make some comment with regard to his act of being surprised to see her there when, even as Ross kissed her on both cheeks, she caught a glimpse of a tall, dark-haired man standing with a blonde woman and another man. But it was the dark-haired man that held Phelix riveted. She felt a deafening silent thunder in her ears, but even as she tried to deny that *he* was here after all, it took everything she had to keep her expression composed. She glanced casually away, but not before she noticed that he had been looking at nowhere but her!

Her insides were all of a jangle. She had not seen him in eight years, and only twice before then, but she would know him anywhere! She had been just eighteen then, he twenty-eight. That would make him thirty-six now.

Phelix began to get herself more of one piece when she realised that, thankfully, he could not possibly have recognised her. She was nothing remotely like the awkward and, in her view, late-developing teenager she had been then. But that was it—she was out of here!

But, having grown a veneer of sophistication, even if her insides were now feeling like just so much jelly, Phelix knew she could not just simply cut and run. But she wasn't staying, that was for sure! As soon as she possibly could, she would tell either Chris or Duncan that she had forgotten something, had a headache, a migraine, athlete's foot—she didn't care what—and was going back to her hotel. From there she would make arrangements to fly back to England.

Hoping against hope that he was a figment of her imagination, she found she was irresistibly drawn to glance over to him again. It *was* him! He was tall, but even so would have stood out from the crowd of people milling around.

She slid her glance from him to the other man standing with him, and on to the close to six feet tall glamorous blonde woman. His girlfriend? Certainly not his wife.

Oh, heavens, he was looking her way again. Phelix flicked her glance from him. She was not unused to men giving her a second look, so knew his second glance was no more than passing interest. But, apart from his female companion, herself and several other women, the conference seemed to be a predominantly male affair.

She tried to tune in to what Ross and the other two were babbling on about, but when she felt as much as surreptitiously glimpsed the man leaving his companions, so her wits seemed to desert her.

But—oh, help—he seemed to be making his way in her direction! Dying a thousand deaths, Phelix prayed that he was making his way elsewhere, or that if he was perhaps coming over to say hello to Ross, that Ross would not think he had to introduce them; the name Phelix was a dead give-away.

He halted as he reached them and her mouth dried and her heart raced like a wild thing. 'Ross,' she heard him greet Ross Dawson, and saw him nod to Duncan and Chris. And then he turned his cool grey eyes on her. How she remained outwardly calm as, for the longest second of her life, he studied her, she never knew. And then casually, every bit as if he had seen her every day of his life for the past eight years, 'How are you, Phelix?' he asked.

Her throat was so dry she didn't think she would be able

to utter a word. But the poise she had learned since she had last seen him stood her in good stead. 'Fine, Nathan,' she murmured. 'You?'

'You know each other?' Ross asked.

'From way back,' Nathan Mallory drawled, his eyes still on her. She guessed he couldn't believe the evidence of his vision; the change in her from the frightened timid mouse she had been eight years previously to the cool, collected and polished woman who stood before him now.

'You're here for the conference?' she enquired, and could have bitten out her tongue for having asked so obvious a question.

'One of our speakers had to drop out. As I intended coming this way, I thought I might as well come early and fill in for him.'

She smiled, nodded—she knew darn well his name had not been down on the programme as one of the speakers. She, knowing he was likely to be in Davos next week with the other heads of businesses, had scrutinised the list of speakers very thoroughly before at last bowing to her father's insistence that she come this week as part of the Edward Bradbury Systems entourage.

'If you'll excuse me,' she managed, striving with all she had to hold down the dreadful feelings of anxiety that were trying to get a hold—she hadn't felt like this in years! 'I think I have to register in.'

Somehow or other she was able to make her legs take her in the direction she wanted them to go. And later, having had no intention of still being there but somehow having been swept along, she was in a seat, listening without taking in a word of what the introductory speaker was droning on about.

She had by then started to recover from seeing Nathan Mallory again after all those years. As well as being tall with dark hair, Nathan was handsome—quite devastatingly so. A man who could have any woman he chose. But Nathan Mallory—she drew a shaky breath—was *her* husband! She, for all she went by the name Phelix Bradbury, was in actual fact Mrs Nathan Mallory. Phelix Mallory. Oh, my word!

As she twisted her wedding ring on her finger—the marriage band he had put there—her thoughts flew back to more than eight years ago. She ceased to hear the speaker's voice and was back in the cold, cheerless home she shared with her father in Berkshire. She was no longer in the conference hall, but was in her father's study, back before she had met Nathan.

Her grandfather, cold and forbidding Edward Bradbury Senior, had died shortly after her mother. Phelix had missed her warm and loving mother so much, and later realised that, perhaps needing warmth and comfort at that time, she had been ready to imagine herself in love when Lee Thompson, their gardener's son, home on vacation from university.

It seemed as though she had always known Lee. She had always been shy with people, but he'd seemed to understand that as their romance blossomed.

Though he'd left it to her to seek her father out in his study and tell him that she and Lee were going to marry.

'*Marry!*' her father had roared, utterly astounded.

'We love each other,' she had explained.

'You might love him—we'll see how much he thinks of you!' Edward Bradbury had retorted dismissively. And that had been the end of the conversation—and the end of her romance.

She had seen neither Lee nor his father again. When Lee had not phoned as he had said he would she had telephoned him, and had learned that his father had been dismissed from his job and that Lee had been bribed—for that was what it amounted to—to sever all contact with her.

She had been too shocked to fully take in what Lee was

saying. 'What do you mean—my father will pay off all your student loans?' she had protested.

'Look, Phelix, I'm in hock up to my ears. I was mad to think we could marry and make a go of it. We'd be broke for years! You're not working and—'

'I'll get a job,' she'd said eagerly.

'What could you do? You're trained for nothing. Any money you'd be able to bring in would be nothing at all like as much as we'd need to keep us afloat.'

That was when a pride she hadn't known she had started to bite, and she had taken a deep breath. 'So, for money you'd forget all our plans, all we ever said? All—'

'I have no choice. I'm sorry. I shouldn't be talking to you now. I'm risking the bonus your old man promised me if I—'

'Goodbye, Lee,' she had cut in, and had put down the phone.

After that she hadn't cared very much what happened. But a few days later she had been able to accept that, her pride feeling more bruised than her heart, that she had been more fond of Lee than in love with him. And that in fact what lay at the base of her wanting to marry him was more an urgent desire for change of some sort. More a need for some kind of escape from this—nothingness. For the chance to leave home, the chance to get away from her intimidating father.

And, since it was for sure Lee had not been in love with her either, she'd realised that any marriage they'd made would probably not have lasted. Not that she had seen her father's actions as doing her a favour. She had not. She'd still wanted to get away. But she supposed then that she must have been living in some kind of rose-tinted never-land, because when she'd got down to thinking about leaving and striking out on her own, she had known that she just could not afford to leave. She could not afford to live in even the cheapest hostel. And as Lee had more or less stated—who would employ her?

Another week went by, but just when she had started to feel even more depressed, her father summoned her to his study. 'Take a seat,' he invited, his tone a shade warmer than she was used to. Obediently, she obliged. 'I've just been advised of the contents of your grandfather's will,' he went on.

'Oh, yes,' she murmured politely, wondering why he was bothering to tell her. Grandfather Bradbury had been as miserly as his son, so probably had a lot to leave—but not to her. In any event, she was sure that anything he left was bound to have some ghastly condition attached to it.

'Your grandfather has been very generous to you,' her father went on.

'Really?' she exclaimed, surprised, Grandfather Bradbury had never shown any sign that he knew she existed when he had been alive.

'But I'm afraid you are unable to claim your quite considerable inheritance until you are twenty-five,' he enlightened her. The hope that had suddenly sprung up in her, died an instant death. Bang went her sudden joy at the thought that she could leave home and perhaps buy a place of her own. 'That is, unless…' her father murmured thoughtfully.

'Unless?' she took up eagerly.

'Well, you know he had a thing about the sanctity of marriage?'

To her mind he'd had more of a thing about the iniquities of divorce. He'd had a fixation about it ever since his own wife had walked out on him and, despite all his best efforts, had ultimately divorced him. He had passed his loathing of women breaking their wedding vows down to his son. Phelix's mother had confided in her one time when Edward Bradbury had been particularly foul to her how she had wanted to divorce him years ago. He had gone apoplectic when she'd had the nerve to tell him—delighting in telling her that if she left him she could not take their daughter with her. 'When you're eighteen,' she had promised, 'we'll both go.' And, until that last desperate bid when Phelix had been seventeen, she had stayed.

'Er—yes.' Phelix came out of her reverie to see her father drumming his fingers on his desk as he waited for her to agree that his father *had* had a thing about the sanctity of marriage.

'So—he obviously wanted you to be happy.' Her father almost smiled.

'Ye-es,' she agreed, knowing no such thing.

'Which is why a clause was inserted in his will…' Naturally there was a clause—possibly some snag to prevent her claiming her inheritance even when she was twenty-five, '…to the effect that if you marry before you are twenty-five you will be eligible to receive ten percent of the considerable sum he has left you.'

'Honestly?' she gasped, her spirits going from low to high, then back down to positive zero. Oh, if only this had happened a couple of weeks ago. She could have married Lee and claimed that ten percent and have been free! Well, not entirely free. Only now did she fully accept that she was glad her romance with Lee had gone no further. Marriage to him would have been a big mistake.

'Your grandfather plainly did not want you to suffer financial hardship in any early marriage you made.'

'I—see,' she answered quietly.

'And how do you feel about that?'

Her father was actually inviting her opinion about something? That was a first. 'Well, I wouldn't have minded having a little money of my own,' she dared. With her father forbidding her to take any lowly job which would shame him, he made her a tiny allowance that, at best, was parsimonious.

'We'll have to see if we can't find you a suitable husband,' he, having paid off her one chance of marriage, had the nerve to state.

It was the end of that particular discussion, but less than forty-eight hours later he had again called her into his study and invited her to take a seat.

'That little problem,' he began.

'Problem?'

He gave her an impatient look that she hadn't caught on to what he was talking about. 'The husband I said I'd find for you.'

'I don't want a husband!' she'd exclaimed, appalled.

'Of course you do.' He overrode her initial protest. 'You want your inheritance, don't you?' he demanded. 'Ten percent of it represents a considerable amount of money.'

'Yes, but—'

'It goes without saying that the marriage will be annulled before the ink is dry on your marriage certificate,' he had bulldozed on. 'But that certificate is all I need to take to your grandfather's solicitors and—'

'Just a minute,' she dared to cut in, 'are you saying that you've found a man for me to marry so that I can claim that ten percent?'

'That's exactly what I'm saying.'

She couldn't believe it and stared at him dumbfounded. 'Is it Lee?' she asked out of her confused thoughts.

'Of course it isn't him!' Edward Bradbury snapped.

'But—but you have found someone…'

'God Almighty!' her father cut in, exasperated. But then, obviously counting to ten, 'Yes, that's what I've just said.'

Her tutors had said she had a quick brain—Phelix wondered where it was when she needed it. 'You're saying that as soon as I've got that—um—marriage certificate that the solicitors want to see, I can divorce—er—this man?' She wasn't going to marry anybody! Besides, her father hated divorce—there was something fishy going on here.

'You won't need to divorce him. Since you'll never live with him, an annulment will suffice.'

In spite of herself, with freedom beckoning, Phelix had to own to feeling a spark of interest. Even perhaps the small stirrings of a little excitement.

'How old is he?' she asked, telling herself she was not truly interested, but not relishing the idea of marrying one of her father's Methuselah-like cronies.

'I've checked him out. He's twenty-eight.'

That spark of interest became a flicker of flame. Twenty-eight? That was all right. She could marry and claim that ten percent, and… 'And he, this man, he's willing to go through a form of marriage with me so that I can claim some of my inheritance?' she questioned. Even while wanting to get away from the environment she lived in, she discovered that she did not trust her father enough to go into this blindly.

'That's what I've just said,' he replied tetchily.

At that stage Phelix had not known just how diabolical and underhand her father could be if the occasion demanded it. But, even so, something just didn't seem to her to tie up.

She started to use what her teachers had said was her good brain. 'What is in it for him?'

'What do you mean, what's in it for him?'

Phelix had no idea of her potential. All she saw was that she was a dowdy, unemployable newly eighteen-year-old, with little to recommend her. And while it was true that by the sound of it her marriage would be annulled as quickly as made, she could not see any man willingly marrying her just because her father asked him to.

'Does he work for you?' she asked, suspecting that some poor man was being pressured in some way to do the deed.

Edward Bradbury's thin mouth tightened at having his slip

of a daughter daring to question him. 'He and his father have their own scientific electronics company,' he answered shortly.

She knew she was making her father angry. Indeed knew she should be jumping at this chance to have her own money. But, 'I don't get it,' she persisted.

'For heaven's sake!' her father erupted on a burst of fury. But he managed to control himself to state more calmly, 'If you *must* know, I heard a whisper that Nathan Mallory and his father are in a hole, financially. I approached the son and said I'll bail him out if in return he'll do this small thing for me.'

Her father was helping out a competitor? She found that hard to believe. On the other hand, as her need for freedom gave her a nudge and then a positive push, what did she know about what went on in big business?

'You've said you'll give him some money if—'

'Not *give*!' That sounded more like her father. 'I've said that in return for him marrying you—a marriage he will not be stuck with—' thank you very much '—I will that day hand over a substantial cheque, a loan repayable two years hence. Now, anything else you need to know before…?'

By the sound of it she would be doing this Nathan Mallory as much of a favour as he would be doing her. That made her feel a little better. 'He—er—knows it isn't permanent?' She found she needed to qualify. 'The marriage, I mean. You're sure he knows…'

Her father did not attempt to spare her feelings but, as harsh as he more normally was, told her forthrightly, 'I've seen a sample of the fashionable beauties he favours—take my word for it, he'll be at his lawyers annulling your marriage before the first piece of confetti has blown away.'

It had not turned out quite like that. Nor had there been any confetti. In fact it had turned out vastly different from the way

Edward Bradbury had had in mind. He had thought they could
be married by special licence and it would all be over and done
with within a week. But in actual fact they'd had to appear at
the register office in person, and give fifteen clear days' notice
of their intent to marry.

So it was that, three weeks before the proposed marriage
date, Phelix had presented herself at the register office and met
for the first time the man she was to marry. Had she been
hoping that her father would be there to ease any awkward-
ness, then she would have been disappointed. He had an 'important business meeting.' Why would he need to be there, for
goodness sake!

'How will I know him?' she'd asked anxiously.

'He'll know you.'

From that she'd gathered that her father had given him a
description of her. As it appeared he had, for a tall dark-haired
man had been there a minute after her and had come straight
over to her. 'Hello, Phelix,' he'd said, and she had almost died
on the spot. Already, aged twenty-eight, there had been an air
of sophistication about him. Oh, my heavens—and she was
going to marry him!

'Hello,' she'd answered shyly, knowing she was blushing,
but calming herself by remembering that this was not going
to be a marriage, just a ceremony.

'We seem to have a minute or two to wait. Shall we sit over
here?' he'd suggested, his tone cultured, well modulated.

Lightly he touched a hand to her elbow and directed her to
a corner of the room which for the moment they had to themselves. She wanted to say something, anything, but even if she
could have thought of anything remotely clever to say she felt
too much in awe to say a word.

But not so him, and it appeared, while being perfectly civil
and polite, he wanted there to be no misunderstanding of the

reasons why they were both doing what they proposed to do. Because without further delay, he asked, 'You're quite happy to go through with this, Phelix?'

Shyly she nodded. 'Yes,' she answered, her voice barely above a whisper.

'And your reasons are as your father stated?' he pressed, clearly wanting everything cut and dried before he committed himself further.

'My gr-grandfather… Um, I can't claim my inheritance from my grandfather until I'm twenty-five. But if I marry I can have ten percent of it,' she began, her voice growing stronger. 'And—er—the thing is, I'd quite like to have some money of my own.'

'You're thinking of going to university?' Nathan enquired.

'No,' she replied, feeling it would be disloyal to reveal that her father had vehemently vetoed that suggestion long since.

'You don't work?'

She blushed again. How could she tell someone who must obviously respect her father that her father was so controlling that anything she suggested, or her mother when she had been alive, had always been very firmly trodden on by Edward Bradbury?

'No,' she repeated. And, fed up with herself that she seemed to be totally spiritless, 'I believe you have financial considerations too, for going through with this?' she said.

Nathan Mallory looked at her then, taking in her long pulled-back hair that revealed her dainty features, observing her splendid complexion, seeming to drink in her face with his steady grey eyes on her wide green ones. 'It will be years before I'm financially in a position to marry for real,' he stated. He was serious still as he dotted the last i and crossed the last t. 'You understand, Phelix, that our marriage ends at the register office door?'

'That will suit me perfectly,' she responded primly. And suddenly he had smiled—and she had fallen a little in love with him.

CHAPTER TWO

A BURST of applause brought Phelix back to the present. 'That
was pretty good, don't you think?' Duncan Ward, seated next
to her, brought her the rest of the way back to the world of
commerce.

'I'll say,' she responded, having not taken in a word.

'Coming for coffee?' called a voice from the aisle. It was Ross
Dawson who had detached himself from the group he was with.

Phelix turned to her two colleagues. 'Shall we?' she asked.
Chris Watson adopted a bland expression, knowing full well
he had not been included in Ross Dawson's invitation.

'I'm so dry I couldn't lick a stamp,' he accepted.

A few minutes later Phelix was waiting with Duncan while
Chris and Ross went to get them coffee.

'Are you staying the full week?' Duncan asked. He and
Chris had flown out on an earlier flight, and this was their first
chance to catch up.

'My father thinks it will benefit the company if I stay for
the end of speeches get-together on Monday evening.' She still
couldn't see how. Though her urgent need to bolt of a couple
of hours ago did not now seem as urgent as it had. Plainly
Nathan, after coming over and asking 'How are you?' while
being perfectly happy to acknowledge that he knew her, had

no intention of telling anybody that he was her husband any more than she had.

She glanced to her left as Ross and Chris joined them—her eyes seemed somehow to be drawn in that direction. Nathan was there in her line of vision, talking to the tall blonde.

With her insides churning, Phelix flicked her glance from him. It seemed to her then that Nathan Mallory had always had some kind of effect on her. Right at this moment she again felt like taking off. But, having discovered over the last eight years that she had far more backbone than she had up to then always supposed, she made herself stay put and smiled, laughed when amused, and generally chatted with her three male companions.

'Have lunch with me?' Ross asked as they made their way back to their seats.

'Sorry. I've some work I want to look through.'

'You can't work all the time!' he protested.

Sitting listening to speeches, even if she didn't take in a word, hardly seemed like work to her. 'There's no answer to that,' she replied, smiling gently at him. It wasn't his fault that on the man-woman front he did nothing for her.

'Dinner, then?' he persisted.

She almost said yes if it included Chris and Duncan. But from their point of view they probably wanted to let their hair down away from the boss's daughter.

So she smiled. Ross was harmless enough. 'Provided you don't ask me to marry you again, I'd love to,' she agreed.

'You're hard-hearted, Phelix. If ever I catch up with that mythical husband of yours, I shall tell him so.'

'Seven o'clock at your hotel.' She laughed, and glanced from him straight into the eyes of Nathan Mallory. He was no myth.

She smiled, acknowledging him. For a split second he stared at her solemnly. And then he smiled in return—and her heart went thump!

* * *

Phelix was in her seat, determined not to let her mind stray again. The current speaker was a bit dry, but she concentrated on key words—'state of the market' and 'systems and acquisitions'—and still couldn't see what she was doing there—apart from Ross Dawson, of course, and the idiotic pipedream her father seemed to have that if she and Ross Dawson became one, Edward Bradbury might one day rule a Bradbury, Dawson and Cross empire.

No chance. Ross had spoken of her 'mythical husband.' Quite when she had let it generally be known that she was married she wasn't sure.

Probably around the same time as she had discovered the extent of her father's unscrupulous behaviour.

Probably around the same time her backbone had started to stiffen. Prior to that, having learned a passive 'anything for a quiet life' manner from her mother, she would never have dreamed of going against her father's wishes. Though, on thinking about it, perhaps Nathan standing up to him had been the wake-up call she had needed.

Realising she was in danger of drifting off again, Phelix renewed her concentration on what the speaker was saying. 'Face-to-face meetings are better than a video link,' he was opining. What that had to do with their businesses she hadn't a clue, and knew she was going to have to pay closer attention. Though in her view it was still farcical that she was there at all.

With quite a long break for lunch, Phelix took herself off back to her hotel. Her father had wanted her to 'network' so he said. Tough! That was a lie, anyway.

Up in her room, she went to open her laptop. But, feeling mutinous all of a sudden, she ignored it. She didn't feel like working. She took some fruit and the cellophane wrapped slice of cake from the platter residing on a low table, added the chocolate that had been placed on her pillow when her bed had been turned down last night, went out to the balcony and stretched out on the sun-lounger.

The scenery was utterly fantastic. In the foreground a church—complete with clockface to remind her that she had to attend the conference centre that afternoon—and behind, towering, majestic mountains. Forests of pine trees right and left. Tall… Somehow she found she was thinking of tall, towering Nathan Mallory—and this time she let her thoughts go where they would.

They had married, she and Nathan, on a warm, humid day. She had worn what she had thought then, but blushed about now, to be a smart blue two piece. She supposed she must have worried a bit, after she had bought it because it had fitted her then. But on her wedding day, it had literally hung on her. Nathan—a stern-faced Nathan—had worn a smart suit for the occasion.

Because he'd been waiting for an extremely important business telephone call her father had been unable to attend, but had said he would be home when they got there. And that had annoyed Nathan because it had meant he would have to go back with her to her home to exchange their marriage certificate for the cheque that would save Mallory and Mallory from losing everything.

'I'm s-sorry,' she'd stammered, half believing from Nathan's tough look that he would change his mind about going through with it.

But apart from muttering, 'What sort of a father is he?' Nathan had kept to his part of the bargain—even to the extent of holding her hand as they came away from the register office.

'Is that it?' she'd asked nervously.

'That's it,' he had confirmed. 'I expect there'll be a few more formalities to deal with to undo the knot…'

But the knot had never been undone. It should have been.

They had originally planned it should be so. But, as matters had turned out, their marriage had never been annulled.

'Where did you leave your car?' Nathan had asked.

'I—um—don't drive,' she'd answered, newly married and starting to dislike the wimp of a creature she, through force of circumstance, had become. As soon as she had that ten percent she was going to have driving lessons, despite what her father said. She would buy a car...

'We'll go in mine,' Nathan had clipped, and had escorted her to the car park.

Her home was large, imposing and, despite Grace Roberts' attempts to brighten it up with a few flowers, cheerless. Grace had had no idea that the daughter of the house had that day married the handsome man by her side, and had been her usual pleasant self to Phelix.

'Your father had to go out urgently,' she said. 'But he left a message for you to leave the document in his study and said he'll attend to it.'

Hot, embarrassed colour flared to Phelix's face, a horrible dread starting to take her that her father might be intending to renege on the part of the deal he had made with Nathan Mallory. That Nathan, his competitor, having kept his part of the bargain, had been hung out to dry!

'Thank you, Grace,' she managed. 'Er—this is Mr Mallory...er...'

'Shall I get you some tea?' Grace asked, seeming to realise she was struggling.

'That would be nice,' Phelix answered and, as Grace went kitchenwards, 'My father must have left an envelope for you in his study,' Phelix suggested. Hoping against hope that her fears were groundless, and that there would be an envelope on the desk with Nathan's name on it, she led the way to the study.

But there was no envelope. Scarlet colour scorched her

cheeks again, and she felt she would die of the humiliation of it. 'I'm s-sorry,' she whispered to the suddenly cold-eyed man by her side. 'I'm sure my father will be home soon,' she went on, more in hope than belief. 'Shall we have tea while we wait?'

Apart from Henry Scott, who had occasionally in the past called at the house with important papers for her father to sign, Phelix was unused to entertaining anyone. If her father had been delayed, her mother had always offered Henry refreshment of some kind.

So copying her mother's graceful ways, even if she was feeling awkward, Phelix gave her new and promised to be temporary husband tea.

It was Grace Roberts' evening off—she was going to the theatre and would be staying with a friend overnight. 'You've everything you need?' she enquired, with a professional look around.

'Everything's fine, thank you, Grace. Enjoy the theatre,' Phelix bade her.

'Grace has been with you for some while?' Nathan, with better manners than her father, stayed civilly polite to ask a question he could have no particular interest in knowing the answer to.

'About six years—she adored my mother.'

'Your mother died recently in a road accident, I believe?'

Phelix did not want to talk about it. Never would she forget the horror of that night. The day had been a day similar to today. Warm, sticky, and with thunder in the air.

'I'm truly very sorry,' she said abruptly. 'I can't think what's keeping my father.' And, feeling sure that Nathan did not want to spend a minute longer with her than he had to, 'Look, if you've somewhere you've got to be, I can give you a ring the moment my father comes in.'

Nathan Mallory stared at her long and hard then, and she

could not help but wonder if he suspected she was giving him the same run-around that her father seemed to be giving him.

But, deciding to give her the benefit of the doubt, 'I'll wait,' he clipped. 'That cheque is my last remaining option.'

And Phelix knew then from the set of this man's jaw that, in order to save his firm for him and his father, Nathan Mallory was having to bite on a very unpleasant bullet. Having completed his side of the bargain, he now had to wait for the man who had offered him the deal to complete his part. Yet Phelix just knew, as she looked numbly into Nathan Mallory's stern grey eyes, that everything in him was urging him to leave. That if there was any other way he would have taken it. *She* felt humiliated, but that must be nothing to what this proud man must be feeling. And yet for his business, for his father, it was, as he said, his last remaining option.

'D-does your father know about today?' she asked tentatively.

'I thought I'd prefer to have that cheque in my hand before I told him.'

That made her feel worse. 'I'm sorry,' she said quietly. 'I truly am.'

He looked at her again, and his expression softened slightly. 'I know,' he replied.

And the next two hours had ticked by with still no sign of her father.

'Will you excuse me?' she said at one point, and went to her father's study to make a call to her father's PA. But Anna Fry said she had no idea where he was. 'Is Mr Scott free?' Phelix asked. And, when she was put through, 'Henry? Phelix. Do you know where my father is? I need to contact him rather urgently.'

Henry did not know where he was either. But, alarmed at her anxious tone, he was ready to come over at once to help with her problem, whatever it was. Phelix thanked him, but said it was nothing that important.

So she went back to Nathan, gave him the evening paper to read—and started to grow anxious on another front. The sky had darkened to almost black when she heard the first rumble of thunder. Thunderstorms and their violence terrified her.

She tried to think of something else, but at the first fork of lightning she was again reliving that night—the night her mother had died. There had been one horrendous storm that night. She had been in bed asleep when the first crack of thunder had awakened her. She had sat up in bed, half expecting that her mother would come and keep her company—her mother did not like storms either.

It was with that in mind that as the storm had become more fearsome, Phelix had shot along to her mother's room to check that she was all right. Only as she had quickly opened the door a fork of lightning, swiftly followed by another, had lit up her mother's room—and the scene that had met her eyes had sent her reeling. Phelix had plainly seen that her mother was not alone in her bed. Edward Bradbury was there too.

'What are you doing?' Phelix had screamed—he was *assaulting* her mother!

Her father had bellowed at her to leave in very explicit, crude language. But at least her interruption had had the effect of taking his attention briefly away from her mother, and her mother had been able to dive from the bed and pull a robe around her shoulders.

'Go back to bed, darling,' she'd urged.

Phelix had not known then which terrified her the more: the violent storm or the dreadful scene she had happened across which was now indelibly imprinted on her mind for evermore.

But there was no way she was going to leave. 'No, I'll—' But she had been urged from the room.

'We'll talk about it in the morning,' her mother had promised, and pushed her to the other side of the door. They had been the last words she had ever said to her. By morning she'd been dead.

A fork of lightning jerked her to awareness that she was in her father's drawing room with the man she had that day married. It looked as if it was going to be another of those horrendous storms. Rain was furiously lashing at the windows, and as another fork of lightning speared the room Phelix only just managed to hold back from crying out.

'W-would you mind very much if I left you to wait by yourself?' she asked, feeling that at any moment now she would disgrace herself by either shouting out in panic or bolting from him.

'Not at all,' Nathan replied and, realising he would probably quite welcome his own company, she fled.

Hoping she could get into bed, hide her head under the bedclothes and wait for morning, when her father would have paid Nathan the money he'd promised, Phelix quickly undressed. No way, with that storm raging, was she going to take her usual shower.

She got into bed, but left her bedside lamp on. She did not want to lie in the dark, when she would again see that ugly scene in her mother's bedroom that night. Phelix closed her eyes and tried to get some rest. It was impossible.

She had no idea what time it was when, wide awake, she heard the storm which she had hoped had begun to fade return with even greater ferocity. It seemed to be directly overheard when there was a violent crack of thunder like no other—and then the lights went out.

Only vicious forks of lightning, in which she again saw her father's evil face, her mother's pleading, illuminated her bedroom. Striving desperately to banish the images tormenting her mind, Phelix made herself remember that she might still have a guest—a husband she had abandoned to his own devices.

Pinning her thoughts on Nathan, who had already been dealt a raw deal by her father and who might now be sitting in the drawing room in the dark, Phelix left her room and raced down the stairs. 'Nathan!' she called, her voice somewhere between a cry and a scream as thunder again cracked viciously directly overhead.

In the light of another fork of lightning she saw he was still there, had heard her, had come from the drawing room and had seen her.

'You all right?' he asked gruffly.

Words failed her. The fact that he was still there showed how very badly he needed that money. 'Oh, Nathan,' she whispered miserably, and in a couple of strides he was over to her, his hands on her arms.

'Scared?' he asked gently.

'T-terrified.' She was too upset to dissemble.

Nathan placed a soothing arm about her shoulders. 'You're shaking,' he murmured.

'It was a night like this when my mother was killed,' she replied witlessly.

'Poor love,' he murmured, and she had never known that a man could be so kind, so gentle. 'Come on, let's get you back to bed,' he said.

And, when she was too frozen by the empathy of the moment to be able to move, he did no more than pick her nightdress-clad body up in his arms and carry her up the winding staircase, his way lit by fork after fork of blinding lightning.

Phelix had left her bedroom door open in her rush, and Nathan carried her in and placed her gently under the covers of her bed.

'Don't leave me!' she pleaded urgently as another cannon-shot of thunder rent the air.

She was immediately ashamed, but not sufficiently so to be able to tell him she would be all right alone, and, after a moment of hesitation, Nathan did away with his shoes, shrugged out of his suit jacket and came to lie on top of her bed beside her. It was a three quarter size bed, but for all she was five feet nine tall there was not much of her.

'Nothing can harm you,' he told her quietly, and in the darkness reached for her hand.

She had gone down the stairs with some vague notion that he would feel uncomfortable sitting alone in a strange house in the dark. But here he was comforting her!

Again she felt ashamed. Then lightning lit the room, and she was again in that nightmare of unwanted visions of that night in her mother's bedroom not so long ago. She clutched on to Nathan's hand.

'Shh, you're all right,' he soothed. 'It will be over soon.' And, maybe because her grip was threatening to break his fingers, he let go her hand and to her further comfort placed an arm around her thin shoulders. Instinctively she turned into him, burying her face in his chest.

Quite when, or how, she managed to drop off to sleep, she had no notion. But she was jerked awake when her bedside lamp suddenly came on—power restored.

'Oh!' she exclaimed, sitting up. 'Oh!' she exclaimed again. Nathan was still on the bed with her. He got to his feet and stood, unspeaking, looking at her. 'Oh, Nathan, I'm so sorry,' she apologised. The storm was over; normality was back.

He surveyed her troubled eyes, her blushing complexion—and more shame hit her. This man had married her—for nothing. He had trusted her father's word—for nothing. She wanted to cry, but managed to hold back her tears. This man, her husband, had suffered enough without him having to put up with her tears too.

'You didn't have dinner!' she gasped, suddenly appalled, although she could not have eaten a thing herself. But just then the headlights of a car coming up the drive flashed across the window. 'My father's home,' she offered jerkily, though was not taken aback when Nathan declined to rush out to meet him.

'I'm surprised he bothered,' he answered, bending to put on his shoes. But Phelix did not miss the hard note that had come to his voice.

'What will you do?' she asked, feeling crushed, sorrowfully knowing for certain now that her father did not intend to honour the deal he had made.

'Frankly, I honestly don't know,' Nathan answered tautly, and suddenly Phelix could not bear it.

'You can have my money,' she offered. 'I don't know yet how much it will be, but you can have it all. I'll—'

Nathan smiled then, a grim kind of a smile. 'Enough is enough,' he said.

'You—don't want it?'

Nathan shook his head. 'Not to put too fine a point on it, little one, I'd cut my throat before I'd touch a penny of Bradbury money,' he replied bluntly.

That 'little one' saved his remark from being as wounding as it would otherwise have been—and then they both heard the sound that told them that her father was coming up the stairs.

With the light of battle in his eyes, Nathan grabbed up his jacket and went out to confront him. Phelix hated rows, confrontation, but it started the moment her father saw Nathan coming from her bedroom.

'What the hell game do you think you're playing?' Edward Bradbury roared.

'I might well ask you the same question!'

'I checked—you married her.' There was a satisfied note in her father's voice.

'I kept my side of the bargain,' Nathan agreed coldly.

'Hard luck!'

'You're saying that you never had any intention of handing over that cheque?'

'I thought you'd have twigged before now,' her father gloated—and that was when Phelix discovered she had more backbone than she had thought. Which made it impossible for her to sit there and listen to the way her father, so careless of her, was so blatantly pleased with himself. 'You can forget all about getting a cheque from me,' he crowed.

'Father!' Phelix rushed from her room and out to the landing, ashamed, disgusted, and never more embarrassed to have such a parent. 'You can't possibly—'

'Don't you *dare* tell me what I can and cannot do!' her father bellowed.

'But you owe—'

'I owe him nothing! He can forget about the money, and—'

'And you, sir,' Nathan cut across—furiously, 'can shove your money!' And somehow or other—perhaps in the thinking time during the long hours of his wait, perhaps with Phelix offering him the money she was due—Nathan seemed to sense now, when he hadn't seen it before, that there was more in this for Edward Bradbury than allowing his daughter to have her own money. 'And while you're about it,' he went on, his eyes glinting fury, 'you can forget about the annulment too!'

That stopped Edward Bradbury dead in his tracks. 'What are you saying?' he demanded, looking more shaken than at any time Phelix had ever known.

'Exactly what it sounds as if I'm saying!' Nathan Mallory stood up to him.

Phelix saw her father's glance dart slyly to her bedroom—and saw unadulterated fury sour his expression, none too sweet before. 'Is this true?' he turned to demand of his nightdress-clad daughter, his voice rising to a screaming roar when she was not quick enough to answer him. *'Is this true?'* Hot colour flared to her face. She might be naïve in certain areas, but she knew what he was asking. *'Is it?'* he shouted.

Her throat felt suddenly dry. She wasn't sure what was happening here, but by the sound of it—if she'd got it right—Nathan wanted to score off her father by letting him think they had been—lovers.

Colour flared to her face again. Even her ears felt hot. But just then she truly felt that, in the light of her father's conduct, she owed more loyalty to Nathan, the man she had married, than to her father.

'If you're asking have I slept with Nathan since our marriage, Father, then the answer is yes. Yes, I have,' she answered. She did not dare look at Nathan as she said it, but realised full well what the huge lie implied—just as she realised that she must have said the right thing.

Because without a word to her Nathan, his chin jutting, leaned to her father, told him to, 'Put that in your dishonourable drum and bang it, Bradbury,' and walked down the stairs and out of the house.

And that was the last time she had seen him. Though even with her father's plan for the marriage annulment scuppered it had not prevented Edward Bradbury from searching for an alternative route to get the marriage annulled. He'd still been nefariously plotting when, a few days later, Phelix had discovered exactly why that annulment was so important to him.

Feeling sickened that her own flesh and blood could care so little for her that he could so deliberately attempt to cheat her, Phelix had lost what little respect she'd had for her father. For the first time ever she had dug her heels in and refused to listen to any further talk of an annulment, or for that matter a divorce.

Had Nathan wanted a divorce or an annulment she would

have agreed at any time. But he had not made any represen-
tation to that effect.

The church clock in front of her chiming the quarter hour
brought Phelix back to the present.

Knowing she had to get back to the conference, she jumped
up from the sun lounger, her thoughts promptly shooting back
to Nathan Mallory. The night of their wedding was the last
time she had seen him or had had any contact with him until
today. She remembered his gentleness, his arm about her…

Stop it! She made her way to the conference knowing she
was going to have to stop drifting off to relive matters that had
taken place so long ago. She supposed it was just seeing
Nathan again so unexpectedly that had set her off.

It was for sure she would have given Davos a very wide
berth had she thought for a moment that he would be here this
week. She had been aware, of course, that Mallory and
Mallory had long since pulled themselves out of the financial
crater they had been in. They were now one of the most top-
notch companies in the business. But she had been certain that
the heads of such large companies would not be bothered with
this week's conference, but would be circling around from
next week, when the big noises from JEPC Holdings would
be leading the show.

And yet, as she entered the conference centre, did it matter
that Nathan Mallory was here? He had said hello and that was
the end of it.

Nevertheless, as she spotted Duncan and Chris and made her
way over to them, she could not help but be glad that, although
still slender, she had filled out a little, had curves in the right
places, and had developed a sense of style that suited her.

She took her seat and noticed Nathan Mallory seated some
way away. She had done nothing either about an annulment
or a divorce from him. And since she had not received any

papers to sign from him, she could only assume that—although he was now more than financially able to support a wife—there could not be anyone in particular in his life.

After striving to concentrate on what the present speaker was talking about—'Strategy and Vision'—she was glad when they broke for refreshments. She told Chris she was going outside for some air, and made haste before Ross Dawson should waylay her.

It was a beautiful day, sunny and too lovely to be stuck indoors. She strolled out into the adjacent park and felt as near content as at any time in her life. She ambled on, in no hurry, pausing to bend and read the inscription on a monument in tribute to Sir Arthur Conan Doyle, who had apparently brought the new sport of skiing to the attention of the world by skiing over the mountain from Davos to Arosa.

No mean feat, she was thinking, when a well remembered voice at the back of her asked, 'Enjoying your freedom?'

She straightened, but knew who it was before she turned around and found herself looking up—straight into the cool grey eyes of Nathan Mallory. 'I didn't know you'd be here!' she exclaimed without thinking.

'Otherwise you'd have kept away?'

Phelix hesitated, then knew that she did not want Nathan to form an impression that she was as dishonest as her father. It took an effort, but she managed to get herself back together. 'I still feel dreadful when I think of our last meeting.' She did not avoid his question. She knew he would never forget their wedding day and its outcome either. 'You've done so well since then,' she hurried on.

He could have said that it was no thanks to the Bradburys, but by dint of sheer night-and-day labour he and his father had managed to turn their nose-diving company around and into the huge thriving concern that it was today. What he did say was, 'You haven't done so badly either, from what I hear.' He did not comment on the physical change in her, but it was there in his eyes. 'Shall we stretch our legs?' he suggested.

She felt nervous of him suddenly. But he had never done her the least harm; the reverse, if anything. She remembered the way he had stayed with her that awful storm-ridden night when she had been so terrified.

It was not an overly large park, and as she stepped away from the monument Nathan matched his step to hers and they strolled the kind of a horseshoe-shaped path.

'You heard I studied law?' she asked, feeling in the need to say something.

'I'm acquainted with Henry Scott,' Nathan replied. 'I bump into him from time to time at various business or fundraising functions. I knew he worked at Bradburys, and asked him once if he knew how you were getting on. He's very fond of you.'

'Henry's a darling. I doubt I'd have got through my exams without his help.'

'From what he said, I'm sure you would.' Nathan looked down at her. 'You've changed,' he remarked.

She knew it was for the better. 'I needed to! When I look back—'

'Don't,' Nathan cut in. 'Never look back.'

She shrugged. 'You're right, of course.'

'So tell me about this new Phelix Bradbury.'

'There's not a lot to tell,' she replied. 'I worked hard—and here I am.'

'And that covers the last eight years?' he queried sceptically.

He halted, and she halted with him, and all at once they were facing each other, looking into each other's eyes. Her heart suddenly started to go all fluttery, so that she had to turn from him to get herself together. She supposed she had always known that this, 'the day of reckoning,' would come.

She took a deep breath as she recognised that day was here. 'What you're really asking,' she began as they started to stroll on again, 'is what was the real reason my father wanted me married *and* single again with all speed?' She was amazed that, when she was feeling all sort of disturbed inside somehow, her voice should come out sounding so even.

'It would be a good place to begin,' Nathan murmured.

He was owed. Owed more than that she just tell him about herself. And he, she realised, wanted the lot. 'I'm sure you've guessed most of it,' she commented. She glanced over to him, and caught the slight nod of his head.

'I was too desperate in my need to save the company to look for hidden angles in your father's offer. But as I started to take on board that I'd been had, I began to probe deeper. And, while I still didn't know "what", it didn't take a genius to realise—too late,' he inserted, 'that there had to be some other reason why your father wanted you in and out of a marriage in five minutes.'

That 'too late' made her wince. But she was honest enough to know that it was justified. 'You were quicker at picking that up than me,' she remarked, remembering how it had been that night. 'That's why you let my father believe an—er—annulment was out of the question, wasn't it?'

'It was the first time I'd seen him with you. It was pretty obvious from the way he spoke of and to you that an annulment was more important to him than simply doing a father's duty and watching out for you. His prime concern, clearly, was that annulment.' Nathan shrugged. 'As enraged as I was, the question just begged to be asked—if he was so uncaring, why was he going to such extraordinary lengths to help his daughter gain ten percent of her inheritance.'

'You knew that there must be some other reason?'

'By then every last scrap of my trust in the man had gone.

It didn't take long for me to see that, shark that he is, there had to be something in it for him.'

It should, she supposed, have upset her to hear her father referred to as a shark, but what Nathan Mallory was saying was no more than the truth. My word, was he telling the truth! 'There was,' she had to agree. Now that she was in possession of the true facts of her grandfather's will, she was totally unable to defend her father. And since the man she had married had been the one to have suffered most, she did not see how—or why for that matter—she should try to defend her father's atrocious actions either. 'There was something in it for him,' she confessed quietly. 'Something he had no chance to claim should I stay married.'

Nathan looked down at her as they ambled along. 'You're not going to leave it there, I hope?' he enquired evenly.

For a few seconds Phelix struggled with a sense of disloyalty to her father. But he had long since forfeited any right to her loyalty. And Nathan *was owed*! 'My father had plans that would never come to fruition if that annulment did not take place,' she said at last. 'But you'd realised that, hadn't you?'

'Sensed, more than knew,' Nathan replied, but asked sharply, 'Did you know in advance—?'

'No!' she protested hotly, not wanting to be tarred by the same disreputable brush as her father. 'I didn't so much as suspect…I'd not the smallest idea. I was still totally in the dark the next morning, when Henry Scott came to the house with some paperwork he needed to go through with my father. When my father was hung up with some business on the phone, I made Henry some coffee. Grace, our housekeeper, wasn't back,' Phelix vividly recalled.

'She'd had the previous night off—she'd been to the theatre.'

'You remember that!'

'I have forgotten absolutely nothing about that night!' Nathan said grimly.

Her heart did a peculiar kind of flutter. She had lain in her bed. He had cradled her close. 'Er—Grace is still with us. She should have retired ages ago, but… Anyway.' Phelix strove to get back to what they were saying, and came abruptly down to earth when close on that memory she thought of her father returning home that night. 'I was a bit down—still coming to terms with my mother's sudden death, and— Well, anyway, Henry—with the patience of a saint, I have to say—dragged from me what had happened.'

'You told him you'd got married?' Nathan's tone had sharpened.

'There's no need to sound so tough! I was very upset over the way you had been treated! I told him my father had defaulted on some money he'd promised a businessman—er—who was down on his luck—to marry me. But I never said who the man was, and I never would. Nor, you can be sure, would my father.'

Nathan nodded. 'So you told Henry Scott that you'd married, and why?' he prompted.

'And I'm glad I did,' she answered. 'Henry's got a shrewder head than me. He asked if I'd seen my grandfather's will. I hadn't, of course. So Henry then asked me what the letter from my grandfather's solicitors had said.'

'But you hadn't received any letter from them,' Nathan stated.

'You're shrewder than me too,' she commented.

'You were standing too close to the picture to see it as Henry Scott and I see it.'

'I suppose you're right. Anyhow—' she broke off. 'I must be boring you with all of this.'

'Don't you dare stop now,' Nathan ordered. 'I've waited eight years to hear this!'

Phelix flicked him a sharp look. Oh, my, was he owed! 'I'm—er—trying not to be too disloyal to my father here…' she began—and had her ears scorched for her trouble.

'Good God, woman!' Nathan snarled fiercely, halting in his stride. 'You think that man deserves your loyalty?' Phelix stopped walking too and looked up into Nathan's angry grey eyes. 'For his own ends—whatever they were—he *used* you! In doing so he thereby gave up all right to any loyalty from you!' But suddenly then Nathan seemed to pause in his anger, somehow seeming to collect himself, and he was much less angry when, quietly, he promised, 'You have my word, Phelix, that whatever it was your father was up to I won't broadcast it.'

Phelix looked from him. Never would she ever have thought the day would come when she would stroll in a park with a man she barely knew, even if admittedly she was married to him, and reveal the full extent of her father's treachery. But, as Nathan had intimated, some sort of an explanation was eight years overdue.

But here she was hesitating. Yet had not her father been instrumental in trying to ruin Nathan? Because by going back on his word about the money that was what could have happened. Perhaps Nathan was fully entitled to know the real reason behind that marriage deal.

'Anyway…' She took a steadying breath, started to walk on, and, as Nathan suited his steps to hers, she plunged. 'Henry—who seems to know just about everybody—telephoned me when he got back to his office and told me he had made an appointment for me with my grandfather's legal people.'

'You didn't tell your father?'

She shook her head. 'I think it was about then that I started to grow up.' She took another steadying breath, and relived the shock of what she had learned when she had kept that appointment. 'Anyhow, the lawyers were quite astounded, and

couldn't understand why I hadn't received any of their letters.'
It had all become clear to her then why her father had suddenly started spending his mornings working from home—
he had wanted to be there when the post arrived. 'But I was
as astonished as they had been that their correspondence had
gone astray when they read that Grandfather Bradbury, a man
who'd had a thing about divorce, had left me money condi-
tionally. As my father had told me, should I marry before I
was twenty-five I was to receive ten percent of the whole cash
sum. But—and this is what I did not know—should that marriage fail, either by annulment or divorce, before I reached
twenty-five, then the remainder of the money and a considerable portfolio of shares, including thousands of shares in
Edward Bradbury Systems, were to go with immediate effect
to my father.'

'My God! The man's a—' Nathan broke off. 'So that was
what he was after—your shares! An annulment would have
given them to him straight away.'

'An annulment is fairly instant. To divorce, a couple have
to be married for more than a year.'

'And your father did not want to wait that long to get his
hands on those shares?'

'He did not,' she had to agree. And, having come to the end,
with everything said that Nathan had waited long enough to hear,
she turned to him. 'That's it, I'm afraid. The whole sorry tale.'

Looking at him, she saw with surprise a hint of a smile
come to the corners of his mouth. 'So how do you feel now
about having snookered his plans?'

Her lips twitched. She had to smile too. She had aided and
abetted Nathan by going along with his hint that an annulment
had been forfeited. 'In all truth, I *had* slept with you,' she
murmured lightly.

'Tut-tut,' Nathan scolded. 'My memory's better than that.'

She could feel her cheeks growing warm. She hadn't blushed in years. Time to change the subject.

'I know he's my father, but he didn't deserve any less.' The subject was done with, the explanation Nathan was owed made—the least he was owed and, 'What do you think of the conference so—?' she began lightly.

'You're wearing a wedding ring!' Nathan abruptly cut in.

'That's probably because I'm married.'

'You're living with someone?' he demanded sharply.

She shook her head and just had to laugh. 'Now run for the hills!'

Nathan stared at her, seemed to like the sound of her laughter. 'I hope I'm braver than that,' he murmured. 'I'll prove it,' he added. 'I'll take you to dinner.'

Somehow—perhaps because she was a little on edge from having revealed the unpleasantness of what she'd had to reveal, or perhaps because she had been her own person for so long now—it niggled her a little that instead of asking he should just assume he would take her to dinner and that was all there was to it.

'I'm sorry,' she stated politely. 'I've arranged to have dinner with someone else.'

They had halted again, and Nathan held her glance for long moments. And then slowly he drawled, 'Don't I, as a mere husband, get priority?'

Her heart seemed to give a giddy kind of flip at Nathan claiming to be her husband. But somehow she managed to appear outwardly cool. 'I can't imagine you being a "mere" anything,' she answered. And all at once they were both grinning—and suddenly she was falling a little in love with him all over again.

CHAPTER THREE

THIS would never do, Phelix berated herself as she dressed to have dinner with Ross that night. All she seemed to think about was Nathan Mallory. It just would not do.

Had she been too friendly with him? How else should she have been? She should, she felt, be feeling a little disloyal to her father, but strangely she wasn't. She concentrated her thoughts on her father.

It had been a tremendous shock when the lawyers had told her the full contents of her grandfather's will, she recalled. Shaken rigid still did not cover how she had felt! She had been rocked, utterly amazed as the extent of her father's treachery had sunk in. Had that annulment taken place she would have lost everything bar that ten percent of actual cash willed to her. Her father would have grabbed everything else from her. Not by accident, but by evil, scheming design.

Only then had she started to realise why he had objected to her wanting to marry Lee Thompson. Had she married Lee she would have lived with him as his wife, with an annulment out of the question. Even should that marriage have ultimately ended in divorce it would have taken too long. Apart from the fact her father could not have hoped to hide the contents of her grandfather's will for as long as a year, he had not wanted to wait a moment longer than he had to to claim her shares.

And she had known nothing of what he had planned! But Nathan, without a clue as to what her father had been up to, had been far more aware than her. He must have started to work out that there was something rotten going on while he'd waited all those long hours for her father to return home.

There had been no annulment anyway, and, since Nathan was long overdue some kind of an explanation, she was glad she had today told him what she had.

Deciding to drive to Ross Dawson's hotel, Phelix went to collect her hired car reflecting that the marriage was neither annulled nor, when at any time after they had been married a year, Nathan could have applied for a divorce, had he done so.

'As stunning as ever!' Ross exclaimed the moment he saw her.

She smiled. 'You're so good for my ego.'

'I speak only the truth,' he replied, and escorted her into the dining room.

Phelix had always found him straightforward and uncomplicated, and to a certain extent felt relaxed in his company. He was one of the few men she dated, and even so he had known from the outset that she was married, and that nothing was ever going to come from her agreeing to have the occasional dinner with him.

That did not prevent him from trying, however. 'Does your husband know where you are tonight?' he asked as they consulted their menus. He was forever trying to fish for information on the man he more often than not called her 'mythical husband.'

But tonight, instead of side-stepping his question or fobbing him off with some kind of non-answer, she replied, 'As a matter of fact,' she replied, and was pleased to be able to answer without prevarication for once, 'he does. That is, he knows I'm in Davos.'

'He does?' Ross looked a touch taken aback.

'He does,' she confirmed.

'But you're still living with your father? You don't live with this phantom husband?'

'He travels a lot.' She knew for a fact he had journeyed to Switzerland.

'He's not in England either at the moment?' Ross pressed.

'He's abroad.'

'Where?'

Phelix was starting to wish that she had opted for a non-answer. 'Do you really need to know?' she asked.

'I'd like to meet him.'

'Why?'

'Because I'd like to tell him to give you a divorce—so you can marry me.'

At which point Phelix just had to burst out laughing. And in doing so she glanced up—straight into the icy cold eyes of Nathan Mallory, the very man under discussion.

He and his female companion had obviously just come into the dining room. Phelix would have offered a friendly kind of hello, but the word, along with the laughter on her lips, froze when with the barest inclination of his head in acknowledgement that he had seen her, Nathan walked straight by her.

'Will you?'

With her heartbeats playing double time, Phelix jerked her attention back to Ross Dawson, who had not noticed the tall couple pass behind him. 'Will I what?' she queried absently. She was feeling hurt by Nathan Mallory's cool attitude—nor did she care too much that he had the tall blonde in tow.

'I've just asked you to marry me.'

'You said you wouldn't!' Already Phelix was denying that she cared a scrap that the cold, unfriendly brute had so soon changed from the friendly man she had strolled in the park with that afternoon. Nor, when he had stated he would take *her* to dinner that evening, that it had not taken him very long to tell some other female that she had been elected.

'Are you really married?' Ross was asking.

And Phelix heaved a heavy sigh. 'I'm sharing a meal with you, Ross, because I like you. My marriage,' she went on, and meant it, 'is not up for discussion.'

Ross sighed too. 'You're saying I'm to either accept that or dine alone?'

Put like that it sounded a bit blunt, but… 'That's what it amounts to, Ross. I'm sorry.'

'Your old man would like us to get together,' he tried.

That seemed to her to be one very good reason not to. But, while it had not seemed so tremendously disloyal to discuss her father with Nathan, there was no one else apart from Henry to whom she would allow that privilege.

She attempted to change the subject. 'What do you think of the conference so far?'

'I do love you, you know.'

'Then eat your spinach—and behave yourself.'

He laughed, and she knew she was more fond of him than just liking. But as he complained, 'Chance to do anything other than behave myself with you would be a fine thing,' she knew that love him she did not.

More than a dozen times as their meal progressed Phelix felt the pull to look over in the direction of where she knew Nathan and the blonde were sitting. But somehow, and it was not easy, she managed to keep her eyes from straying in that direction.

But she was glad when the meal was over. Though when she and Ross were ready to leave the dining room she was still concentrating on not looking to where Nathan was. He thought, after the friendly way they had been with each other that afternoon, that he could just more or less ignore her? Okay, so he had inclined his head a touch, but a friendly hello wouldn't have hurt him.

Realising she was making too much of what she was letting herself believe was a snub, Phelix was glad she had some superb clothes. The green, just above the knee, dress she was wearing was one such article. Poised, generally aloof, but smiling at her dinner partner, she walked from the dining room with Ross Dawson staking his claim by placing a guiding arm lightly across her back. She had shrugged his arm away from her the last time he had done that, and did so again—but not until they were out of sight of the dining room.

'Something to drink to finish off with?' Ross asked.

'Better not.'

'You can't be going back to work!'

'Why not?' enquired she who had not opened her laptop since she had got there!

'I'll walk you back,' Ross offered.

'I drove here.'

'One of these days…' he promised.

'Goodnight, Ross.' She smiled, but found he was still escorting her to where she had parked her car.

He kissed her on both cheeks, gripped her arms as though he would like to pull her to him, but decided, in the hope of seeing her again soon, against it. They bade each other a smiling farewell.

But Phelix was not smiling as she let herself into her hotel room. How dared he more or less ignore her? Who did Nathan Mallory think he was? Just because he was dining with that luscious blonde!

For a further five minutes, totally unused to men treating her that way, Phelix railed against him. But it was when she found herself thinking that for two pins she'd divorce the swine that her sense of humour surfaced—and she just had to laugh at herself.

They had been married for eight years—and never a cross word. And in truth, no matter how cranky he was, she did not want to divorce him. Perhaps, once this conference was over, it would be another eight years of complete harmony before she saw him again.

Phelix showered and brushed her teeth, but when she climbed into bed she was starting to realise that if she was to be brutally honest she would *not* like another eight years to pass with never a sight of Nathan.

It was during her early-morning swim the next morning that she recalled her last waking thought before sleep had claimed her. But she was then able to dismiss it as nothing but a load of tosh.

She was still telling herself that she wouldn't give a button if she never saw him again when, making her way to breakfast, she bumped straight into him! As she stepped out of the lift he was coming from the direction of the breakfast dining room.

'Phelix,' he acknowledged her, covering his surprise better than she thought she covered hers that, by the look of it, they had opted to stay at the same hotel.

'Nathan.' She nodded, and did a smart, head in the air left turn away from him.

She was feeling all shaky inside when she sat down at her table. But for his surprise at seeing her there would he have spoken at all? she wondered. And was he staying here or had it been more a temporary stop-over—with the blonde?

Deciding that she did not want to know, Phelix suddenly discovered that she was not very hungry. Her small amount of cereal and coffee did not take long to consume, but she all at once felt hesitant to leave the room. What if…?

Phelix immediately took herself in hand. Heavens above,

was she worried that she might bump into Nathan again? How ridiculous was that!

She did not see him in the hotel when, cross with herself, she left the breakfast room. Nor did she see him again when she made her way to the conference centre. But she did see him again, in the same seat he had occupied yesterday. She was more aware of him than she was the present speaker. But then, that speaker having come to an end and been applauded, she watched as Nathan Mallory, having stepped into the breach for the person who had been scheduled to speak, left his seat to address the assembled audience.

For no known reason she felt all churned up inside, but started to relax as Nathan began, quite obviously at ease with his subject. Most peculiarly, when apart from that slip of paper—their marriage certificate—he was nothing to do with her, her heart filled with pride. She watched him with riveted attention as he spoke clearly, concisely and confidently. Then all at once he seemed to look directly at her and—hesitate. But it was only for the briefest moment before he was going smoothly on again.

When he came to an end he received well-earned applause— and Phelix was at one and the same time proud and choked. She felt a desperate need to be on her own, and was glad that at that moment there was a general break for refreshments.

'Coffee?' Duncan asked before she could make a bolt for it.

'I'll—er—get back to my hotel. I need to make some phone calls,' she replied, ready to invent anything in her need to be alone.

With other delegates congesting her way, her exit was not as speedy as she had hoped. But at last she was outside the conference centre and walking quickly along the Promenade— the main street—towards her hotel.

Oh, Nathan! He had been wonderful. Just looking at him…

No! Stop thinking about him! She did not know what it was about him, but he was having the strangest effect on her. She admired him tremendously. Why wouldn't she? There had not been a sound to be heard when he had been giving his speech.

That did not explain, though, why she had been feeling so mixed up inside about him that she had needed to get out of there.

Phelix suddenly became aware then that she had walked quite some way, and she began to slow her pace. She was not sure that she wanted to go back to her hotel.

But it was then that she saw that she was nearing the Schatzalp funicular that would take her a good way up the towering mountain. Davos was said to be the highest town in Switzerland. The funicular was just what she needed to carry her up and away. She needed to clear her head. Perhaps the pure air up there would help her do it.

Regardless that she should be taking her seat at the conference, Phelix executed a smart right turn and inside the next five minutes was seated in one of the compartments, waiting for the vehicle to start its climb.

But so much for her hoping to escape her mixed-up feelings! Because before the car could set off someone else had joined her compartment, and as shock hit her, and warm colour surged to her face, her emotions went chaotic. Stumped for anything to say, she just sat and stared at the tall dark-haired man who had just entered.

'Bunking off?' Nathan Mallory enquired equably.

Somehow, and from where she had no idea, Phelix managed to find a cool note. 'All work, etcetera,' she returned calmly as he took a seat on the bench next to her. She then sought feverishly for something else to say. 'Good speech, by the way,' she remarked lightly. And, as she realised that he had probably decided to go up the mountain to clear his head too, 'Er—if you want to be alone…' she began.

'Had I wanted to do that, I wouldn't have followed you from the conference,' he replied evenly.

'You followed me?' she asked in surprise as the vehicle started off. Last night he hadn't wanted to know her—this morning either for that matter. Yet now...? She opted to go for the impersonal route. 'It's no good talking to me about business. I'm on the legal side, so wouldn't know—'

'I've no interest in your family's business,' Nathan butted in, and seemed more interested in enjoying the ride than in enlightening her as to why he had followed her. Presumably he wanted to speak with her about something.

When they alighted from the vehicle some five or six minutes later, Nathan seemed content to wander around the kind of plateau a good way up the mountain that housed a café-restaurant and a small souvenir kiosk.

'Shall we have coffee?' Nathan asked, instead of telling her this time.

There was a large hotel further along, but it appeared to be closed, so they made their way to the café-restaurant, opting to have coffee outside, where they could take in the air while admiring the spectacular view.

Phelix had to admit that her emotions were still a little erratic, but she had not spent years outwardly being in control for nothing.

Nathan ordered their coffee, which arrived with a little heart-shaped biscuit. But if he had followed her for a reason, and it was not her family's business, she decided it must either be his business or—and oddly her heart gave a small lurch—personal.

But, apart from a few words of idle conversation, he seemed in no hurry to begin. And from her point of view, as she began to accept the moment and to just enjoy her splendid surroundings, she was in no hurry should he have decided to end their marriage. Although of course with the length of time they had lived apart, when he could have obtained a divorce at any time, there was absolutely no need for him to discuss it with her at all.

The view truly was breathtaking, and Phelix looked into the distance, watching brave hang-gliders soaring over the mountains that surrounded them. She did not want a divorce. It suited her very well to be married. But her family, or more precisely her father, had served Nathan with the sticky end, and if a divorce was what Nathan wanted, a divorce was what he would have.

Her attention was drawn to the nearby red-berried rowan trees to her left, and she found she was asking, 'Are you staying at the Schweizerhof?' and immediately wished that she hadn't. If he had been merely visiting, she didn't think she wanted to know.

'I thought my team might be more relaxed if I stayed elsewhere,' he replied.

'There are three of you?' she queried, discovering she wanted to know his connection with the blonde, but trying to hide it.

'There were always meant to be three,' Nathan answered, not helping her at all.

'That would be you, substituting for your employee who couldn't make it, the other man, and…' she just could not hold back from asking, '…the blonde lady? Sorry,' Phelix apologised immediately. Grief, what was wrong with her? 'Perhaps the lady's more of a friend than…'

Nathan stared at her every bit as if he knew what she was thinking, and for a split second she hated him. 'Dulcie Green is a scientist,' he revealed. 'Brilliant in her field,' he added. 'We're very lucky to have her. But between you and me,' he murmured conspiratorially, 'I'd as soon have had dinner with my wife last night.'

Phelix laughed. Whether he was being serious or just plain charming, she had to laugh, though she guessed from his remark that he had taken Dulcie Green to dinner out of courtesy, when perhaps his other team member had been engaged elsewhere.

'How about you?' Nathan asked. 'You're not staying with Ward and Watson.'

It did not seem polite to mention that she would have been had her father had his way.

But before she could do more than shake her head. Nathan asked abruptly, 'Where's Dawson staying?'

She looked at him in surprise. 'What's Ross got to do with anything?'

He ignored her question. 'What is he to you?'

'What do you mean—what is he to me?'

'You know what I mean,' Nathan replied shortly.

From the way she remembered it—and she had known all along where Nathan's table was even if she had managed to keep her glance from straying—Ross had had his back to Nathan. Though she supposed he could have caught a glimpse of Ross's face when they'd stood up to leave.

'Er.' She had no idea how to answer that statement.

'Does he know that you're married?'

Really, there was something of the terrier about Nathan Mallory, she decided! He wasn't leaving the subject of her relationship with Ross Dawson alone, anyway.

'He knows,' she replied. 'I'm not sure that he believes it— for all I tell him often enough—but he knows.'

'Do you intend to marry him?'

Phelix looked into Nathan's cool grey eyes, and away again. But, bearing in mind that Nathan had followed her, and must have done so for some reason, she thought she might ask a few questions of her own. 'I'm more than happy with the state of my present marriage, thank you. If you are?' she added, giving him an 'in' should he have followed her to tell her that in his view their marriage no longer served any useful purpose.

He did not take up the opening she had given him, and nor did he answer her question either, but asked instead, 'I take it from that that there's no one special?'

'Who has the time?' she lobbed back at him. But then she looked across to him and, observing the virile look of him, 'Well,' she qualified with a light laugh, 'you would. You'd make time. But…'

'But you've been busy getting on with your career?'

She shrugged her shoulders slightly. 'You must know how it is. You must have worked long hours—evenings, weekends too—to get where you wanted to be.'

'As did you,' he agreed, with a smile for her that just about melted her bones. 'So there's been no one special?'

She would have loved to ask him the same question, but changed her mind—she didn't think she wanted to know about the women in his life.

'No,' she replied—then suddenly remembered Lee Thompson.

'But?' Nathan queried, spotting her small moment of hesitation.

'There nearly was,' she said, but found that she didn't want to talk about anything unpleasant. 'I've finished my coffee. I think I'll make tracks.'

Nathan stood up with her and glanced about. 'We'll walk down,' he decided. She opened her mouth to protest; she just wasn't used to other people making such decisions for her. 'You've got the right shoes for it,' he added, his eyes on nowhere but her face, that alone telling her that he must have observed everything about her, right down to the flat heeled shoes she was wearing.

Her protest died unmade. She had just realised that she would like nothing better than to take the footpath down to Davos with him.

'Do you manage to get much exercise?' she asked, apropos of nothing, as they took the signposted Thomas Mann Weig to the zig-zagging mountain path.

'As much as I can. It's good to be outdoors. You?' he asked as, at a steady pace, they started on the walk that from a sign she had seen she calculated would take them forty or so minutes.

'We have a pool at home. I swim most mornings,' she replied, and enchantment started to wash over her as she paced with Nathan through the mountain pines, spotted the odd red squirrel shooting up them, and observed birds she did not know the name of flying by and settling in branches.

'You've had lovers, of course?' Nathan enquired after a while, quite unabashed at asking that which he wanted to know.

'We're still talking about exercise, I take it?' she enquired dryly.

He had the grace to grin, and her heart skipped a beat. 'No, actually,' he replied. 'Rather belatedly, I think I should just like to know more about this quite stunning woman I've been married to all this time.'

Her mouth fell open in surprise. Though she did not know which surprised her more, the fact that Nathan thought her stunning or the fact that he wanted to know more about her.

'Was that why you followed me, because…?' Had he really wanted to know more about her?

'Not solely because I want to know more of your love-life,' Nathan replied. 'Though I must admit I'm a shade intrigued that you wear a wedding ring.'

'You think I shouldn't?' she asked shortly.

'No need to get edgy,' he answered. 'Is it the same one I put there?' he asked.

'I never thought you'd mind. I mean, it's not as if anyone knows who I'm married to—'

'I don't mind,' he cut in.

'And it came in more than useful when I didn't want to date but needed to concentrate solely on my studies.'

Nathan took that on board. 'I bet it irritates the hell out of you father.'

'You could say that,' she replied lightly, recalling the thunderous row they'd had the first time had he noticed the ring on her finger. Though it had been more him bellowing and threatening and her standing firm for once and being determined not to take it off.

Nathan tried another tack. 'With or without that wedding ring, men are going to want to date you.'

'I've dated a few times,' she admitted, and was aware of Nathan's sharp glance at her. 'Nothing serious.'

'You're saying you've not had a lover?' Clearly he did not believe it. 'Dawson…?' he began.

'I'm not comfortable with this conversation.' She cut him off shortly. But immediately relented. She did not want to part bad friends. 'Not Ross, not anybody,' she added as they turned a bend in the path. But as Nathan abruptly halted, and she bumped into him, so in her too-speedy effort to take a pace away her foot slipped on a small collection of scree. But for Nathan catching hold of her, she would have fallen.

He held her close up to him, and suddenly her emotions were going haywire. 'No one?' he questioned. 'You've never…' Her mouth went dry—he was looking at her with a kind of warm look of surprise in his eyes.

'Absolutely never,' she murmured, and suddenly she just knew, as his glance went down to her parted lips, that he was going to kiss her.

But she was already shaken that he was so close, his hands on her arms still holding her to him, and she was not ready. She jerked away—and instantly wanted the moment back again. She wanted him to kiss her, wanted to feel that warm, wonderful mouth on hers. But too late now. She knew she would never again have the chance to feel his kiss.

Nathan made no attempt to hold on to her, but let her go and put some space between them as they carried on down the zig-zag path. And as Phelix began to get herself more of one piece again, she began to be certain that she had been totally wrong to imagine that Nathan had been about to kiss her; she could only blame that sudden heightened awareness of him that her emotions had gone off at a tangent.

They were walking side by side but with a fair space between them, and she was striving hard to concentrate on squirrels, birds, trees and pine cones—on anything but him—when, out of the blue, Nathan enquired, 'Do you have a hang-up about men, Phelix?'

That almost stopped her in her tracks. But she'd had years of experience in hiding her feelings, so she walked on and, in the same conversational tone he had used, 'Because I've never had a lover?' she asked.

'Not totally,' Nathan replied. 'You're twenty-six and are entitled to—have had experiences. But, at a guess, I'd say you had one fairly foul childhood. Your mother died tragically, and I doubt your father is the most sensitive of men.'

'You're psychoanalysing me?' she protested.

Nathan shook his head. 'What I am is feeling guilty that I never made contact with you in all this time to check that everything was going all right with your world.'

'You owe me nothing!' she exclaimed abruptly.

He was unabashed. 'I gave you my name. I should have done more.'

'Nonsense!' Phelix retorted sharply—and immediately regretted her sharp tone. She didn't know what was wrong with her, blowing first hot and then cold, annoyed one minute and then regretting it—she did not want to be bad friends with him. 'Anyhow, apart from the fact that you must have had one almighty row to hoe in those days of you and your father doing everything you could to turn your company around, you found out from Henry Scott how things were with me, what I was doing with my life.'

'Ah, yes, Henry,' Nathan murmured, but just then they came to the signposted junction where one road would lead in the direction of the conference centre, the other to Davos Platz and her hotel.

'I'm going this way,' Phelix said as they came to an amicable kind of halt.

'I'm committed to lunch with some people,' Nathan stated, and sounded as if he regretted that he had to go the other way. Charm, pure charm, she decided. 'I'd ask you to come along,' he added, 'but you work for the opposition.'

'I might have accepted—had I thought I was trusted,' she responded loftily.

But suddenly, as they stared into each other's eyes, they both started to smile. Her heart turned over.

'Want to come?' he invited after all.

And she felt all choked up suddenly. Oh, dear heaven! 'Better not,' she answered huskily from a suddenly constricted throat. But—before she could take her intended swift step away—Nathan just then took a step towards her.

'You are one very beautiful woman,' he said softly, and bent and kissed her cheek.

He took a step back, and she just had to let go a shaky breath. 'You're not so bad yourself,' she managed, and turned swiftly to the path she must take in fear that she might change her mind and ask if she could have lunch with him after all.

She walked away from him blindly, her mind in an uproar, her emotions in an uproar. Oh, how had it happened? Phelix

swallowed, feeling devastated as a truth she could not deny
hit her full force. She loved him! Heavens above—she loved
Nathan Mallory!

Oh, help her, someone—she had fallen in love with
Nathan. She was in love with him, Nathan, her husband—and
any time now he could ask for a divorce!

CHAPTER FOUR

PHELIX was unseeing of anything as she made her way back to her hotel. She would have liked to have believed that what she felt for Nathan was mere infatuation. But it was not, and she knew that it was not. Oh, what had she done?

It had happened so quickly she could barely believe it, but it was there. Staggeringly, utterly staggeringly, it was there and would not go away. She was totally and completely in love with Nathan Mallory!

With her head in such a whirl, Phelix was back in her room before she had space to realise how very much Nathan must trust her. Had she gone with him to lunch he would have introduced her as Phelix Bradbury. That alone would have told the people he was lunching with who she was. Might even have jiggered up any deal he was making. It went without saying that her father, as hard-headed a businessman as they came, would—unless he'd had a complete personality change—have upset a few people in his day.

But she was more concerned with Nathan than with her father or any stuffy old business. How she had come to fall so hopelessly in love with Nathan she had no clue. Although it was true to say that she had always had a soft spot for him. She recalled his gentleness with her eight years ago, when she had been something of a scared rabbit. She still loathed thunderstorms and knew, with those images of her father assaulting her mother still sharp in her mind, that she always would.

But Nathan, without knowing more than the bare bones that her mother had been killed during a storm, had held her and cradled her to sleep—so how could she not have a soft spot for him?

But this would never do. Realising that, apart from a small bowl of cereal at breakfast and that heart shaped biscuit at the café at Schatzalp, that she had eaten little that day, she left the hotel, found a café and had a snack, and then thought she had better make tracks for the conference. She had 'bunked off' that morning—she mustn't let the side down. Besides which, even if they never got to exchange so much as a word, she felt a great need to just see Nathan again.

She was in for a disappointment, however. She did not see him. What she thought of as his normal seat was empty, and stayed empty all afternoon. The blonde was there, and so was the other member of his team, but of Nathan Mallory she saw not a sign. And her heart began to ache.

And this, she started to know, was how it was going to be. And how could she bear it? She began to comprehend that now, with his speech over—the sole reason for him being there—and his lunch meeting over too, there was every chance that Nathan was on his way back to London.

'Are you going to have dinner with me tonight?' Ross Dawson caught up with her before she could leave the conference centre that afternoon.

Her appetite had disappeared again. As nice as Ross was, she wanted neither food nor his company. 'No can do,' she offered with an apologetic smile.

'You can't be working!' he protested. 'You're always working back home! But here—'

'I'll see you tomorrow, Ross,' she cut in firmly. She listened to a few more grumbles from him, and in order to escape—when he saw that there was no changing her mind—she agreed to have lunch with him the next day.

It was still a glorious sunny afternoon, and back at her hotel Phelix went onto the balcony and from the sun-lounger tried to come to terms with what had happened to her, and her inability to do anything about it. She loved Nathan and he was on his way back to England; were it to be another eight years before she saw him again she did not know how she would bear it.

But her love for him was too new for her to focus on what she should do about it. Or how she must look forward to a future without him—a future where she would never see that smile, that wicked grin.

She felt cold suddenly, and realised that, for all the mountains were sunlit, the sun had gone over the top of the mountain nearest to her.

Leaving her lounger, she decided to kill some time by taking a shower. She wasn't hungry, but if she did feel peckish later she would order something from Room Service.

Nathan was in her head the whole time she was taking her shower; she was starting to realise the futility of attempting to push him out.

She was in the act of drying herself when there came an unexpected knock on her door. Thinking it might be one of the hotel staff, come to service the mini-bar or check up on something, Phelix swiftly donned the hotel's courtesy towelling robe and went to the door.

It was not a member of the hotel staff who stood there, however, but—to set her heartbeats drumming—none other than Nathan Mallory! 'I—er…' she gasped, a riot of emotions going on within her. Unspeaking, he stood silently looking at her. Her face was scrubbed clean of make-up, and as she sought for something fairly sensible to say, she knew her face was scarlet. 'I thought—thought you'd gone back to London,' she managed, albeit jerkily.

'Would I?' he replied laconically.

She was at a loss to know what to make of that for an answer. All she knew was that she was delighted to see him, and that he must want to see her, or why would he ask Reception for her room number?

'You're staying for the rest of the conference?' she asked, burbling on when it looked as if he *was* staying, 'I sort of thought, with your speech done, and the top brass not needing to be here until next Wednesday—' She broke off, amazed that the person she knew herself to be, that fairly reserved person, was babbling away like a nitwit. She compounded that thought when, suddenly aware that she was standing there in a robe that had come open at the top and which, from his height, must be giving Nathan a bird's-eye view of the top of her swelling creamy breasts, she exclaimed, 'I've got nothing on!' And there was Nathan's half smile again, and she loved him.

'I guessed,' he drawled, adding as he stretched out warm fingers and went to pull the edges of her robe together, 'With any other woman I might have construed that as an invitation.' A thrill shot up her spine as the backs of his fingers brushed briefly against the swell of her breasts. 'But knowing you, little Phelix, I'd say you're warning me that you're feeling a shade uneasy and wouldn't mind it I stated my business and left you to get dressed.'

Was she? She was too emotionally confused to know what she had meant. Other than she did not want him to disappear if it meant she would never see him again.

'So?' she enquired, holding down a beaming smile and aiming for pleasant.

'So I thought I'd stop by and, since you refused my invitation to lunch, see how you felt about dinner?'

Don't smile, don't smile. By a supreme effort she held the smile down. 'With you?' she asked pleasantly.

'Just me,' he confirmed. 'You've ample time to tell Dawson you can't make it.'

She had to laugh—she just did. 'Where?' she asked, her heart suddenly starting to sing.

Nathan looked pleased that she had just accepted to have dinner with him. 'Presumably you'd like to stay well away from Dawson's hotel?'

'It might be politic,' she agreed. She had, after all, turned said Dawson's dinner invitation down.

'What's wrong with here?'

Absolutely nothing! Absolutely, wonderfully nothing! 'Here would be good,' she agreed.

His eyes held hers. But a moment later he stepped back. 'I'll call for you at seven.'

That did not leave her very much time. 'Fine,' she replied, and casually stepped back into her room. Though once the door was closed she was galvanised into action. What was she going to wear? Suddenly she was starving.

She was dressed in a knee length dress of amber-gold-coloured silk when Nathan next knocked on her door. She did not keep him waiting. 'Phelix,' he said—just her name—and she went weak at the knees.

It was the start of the most wonderful evening of her life. Nathan escorted her down to the lounge area and saw she was seated on a sofa, while he took the chair to the left of her. Which suited her fine, because she was able to look at him whenever she chose. That, of course, meant that equally he could look at her, but she'd had time to give herself a small lecture that had gone along the lines of not by word, look or deed, would he know how things were with her.

An assistant came from behind the adjacent bar to enquire if they required anything. Phelix opted for a gin and tonic while Nathan had a Scotch.

'You're not in any hurry to eat?' Nathan thought to ask.

If it meant extending the hours she was with him Phelix would have been quite happy not to eat until midnight. 'Not at all,' she replied evenly. And, because she felt something else was needed, 'It's just lovely to be able to relax.'

'You still work long hours—at home?'

She smiled at him, wondered if perhaps she maybe ought to ration her smiles, but didn't seem to be able to stop herself from smiling. It was a fact: it was a joy just to be with him.

'You know how it is,' she replied, knowing for certain that a man in his position didn't just cut and run when the clock struck five.

'You enjoy your work?' Nathan asked.

'I do, actually. Mainly, I think, because I work under Henry. I've learned so much more from him since I qualified.' And, as the thought suddenly struck, 'I do work, you know. Just because I'm the boss's daughter, so to speak, I—'

'I don't doubt it,' Nathan cut in easily. 'Knowing your father I'd say you earn every penny of your salary and more.' She was feeling a little foolish. There had been no need for her to defend herself. But Nathan was giving her no time to feel a fool, and was going on, 'Whose decision was it that you should go into the firm?'

Phelix thought about it, but somehow, instinctively, she seemed to know that Nathan would not break any confidence she shared with him. 'I think it was more or less part of the deal I made with my father.' And, when Nathan looked interested to hear more, 'Well, he'd always bossed me about, as you probably know. Always been—er—a bit difficult. But as—um—difficult as he sometimes is, I just couldn't get over the way he'd gone back on his word to you.'

'Forget it,' Nathan inserted quietly, but she knew that he never would. Or forgive either, for that matter.

'Does your father know?' she asked as the impulse struck her.

'About the marriage?' Nathan studied her for a moment before replying honestly, 'I was saving that information until I could wave the cheque and tell him to stop worrying. I would have then told him how I'd earned it.' He paused. 'There didn't seem much point in upsetting him by telling him afterwards.'

'I'm sorry,' she said huskily.

'You are not the one who should apologise,' Nathan stated, his expression softening. 'Go on,' he instructed, 'what made you opt to train in law and go into the family firm?'

Phelix hesitated. 'It'll bore the socks off you.'

'I doubt you could ever do that,' Nathan said lightly, and her heart turned over.

'Well—' she started abruptly. Well—what? 'So—um—well—er—the reason I was originally so keen to have that initial ten percent of my inheritance was because to have that money would have meant I'd have the financial backing to leave home.'

Nathan did not query her being unhappy there, he must have known the answer, and stated instead, 'But you're still living there?'

Phelix began to wonder about Nathan's occasional bumping in to Henry, for the fact that she was still living at home must, she felt, have come from Henry.

'That was part of the deal. When Henry suggested I train in law and I started to get keen on the idea I knew—er…' She halted—whatever she said, her father wasn't going to come out of this sounding too good.

'You fancied training? Were keen on it?' Nathan took up. 'And?' he prompted.

She loved him. How could she hold back? 'Well, I knew I'd probably need all my inheritance to fund my training.'

Nathan, perhaps sensing she was struggling not to be disloyal to her father, for all her father had long since forfeited any right to her loyalty, made no comment on what he thought of her skinflint parent—he knew to his own cost that Edward Bradbury put money before honour.

'You paid for your own training—and stayed with your father because you couldn't afford to move out?' he enquired evenly.

'Not totally. My father went up in the air when I told him what I wanted to do.'

'He gave you a hard time?'

And then some! But she didn't want to think about that. 'The balloon went up again when I told him I was moving out.'

'He wanted you to stay home?'

'Not particularly, I don't think. But he knew that if I went Grace would leave too. She runs the house like clockwork—he'd never get another housekeeper half as good and he knew it.'

'So you stayed just so he would have a well-oiled home to live in?'

'Not totally. My conscience was plaguing me, naturally.'

'Naturally,' Nathan agreed, with a sort of gentle look for her.

Her heart acted up again, causing her to have to concentrate extra hard on what they were discussing. 'There was a lot going on at the time. Henry guiding me about training, interviews, and so on, and then there was Grace. She'd made a comfortable home for herself with us and was due to retire in a few years' time. She'd told me many times, and meant it, that when I went she was off. But was it right, with her pension not yet due, that she should start to look for other work at her age? Anyhow, when I confided in Henry he said that as I rarely saw my father I might just as well live at home as not.'

'And that was all right with you?'

'It seemed the best compromise. My father didn't like that I was determined to study law, but, as he was certain I was never going to stick it out until I qualified, he agreed.'

'He thought it would be a few months' wonder and then you'd pack it in?'

'Something like that—and I've talked quite, quite enough,' she said firmly. Had she ever! She hadn't opened up like that to anyone—except maybe Henry—and he knew her circumstances anyway.

'You still haven't told me whose decision it was that you went into the firm,' Nathan reminded her.

She had told him everything else, she supposed she might as well add that little bit. 'My father pointed out that I would be doing the Bradbury name a great disservice if I worked anywhere else.' What he'd actually bellowed was that he wasn't having her giving some rival firm details of his business—not that she would, even had she known any. 'Anyhow, Henry wanted me with him, and I wanted to work with Henry, so we all got out of it with honour intact.' She inwardly winced—how could she mention honour and her father in the same breath in front of Nathan?

But, whatever he was thinking, Nathan refrained from saying it, and instead stated, 'You're very fond of Henry.'

'He was a great friend to my mother. He has helped me tremendously, and I love him dearly. And now I really am going to shut up,' she declared, and was determined to not say another word.

Nathan glanced at her determined expression. And smiled that smile that would have had her telling him anything he wanted to know. 'Hungry?' he asked.

They went across to the dining room and were greeted and seated and presented with a mouthwatering five-course menu. And it *was* mouthwatering, and it was the best meal, the best companion and the most magical time ever.

She discovered with her grilled tuna and vegetable salad starter that Nathan could talk on any subject. And found with the apple curry cream soup that she chose to follow that he seemed to really want to hear her opinions and ideas. They both had a green salad to follow, and never seemed to have a stilted moment.

With the beef, potato noodles and spinach they both ordered next, Nathan wanted to know what she did for pleasure, and asked lightly about her male escorts. 'I occasionally go out with someone from work. I don't seem to have a lot of time to meet anyone socially,' she replied.

'And you'd be extremely selective even then,' he stated, seeming to know that about her.

Over the final course—Phelix opted for a sorbet, about all she could manage—she asked him about his social life. 'How about you?' she asked, not certain that she wanted to know. 'Er—anyone special?'

Nathan looked at her, seemed to enjoy what he saw, and for a moment or two did not say anything, so that she began to think that perhaps she had overstepped the privacy mark. Though he hadn't hung back from asking her anything *he* wanted to know, had he?

Then suddenly he smiled and gave what seemed to her, in her in loving and not-thinking-straight mind, to be a tender look, as he answered softly, 'No one I'd want to divorce you for, Phelix.' Her heart thundered and she had to look away. How intimate he had made that sound. But in the next second, obviously having noted she had finished her sorbet, 'Coffee here or in the lounge?' he enquired.

'Lounge,' she opted. She knew she was being greedy, but

if they had coffee at the table it would not take long to drink, whereas if they went into the lounge perhaps they could linger a little while longer. And the plain truth was she never wanted the evening to end.

By a mutual sort of choice they returned to the seats they had used before. The lounge was fairly deserted, she noted, and that was fine by her. Nathan ordered coffee and turned to her.

'So who was he?' he asked casually.

'Who?' She was, for the moment, completely foxed.

'Your somebody special?'

'I don't have a "somebody special",' she replied honestly.

'Shame on you,' he scolded. 'Only this morning—while we were having coffee—you told me that there nearly was someone special.'

'Honestly!' she gasped. 'Do you forget nothing?'

'Not when it was plain you were trying to avoid talking about it.'

'I'm sorry. I must have made it sound too important,' she said lightly. She didn't want to tell him about Lee Thompson, so wouldn't.

'Was it important?' Nathan persisted.

Terrier, did she say? 'If you must know, he got away.'

'This was before I came on the scene?'

She was starting to get annoyed—and did not want to be. 'Yes,' she answered shortly.

Nathan leaned forward. 'You're lovely when you're cross,' he breathed.

What could she do? She burst out laughing. And he, as if enjoying seeing her laugh, studied her for a few more moments before sitting back in his chair again.

And suddenly she could not be annoyed with him any more. 'Lee Thompson. He was the gardener's son, home from university. We were going to be married.'

Nathan's brow shot up. 'The devil you were!' he exclaimed. 'You were lovers?' he demanded.

'I thought we were, but—um—not in the actual physical sense, if that's what you mean.'

Nathan relented, taking her naïvety back then on board with a kind look, but he still wanted to know all that there was to know, and he pressed, 'What happened?'

She had already come close to falling out with Nathan and she truly did not want that. So she took a deep breath and, there being only one way to say it, said, 'My father happened.'

'He didn't want you to marry?'

'I told him that Lee and I wanted to get married—he hit the roof.'

'How soon was this before I came on the scene?' Nathan asked, and Phelix knew then that he was, with his lightning brain, well on the way to sifting it all through.

'About a couple of weeks,' she filled in.

Nathan nodded. 'Your father wouldn't want you to be permanently married to anyone,' he said. He broke off as their coffee arrived, then continued, 'He wanted you in and out of marriage fast. Which wouldn't have happened had he let you marry a man of your own choosing.'

'I worked that out later.'

'What happened to Lee?'

Phelix wrinkled her nose in distaste. 'My father paid him off—with a bonus not to contact me, so Lee said when I phoned him. My father sacked his father at the same time. It was all very unpleasant.' She took a shaky breath as she recalled it all, but ploughed determinedly on, knowing by then that Nathan wanted to hear everything. And, after the way he had been treated, she overcame her inclination to hold back. 'Anyhow, in almost the next breath my father was telling me of the ten percent I would inherit if I married before I was twenty-five.'

'And you started to smell freedom from your father's tyranny?'

She wouldn't have put it quite like that. But tyranny, she supposed, was about right. 'Well, not at first. But a couple of days later, when he said he'd found someone for me to go through a marriage ceremony with—no strings—it didn't take me long to see that with money I could leave home and make a life for myself.' She smiled wryly. 'That simple! I could kick myself now, when I think of the hard time he gave my mother, when I think of how I knew how ruthless and uncaring he could be. Yet not once did I stop to wonder what was in it for him. Or why, when he had stopped me from marrying Lee Thompson, he was promoting that I should marry someone else. I just assumed he was tired of supporting me financially.'

'You were innocent of mind and everything else,' Nathan said gently. 'Add to that you were winded by Lee Thompson's defection, not to mention you were most likely still suffering trauma over your mother's death. You wouldn't have stood a chance of not being taken to the cleaners, so to speak.'

Phelix smiled at him. She loved his gentle tone. She loved him. She caught her breath. Heavens above, she'd be drooling over him in a minute!

'Anyhow,' she said brightly, while she sought to find some kind of a brain, 'you—um—knew. You soon saw that there was more to my father promoting an annulment than was showing on the surface.'

'I didn't know the what of it,' Nathan responded. 'But when he so blatantly welshed on an agreement we had shaken hands on, I was ready to put any spoke in his wheel that I could find.'

'You decided your only recourse was to tell him he could forget about the annulment?'

Nathan nodded cheerfully. 'I was working solely on instinct,' he recalled. 'And you played along magnificently.' Oh, my word, had she ever! 'Have you told him yet?' Nathan asked.

'Told him…?'

'That an annulment was on the cards after all?' he answered, a look of humour in his eyes.

She wanted to laugh. This love, her love for him, was making her light-headed. 'I'm saving that for our next big row,' she replied solemnly. But couldn't keep it up. She just had to laugh.

Nathan stared at her for long, long moments, and then his face was splitting into the most infectious smile. 'If I asked very nicely, would you let me be the one to tell him?' he asked.

'You have a wicked streak in you, Nathan Mallory,' she informed him, and loved him like crazy—and started to get scared of what it was doing to her. 'I think I'll go now,' she stated, and could not in all truth say whether she was glad or sorry when Nathan made no move to prevent her from returning to her room.

'I'll come with you,' he agreed. 'We're on the same floor.' She glanced at his bulky keyring on the table in front of them, noting that his room was but four doors down from hers.

Together they left the lounge area and took the lift to the fifth floor. She did not want to part from him, and tried to be sensible, but sense and love, she was discovering, had little in common.

'You're staying on until next week?' she queried politely.

'Might as well,' he replied. 'You?'

'I'm flying home next Tuesday.' All at once she began to feel a little uptight and, when they'd had no trouble conversing freely all evening, suddenly found she was having to search for something to say. 'It's beautiful here, though, isn't it?'

Thankfully the lift came to a halt, and they walked the short way to her room. Nathan had to pass her door to get to his own, but as they came to a halt outside her door, and her lips started to form the words to say goodnight, Nathan asked, 'Did you love him?'

Her green eyes shot to his. 'Who?' Her head was so full of the man she had married, it seemed to have slowed down her normally quick-thinking processes.

'Thompson? You were all set to marry him, remember? Did you love him?' Nathan repeated.

'No,' she replied, valuing honesty above all else. 'I told myself I did, of course. And my pride was bruised that I could be dumped for money. But in next to no time I was very much relieved that I hadn't married him. I—didn't love him.'

'Poor sweetheart,' Nathan murmured softly, and, if that wasn't enough to melt her bones, 'I'm sorry your pride was bruised,' he added. They gazed into each other's eyes, and the next moment he bent down and kissed her.

He did not otherwise touch her. With a hand on the doorframe at either side of her he gently, lingeringly, laid his lips not on her cheek, as before, but on hers. And she—she stood transfixed, her heart thundering— And was suddenly terrified that, in the absence of him putting his arms around her, she might put her arms around him—and hold him tight.

When at last he raised his head and, looking tenderly down into her slightly bemused face, took a small step back, Phelix was ready to faint away. 'I—er—had a lot of growing up to do,' she mumbled, from some semblance of her brain.

'You have, if I may say, done that beautifully,' he commented.

And she smiled, laughed delicately in her nervousness; the sophisticated image she had been at pains to show the world was absolutely nowhere in sight. 'You say the most wonderful things,' she said lightly, and, grabbing at a 'now or never' moment, 'Goodnight, Nathan,' she added quickly.

He looked at her as if he might kiss her again—she was going to give her imagination an almighty talking to—but instead took her key from her and opened up her door. 'Goodnight, Phelix,' he answered.

She did not wait for any more, but went smartly in and closed the door. Oh—heavens! His kiss—that light, lingering, yet passionless kiss—had been mind-blowing!

In something of a daze she went further into her room. The whole wonderful evening had been mind-blowing. Dreamily she started to relive moment after moment—and then her bedside telephone rang.

Nathan! Her heartbeats picked up again. Why Nathan would be ringing her when they had only just said goodnight she hadn't a clue, but she had to take a deep and steadying breath before she picked up the instrument.

'Hello,' she said huskily—and fell to earth with one enormous crash.

'What the hell game do you think you're playing?' roared her father in a none-too-dulcet tone.

No! No! She did not want to talk to him. *He spoilt things!* She did not want to come out from this bubble of near euphoria that had encompassed her.

'Good evening to you too, Father,' she replied, with a calmness brought about by many years of practice.

'I didn't have you booked into *that* hotel!' he bellowed.

'Well, it's very nice here. Was there any special reason you wanted me to stay elsewhere?' she enquired innocently.

'I've been trying to get hold of you!' he blazed on. 'When nobody seemed to have seen you I had no recourse but to ring Ross Dawson.'

Thank you, Ross. 'What did you want to contact me for?' Well, at least her father was not pretending not to know that Ross was there.

'Do I have to have a reason?'

Most definitely! 'Is everything all right at home?'

'No, it isn't all right! Grace has given notice!'

'Grace wants to leave?' Phelix was shocked.

'She's left!' he retorted irritably.

'Grace's left? But—'

'We had a row. I told her nobody talks to me like that—and off she went!'

'You mean—you sacked her?'

'No, I don't mean that!' he snapped—and Phelix guessed that was probably right. Blow up furiously at Grace he might, but he still valued her housekeeper skills too much to want to deprive himself of them. 'What have you been doing?' he demanded. 'Ross Dawson said he'd invited you to dinner and that you'd declined!' Thank you again, Ross! 'Why?' Edward Bradbury demanded. 'Surely even *you* can see the benefits of keeping in with the Dawson clan? Surely—'

'Actually,' she cut in, starting to feel slightly nauseated that her father saw everything from a monetary angle, 'I had dinner with somebody else.' As soon as the words were out she regretted them. This was private between her and Nathan. Their evening together had been good—it had been pretty near perfect—and her father seemed to make it his business to spoil everything.

'Who with?' As she should have known, he wasn't leaving it there.

But, perhaps because of her aversion to being anything like him, with his underhand ways, or maybe after that one mighty lie eight years ago, or it was her otherwise essential honesty, but Phelix had no intention of stooping to his level.

'If you must know, I had dinner with Nathan Mallory,' she told him up front.

For all of one second there was nothing but silence. But then, with a roar that threatened to perforate her eardrum. 'Nathan Mallory's *there*!' he exploded. Vesuvius had nothing on him. 'You've dined with him *tonight*?' he exclaimed, outraged.

'Very pleasantly,' she replied, calm under fire, and far from ready to deny something she thought of as good and decent—and more than a tiny bit sensational.

'Well, you just keep away from him!' Edward Bradbury thundered.

She was twenty-six, and this man who had done absolutely nothing for her except sire her thought he could suddenly come the heavy father! 'Any particular reason why I should?' she asked—to earn more of his wrath.

'He's not to be trusted!' he had the gall to hurl at her.

Talk about the pot becalling the kettle! She was astounded. 'I think he is!' she defended, and, getting angry despite all her efforts to stay calm, 'I also think I'm old enough to make my own decisions.'

'Don't you dare…' He began to threaten, but changed rapidly to demand, 'Are you saying that should Mallory ask you out again, despite me expressly forbidding you to accept, you'd go?'

Phelix had no idea if Nathan would ask her to have dinner with him again or not. But she had not the slightest intention of being brow-beaten by her father.

'That's exactly what I'm saying!' she retorted firmly.

And received another earful. 'We'll *bloody well* see about *that*!' Edward Bradbury shouted, and slammed down the phone.

CHAPTER FIVE

PHELIX awoke early on Thursday morning. She had not slept well, and some of the thoughts and worries that had plagued her after father's phone call were still unresolved.

She was too churned up to stay in bed, and went and took a shower, her head full of doubts, Nathan at the core. She thought of him—and knew that her father would spoil things for her with Nathan if he could. Not that there was anything to spoil, she reprimanded herself sharply. She'd had coffee with Nathan, and had enjoyed a wonderful dinner with him. He had lightly, if lingeringly, kissed her. But that could hardly be said to be any kind of a 'thing'.

She might be in love with him, but she was suddenly sure he would be amazed if he thought she had imagined anything more in that light kiss than he had intended.

And anyway, a kiss to her cheek and one light kiss to her mouth was no sort of a declaration. Nor, with her father and Lee Thompson being the two men who had attempted to mess up her life, was she anywhere certain that she wanted it to be. She might be twenty-six, but in the cold light of day she did not think she was ready for any sort of a relationship.

Self-preservation it might be, but she was wise enough to know that should the impossible happen, and Nathan might want to take things further, then she, the one in love, was the one who was going to get hurt—seriously hurt—when it came to an end.

Battling against memories of her gentle mother and the heartbreak she had suffered when she had fallen in love with Edward Bradbury, there was no way Phelix was going to go down that road. Needing to outrace her thoughts, she got into her swimsuit, donned the hotel's white bathrobe and went down to the hotel's swimming pool.

Phelix had swum ten lengths when she realised she was being ridiculous anyway. For one thing Nathan was nothing at all like her father, nor Lee Thompson. Oh, she didn't doubt that Nathan could be tough when his business demanded it, but she had seen his gentle side. But, for another, she was creating a problem where there just wasn't one. Nathan, though married to her he might be, just wasn't interested.

And that gave her pause for thought. How could he be interested when he could not possibly want to do anything that might block an easy 'out' of their marriage? *Oh!*

She had been treading water when someone swimming underwater grabbed a hold of her ankle, cutting off all thought, letting her know that she no longer had the pool to herself. But before she could sink too far under a pair of safe hands were at her waist, pulling her to the surface.

Breaking through the water, she shook her hair back from her face—to find she was looking straight into the mischievous laughing grey eyes of the man who consumed most of her thoughts.

'Good morning, Miss Bradbury,' Nathan greeted her, his hands still at her waist as they both trod water. In an instant, just seeing him negated every one of the anxieties that had awoken with her.

'You do realise it will take for ever for me to dry my hair,' she told him primly, her heart singing.

'You've nothing to hurry for,' he replied, unperturbed.

And she loved him, loved him, loved him. 'You didn't say you swam,' she commented, vaguely remembering that she had told him that she swam most mornings, but overwhelmingly aware of his broad naked chest and the dark wet hair clinging there.

'I've just taken it up,' he answered, his thighs brushing against her thighs, threatening to blow her mind.

'You brought your swimming gear with you?' And, sudden panic turning her insides over, 'You're not…?'

'In the buff?' He grinned. 'Relax, Phelix—there's a sports shop across the road.'

He'd purchased some swimming shorts yesterday! But with Nathan so near, his hard-muscled thighs brushing hers again, just the feel of his naked skin against her own skin was threatening to block out all thought.

'Well, I'd better—' she began edgily, never having imagined herself in this situation.

'Don't be alarmed, Phelix.' Nathan cut her off, every bit as if he knew that the intimacy of his near enough naked body next to hers was causing her to want to erect barriers. He let go of her. But as she swam to the side he swam to the side with her.

'I'll—er…' she began, starting to clamber out of the pool. 'I'll see you later.' That sounded too much as if she was trying to make a date with him. Oh, grief! 'At the conference—er—probably—'

'Or,' he cut in, treading water, his grey eyes taking in her long-legged shapely form prior to his gaze meeting hers, 'Or we could both bunk off and spend the day…'

Phelix abruptly turned from him. Suddenly, while happily knowing that there was nothing wrong with her shape and size, she began to feel totally vulnerable. Hastily taking up one of the towels set out for use, she wrapped it round her head and shrugged quickly into her towelling robe. Only then did she feel able to consider what was on offer.

In actual fact there was no contest. When it came to sitting in that conference hall, trying to keep her thoughts from straying, and the choice of 'bunking off' to spend the day with Nathan Mallory, the conference did not stand a chance.

Suitably towelled and robed, she took a deep breath—but went to pieces again as Nathan got out of the water too and reached for a towel. Oh, heavens, he was magnificent.

'I—er—promised I'd have lunch with Ross Dawson!' she found, out of an entirely woolly head.

'The hell you did!' Nathan rapped sharply.

'It was that or dinner last night.'

'In that case I'll forgive you,' he relented, and, with a smile that made her too weak to refuse any other offer he made, 'I've some business to take care of first. How about I call for you around ten? I'll take you to this place I know for coffee. Put your flat shoes on,' he instructed.

She thought, only briefly, of telling him of her father's call. But her father had no part in this—whatever this was. 'You're on,' she agreed, and felt a need to kiss him, and wondered if she had completely lost her senses. 'See you,' she said quickly, and got out of there.

It seemed hours to go before ten. But she put those hours to good use. She showered and shampooed her hair, used the bathroom hairdryer to good effect—but then she began to have doubts. When she was with Nathan everything seemed so right, nothing worrying or complicated. But the minute she was away from him doubts seemed to rain their spiteful darts down on her.

What she was doubting, she was not sure. Nathan wasn't asking her to rob a bank or do anything criminal. All he was asking, in the absence of her being able to spend the day with him, was that he take her for coffee—flat shoes required. Given that her father would be furious if he ever heard she wasn't 'networking', what could be more innocent than that? With any man other than Nathan she would not have wasted a moment considering the ifs, ands or buts, but would have gone along with the idea or not, as she fancied. Love, she was discovering, when at war with the strait-laced emotion-stifled austerity of her upbringing, was a string-jerking puppet master.

Deciding to leave ferreting away and not to give doubt another chance, Phelix instead channelled her thoughts to Grace. There was no way Grace could be allowed to leave just like that! Phelix determined to get in touch with her as soon as she could. Grace always made certain Phelix had her friend's telephone number whenever she went to stay with her. Midge was sure to have heard from her. Phelix decided to give Midge a ring when she was back in London.

Intent on thinking only of what she must do with regard to Grace, Phelix suddenly found she was wondering had Nathan purchased his swimwear especially because he knew that she swam most mornings? Surely not! She was being fanciful. As if he would! The poor man just felt like some exercise, that was all. For heaven's sake, get your act together!

Unsure what strange intuition was putting such weird notions into her head, Phelix left her room and went down to breakfast. She half hoped—didn't hope—that Nathan might be in the breakfast dining room. And did not know whether she was glad or sorry when there was no sign of him. Quite plainly he'd either had breakfast or was having a working breakfast in his room.

The notion that he probably felt like some exercise was borne out, though, when at ten o'clock he tapped on her door and, when she opened it, glanced down to her flat-heeled shoes and nodded approvingly.

'Fancy a walk up a mountain?' he asked.

Her lips parted in surprise. She saw him glance to her mouth—the mouth he had last night kissed—and she tried desperately to get her head together. He only had to look at her and she was just so much jelly.

'The same one we walked down yesterday?' she enquired, somehow managing to make her voice sound even. So *that* was where this place was that he knew for coffee.

'You'll enjoy it,' he stated.

It had taken them over half an hour to walk down. Heaven alone knew how much longer it would take them to walk up. 'I'm sure,' she murmured, and left the hotel with him, to walk some way along the Promenade until they found the path that would lead them ever upward.

They set off walking steadily up the zig-zag path, sometimes exchanging conversation and sometimes not. And it was all too fantastic for Phelix. She wanted to store up this time she spent with him. To enjoy it and to look back on it with no regrets. She would be leaving on Tuesday—it was highly unlikely that she would see him again after that.

She had been reluctant to attend the conference, but these last two days—yesterday and today—had been magical. Yesterday Nathan had followed her…

'Yesterday,' she plunged, before she had thought it through—and was then committed to going on. 'Given that I've talked and talked about my side of our—er—marriage bargain…' She wished she hadn't got started, but too late now—she would look foolish if she stopped. 'Was that why you followed me? Because you wanted to know about why I work for my father—about…er…?' Her voice tailed off. Of course it was, idiot! What else could it have been? Heavens, she had talked so much he must have had earache.

'Tell me about Henry,' Nathan suggested, before she should feel more idiotic than she already did.

That stopped her dead in her tracks. 'Henry Scott?' she stood rooted to ask.

Nathan halted too. 'Henry Scott,' he agreed.

'Henry…' She began to walk on, and Nathan fell into step with her. At first she thought he had thrown Henry into the conversation because, perhaps noticing that she was feeling a little foolish, he was merely changing the subject.

But, glancing at Nathan, she saw there was something in the serious look of him that seemed to more than suggest to her that his question about Henry was not without purpose, that he really wanted to know about him.

'Was Henry some of the reason you followed me yesterday?' she asked. With Nathan looking so sort of determined somehow, it struck her then that Henry seemed to have a great deal to do with why Nathan had followed her. Though for the life of her she couldn't think why.

'I'd like to hear more about him.'

'You do know that Henry has my absolute loyalty…?'

'As I suspect you have his,' Nathan inserted.

'True,' she agreed, and, that established, 'So what do you want to know that, given those parameters, I can tell you?'

'You said you loved him, and I've taken it as a two-way feeling.'

That seemed to her to be more about her and Henry than just Henry. But she could see no reason not to reply. 'Henry looked out for my mother. He…'

'They were having an affair?'

'No!' Phelix exclaimed sharply. But calmed down to add, 'No, I'm sure not. It was just that, well, her life wasn't easy. She was much too gentle a person to be married to a man like my father. And Henry—he was always sort of there for her. He recognised that gentleness in her, and cared for her. When she died he transferred that caring on to me.' Phelix broke off as she recalled the many times that Henry had metaphorically held her hand. 'I'd have been lost without Henry so many times. Not just in business, but things were pretty bleak when my mother died. He always seemed to be there in my down moments.'

'Not your father?'

As if! 'What's your interest in Henry?' she asked, ignoring the question. Nathan knew the answer anyway, she felt sure.

'He knows,' Nathan replied.

'Who knows?'

'Henry.'

'Knows what?' she queried, having lost him somewhere.

'Henry Scott knows that I'm the man you married,' he stated, as if he absolutely knew that for a fact.

That stopped her dead in her tracks again. 'He can't know!' she protested. 'I didn't tell him—didn't tell anybody!' Nathan still looked absolutely certain. 'How do you think you know he knows?' she challenged, winded by just the thought of it.

They had come to a halt by a thoughtfully placed bench. Nathan took hold of her arm and led her over to it. By unspoken mutual consent they took their ease on it. 'Something you said on Tuesday set me thinking,' he said, to enlighten her.

From where Phelix was seeing it, she hadn't a clue what she had said on Tuesday that had given him pause to think that Henry knew the name of the man she had married. 'When we were in that park next to the conference centre?' she asked, realising that it had to be there, because apart from exchanging a few courtesy words of greeting on Tuesday morning they hadn't had any other conversation that day. Nathan nodded confirmation anyway, and she just had to ask, 'What? What did I say that set you thinking?'

Nathan looked into the distance. It was another beautiful day, the view as magnificent as ever. 'A couple of things, actually,' he responded after a few seconds. 'You said Henry knew you were very upset over the way your marriage partner had been treated. You also said that Henry seemed to know everyone and…'

'You thought from that that Henry had guessed the name of the man I'd married the day before?' How, for goodness' sake?

'Not then—that was a side issue,' Nathan replied. 'But when I tied it in with other matters—that he should know my name and want to do something on your behalf to honour a deal that you, by the sound of it, were feeling so wretched about—it all started to slot in most convincingly.'

'It's been said,' Phelix chipped in dryly, 'that I have quite a bright head on my shoulders. So why haven't I a clue what you're talking about?'

Nathan turned and gave her that half smile that turned her bones to water. 'Probably because you don't know the half of it,' he said softly.

Oh, Nathan! Swiftly she stiffened her limpid spine. 'But you're going to tell me?'

He nodded. 'I've been examining the facts. One—Henry thinks the world of you. Two—he knew you were upset. I'm sure you would have confided in him about the Lee Thompson affair?' Phelix nodded confirmation, and Nathan went on. 'From that Henry would know that your father had sold you twice—or would have, had he not shot himself in the foot, so to speak, by not paying up the second time. Point three—and I'm guessing here—you told Henry how you'd offered me all of that ten percent of your inheritance and—'

'I did—and that you'd refused to take it.'

Nathan took that on board, and said, 'From my small dealings with Henry Scott, I would say that he is a most honourable man.'

'He is!' Phelix exclaimed. 'He's one of the finest men I know.'

Nathan gave a brief nod. 'Which would make him want to do whatever he could on your behalf to repair the situation.'

'You think so?'

'I've been certain of it ever since Tuesday,' Nathan replied.

'When I said Henry knew I was upset over the way you were treated?'

'And how Henry seemed to know everyone,' Nathan confirmed, going on, 'You may remember that your father and the deal I made with him was my last-ditch desperate attempt to save my company...'

'Oh, Nathan!'

'Don't!' he said sharply. 'You are in no way to blame.' She wanted to say thank you, but suddenly felt too choked to speak. 'Anyhow, I was sunk, or thought I was. My father and I were on the verge of ruin with nothing more I could do about it. Then, just two days later with just about twenty-four hours to go before I must make an announcement that Mallory and Mallory were finished, a note was delivered to my home that started to give me hope.'

'A note?' she repeated, starting to be even more intrigued. 'Who from?'

'It was unsigned. I never discovered who from,' he answered. 'By the time I'd read it, the despatch rider who had delivered it was roaring away on his motorbike.' He paused for a moment to mention, 'In those early days I was too busy getting the firm afloat again to over-worry about who had sent it.'

'You just got on with it, head down, no time to look at side issues?'

'That's about it,' Nathan acknowledged. 'I've wanted many times in more recent years to find out who sent that note, but the trail has long gone cold,' he revealed. And then he asked, 'Ever heard of a man named Oscar Livingstone?'

Who hadn't? 'He's some sort of arts philanthropist—er—a theatre backer,' she replied. And added innocently, quite unprepared for Nathan's reaction, 'Henry was up at Oxford with him.'

'I *knew* it!' Nathan exclaimed, and suddenly she was feeling the benefit of his full smile head on. 'I *knew* it!' he repeated, and the next she knew Nathan had caught a hold of her shoulders, pulled her to him, and was planting an exuberant kiss on her slightly parted lips.

She had to smile, she just had to. 'I wish I *knew* it,' she said lightly, feeling quite bemused.

And could not believe it when Nathan divulged, 'Oscar Livingstone at that time—totally unbeknown to me or to anyone who didn't know him well—was also looking to invest in a company that, while having potential to go places, was struggling to make it.'

She stared at him wide-eyed. 'Oscar Livingstone invested in your company?' she asked, startled.

'We could never have made it without him.'

'But…' She was stunned.

'Exactly! How did he hear about us? My father and I had been keeping the state of our finances very quiet. Only obviously your father somehow knew how truly dire our situation was.'

'And my father was unlikely to put your name—his competitor—forward.'

'Understatement of the year,' Nathan commented shortly, but added, 'Oscar Livingstone would not reveal who it was who had put our name forward. But it was your man Henry. I'm convinced of it.'

Phelix would love it to have been Henry, but did not see how it could have been. 'H-how…?' She was too shaken to work it out, but tried anyway. 'I mentioned on Tuesday that Henry seemed to know everyone.' She went through it piece by piece. 'I also said how I'd told Henry how very upset I was over the way you had been treated. And…'

'And Henry, I'm guessing, would want to do whatever he could to put that right for you.' Nathan helped her out.

'You think so?'

'I'm sure of it the more I think about it. And for all I was initially too over-worked to have time to do anything but be grateful that somebody else *had* interfered, I've never forgotten or ceased to be grateful.'

'But—how…?'

'How did he know it was me you had married the day before?' Nathan asked, and answered, 'By the simplest of methods. He had the date; all he had to do was nip into the register office and ask to see the current register to find out who. In no time he would have discovered not only the name of the man who had been married to Phelix Elizabeth Bradbury on that date, but also the man's home address and his occupation—the rest of his enquiries would follow on easily.'

'Good heav… Why didn't I think of that?'

'There was no need for you to think of it. As it was, without your knowing it, by confiding everything to Henry you did more than repair the damage. A day afterwards, presumably after Henry had checked me out, I received an anonymous note saying, "Oscar Livingstone is waiting to take your call." There followed what I now know to be Oscar Livingstone's private telephone number.'

'You rang it?'

'I was desperate. If it was a hoax, so be it. I rang it,' Nathan confirmed, 'and was never more glad that I did when the great man invited my father and I in for a chat.'

'He backed you?'

'He backed us, but refused to be drawn as to who had told him about us.'

Phelix looked at him with shining eyes. 'It had to be Henry,' she said.

'That's what I think,' Nathan answered with a gentle look for her. He stretched out a hand as though about to touch her face. But abruptly drew back and got to his feet. 'Coffee,' he said decisively.

Together they climbed the rest of the way up to the restaurant area. Each busy with their own thoughts, they said little.

Phelix's head was full of what Nathan had told her. Henry—good, kind, wonderful Henry. He had known how very dreadful she had been feeling about Nathan, had known when she had told him how she had offered Nathan all of her ten percent that she would want to do anything she could to recompense him. And by the simplest of methods, having discovered the name of the man she had married—for she had only said that the man she'd married was a businessman undergoing severe financial problems—Henry had done what he could to fully redeem her honour.

They reached the plateau and, the sun shining brilliantly, again opted to have their coffee outside. 'I'm still trying to take it in,' she said as the waitress brought their coffee.

'You'll adjust,' Nathan assured her.

'Have you?' she asked. 'You've had two days in which to get your head together. Have you adjusted yet?'

'More settled than adjusted, I think,' Nathan replied. And then asked, 'Is this just between you and me, Phelix?'

She thought about it. It was such a wonderful thing Henry had done, she did not think she could just—let it go. 'May I not thank Henry?' she questioned sincerely.

'You'd keep it to yourself just for me?' Nathan asked, his grey eyes warm on her green ones.

'If you insist,' she replied quietly, her heart starting to pound at the warmth in his look for her.

Nathan did not insist, but asked, 'Would you let me know when you've thanked him?' And her heart pounded the more. Because she had been certain that after next Tuesday, if not before, all her contact with Nathan would end. But here he was, asking that she let him know, and since she would not have chance to personally thank Henry until she went into the office the following Wednesday, she would at least be in telephone contact with Nathan. 'I'd like to thank him myself.'

'Of course,' she murmured.

Her defences were already down, she was ready to melt under Nathan's warm regard, and so was rendered utterly speechless when, quite out of the blue, 'Would you take my heart, Phelix?' he asked softly.

With her own heart thundering against her ribs, she stared at him. But, confusion reigning, she had to glance away. Down to the table—which in actual fact was most fortunate. Because only then was she able to see the plastic-wrapped heart-shaped biscuit he was offering.

Not trusting her voice, she shook her head. Oh, what an idiot love had made her! As if Nathan would ever truly offer her his heart! It took her a few moments to gather sufficient control to be able to murmur lightly, 'Don't want to spoil my appetite for lunch.' She flicked a glance to his face and saw that his warm look had disappeared, to be replaced by a stern look. She thought for one inane moment that he was annoyed, or jealous, even, that she was lunching with Ross Dawson.

Her imagination was having one hysterically mad field-day, she soon realised. Honestly! Though she felt a little better when, his stern look gone, 'I refuse to allow you to have lunch *and* dinner with Dawson,' Nathan told her forthrightly.

Was he asking her to have dinner with him that night? Oh what should she do? What she did—since the only communication she might have with Nathan after she left Switzerland would be that telephone call to confirm that she had thanked Henry—was to decide at that very moment that she was going to see as much as she possibly could of Nathan, and enjoy every second of it.

'If you're very good, I'll take you to dinner tonight,' she invited prettily.

He stared into her laughing eyes. 'Call for me at seven,' he accepted.

Shortly afterwards Phelix glanced at her watch. 'I'd better start making tracks,' she said lightly. She knew she was being greedy, but she did not want to start 'making tracks.' She wanted to spend more time with Nathan. She looked at him, this man she had married, and her insides somersaulted. 'I'd—er—better take the funicular down,' she added brightly, striving for some sort of normality, striving to hide the least suspicion of a love-light in her eyes.

Together they descended, and well within the next ten minutes they were standing together on the pavement of the Promenade. 'Coming this way?' Nathan asked when she hesitated. He was half turned towards the conference centre.

She denied herself the pleasure. 'I'd better pop back to the hotel and freshen up.'

Nathan looked at her long and hard. 'You do realise that you're my wife,' he murmured, more as though to himself than to her—and her heart started playing a merry tune once more.

'Which leaves me with certain privileges,' she answered lightly. And some creature within her with whom she had never been acquainted before suddenly took charge, and Phelix did no more than reach up and kiss him—and did not know which one of them was the more surprised, him or her. 'Er—thanks for the coffee,' she said quickly, and turned hastily about.

She was still wondering about this new and impulsive creature love had turned her into when she reached the sanctuary of her room. Good heavens, they just weren't 'kissing' husband and wife! Though it was true Nathan had kissed her a couple of times.

But she must not read anything into that, she counselled, as she changed into a smart trouser suit and a crisp white shirt. Not that she wanted 'anything' to *be* in it.

As before, Phelix stated to worry about her friendship with Nathan. Everything seemed so right when she was with him. But the moment they parted she began to wonder if she had given away her feelings for him. She would just die if she had, and did not doubt that if Nathan had seen how she felt about him, he would be consulting a divorce lawyer the first chance he had.

He did not want her love. And, on thinking about it, she did not want to give it to him. She knew that she didn't have too much faith in men—though she would never forget Nathan's gentleness with her on their wedding night, or rather, the night following their marriage. She found she was wondering what kind of a lover he would be—and hastily brought herself up short.

Good heavens! What on earth was going on in her head? All his fault of course, but he did have the most wonderful mouth! She recalled his bare chest down at the pool that morning, his long straight legs when he'd got out of the pool and stood with her, water hanging on one of his nipples. For heaven's sake…!

As if to escape the demons that had been nowhere a part of her until she had become reacquainted with Nathan Mallory, Phelix hastily left her room.

She went quickly along the Promenade and decided that she would cancel her dinner date with Nathan that night. Then she countermanded that notion. Botheration, she loved him! Tuesday would come too soon, and with it her return to England. She should be glad about that. Perhaps once she was back in her old routine everything would settle down again.

But she had tasted the uplift of spirits that came each time she saw the man she loved. The welter of emotions, highs and lows, that came with being with him and with not being with him. Life, she knew, was going to be very dull when she lost all chance of seeing Nathan again.

She half wished that she had not come to Davos. That she had not seen him again. Were it not for one of his scientists being unable to make the trip, she would not have seen him.

But how could she half-wish anything of the kind? Until she had fallen in love with him she had been asleep. Falling in love with Nathan had brought her awake—made her feel alive. Just thinking about him made her…

But she would settle down again. She would have to, she resolved. She had a good career. Under Henry's guidance… Oh, how could she ever have forgotten Henry? Dear, kind, good Henry. It was the things Henry did, the way he behaved, that time and time again had restored her faith that there were good men around.

Instinctively she wanted to telephone him and thank him from the bottom of her heart for what he had done. She somehow knew without question that it was Henry who had instigated the saving of Mallory and Mallory.

But this was too big for a telephone call. She needed to thank him in person. And would, the first chance she had.

Meantime, she had to meet Ross Dawson for lunch. Only somehow lunch with Ross did not have the same thrill as dinner with Nathan. 'Call for me at seven,' he had said.

A smile curved her lips—she could hardly wait.

CHAPTER SIX

HER lunch with Ross Dawson was a pleasant enough affair. 'I didn't see you at the conference this morning?' he more enquired than commented as soon as they were seated.

'Was it interesting?' Phelix evaded. There was no reason why she could not have told him that she had walked a good way up a mountain to have a cup of coffee. But he might ask who with, and somehow her time with Nathan was special and private.

'It'll be more interesting next week when the top boys from JEPC Holdings hit town.'

'So I believe,' she replied. If Ross was fishing to find out how much she knew then he was going to be disappointed. Apart from the fact that she knew only the bare bones of the outsourcing contract that was said to be in the offing, she did, regardless of her father's doubts, have a certain loyalty to her father's company.

'Did your father manage to get you last night?' Ross, seeing he was getting nowhere with his feelers, changed the subject.

'He did. Thanks for letting him know where to find me,' she answered lightly. There was no need for Ross to know that her relationship with her father was not what she would have wished. She had not forgotten her father's furious 'We'll see about that!' when she'd said she would go out with Nathan

Mallory again should he ask her. Though what he thought he could do about it, she failed to see.

She and Ross chatted amicably through their meal. But as they left the dining room, 'Fancy dodging out of the conference this afternoon?' he asked.

'What sort of a girl do you think I am?' she asked, and had to laugh when Ross replied he knew what sort of a girl he'd like her to be.

Her laughter died when, out of nowhere, it seemed, there was Nathan Mallory! She saw him favour Ross Dawson with a stern look, though he was quite pleasant to him when he asked, 'Good lunch?'

'Depends who you're with,' Ross replied with a warm look to her.

Nathan gave a small inclination of his head to acknowledge her, and walked on by. Somehow, her insides in knots again just from seeing him, Phelix carried on walking as if she hadn't a care in the world. But she was giving serious thought to going home to England. It had been less than a couple of hours since she had last seen him, for goodness' sake, and just seeing him again was making her feel all over the place. She had grown used to being the one in control of her life, but that control appeared to be slipping. It was very off-putting!

She saw Nathan again that afternoon. He was with other people but glanced over to her, and seemed about to smile. Phelix inclined her head a little to return the compliment, and saw him grin—and felt a huge mirthful grin of her own coming on; her lips tweaked but she hastily looked away. Honestly—what was this man doing to her?

Having deflected Ross Dawson's hope that she would have dinner with him that night, Phelix left the conference at the end of the afternoon session and—deny it though she might try, toy with the notion of haring back to England though she had—she knew that she wanted nothing more than to see Nathan again. And, joy of joys, in a very few hours that was exactly what she would do.

She walked smartly back to her hotel, wishing she had brought a more extensive wardrobe with her. Perhaps tomorrow she would cut the conference—her father would have a fit—and go in search of a dress shop.

She was taking a shower when she started to laugh at herself for her own idiocy. Oh, my word. Nathan hadn't even asked her out tomorrow evening, and already she was planning to update her wardrobe! Serve her right if he decided that dinner two nights in succession was more than enough. And yet that grin this afternoon, and her response to it. Was it just she who had felt a moment of magic in the air between them?

Her phone was ringing as she left the bathroom. She paused, took time out to swallow down a spasm of nervousness—it might just be him—and picked up the phone.

'Hello?' she enquired nicely—and had her dream shattered!

'Phelix?' Edward Bradbury barked.

Her father! Her spirits plummeted. 'Yes,' she replied.

'You'd better come along here and meet me,' he ordered.

She sank down on the bed, his 'We'll see about that' of last night taking on ominous reality. 'Where—are you?' she managed to ask, hoping against hope.

'In the hotel where you're supposed to be!'

'You've flown in…?'

'We've important business to discuss. You can have your dinner here. We'll—'

She started to recover. 'I've already arranged to have dinner elsewhere.'

'Perhaps you didn't hear me. We have business to discuss!'

'Perhaps you didn't hear *me*. I'm having dinner here.'

There was a moment's tense silence. 'Very well,' Edward

Bradbury agreed disagreeably, and she thought for one lovely moment that he was giving in. She should have known better. Because, shrewdly taking it that she was not intending to dine alone, 'You'd better get your hotel to change your reservation to dinner for three,' he rapped.

Sadly, she had never been able to grow to like him, and just then she positively disliked him. 'I'll come to you,' she said woodenly, and could have wept.

Having yet again established his power to manipulate, he had nothing more to say, and Phelix put down her phone knowing that to give in had been the only thing she could have done. To share dinner with Nathan *and* her father was unthinkable. And, after the way her father had behaved to Nathan, she was astounded that he would have had the gall to impose himself on their table—for there was no doubt in her mind that her father knew that she had planned to dine again with the man he had arranged for her to marry.

She took off her robe and dressed without enthusiasm in the green dress she had worn two nights ago, when she had dined with Ross Dawson.

Hastily pulling a brush through her hair, she knew she should not delay in contacting Nathan to tell him of her change of plan. She had no idea of how he would react—more than likely shrug his shoulders and arrange to dine with someone else. But what option did she have? Her father would spoil everything. And, while she had little idea of what 'everything' was, all she knew was that she wanted to laugh with Nathan again and be happy just to be with him again—and that just wasn't going to happen with her father present.

She thought about telephoning Nathan, but, perhaps because she was already hungry for the sight of him again, she opted to go along to his room.

His room was but a few steps down from her own, but she

had started to feel anxious before she had taken more than a couple of paces in that direction.

She knocked on his door and endeavoured to put a 'not too much put out' expression on her face. Nathan, shirt and trouser-clad, came to the door. She thought he was about to smile when he saw her, but he did not, so she concluded he had either not been going to smile or had picked up that something was a trifle amiss.

'Would you like to come in while I get my shoes on?' he enquired, when for the moment she had lost her voice.

He thought she had come early to call for him! 'I—er—can't make dinner after all!' she found her voice to tell him in a rush. Oh, how dear he was to her; she could have cried.

Still he did not smile but studied her face for a second or so before enquiring, 'Had a better offer?'

She supposed that was preferable than his just saying fine and closing the door in her face.

'M-my father's here,' she stammered, wanting it said and done—though she did not care at all for the hostile expression with which Nathan greeted the news.

He said nothing, however, of the fact that Edward Bradbury was in town about five days early, but queried, 'Here? At this hotel?'

'No, no,' Phelix replied.

But before she could go on, 'And this has got what, exactly, to do with me?' Nathan asked coolly—and something inside her froze.

She had said what she had come to say. There was nothing more she could add. Pride came to her aid and up went her chin. 'Not a thing,' she replied, her tone coldly aloof, and turned abruptly about and went quickly back to her own room. His door had slammed hard shut before she got there.

It was the end, and she knew it. She was dining with her

father because she did not want him to spoil this—this nebulous thing, this, her time with Nathan. But it was spoilt already. Nathan was unlikely to ask her to dine with him again. And, after the way he had just so decisively closed the door, neither would she ask him.

She drove to her father's hotel, wanting her dinner with him to be over and done with as quickly as possible. She could barely remember the last time she and her father had sat down and shared a meal together—and they lived in the same house!

He was in the lounge studying some papers when she went in. There were other people there who must know who he was, but—and she thought it was so sad—her father was sitting alone.

Although, on reflection, anyone who approached him when he was reading through matters financial was bound to receive short shrift.

'Father,' she said, standing in front of him.

He did not stand up to kiss her cheek in greeting—she'd have died on the spot if he had. But, indicating the seat opposite, 'Sit down,' he said.

'Good journey?' she enquired politely. She should have known better. They just did not do small talk.

'What's Mallory doing here?' he demanded, and was at his churlish worst.

'The same as you, I shouldn't wonder,' she responded—other fathers doted on their daughters; fat chance!

'I forbid you to see him again,' he attempted brusquely.

'You gave up the right to forbid me to do anything on the day I married him and ceased to be your responsibility!' she answered, her tone low. She was conscious, unlike him, of other people around.

'Hmmph,' he grunted, and still trying to bully her, 'While you're living under my roof—' he began, but stopped when—

as a new and wonderful thought suddenly struck her—Phelix's expression lightened and she started to smile.

'If I can't persuade Grace to come back, it could be I won't be living under your roof for very much longer,' she stated.

'Don't be ridiculous!'

She refused to be crushed. 'Look, do we need to carry on with this farce of a dinner?'

'You've cancelled your arrangement with Mallory?' She nodded—and saw from what passed as his smile that she had at last done something to please her father. The smile did not last. 'So what have you discovered?' he wanted to know.

'About what?'

'You've been here since Monday! Surely you've picked up something about what's going off with the outsourcing deal?'

Now did not seem an appropriate time to tell him that not only had she cut quite a few of the speeches and lectures, but also had not mingled to eavesdrop. 'Everyone seems to be playing their cards very close to their chests,' she replied instead. And, thinking of the evening she had given up and the limited chances she would have of seeing Nathan now that her father was here, she was suddenly totally fed up with this verbal sparring. 'You said you had business you wanted to discuss. What business would that be?' she enquired, knowing in advance that her father was far more likely to arrange a meeting with Henry than with her on anything to do with matters legal.

Her father looked away from her, someone just coming in catching his eye. 'Ah, here's Ross!' he exclaimed, a welcoming smile on his face. 'I've invited him to join us.'

It would not have taken much for Phelix to walk out there and then. She had given up her evening with Nathan in order to avoid an unpleasant threesome dinner at her hotel, and all along her father had planned this! If nothing else, it was embarrassing.

Good manners instilled in her by her mother came to her aid. 'Surprised to see me?' Ross asked, his eyes twinkling with pleasure at her father's invitation that he join them.

'Always a joy to see you, Ross,' she replied, and did not know if she was glad or sorry that he was there. With Ross in attendance there was no way her father was going to discuss business. On the other hand, since she and her father had never gone in for small talk, Ross's presence might help the evening along.

But oh, how much better the evening would have been had she not had to come here at all! Had she followed her instinct she would have got out of there there and then, leaving her father with Ross for a dinner companion—that would obviate her father turning up at her hotel. But, the die cast, she could hardly speed back to her hotel and knock on Nathan's door and tell him that their dinner together was on after all. Besides, after his cool 'And this has got what, exactly, to do with me?' there was no way her pride would allow her to do anything of the sort. And in any case, he would by now most likely have found himself another dinner companion.

Phelix did not like that last thought, and so turned to Ross and tried to pretend that she was glad they had met up again.

She discovered that she had little appetite for food, but while her father and Ross skated around business issues she entered the conversation whenever she felt called upon to do so. But her heart wasn't in it. Her mind for the most part was back at the Schweizerhof with Nathan. The whole of her heart back there with him.

They were midway through their main course when such a terrible yearning came over her to be with Nathan that when she saw him enter the dining room she thought for a moment that it was purely her imagination that had conjured him up.

But it was not her imagination, it was him and, after a dark glance to her table when he surveyed her two escorts, he did no more than start to make his way over to them.

Her heart rejoiced. Her insides might be acting up like nobody's business, but her heart rejoiced just to see him. He was on his own, not a blonde, a redhead or a brunette of her imaginings in sight. Would he ignore her? Should she ignore him? Would he walk by without a word?

She averted her gaze, adopted a distant air as if it mattered not one single bit to her if he ignored her. But, while she was very much aware of him nearing their table, she would not have been at all surprised had he arrogantly walked on by.

But he did not walk past, and nor did he ignore her. And, while her insides were having one wild time within her, he did no more than stop directly at their table.

Ignoring her father, he nodded briefly to Ross, and then, his dark expression disappearing as he transferred his gaze to her, 'Meet me for a drink after your dinner,' he invited.

Her heart was pounding so loudly she was surprised no one could hear it. As it was, she had about one second in which to forgive him his previous cool manner with her before he strode on. She loved him—love forgave all.

'That would be—nice,' she accepted. Nice! It would be marvellous!

But as usual her father was there, to attempt to exert his power over her. 'My daughter has business to discuss. It will be too late...'

Nathan ignored him and, to make her insides flip, he caught a hold of her left hand. And did no more than lift it to his lips and, exactly where her wedding band rested, he kissed it. 'I'll wait,' he said, and was gone.

Phelix was still on cloud nine, and her father still furious, so it was Ross who was the first to recover from the small but unexpected scene. 'How well do you know Nathan Mallory?'

he asked, looking a shade put out that she had agreed to have a drink with another man while she was dining with him.

'As Nathan mentioned, we know each other from way back.'

'You two have history?' Ross wanted to know.

'Good heavens, no!' Edward Bradbury chipped in. 'Phelix is just too polite to say no to one of our competitors.'

'She's said no to me,' Ross grumbled.

'She's just playing hard to get,' Edward Bradbury mollified him, as though she wasn't there. Phelix cared not—Nathan had forgiven her, he was no longer cool towards her, and, best yet, she would see him later.

Though, if her father had anything to do with it, later would be too late. He was in no hurry to finish his meal, and was insistent that they had an after-dinner brandy or two.

'I'm driving,' she refused.

'Then you'll stay and have coffee,' he asserted. And for Ross's benefit, 'Your poor old dad hasn't seen you all week!'

Feeling sickened at the hypocrisy of it, only good manners in front of Ross Dawson prevented her from telling her 'poor old dad' that she didn't remember seeing much of him the previous week, or the week before that for that matter.

But, given that she was yearning to be elsewhere, Ross Dawson was good company, and as they returned to the lounge he gave Edward Bradbury colourful highlights of some of the speakers and their speeches.

'You must be tired after your journey.' Phelix addressed her father when she thought, all proprieties observed, that she had spent a long enough time with them. If she didn't get a move on Nathan would begin to think she had changed her mind about having that drink with him. She had assumed, in fact was pretty certain, that he had meant that drink to be back at their hotel. She just could not bear to think that he might have given up on her and gone to bed.

'Not at all!' her father answered robustly.

'Well, I'd better make tracks…'

'I've brought some paperwork with me I need to go through with you,' he announced. Phelix looked pointedly at her watch.

It had gone eleven-thirty by the time she thought she had been quite polite enough. She had said goodnight to Ross and had accompanied her father to his suite, where he had shown her paperwork she had already seen and then discussed at great length pieces of work that were entirely nothing to do with her. All, she knew, in an attempt to prevent her from having that drink with Nathan Mallory.

Frustrated by the nonsense of it beyond bearing, she told her father bluntly that she saw little point in delaying going back to her hotel.

'What about Ross Dawson?' he demanded.

'What about him?'

'He wants to marry you! It would be a tremendous advantage to—'

'Forget it, Father. I will never, *ever* marry Ross Dawson.'

'You're being unreasonable!' Edward Bradbury erupted angrily. 'Ross is a fine man. He'll—'

'I'm well aware of what Ross is,' she butted in. 'And I agree that he's a fine man. But he's not my man. I will *not*,' she emphasised, 'ever marry him.'

'You'd rather stay married to that—that—'

Her father was starting to grow apoplectic. 'His name is Nathan Mallory,' she interrupted him calmly. 'And I'm going—'

'You're going back to have a drink with him!' he blasted her, outraged at not getting his own way, furious at the fading picture of Bradbury, Dawson and Cross.

'If he hasn't got tired of waiting.'

'Let's hope he has,' he spat. 'He's no good to you!'

And you are? 'Goodnight, Father,'

'Watch him—he'll stop at nothing get back at me!' he rapped, and, when that did not dent her, 'You be here first thing in the morning!' he ordered, and turned his back on her.

It was nearing midnight when Phelix, her car parked, entered her hotel. She felt near to tears knowing that she would be wasting her time going to the bar. Nathan would not be there.

He wasn't in the bar. Where he was, was in the adjoining lounge area. Hardly believing it, she saw him stand up as soon as he saw her, and she hurried over to him, her heart singing. 'I didn't think you'd be here!' she said in a rush.

'I said I'd wait,' he replied, his eyes taking in the anxiety in her eyes. 'Come and sit down,' he suggested, and a second or two later they were seated where they had been the previous evening. 'What would you like to drink?'

In point of fact she did not want a drink. But neither did she want to cut short her chance to spend some time with him. 'Perhaps a coffee,' she answered.

They both had coffee, Nathan seeming to be as pleased that she was there as she was to be there. 'You knew your father was on his way here?' he asked, civilly enough, but she sensed a hint of censure behind his question.

She did not want to be bad friends with him ever. She shook her head. 'He rang last night, when I got to my room. Er—Grace, our housekeeper, has finally had enough and has walked out.'

Nathan took that in, and asked, 'He told you he would arrive today?'

Again she shook her head and, realising Nathan could be thinking she'd had all the time in the world to mention it that morning, 'No,' she replied.

'So—he arrived completely out of the blue?'

'Do all your coffee companions get this third degree?' Her

father had given her one grilling. Love Nathan though she might, she did not fancy another.

Nathan looked at her steadily for several long seconds then, quite clearly, stated quietly, 'Only the ones I care about.'

Oh, Nathan—her heart kicked off a riot. 'Oh, that's all right, then,' she murmured as nonchalantly as she was able. Oh, my word! Though don't read too much into that, she instructed. He wasn't intimating that she was anyone special, just one of his—many, she was sure—female coffee-drinking companions.

'Did you happen to mention, during your conversation with him last night, that I was in the vicinity?' Nathan wanted to know.

She had to give him top marks. Though guessed he was far from blinkered where her father was concerned. 'I might have mentioned that I'd had dinner with you,' she replied lightly.

'I bet he loved that,' he commented, and asked, 'Are you having dinner with him and Dawson again tomorrow?'

'Not if I can help it!' she replied promptly, but confessed, 'Actually, it was either I joined my father at his hotel or he would have come to dinner here.' And, hurrying on, 'I didn't know Ross would be there tonight.'

'Your father wants you to marry Dawson?'

'That's hardly likely with a Mallory blocking the way,' she commented, knowing that Nathan would appreciate the subtleties that while she was married to him her father's plans didn't even get off the starting blocks.

'Always a pleasure to be of use,' he remarked, his lips twitching. But, sobering, 'You're not interested in Dawson—that way?'

'I like him; he's good company. But, no, I'll never marry him,' she replied, and learned something else about the man she was married to—he seemed to have an unerring instinct about that which he did not know. Although she supposed she already knew that from eight years ago when, without knowing why, he had known that annulment was important to her father for some reason. 'He's asked you, though? Dawson? He's keen to marry you?' And, when she did not answer, 'He's in love with you?'

'I—er—don't think I feel too comfortable discussing how someone else feels about me,' she replied. 'It—er—doesn't seem fair.'

Nathan looked at her solemnly for a moment or two, and then smiled that smile that melted her bones. 'Do you know something, Phelix Bradbury, you are one rather special person.'

She looked away from him, her insides dancing a jig. He cared a little for her—he'd more or less said so. And now this, that she was one rather special person. It was all too much.

'Well—um—this won't get us bright-eyed and bushy-tailed in the morning,' she offered brightly, glancing at their empty coffee cups. She instantly wanted the words back, but too late now. Nathan had taken the hint and was on his feet.

Together they walked over to the lift. Together they rode up to the fifth floor—and never once did he ask her what she was doing tomorrow. It could have been, of course, that he was aware she would be under pressure from her father tomorrow. Or it could have been that he had no desire or intention to ask her to dinner only to have her father usurp him.

Either way they were at her door, the key in the lock, when Nathan glanced down at her. Last night he had kissed her. She wanted him to do so again. 'Goodnight,' said the contrary person inside of her who was determined she waited for no man's kisses.

She looked up then, and there was that look in Nathan's glance that said, What sort of a man do you think I am to let you go to bed unkissed? She gave in, she half smiled—he needed no further encouragement.

Last night he had lingeringly kissed her without otherwise touching her. Now he drew her gently to him. And it was bliss. Utter bliss!

'Goodnight,' he said softly, as he pulled back.

'G-goodnight,' she stammered, but her fingers were all thumbs suddenly and she couldn't get the door open.

Smoothly, Nathan took over. He opened up her door and switched on the light. She went inside, her heartbeats drumming. Joy of joys, Nathan stepped inside with her—and closed the door behind him.

'This is more private,' he said, and took her in his arms again.

Gently, he kissed her again and, as if starved, she willingly accepted his kiss. He broke his kiss to look down at her, as though to ascertain how she was feeling.

He must have seen that she was feeling never better because, moving further along the short hallway into her room, he once more took her into his arms. Nathan, Nathan… She wanted to cry his name, but was too choked to speak.

He raised his head to look down at her. 'All right?' he asked softly, as if afraid she really did have a hang-up when it came to such intimacies.

'All very all right,' she answered huskily. And loved him, loved his tender smile, and was all his when he gathered her to him and kissed her with a growing urgency.

She returned his kiss, felt his body against hers, and wanted to get even closer. But as that kiss ended and she opened her eyes the large alcove where the double bed was came into focus. And that was when she saw that the room staff had been in, and that the white and frothy very feminine nightdress that she had popped under her pillow that morning had been elegantly draped over the turned-back bedcovers, and suddenly everything seemed to her to be so much more extremely intimate—more extremely intimate than she was ready for.

'I—er…' she began, and Nathan's eyes followed her shaky glance to the bed.

And he was wonderful. She guessed many men would have endeavoured to push past that unseen barrier she was erecting, but not Nathan. Even though he probably knew that barrier was not insurmountable, he made no attempt to push through, but, letting her go, he teased lightly, 'Feet feeling the chill?'

'Oh, Nathan.' She laughed. But it was true, she was getting cold feet. 'Do you mind?'

He placed a light kiss to her parted lips. 'You must never, ever do anything that doesn't feel one hundred percent right to you,' he said, taking a step back.

'It—isn't—you,' she said chokily.

'I know that, my darling,' he replied tenderly.

And for just that she wanted to be back in his arms. But that bed, that nightdress, and the strictness of her childhood, the repressions of her adolescence, were not so easy to overcome.

'Goodnight, Nathan,' she bade him.

'Goodnight, sweetheart,' he answered, and went quickly, leaving her staring at the door. Was it any wonder that she loved him?

CHAPTER SEVEN

PHELIX lay awake for hours that night. How could she sleep? Nathan had called her his darling, had called her sweetheart, had intimated that he cared. Well, sort of. He cared for her—along with other females of his acquaintance, the sober part of her head reminded her. Yes, but he had also said that she was special.

She sighed, and turned over in her bed. None of which meant that he felt the same way about her that she felt about him, of course. But he had kissed her. Had held her close and kissed her—and had been understanding of whatever it was that held her back.

She loved him, she loved him, and she was not going home until Tuesday. Surely if it was true that he did care for her a little, if it was true that, for a little while anyway, she was his darling, then surely between now and Tuesday they would find space to spend a little time with each other?

Phelix turned over in her bed again as the unwanted thought pushed through the pleasantness of her world that she was making a giant something out of nothing. Was she presuming too much?

Doubts started to intrude. For heaven's sake, what had the poor man done but been gentle, been tender with her? He had spoken a few endearments that in some circles might be considered throwaway, and here she was imagining far more than he could ever be meaning.

Those doubts began to multiply. Nathan would be off to his lawyers instigating their divorce sooner than *that* if he had the smallest notion of the way she had perceived his—his manner with her.

With doubts crowding in, sleep impossible, Phelix realised that if she wanted to continue to be friends with Nathan—and who said that friendship would extend beyond next Tuesday when she left for England, for goodness' sake?—then she had better be on her best guard to hide how even the smallest smile from him could affect her. If she went for a swim in the morning and Nathan was there…

At last from sheer weariness she dropped off into a light sleep. But it seemed no sooner had she closed her eyes than her telephone rang to wake her. She sat up, putting on the light and picking up the phone while at the same time checking her watch. Half past five!

'Hello?' she queried.

'I've booked you out on an early flight.' She heard her father's irascible tones. 'You'd better get your skates on.'

Phelix came quickly alert. She felt that during the past few days in foreign climes she had sloughed from her a little of her father's stifling pressure. She certainly was not ready to be manipulated by him at his merest whim.

'I haven't any plans to go anywhere,' she defied, certain as she was that this was just one more instance of him wanting control over her. She had opposed him last night when she'd agreed to have a drink with Nathan Mallory. This, without question, was her father's way of ensuring that she never had another drink with Nathan. Just as if she was some errant schoolgirl, and purely to keep her out of Nathan's sphere, he thought he could send her home! 'I've decided to stay here until next Tuesday as planned,' she stated unequivocally.

'If that's what you want to do that's fine by me,' he agreed pleasantly.

Something was wrong! This wasn't the father she knew and distrusted. 'Good,' she said. 'Thank you for waking me at five-thirty to have this little discussion.'

'Why, you cheeky b—!' That was more like him, but he managed to swallow down his ire. 'If you want to stay, that's up to you,' he went on. 'I'm sure Henry Scott will recover well and—'

Animosity with her father was forgotten on the instant. '*Henry*! What's the matter with Henry?' she asked urgently. 'Is he ill?'

'I took a phone call late last night—not so late in London. They're an hour behind us,' he inserted inconsequentially when she was more interested to know what was amiss with Henry than what the hour had been when her father's mistress had telephoned him. 'Apparently Henry collapsed yesterday and was carted off to hospital.'

'What's wrong with him?' she asked quickly.

'I didn't get more details, can't tell you which hospital, but it seems that he is asking for you.'

Oh, Henry, Henry. She swallowed down her feelings of panic. 'And you've arranged an early flight for me?'

'It was the first flight I could get. I thought you might want to go to him.'

'Thank you, Father,' Phelix said quietly, feeling a little amazed at his thoughtfulness—and also feeling a little ashamed of herself. He did have a good side, even if he did manage to keep it extremely well hidden.

'Think nothing of it,' he answered, and proceeded to give her details of the flight he had arranged for her.

Knowing that she had little time to spare after that phone call, Phelix took a hasty shower and then scurried around packing her case. She knew she would not be returning. By the sound of it Henry must have suffered a heart attack of some kind, and was asking for her. She must get to him with all speed.

But yet, with all the urgency of her actions, with most of her emotions taken up with fears for Henry, she could not help but think of Nathan.

She quite desperately felt that she wanted to perhaps write him a note and slip it under his door when she went. But against that was her fear that she was reading far more into their 'friendship' than he had intended. Wasn't he more likely to shrug, probably, hopefully, think It was nice knowing you, but add, It wasn't necessary for you to write.

She glanced at the phone as she was leaving. No, she decided firmly, when everything in her pulled her to have a quick word with him. Besides, it was too early to disturb him, and anyway…

Phelix was on her way when it dawned on her that while she had told Nathan a great deal about herself, he had told her little about himself. She knew she was highly vulnerable where he was concerned, and was then glad that she had not contacted him to say she was leaving.

What did she expect him to say, for goodness' sake, except—Bye! And that would have left her feeling an idiot, that she had disturbed him at that time in the morning. Well, at least she had spared herself that embarrassment.

Aware, though, of her vulnerability over him, Phelix used her years of bottling down her feelings to concentrate on the job in hand. Her first priority was to get to Henry.

It was a warm, sultry day when her plane landed in London. As she had no idea which hospital Henry was in, she decided to make a short stop at her office, where someone would obviously be able to tell her where Henry was to be found, and also the latest news on his progress, if any.

With fear clutching her heart at that last thought, Phelix raced to the Edward Bradbury building and straight up to the legal department. She was still in fact in the corridor, when the first person she saw was a fit and well looking—Henry Scott!

'Phelix!' he exclaimed in delight. 'I didn't expect you back today.' And, his eyes on her face, 'You look pale. Are you all right?'

Never better—now! 'I've—had a bit of a rush,' she replied, and as he looked at her, so she looked for any sign that he was unwell. 'I heard you were at death's door.' She was too shaken to hold it back.

'Oh, they don't want me up there just yet,' he answered breezily. And, as if where they were was much too public, 'Come into my office and tell me about your trip,' he invited.

'What happened with you?' she wanted to know the moment the door was closed and they'd moved over to a couple of chairs.

'Your father?' he guessed. 'He phoned you?'

This was no time to prevaricate. And in any event there was not much about her father and his 'little ways' that Henry did not know of. 'He's in Davos,' she informed him, and saw Henry's look of surprise.

'That snippet hasn't filtered down to me yet,' he stated, and they both knew that her father, probably suspecting that Henry would ring her to tell her that her father was on his way, had deliberately kept that information from him.

'He contacted me this morning to tell me you'd collapsed and been taken to hospital,' Phelix revealed. She felt it more important then to find out about the present state of Henry's health than to start getting angry that her father might have deliberately panicked her as some sort of reprisal for daring to defy him by meeting up with Nathan Mallory last night. 'You *did* collapse?' she wanted to know.

'Nothing too dramatic…' Henry began, and she *was* panicked.

'What happened?' she asked swiftly.

'Nothing other than the fact I had a forgetful moment in my old age and, when it's become second nature to me over the years, I somehow managed to mistime my insulin shot.'

'Insul… You're a diabetic?' she asked, startled.

'True.'

'I didn't know!' she protested.

'There's no reason why you should know. It's well under control—normally.'

'But not yesterday?'

'An oversight on my part. It won't happen again.'

'You blacked out?'

'It was a bit of a pantomime.' He made light of it. 'I went shopping instead of having lunch—and the next I know I'm coming round in hospital. They'd obviously done a sugar test when I stayed unconscious, taken the appropriate action—and kept me there until they considered I was well enough to leave.'

'Should you be here? Shouldn't you be resting?'

'Now, don't get in a stew, there's a good girl,' he said warmly, his tone fatherly. 'I'm absolutely fine. It was a one-off.'

She looked at him and realised he did not want any fuss, that he wanted to play it lightly. 'The way I heard it, you were asking for me,' she commented, seemingly off-handedly.

'Who else would I call for as I came out of it,' he teased, 'but my very good friend, Phelix?'

She smiled, feeling heartily relieved that while his collapse had been serious he had been quickly attended to. It passed through her mind to wonder if her father knew far more about Henry's collapse than he had told her. Most probably, most certainly, she realised, he did.

But, having ascertained that Henry had suffered no permanent damage, there was something more important on her mind just then than that her father had manipulated her out of one country and away from a man he did not want her to have anything to do with and into another country.

'You've been a very good friend to me too, Henry, haven't you?' she asked.

'Oh, my, you're looking serious,' he said lightly, non-committal until he found on what she was meaning.

Phelix knew then that, having always guarded over her, he was unlikely to admit anything that he considered was likely to cause her the smallest distress. Which meant that she was going to have to bring what was in her mind out into the open.

'You know the name of the man I married, don't you, Henry?' she asked, and, knowing that he would not lie to her, waited.

And, having weighed up all the pros and cons, 'I've always known,' he admitted. 'From day two.'

'You went to the register office?'

'Don't be cross, Phelix,' Henry soothed, when she was not at all cross with him. 'You were so very upset, and while I could do little about what had taken place, I'd have been failing in my duty to your mother if I hadn't checked who the man was and what consequences, if any, might be in store for you.'

'Oh, Henry,' she said softly, and asked then what she supposed she had over the years grown to know, 'You—loved my mother, didn't you?'

Henry looked from her briefly, but turned back to answer quietly, 'Felicity was a saint.' Going on to reveal, 'It was my sincerest hope that I might one day be able to ask her to marry me.'

Phelix felt tears prick her eyes. Strangely, she was not startled to hear what Henry had just said. It was just painful that, when her mother could have had a much better life with Henry, for her child's sake, she had stayed with her mean, abusive husband.

'Oh, dear, dear, Henry,' Phelix murmured. 'You knew she had a rough time with my father?'

'I would only have made matters worse had I gone to sort him out,' he admitted.

'You stayed on here, working for him?'

'I didn't want to. I turned down several better offers. But if I'd given up my work here, I would also have given up the chance to do any small service I could for Felicity. And,' he opened up, 'when Felicity was taken from me—even though I knew she was not mine…'

'You stayed on here—for me?' Phelix guessed.

'I could see you might go the same subjugated way your mother went. I wasn't having that. Not that I needed to,' Henry said with a smile. 'I think you started to find yourself on the day you married Nathan Mallory.'

'And you encouraged me—every step of the way.'

'It was always there in you.'

'Just needed a little nurturing?' she offered lightly.

'Had things gone as I wanted, you'd have been my daughter—my stepdaughter,' he qualified. 'Naturally I encouraged you.'

Phelix knew he would have made a superb stepfather, and felt quite choked for the moment. But he had always looked out for her anyway. Inwardly she mourned for the life her mother might have had, for what might have been. But, getting herself back together, she asked that which had to be asked, 'Was it you who sent that note to Nathan Mallory?'

'What note would that be?'

'You're hedging,' Phelix accused. 'I *know* it was you.' And she nudged when he did not answer. 'Eight years ago? Your friend Oscar Livingstone—remember?'

'Good heavens!'

'Exactly. When I told you of the shameful way Nathan had been treated you had him checked out and then you contacted Mr Livingstone. Following on from your conversation with him, you sent a note by messenger to Nathan suggesting he phone him.'

'Good heavens!' Henry exclaimed again. 'I knew you were bright, but how on earth did you work that out?'

'I didn't. I had help. Nathan Mallory is in Davos. We got talking…' Her voice faded. She remembered Nathan's strong arms about her, recalled his wonderful kisses…

'Nathan Mallory worked it out?' Henry did not seem surprised to hear that Nathan had been in Switzerland at the same time as her. 'How come?' he asked.

'Um—as I said, we got talking. I told him about you coming to my home the day after the wedding and how I'd told you everything but the name of the man I married. I also happened to say how you seemed to know everyone, and Nathan worked it out from there.'

'How did you get on with him?' Henry asked.

Phelix felt herself blushing. 'Very well,' she answered. Adding quickly, 'We had dinner one night and I was foolish enough to mention it to my father when he phoned.'

'I bet he caught the first plane out,' Henry said cheerfully.

And Phelix had to laugh. 'Do you know, Henry, I think you have a streak of wickedness in you?'

'And all these years I've been trying to keep it hidden.'

Phelix got up from her chair, and when he stood up too, she went over to him. 'Thank you so very much for saving Nathan from losing everything,' she said softly, and stretched up and kissed him.

'He's more than proved himself worthy of saving,' he answered sincerely. And, musing aloud, 'Do you think I should try to contact your father to tell him to stop worrying about me?'

'You *are* wicked!' Phelix branded him, and they both smiled.

She went to her office after leaving him, but was all of a sudden overcome by such a feeling of restlessness that she found it impossible to settle. She checked through to see if there was anything urgent pending. And then, telling herself that she wasn't expected in her office until next Wednesday, she, for about the first time in her working career, turned her back on the diligence of her nature, phoned through to tell Henry where she was going, and went home.

Home was quiet without Grace there. And to rattle around in the cold mausoleum of her home did absolutely nothing to ease her restless feelings.

She unpacked her case, threw some laundry in the washing machine and, time hanging heavily, wondered if perhaps she would not have been better to have stayed at work.

Though in her heart she knew what was wrong with her was more a restlessness of spirit than a restlessness because she had nothing to do. Less than twenty-four hours ago Nathan had kissed her...

While Phelix was glad that Henry had quickly recovered, she began to see it as fact that her father, with his 'We'll see about that,' had totally and without the smallest compunction used Henry's temporary indisposition to remove her from Nathan Mallory's orbit.

And she had fallen for it! He had left it until the last minute to tell her of her flight. Not that she could regret dashing home to check on Henry the way she had, but oh, how she longed, positively ached, to be back where she might see Nathan again. They had been staying in the same hotel, for goodness' sake. Surely she would...

Phelix spent the next half-hour going around in mental circles. With her whole physical being she wanted to be back in Davos. With the whole of her logical thinking brain she knew her small 'dalliance' with Nathan was over. Just as she knew she had been right to leave as she had without letting him know. Her face burned with the thought of the idiot she would have made of herself had she slipped any kind of a note beneath his door.

It was over, finished. Possibly, from his point of view, never begun. Good grief—he would be amazed if he thought she had read anything more into his kisses than, for him, a small pleasure of the moment. Think of something else, do!

In an endeavour to do that very thing, Phelix went to the kitchen where Grace kept a board with a list of phone numbers. And in the next minute she was speaking to Grace's friend Midge.

'I wondered if you'd heard from Grace recently?' Phelix began, after saying who she was.

'Grace is here now. Just a minute.'

And within that minute Grace was on the line. 'You're back?' she asked.

'Came back today,' Phelix replied, and asked, 'What happened, Grace?'

'I've been cooking him his favourite steak and kidney for umpteen years now—and suddenly he decides I'm not making it right!' Grace exclaimed indignantly.

'You had words?'

'The fur flew!' Grace laughed.

'You're obviously feeling better about it now.'

'I'm still not coming back, if that's what you're asking.'

'It isn't,' Phelix replied. 'I just wanted to make sure that you're all right?'

'I'm fine. I'm staying with Midge for a short while, while

I consider my options. But actually, Phelix, and don't take it personally, but it's something of a relief to be out of that house.'

Phelix did not take it personally. She was having the same sort of feelings herself. She stayed chatting to Grace for quite some time, and ended the conversation by asking Grace to let her know if she needed help of any sort or in any way. She made a mental note to include a hefty bonus in Grace's salary and to try to keep in touch, and rang off, wishing that she, like Grace, could just pack her cases and be off.

She admitted that the idea had tremendous appeal, but supposed she had better hang around until a new housekeeper had been found and installed. She— A distant rumble of thunder interrupted her thoughts. A thunderstorm had been threatening for some while.

The air stayed sultry, but to Phelix's relief the storm stayed in the distance. She went to bed that night with the threat of a thunderstorm miles away from her mind. Thoughts of Nathan Mallory had taken precedence. He was her one love. She, as far as he was concerned, she did not doubt, was one of many—and love didn't come into it.

The air was still heavy when she got up the next morning. It needed a thunderstorm to clear it, but she would far rather be in Switzerland when at last the storm broke. Switzerland and Nathan were back with her.

She attempted matters practical. She had spent time yesterday clearing up a backlog of dishwashing that her father had not deigned to clean his hands with. That Saturday morning Phelix set about putting the house in some sort of order.

Having vacuumed and polished, with Nathan her companion the whole while, Phelix went out for fresh milk and a few other oddments. Her appetite had gone, but she would try and find something tempting to eat.

By eight o'clock that night, having munched her way

through a salad, finishing off with a banana, Phelix went up to her room to shower. The air was oppressive, and she knew if she did not take her shower now there was no way she was going to do so once the storm that had been threatening well and truly broke.

She felt marginally refreshed after her shower, but was wide awake. In any event, it was much too early to go to bed.

Doubting that she would sleep anyway, she slipped into a lightweight black silk leisure suit. It was something she seldom wore, but it was too hot for anything heavier. But with no one else in the house, she might as well take a book to the drawing room sofa.

By ten o'clock she knew it was a ridiculous idea. She was going to have to do something about Nathan Mallory. He was interfering with her head big time.

Determined to stick it out until eleven, Phelix again tried to get interested in her book—only this time for a violent clap of thunder to tear her concentration to shreds. Feeling hot and clammy, she strove to keep calm—but nearly jumped out of her skin when at that precise moment the doorbell sounded.

She went swiftly from the drawing room to the front door, and as another clap of thunder rent the air she forgot entirely her more normal caution to check through the spyhole to see who was there before opening the door, and urgently pulled it back.

Shock made her momentarily dumb. 'Nathan!' she gasped when she had her breath back, still half ready to believe that she was imagining that he stood there. A fork of lightning lit the sky. 'Come in!' she invited hastily. 'You'll get soaked out there!'

Phelix took a shaky breath as—tall, superb, and so loved— Nathan Mallory stepped over the threshold. She quickly closed the door, her heart hammering to see him again so amazingly unexpectedly, so wonderfully unexpectedly, as she strove hard to find some sense of normality. What was he doing here? She had imagined him in Switzerland. He should *be* in Switzerland!

'What brings you to this neck of the woods?' she asked lightly, while trying to keep a lid on her soaring excitement. He wasn't here to see her father. Indeed, she would have thought that he would never want to set foot inside her home again after the last time. But he *was* here! So Nathan, having left Switzerland for some reason, *must* have come to see her!

'My car broke down nearby,' he replied, but there was such a look in his warm grey eyes that she knew he was lying.

'Try again?' she invited. 'No car of yours would ever dream of breaking down.'

He grinned, and she loved him. 'I was bored,' he offered.

She looked him over. Dark-haired, mind-blowingly impressive—and wearing an immaculate suit, collar and tie. 'All dressed up and nowhere to go?' she queried.

'I took her home,' he admitted, adding quickly, 'Didn't stay.'

Phelix did not know which she was first—jealous that he had taken out some other woman, or delighted that he had been bored with the other woman's company. Then she became conscious of her thin trousers and top, became aware that Nathan was now flicking his glance over her the way she had flicked her glance over him. And she just knew, as his eyes traced briefly over her breasts, that he knew she was not wearing underwear.

'It was hot!' she said, in a rush to explain her thin attire— and bang went the air of sophistication she was trying to achieve.

'Oh, love,' he murmured.

But she was feeling awkward and vulnerable, and was not waiting for anything else he might add. 'Coffee?' she offered jerkily. 'Shall I make you some coffee?'

Nathan looked at her tenderly, every bit as if he knew how she was feeling. 'I'd love some coffee,' he accepted quietly.

Trying to not break out into a sprint, Phelix went quickly along the hall. 'If you'd like to wait in here?' She put her best hostess hat on at the open drawing room door.

'Can I help?' he offered.

'No,' she refused lightly. 'It will only take me a couple of minutes.'

She left him at the drawing room door and went quickly to the kitchen. She was glad she had offered him coffee, glad he had accepted, but knew that she must put in some very hard work in those couple of coffee-making minutes to try and get herself back to one piece again.

And then abruptly there was an almighty crack of thunder and she saw her mother's face, saw her pleading with her father, and on the heels of that first crack another horrendous clap—it must have been directly overhead. The lights flickered and went out, and she thought she might have cried out. But even as she was striving to hold herself together the lights came on again, and Nathan was there.

He placed his hands on her shoulders and turned her to him, his arms coming round her to hold her safe as he pulled her to him. 'Still bad?' he asked softly, understanding.

She nodded into his shoulder. She felt safe with him. 'I'm all right now,' she said shakily, drawing back to look at him, and making to move out of his hold.

'Don't be a spoilsport,' he teased gently. 'You know how much I enjoy having you in my arms.'

'Oh, Nathan,' she wailed, but, as perhaps he had hoped, he had drawn a smile from her. 'Coffee,' she said determinedly, and would, she thought, have found the strength to have pulled out of his arms. But then he bent down and gently kissed her—and she had no strength to do anything after that.

'I'm not really interested in coffee,' he commented.

There was that look in his eyes that said he was interested

in her, but she felt so mixed up just then she was not at all sure that she was reading the signals correctly.

'And—um—you haven't truly broken down in your car?' She strove for some clarification.

Nathan shook his head. 'I parked it on the side of your drive. I wanted to see you, Phelix,' he added softly.

Oh, Nathan! Her spine was beginning to melt. 'That's—um—nice,' she managed, and he laughed lightly in delight with her.

'You can do better than that,' he suggested.

And, looking up into his tender grey eyes, she knew that she could. She stretched up and kissed his cheek, and held him close. 'Better?' she asked, pulling away, but only to feel his arms about her tighten before she could move too far.

'Hmm—I think I should warn you—there's a chance we could be getting into serious territory here,' Nathan, his hold still firm, thought to mention.

Phelix looked at him—and needed help. 'I'm not sure how I feel about that,' she replied honestly, and didn't think she liked it when Nathan relaxed his hold on her and seemed about to step back. 'But that doesn't mean I wouldn't like to—er—um...'

'Do a little research?'

Phelix got cold feet again. 'I'll make that coffee,' she said firmly, and would have been the one to step away, only he held her steady.

'There's no call to be totally unfriendly,' he rebuked her. 'Why not stay just where you are and give me one good reason why you didn't let me know you were doing a flit?'

From Switzerland, obviously. She should have let him know. *Now*, with Nathan here, she felt she should have done so. 'I wanted to let you know, but...' She just couldn't tell him that she had not done so because she had not wanted to presume on their friendship—or whatever it was.

'But you preferred me to find out from your father?'

'Did he tell you I'd…?'

'He came to the hotel to settle your hotel bill, so he said. But since I'm sure you would have settled it yourself, to all purposes and effect he came and waited until he saw me, in order to let me know how you'd phoned him to ask him to arrange for you to catch the first flight you could.'

'It—wasn't quite like that,' she confessed. She loved the way Nathan was holding her. 'Um…' She tried to get her thoughts together.

'You didn't leave because you thought I'd come on too heavy when I kissed you the way I did?' he queried seriously.

And she stared at him, startled, amazed that he should have thought such a thing. There seemed to her then only one way to show just how wrong he had been if he'd thought that.

Raising her head, she stretched up and, ignoring his cheek this time, she touched her lips to his. No brief meeting of lips; she kissed him long and lingeringly. She had to admit to feeling a shade flushed when she pulled back from him.

Nathan looked steadily into her wide green eyes. 'I'm convinced,' he said softly, and then proceeded to take over from where he had left off on Thursday evening.

Somehow or other his jacket and tie were hanging on the back of a chair, and Phelix felt the warmth of his chest burning into her through her thin covering when, holding her firmly in his arms, his lips met hers, seeking and finding a response.

'You're beautiful, my darling,' he breathed as their kiss broke and he gazed tenderly down at her. And as she thrilled to his endearment, rejoiced that Nathan the man she loved thought her beautiful, he kissed her again.

Her arms went up and around him. He was warm and wonderful and she was enchanted to be in his arms, to be kissed and held by him.

Then suddenly she was not so sure. She loved him. She knew that she always would. But as his warm seeking hands found their way beneath her thin top, something she had no control of seemed to be tripping her up.

She felt his hands on the bare skin of her back, caressing upward—proof there if needed, when there was no bra to hinder his caresses, that she had nothing else on.

Nathan kissed her again, a long enchanting kiss, and she started to breathe a little more easily. But then those seeking hands began to search beneath her top around to the front of her—and she abruptly jerked back, taking a step away from him. His hands fell from her.

'I'm s-sorry,' she apologised, feeling uptight again, embarrassed and...

'You've nothing to be sorry for,' Nathan assured her calmly, his eyes on her as if reading her face.

'You'll think I'm a t-tease, or something,' she stammered.

'Don't you think I know you better than that?' he asked quietly.

There was perhaps about a yard now separating them. 'Do you know me?' she asked. 'It's less than a week since we met.'

'I've been married to you for eight years, remember?' he queried, his mouth quirking up at the corners as he tried to get a smile from her. 'And, while there's a lot more we need to know about each other, I know that you're good, you're kind, and that you're as honest as the day. I think that's a very good start, don't you?'

A start to what? Her heart was pounding madly. 'I—wanted to leave a note to tell you where I'd gone, but—but I didn't want you to think...' Her voice failed her.

'I think you should learn to trust your instincts more than you do,' Nathan offered quietly.

'You—do?'

'While keeping a natural caution,' he qualified.

And she smiled, and wanted to kiss him, but did not dare risk it. She did not know what was wrong with her, but there was some insurmountable barrier that, no matter how much she loved him, she could not get through.

'M-my father received word that Henry had collapsed—he, my father, arranged for me to get home quickly,' she explained in a rush.

'You're too far away over there,' Nathan commented, but made no move to come any closer.

Trust your instincts, he had said. Phelix took a deep breath and moved close to him. Still he did not touch her. She stretched out her hands and placed them on his waist.

'What's wrong with me?' she asked.

Nathan looked deeply into her eyes. 'Sweet darling,' he murmured lightly, 'with so much right with you, I'd be a little scared of you if there wasn't something just a tiny bit out of kilter.'

'I don't believe you've ever been scared of anything,' she offered, but as lightly, and had to smile.

She guessed Nathan took that as an encouraging smile, because, although he made no move to kiss her again, he caught her to him in a loose hold and instructed, 'So relax, and tell me how Henry is. Was it a heart attack?'

She did relax, and felt good. 'That's what I thought too. I didn't know which hospital he'd been taken to, so I detoured to the office first—and there to my astonishment, looking fit and well, was Henry himself.'

'Your father panicked you for the pure hell of it?'

'Not exactly. Henry had collapsed and had been taken to hospital. But it wasn't his heart—he'd forgotten his insulin shot. I'd no idea he was a diabetic!'

'Poor Phelix,' Nathan sympathised.

'Poor Henry,' she countered, but then smiled broadly as she told Nathan, 'You were right. It was Henry who sent you that note.'

Nathan smiled too. 'After he'd contacted Oscar Livingstone on my behalf,' he filled in. 'You told him of my suspicions?'

'I had to. He wondered how I'd worked it out—I said I had help.'

'I'll set up a meeting with him,' Nathan said, as she had perhaps known that he would.

She looked at him then, and as she looked at him she seemed to read something in his eyes—as if he was quietly waiting—though what for she had not a clue. But she was suddenly filled with so much love for him that she could hardly bear it.

'I want to kiss you,' somebody else in charge of her said huskily.

Nathan's expression did not change. 'If that is what you want to do, Phelix,' he replied softly, 'I have to tell you that I have absolutely no objection.'

'Oh, Nathan,' she cried. 'What if I get cold feet again?'

For answer, he smiled gently. 'I'm a big boy. I'll cope,' he said.

She looked from his eyes to his warm superb mouth, and all at once Nathan was meeting her halfway. And it was such a joy to be held warm and safe and close up to his heart again.

'All right?' he questioned when their kiss broke.

'May I have another?'

He laughed lightly. No pressure. 'I think we can manage that,' he agreed, and suddenly she was in seventh heaven again, as they exchanged wonderful long and sometimes short kisses.

She placed her arms up and over his shoulders and he held her to him, not attempting to touch her more intimately. Though she was aware, when a moment later their lips met again, that his kisses were growing more and more passionate.

A fire started to burn in her for him. She welcomed it, and, barely being aware of what she was doing, she pressed herself to him.

But gently he was easing her a little bit away from him, and as that kiss broke, 'Darling, Phelix,' he said softly, 'I love you so much, but…'

Colour flared instantly to her face. He loved her! Joy such as she had never known broke in her. She kissed him, her own passion soaring. Nathan loved her. It was all she wanted to hear. And, more than that, with those words 'I love you so much' it seemed as if every one of those insurmountable barriers she had subconsciously put up had on that moment collapsed, disappeared without trace.

That was, there was still one barrier there, in that she wanted to tell Nathan that she loved him in return, but shyness seemed to freeze the words to her tongue.

Which made it the biggest mystery to her that, as their kiss ended and they looked at each other, and to her heightened senses it seemed as though for his sanity's sake Nathan might put her away from him, she found her tongue to urgently tell him, 'Nathan, I w-want to make love with you.'

He halted, and looked at her as if he could hardly believe his ears. 'You want to make love?' he asked, as if checking his hearing.

'Yes,' she replied without hesitation. She might be a little red about the ears, but her answer was honest.

Nathan looked deeply into her eyes, and then drew her to him. And the next time he kissed her there was more passion there, and she rejoiced in that passion. He held her close, and then it was that his hands began to caress her back, began to find their way beneath her thin silk top.

He broke that kiss to pull a little way away from her, but his hands were still beneath her top as, unhurriedly, his long sensitive fingers caressed their way to the front of her.

Phelix held her breath in exquisite torture as his hands held her ribcage. 'You're sure?' he asked quietly.

She was feeling very much on uncharted ground, but, 'I'm sure,' she answered huskily—and felt the most sublime pleasure when his hands moved upwards and his sensitive fingers captured her love-swollen breasts, his eyes on hers the whole of the time.

'You're still sure?' he asked.

This was new territory for her. It was the first time she had wanted any man. But Nathan was not just any man, he was the man she loved—her husband. And she adored his touch.

She swallowed on a knot of emotion, but was unwavering when she replied, 'I was never more certain.'

'You darling,' Nathan breathed. 'My brave darling.' And with that, obviously deciding to not make love to her in the kitchen, he gathered her up in his strong arms and strode from the kitchen with her towards the stairs.

'I'm heavier than I used to be,' was the only protest Phelix made as he carried her up the stairs.

'Delightfully so,' he replied, pausing to bend and kiss her—and then moving on to unerringly find the bedroom where they had last lain together.

But this time it was different. This time she was no immature teenager in need of comfort from the storm. This time she was a warm, vibrant and wanting woman!

The only light in the room came from the bedside lamp that Nathan switched on. They kissed and held, and Nathan let go of her briefly to divest himself of his shirt, and Phelix, her heart full, could only wonder at the splendour of him.

She stretched out a hand to his broad naked chest and marvelled at this intimacy they shared. He looked warmly at her, took her hand to his mouth and kissed it, and then drew her closer to him.

The warmth of his uncovered chest burned into her through her thin top. She loved him so. She was his whenever he chose. Though when he made to remove her top, Phelix discovered that she still had a few inhibitions remaining.

She caught a hold of his wrists to stop him. 'I—can't,' she said jerkily, nervously.

Nathan instantly stilled. 'You can't—make love?' he asked, his voice quiet, controlled, with not an atom of anger with her in evidence.

She shook her head, feeling gauche and awkward suddenly. 'The light,' she explained huskily. And adored him when he straight away seemed to understand that she was already making giant leaps from the repression that had held her in a merciless grip, but that she was not yet ready to stand naked before him in full view in the lamplight.

'Sweet love,' he said softly, kissed her gently, and then bent to put out the light.

'Oh, Nathan,' she whispered, and was in an enchanted land she had never known as he kissed and caressed her and kissed her. And as he again went to remove her top, she did what she could to help him.

And then they were standing naked together, and as he kissed and caressed her breasts, taking a hardened peak into his mouth, Phelix was no longer thinking, only feeling.

Nathan held her close, and as Phelix felt his all maleness against her, so she started to tremble. 'You're doing magnificently, my darling,' he soothed, feeling her trembling body against him, and he moved with her to lie down on her bed and—she was enraptured.

They kissed, their legs entwined, and she wanted to touch

him, to stroke him all over—but, a private person herself, she had no idea what was and what was not acceptable.

'Help me to know what to do?' she pleaded softly.

'Oh, darling innocent,' Nathan crooned, feeling her trembling still as he held her. 'Do whatever feels right to you.' And again he kissed her, kissed her lips, her eyes, her throat, and while she could barely breathe from the ecstasy of his tenderness, he kissed her breasts, their pink tips—and she rejoiced in his kisses.

And as desire for him soared in her, so she began to feel liberated. She touched and caressed his nipples, her arms going round him, and they clung to each other. Her fingers played over his back and she marvelled at the wonderful exquisite feel of him.

Nathan came to half lie over her, and she felt his hands on her naked behind, pulling her to him. And knew joy unfettered when, tracing her hands down his back, she was able to likewise hold his superb behind.

Unrestrained, they pressed into each other. But then, when Phelix was feeling quite dizzy with delight, Nathan moved a little away from her and, while still tenderly kissing her, his caressing hands travelled down over her breasts and down to her belly.

Then all at once, as his sensitive touch was gently exploring further, Phelix knew as she thrilled to his touch that they had reached a point of no return. Nor did she want to return. Making love with Nathan was beyond anything she had ever known.

She loved him, and as he wanted her so she wanted him. Though when his exploring fingers became even more intimate, and her breath caught, she could not hold in a small cry of hesitancy.

Nathan stilled. 'Problem?' he queried, as if suspecting he might have suddenly come up against a last minute brick wall of her inhibitions.

And she, fearing he might stop, quickly found her voice to tell him, 'Just a momentary blip of—um—shyness.' She kissed him then, pressing herself hard against him as passionately as she knew, in the hope that he would know from that that she would just about die if he went and left her wanting him like this.

'My sweet love,' he breathed, and as passion between them flared out of control, and as if he knew she would wait no longer, he came to lie over her and eased himself between her parted thighs. 'I love you, sweet darling,' he murmured, and she—she loved him so, and joyously welcomed him.

CHAPTER EIGHT

IT FELT incredible to Phelix to awake at dawn in the arms of
the man she loved. Joy awoke within her as she recalled
Nathan's utter tenderness with her. She had awoken during the
night but, as if somehow anything she might say might take
away the sublime magic, she had stayed still and silent—and
just rejoiced to have Nathan so near.

He had told her he loved her—she wanted to pinch herself
in case it was just a wonderful dream. But it was no dream.
She could feel the heat of his body next to hers beneath the
sheet, their only covering on such a warm night.

Oddly, when she had so wanted to tell him of her own
feelings, of how she loved him in return, she had felt too shy
to voice those words that were in the very heart of her, those
words that were a stranger to her.

Her shyness was totally ridiculous, she knew, when she
considered the absolute freedom she and Nathan had shared
with each other. The absolute, enrapturing freedom.

But Nathan knew what she had been too shy to tell him.
He must know, surely?

Oh, Nathan. They had made love—sublime, perfect, incredible love. Her heart felt full as she recalled the exquisitely
tender way he had been with her. Never had she thought a man

could be so gentle, so caring of her discomfort when slowly, unhurriedly, taking time because of her untried body, he had lovingly taken her virginity.

A small sigh involuntarily escaped her—and her joy soared. Nathan was awake too, and had heard the sound.

'Good morning, Mrs Mallory,' he breathed softly.

'Oh, Nathan.' She turned, her body happily colliding with his. Thrilled by his words, she moved her head to look at him, and warm colour rushed to her face.

'You can still blush?' he teased softly, his grey gaze warm on her.

Again she felt the need to tell him that she loved him, but again shyness kept the words unsaid.

'Er—good morning, Mr Mallory,' she answered, and loved and wanted him when he bent to her and kissed her. 'Oh,' she sighed, and when he pulled her close up to him, she knew that as she had instantly desired him, so Nathan instantly wanted her.

He kissed her again, one arm holding her, one hand caressing her right shoulder. And again they kissed, passion soaring, that hand leaving her shoulder to caress her breast, until suddenly Nathan pulled back from her.

'Is it too soon for you?' he asked, releasing her breast, holding her waist and moving fractionally away, as though striving to turn the temperature down.

For a moment she was unsure what he meant. But, recalling his care of her last night, she suddenly realised that he must be thinking that perhaps her newly tested body might need to recover.

'I want you,' she said simply, and kissed him, and held his warm fantastic-to-the-touch hip so he should come in close again.

He smiled at her, but did not come any closer. 'I'm glad,' he said, and gently kissed her.

But whether he would have made love with her then or not she did not know. What she did know was that in the next second the mood was heartbreakingly shattered, spoilt, abruptly fractured beyond repair, when—with a crack of thunder that sounded as if the heavens had split in two—simultaneously, paralysingly, her father came charging into her bedroom!

Shock made her world spin! Having been so completely enraptured by Nathan that, remarkably, she had been entirely unaware of the gathering storm, she had been unaware too that her father had returned from Switzerland!

Feeling dizzy from being so cruelly torn out from the bliss she had been sharing with Nathan, Phelix stared at her father, completely astounded that with that crack of thunder he had come roaring in.

'*I knew it!*' he bellowed, his face contorted with rage, and, venting his apoplectic wrath on her bed companion, 'That's your car parked on my drive, Mallory! Well, *bloody well* move it—and yourself with it!'

The scene was ugly. Desire died an instant death. No way could it have survived. Surprisingly, as Phelix started to surface from being stupefied, she felt no shame that her father should have found her in bed with Nathan. What did shame her was that he could speak to Nathan the way he did.

'I'm not here at your invitation,' Nathan replied calmly, taking his arms from her and sitting up. Phelix, pulling the bedsheet close up to her, sat up too.

'Too bloody right you're not!' Edward Bradbury shouted. 'Nor likely to be! This is my house and I say who enters it!' he spluttered—and as thunder and lightning joined in the bedlam and her father's face contorted again, so Phelix was once more back in the night when her mother had died. Lightning forked, and again she saw her father's face twisted and evil as he had set about doing her mother harm.

Phelix strove hard not to flinch as her father continued to shout, but she felt the colour drain from her as nausea invaded. From experience she knew she had to appear calm, but it took a tremendous effort and years of self-training to hide just how sick she felt inside.

Outwardly unflustered, she became vaguely aware of Nathan leaving her bed and getting into his clothes. But, with her insides already churning, she had to endure a feeling of humiliation too that, with her father still yelling—pointless to try and argue with him—Nathan should find himself a part of the vile scene. It mortified her that because of her he had become embroiled in such ugly unpleasantness.

Feeling shamed and flattened, she found the two awful scenes alternating in her head: flashes of her father's physical assault on her mother, and his present verbal assault on the man she loved.

She saw Nathan's jaw clench, saw his hands bunch, and had an idea, as her father continued to scream abuse at him to take himself off his premises, that Nathan was having a hard time holding down on the urge to silence the older man with his fists. But her father, his face malevolent as it had been that terrible night, was still roaring at him to get out when Nathan looked across at her, at her ashen face.

'Phelix.' He said her name, which brought her away from that night. But what Nathan would have added she did not wait to hear.

She could not take it. At any moment now her father's language would ripen, and on top of this, she knew she just would not be able to bear the degrading ignominy of it.

'Go, Nathan,' she pleaded, pulling the bedsheet defensively up and around her. 'Please go,' she begged.

His eyes followed her movements with the sheet and he

hesitated, seemed torn. 'I'm not leaving you alone with this madman. He—'

'Do as she says! Clear off before I call the police!' Edward Bradbury erupted.

Nathan ignored him. 'Phelix, you—'

'It's better if you go.' She interrupted him this time, half hoping that he would say, Come with me. But he did not say that, though with her father still proving that his lung power had not diminished over the years, he would have had a job making himself heard. 'He'll calm down once you've gone,' she promised.

Nathan did not look convinced, but asked, in the space provided when her father paused for breath, 'I'm making things worse by staying?'

'I know it,' she answered. And, as Nathan still seemed to be having a mental struggle within himself, 'Please go,' she urged. 'Please.'

Nathan still did not look entirely convinced but, as if conceding that she must know her father and his rages far better than him, asked, 'You'll be all right if I leave?'

Phelix nodded, wanting him gone before her father should mortify her further by resorting to the kind of language he used when his outrage spilled over into foul mouthed obscenity.

'I'm used to him. He'll calm down soon,' she said—hoped.

And wanted to weep when, after long moments of studying her calm expression, despite her insides being all of a heap, Nathan, with her father on his heels, did as she asked and left the room.

In a kind of numb shock she heard them going down the stairs, heard another altercation break out when Nathan detoured to the kitchen for his jacket, tie and car keys. It was still going on when she heard the slam of a car door—and then heard Nathan's car roar down the drive.

Tears came then. Floods of them. Phelix rushed from her room to her bathroom and locked herself in. The storm was still going on overhead as she stood under the shower—she barely noticed.

Last night with Nathan had been magical. Look at it now! In ruins! Smithereens! It wasn't Nathan's fault. Dear God, he had been wonderful. It was her father. He had spoilt it as he spoilt everything else.

She guessed he would come upstairs, possibly come into her room again to turn his vitriol on her. But the shower was her sanctuary. She knew she would not be disturbed.

But after some while she knew that, since she could not stay in the bathroom all day, she had better get dressed and decide what she was going to do. Because it went without saying that this was the end as far as she and her father were concerned.

Drying her eyes, she took a grim if shaky breath and, leaving her bathroom, went into her bedroom. The bed seemed to suddenly dominate it. Feeling compelled, she gave in to a moment of weakness and went and sat on the edge of her bed, on the side where Nathan had lain. She picked up his pillow and held it to the side of her face, her heart crying out for him.

Humiliation deep and bitter racked her that Nathan had had to put up with her father haranguing him. She did not know how she would ever face Nathan again, or if indeed he would want to see her again after that appalling scene. She'd like to bet that in all his home life he had never ever witnessed or been forced to be part of anything that was a quarter as vile as the treatment her father had dealt him.

Swallowing back fresh tears, determined to not cry again, Phelix left the bed and got dressed with her head in a turmoil.

First things first, she decided. But what came first? She was striving to think logically, though with that scene bouncing back at her all the time she was finding logical thinking difficult to hang on to.

But, making a start, she stripped her bed and went and put the sheets and pillowcases in the washing machine. The phone rang—her father answered it before she could get from the laundry room to the kitchen phone. She made a dive for it anyway, but her father must have had the briefest call on record, because as she picked it up all she heard was the sound of the dialling tone. He had obviously ended the call before it had begun.

Her spirits lifted momentarily—had that been Nathan?

Hoping that the caller might have been Nathan, she realised she might be able to find his number by dialling one four seven one. But before she had the chance the phone rang again, cancelling out the previous number. Her father had snatched up the receiver at the same time, but since the call was for him, from Anna Fry, Phelix had no interest in the call and replaced the receiver.

Her spirits zoomed down to zero. If the previous call had been Nathan her father would deny it. No two ways about it, he would not have taken a message for her. It would be pointless to ask him. Not that she felt inclined to ever speak to her father again.

She went back up the stairs to fold her bedding and to pack as many of her belongings as she could. Anything she hadn't got she would do without or collect at a later date. For now she was doing what she should have done years ago—she was leaving.

Phelix took one of her two suitcases and a holdall out to her car, and went back to her room for the other one and a bag containing toiletries and bits and pieces.

She had no mind to see her father, but, supposing his girlfriend's call would have calmed him down, Phelix did not shrink from going to see him. Taking her case with her, and with a car coat over her arm, she went along the hall to the drawing room.

He looked up when she went in, his mouth thinning to an even tighter narrow line when he saw she was carrying a suitcase. She did not wait for him to start, but plunged straight in.

'You'd better set about finding a new housekeeper. I've had a word with Grace; she isn't coming back—and I'm leaving.'

'You don't think for a minute that Mallory will want you running after him, do you?' he asked nastily. 'He's had what he wanted,' he snarled crudely. 'He won't want you turning up on his doorstep now!'

Phelix felt instantly nauseous again. How did she ever come to have such a father? She could only be glad that she had inherited her mother's traits and not his. But, as it was, she was feeling at her most vulnerable, and wanted to get away from him and his cold house as fast as she could.

'I'm not going to Nathan,' she replied, with what dignity he had left her with.

'So where the devil are you going?' he questioned disagreeably.

'I haven't decided yet.' She hadn't, but she doubted he would want her forwarding address. 'I won't be coming back,' she added finally, and, there being nothing else to say, she went to turn from him.

But, as ever, he wanted the last word. 'It worked, then, didn't it?' he snarled.

She really wasn't interested, but years of giving him the courtesy of hearing what he had to say had become something of a well-mannered habit. 'What worked?' she asked, knowing even as she asked that she would be much better just getting out of there.

'Mallory! He set you up!'

She should have guessed. Her father was not the sort to give in gracefully. 'Why?' she asked. 'To get back at you?' she challenged.

He shook his head. 'He set you up, and you fell for it.'

'I don't need to hear this,' Phelix attempted, turning away again.

'Tell you he loved you, did he?' She turned back, her face burning. 'Of course he did!' Edward Bradbury cried triumphantly. 'And you believed him. You must have been a push-over!'

Nausea gripped her. She did not want to hear this. Did not want her father undermining her confidence the way he had so often tried to—and so often succeeded—in the past.

'Well, you soon saw him off, didn't you?' She refused to be subdued.

'Why wouldn't I? It was only on Friday that he was telling me point-blank how he intended to divorce you at his very first opportunity!'

Her breath caught. She had no idea what the situation between her and Nathan now was, had been too enraptured by him to think past the moment. But she did not care at all for the thought that he might have been discussing the subject of their marriage—none or otherwise—with her father. *If* such a discussion had taken place! But—had it?

And Edward Bradbury must have read that hint of doubt in her face, because, 'Ask him,' he challenged. 'The very next time you see him, ask him if he did not say those very words. Unless he's the biggest liar breathing, he'll admit it.'

Phelix could think of no particular reason why Nathan would lie about such a thing. But doubt—about Nathan this time—and uncertainty she did not want, doubt she had thought she had done away with, was there to plague her again. If Nathan had told her father that he wanted to divorce her with all speed, then it must have been a lie when Nathan had told her that he loved her!

She felt on very shaky ground suddenly. 'I know Nathan Mallory far better than you're ever likely to,' her father pressed on. 'He's an unforgiving man and will get back at me any way he can.'

'Can you blame him after what you did to him?' Phelix rallied.

'Any way he can,' Edward Bradbury ploughed on, ignoring what she had just said. 'Even to the extent of using my daughter to do so.'

No! She did not want to hear this! 'I'm sure you're right,' she agreed calmly. Anything to get out of there.

'You *know* I'm right!' her father insisted. 'But it's gone past him getting even with me. It's now more to do with that outsourcing contract.' Phelix looked at him in some surprise. 'Mallory knows damned well that I'm in a better position than he is to snaffle that deal,' he went on. 'That contract is as good as signed in my favour.'

Phelix stared at him. That didn't make sense. 'I can hardly believe that.' She dug her heels in. 'Why, if you've got that contract virtually done and dusted, are all the big chiefs going to Switzerland next week?' she challenged.

'Because certain form has to be observed, naturally. The others don't know what I know in any case. That's why Mallory has come sniffing around after you.' Was she really this crude man's daughter? Sometimes she just couldn't believe it. 'Though, given that any man will take what's on offer,' he sneered crudely, 'it's not you he's after—creeping in here behind my back. He knew I wouldn't be here.' He chipped away a bit more of her confidence. 'He knows you work in my legal department—a misplaced word here, a detail of the contract being negotiated falling in the wrong ear, and what do you know? The Mallorys are back in with a chance—a chance of offering a better contract before all signatures are down.'

Phelix had to concede that—although she doubted very much that she would be the main legal executive dealing with any such mammoth contract—some parts of it might well drop on to her desk.

Doubts were already building up and starting to spear her with their spiteful barbs when Edward Bradbury put the final boot in. 'As soon as he knew you'd be in Davos last week, he flew out to charm you witless.'

Phelix stared at her father. 'Nathan had no idea at all that I'd even be *in* Davos last week!' she protested. Of that she *was* certain.

'*Of course* he knew! He planned it right down to the last detail.'

She would not believe it. 'Nathan wasn't even going to Davos last week. But for one of his people being unable to attend—'

'And who do you suppose ordered that person not to attend?'

'I don't believe you.' She wanted to run, but would not. Her father was not going to have the last word this time. 'Nathan only went because—'

'Because he knew you would be there, and he saw a splendid chance. A whole week to have a crack at you! What could be better?'

'You're wrong!'

'You know I'm not. Any one of his underlings would more normally have stepped in to give that speech without one of the high-ups—Mallory himself—putting themselves out to take it on.'

No! But even as she thought no, her intelligence was telling her that it was true. Nathan could have sent any one of his scientist workforce in his stead. There had been absolutely *no reason* for him to go in person. And it would have been far more likely, surely, for him to send someone else?

Suddenly her whole world was starting to fall apart. But what she lacked in confidence, she had in an abundance of pride.

'I don't believe you!' she stated loftily.

'Don't!' Her father was angry. 'Don't believe me! You just go ahead and make a fool of yourself!' He started to rampage. 'But believe this, I know men better than you do. I know men like Mallory, much, much better than you'll ever know him. So don't imagine for a moment that he wants to stay married to you. Because he doesn't. You're good for his purpose, that's all.' He was starting to raise his voice. 'All he's interested in is finding out what we're doing on the outsource deal. With you on-side he'll reckon he's got it made. The bastard's an expert,' he raged on. 'He knew where you would be all last week! It was no coincidence that he stayed in the same hotel.' He did not wait for her to interrupt when her lips parted, but pounded furiously on. 'Every firm of note is charged up to get that outsourcing contact. You were his insurance in the event Bradbury's got it. He set out to woo you,' he spat. 'Bed you if he had to, but above all else get everything he wanted to know from you—and if it might take longer than a week or so to learn snippets of contract talk and special clauses, he was prepared for that—'

'*Stop it!*' Her father had ranted and raved at her before, but never had it hurt as much as this. 'Stop it,' she mumbled unhappily.

But Edward Bradbury knew that he had planted enough seeds to ensure that Nathan Mallory would get short shrift the next time he approached his daughter.

'Willingly,' he replied. 'Just don't come crying to me when divorce papers land on your desk—any time soon.'

'You can be certain I won't do that!' she answered stiffly,

and got out of there before her father should witness her final humiliation—her tears.

She made it to her car without breaking down, and drove to a lay-by, where she sat for an age getting herself together.

Away from the house, away from her father, she was sure she did not believe a word of it. But those words he had spoken had a nasty way of returning again and again to pick at her.

She just did not believe that Nathan had known she would be in Switzerland last week. She drew a shaky catch of a breath as logic she did not want reasoned that, with the trip being planned quite some weeks ago, if, as he father had said, Nathan had deliberately 'targeted' her, then he could quite easily have found out that information.

Not that he could have known in advance which hotel she was staying in. She brightened up. Henry had switched her hotel at the last minute. So the fact that Nathan was staying in the same hotel must be, as she had thought, pure coincidence and nothing more.

Phelix brightened some more to be able to put her father's diabolical suspicions from her. In any event, prior to Switzerland, the last time Nathan had seen her she had been plain, immature and clueless. He had been kind to her eight years ago, she recalled, but they had not seen each other since then. He had not seen her, so she just could not see him deliberately setting out to 'woo', as her father had put it, the type of female she had been then, regardless of that contract.

Her brightness faded when thoughts she did not want rushed in to remind her of the many, many millions that contract would be worth over the next ten years. It faded further when she recalled how Henry and Nathan seemed to bump into each other every so often. Nathan had known she was a career woman. What else had Henry told him? That she had shed her dowdy image and had scrubbed up rather well? That, surely, would have made the pill easier to swallow?

Suddenly Phelix was back to doubting again. Oh, Nathan, she mourned. It was all so different when she was with him. But those doubts, those doubts that had rocketed in when apart from him in Switzerland, were there swamping her again.

Feeling quite desperate, she made herself remember those times when she had been with him. Those times when he would make her laugh. She had loved laughing with him. Loved him.

She remembered being in his arms last night. Surely no man could be so tender and feel nothing? She had thrilled to his kisses, his touch, his lovemaking...

But her father and his 'he'd bed you if he had to' began to sully that beautiful memory. Surely Nathan had not purposely set about seducing her? Even to the extent of telling her he loved her? She could not believe that. And yet—what did she know of men? Apart from having had little time for much of a social life, what with work and study, she had just never been able to let any man get close to her—before Nathan...

But why would he tell her father he was going to divorce her at his first opportunity? If Nathan *had* said that, of course.

Well, it was for certain she could not ask him. To do so might give him the impression that she was trying to hang on to him—and her pride would not allow that.

Had he said it? Did it matter anyway? They may have made love with each other but that did not signify any sort of commitment on his part. Phelix was feeling so thoroughly mixed up by then that she had no idea what it meant on her part either—other than that she wanted with all her being that he had taken her with love in his heart for her.

By the time she drove away from the lay-by she was starting to feel more confused than ever. She booked into the first respectable-looking hotel she came to, and was by then reduced to feeling totally numb.

She lay on her hotel bed, her head starting to ache from the punishment of her whirling brain. She did not believe it. Did not, would not believe that Nathan had deliberately set her up to get her on his side with regard to any information she could feed him.

And yet—had Nathan set out to make her fall in love with him? Did he *know* that she was in love with him? He must do. He had the evidence that she did not give herself to just any man—which made him special. Oh, she couldn't bear it!

Phelix was again trying to dissect. Had Nathan known she was Switzerland-bound before she had gone there, before *he* had gone there? If so, it would mean that her father was right, that— The ringing of her mobile phone cut into her thoughts.

Very few people had her cellphone number, and she certainly did not want to speak to her father. Though she rather thought he had said more than enough without thinking to phone her to add more.

But it might just be Henry. Perhaps she could ask him... She reached for her mobile. 'Hello?' she said, and nearly dropped it.

'Phelix, are you all right?' Nathan asked.

Tears sprang to her eyes. She swallowed them down. 'How did you get hold of this number?' she asked with what wit she could find.

'With difficulty. I've been ringing Henry—he was out. Are you all right, my darling?' he asked. That 'my darling' threatened to sink her. 'I regretted leaving you with that monster before I'd gone a mile.'

'I'm fine,' she told him flatly.

'I've been ringing your landline—only to get an earful from your father. But we can deal with him later. I'm outside your house now. Say the word and I'll come in and get you.'

Oh, Nathan. 'Er—I'm not at home,' she answered. 'I've—moved out.'

'You have! Good! That was my next suggestion.' She could tell he was smiling. Just that and her backbone was evaporating. It would not do. 'Tell me where you are and I'll—'

'Nathan.' She just had to cut in. That, or go along with whatever Nathan said, regardless of whether he was just stringing her along or not. She knew that she could not ask him if he had told her father that he intended to divorce her, because that would cause him to presuppose that she had thought she would stay married to him. But there was one question that she *could* ask him. 'Did you know I would be in Davos before you decided to go to Switzerland yourself?' she asked him.

And rather thought she had her answer in the slight pause that followed, before, 'You sound serious?' Nathan answered quietly.

Was he playing for time? 'Did you?' she persisted—and could have wept at his answer.

'Yes, I knew,' he admitted. 'What has—'

'Was I—?' She broke off, feeling foolish even before she voiced the question. 'Was I, in any way, any part of your reason for deciding to personally attend?' She made herself continue.

And again there was a pause. 'I confess, little love, you were very much a part of the reason I decided to attend,' he replied.

Gripping tightly on to her telephone, Phelix sank down onto the bed. 'Thank you, Nathan,' she said, thanking him for at least being honest in that. But pride was rearing and pushing her to not allow him to think that she was clinging to him because of what had happened between them. 'I don't think we have anything more to say to each other,' she told him coolly. 'Goodbye,' she added, finality in her tone. She did not wait for him to answer but abruptly cut the call. He, Nathan, her love, *had set her up!*

If Nathan rang again—which she thought extremely unlikely after the way she had just spoken to him—Phelix was unaware of it. She immediately switched her phone off and had not the smallest interest in checking to see if there were any messages.

That Sunday that had started out so blissfully ended as one of the worst Sundays of her life.

She lay awake for hours that night, going over every moment she had spent with Nathan. And every moment seemed to bear out what her father had said about Nathan setting her up to get her on-side.

He had been there from the first, she remembered, coming over to her the moment she had appeared at the conference centre. But not by word or look had he revealed that he had known she would be there.

He had, that very same day, 'bumped into her' in the park. Had asked her to dine with him that night, she recalled. Had the very next day followed her to the funicular.

She had dined with him that same night—and he had been there at the swimming pool the very next morning—and then they had walked up the mountain together.

All in all, she realised, they had seemed to spend a considerable amount of time with each other. And all, as far as he was concerned, in the interests of big business!

After a fitful night's sleep, Phelix awoke and knew that she had had it with big business. She was in no hurry to go to her office. In fact, were it not for Henry, she would not have gone at all. But, at a little before three that afternoon, she sat in her office and typed out a letter, and then went to see Henry.

Luckily he was alone, and welcomed her with a smile the way he always did. Though as she approached his desk his smile changed to a look of disquiet.

'You look troubled?' he questioned straight away.

'My resignation,' she replied, and handed him the letter she had just signed.

'Take a seat, Phelix,' he invited, 'and talk to me.'

She took a shaky breath. Where to start? How much to tell? 'I had a bit of an upset—well, a lot of an upset with my father yesterday.'

'He's home?'

'Unexpectedly,' she answered with a shaky sigh. 'I was with Nathan Mallory.'

'Out—or at home?'

'At home.'

'That wouldn't have gone down well.'

'It didn't. He none too politely told Nathan to leave. Which he did.'

Henry looked into her eyes, sad eyes, as she relived that awful scene. 'And when he'd gone your father directed his spleen on you?'

'You know what he's like!' Phelix swallowed on a lump in her throat, and went on, 'Grace walked out last week and won't be coming back—I couldn't see any point in staying either.'

'You've left home!' Henry exclaimed, and, not needing an answer, 'Where are you staying?' he asked, and offered, 'You can put up at my place if…'

'That's kind of you, Henry, but I'm comfortable where I am for the moment. I'll start looking round for somewhere to rent or buy tomorrow.'

Henry did not press her, but stated, 'Nathan Mallory was trying to get in touch with you yesterday.'

'He rang my mobile.'

'I didn't think you'd object to my giving him your number,' Henry commented, adding, 'Naturally I wouldn't have given it to him if I didn't know him to be a man of the highest integrity.'

That startled her. Henry, nobody's fool, was usually a fine

judge of character. 'You—think he has high integrity?' she questioned slowly.

'Of course,' Henry answered without hesitation. 'I wouldn't have recommended him to Oscar Livingstone had I not heard and received extremely good reports of him. Nothing he has done since has done anything to change my good opinion of him.'

Phelix stared at Henry, her insides starting to knot up. 'You've—er—heard good reports of him?'

'Bearing in mind that seldom a week goes by without I bump into one industrialist or another, had there been anything in any way detrimental being said of Nathan Mallory or his company you can be sure I'd have heard about it,' Henry replied.

And all at once Phelix was suddenly feeling totally mixed up again. But she fought her way through the quagmire that was in her head. 'Would you say, from what you know and have heard of him, that Nathan was capable of pulling any trick in the book to get this JEPC Holdings outsourcing contract?'

Henry looked at her, but, when there must have been questions queuing up in his mind, he instead stayed with the point and answered the question she had asked him.

'I don't doubt that Nathan Mallory can be as hard-headed as the next man when it comes to business—he would have to be to have made such a success of the company after that near financial crash eight years ago, when a lot of companies went to the wall. He's shrewd, Phelix, I'll grant that, but from what I've witnessed of him I would say that to act unfairly is beneath him. I'm afraid that when it comes to dirty tricks it's your father who wears that crown.'

Her breath caught, and she desperately needed to be by herself. But she had just one last question. 'Would you say that he—Nathan—is a man to be trusted?' she asked.

And Henry, without having to think about it, nodded. 'I would say that he is entirely trustworthy,' he confirmed.

Phelix stood up. 'I'll—er—go and clear out my desk,' she said, and urgently needed solitude.

'I'm on my way out,' Henry said, having shown no signs of being in a hurry but appearing to have had all day to talk to her if it would take the troubled look from her face. 'I'll give you a ring at the end of the week. We could catch up over a meal,' he suggested.

'I'd like that,' she agreed, and made it back to her own office to close the door and to sink in her chair, her head in turmoil.

Had she been wrong?

That question haunted and occupied her for the next hour as she sought to untangle fact from emotion, lie and deceit from truth.

And at the end of that hour, with her cheeks pink from the stress of it, a picture had emerged of her—despite her best efforts to the contrary—having still been so much under the insidious and devious influence of her father that she had needed to hear Henry speak highly of Nathan for her to start to see everything from an opposite perspective.

And that left her having to ask: had she not only been wrong, but, in acting the way she had in believing her father, had she wronged Nathan?

With her mouth dry, Phelix went over everything again, starting with Nathan knowing in advance that she would be in Davos. He had come straight over, had not pretended not to know her, but had said straight out 'How are you, Phelix?'

He had not revealed, in stating that they knew each other from way back, that they had actually married each other. But, given that that did not make it any clearer to know why he had made that trip when he had known she would be there, what was more natural than that he would want to have some sort of private discussion with her?

Which was why he had 'bumped into her' in that park that same afternoon. And, having deduced from what she had said that Henry could well have been the one to have put him in touch with Oscar Livingstone, what was more natural, too, than that he would follow her to that funicular so as to have more private conversation?

Not that they had spoken very much about Henry then, she recalled. That had come later. But had that—the two of them being together a lot of the time—all been the act of a man out to get her on-side with regard to what he might glean in respect of that wretched contract? Or, and a very breath-taking or, were all of Nathan's following actions those of a man— starting to—fall in love!

Phelix went hot all over. Oh, my heavens! She tried not to get too excited—it was difficult. She loved him. She knew that she did. But could he—love her? She swallowed hard—and suddenly came alive.

What a fool she had been! Good heavens, hadn't she thought, that night her control freak father had telephoned her at her hotel when she had told him she had dined with Nathan, that her father would spoil it for her if he could?

And he darn near had! Might well still have done. Would Nathan ever want to speak to her again? She doubted that any- one had ever terminated a telephone conversation with him so abruptly, or so finally either. She, with her cool, 'I don't think we have anything more to say to each other.' Oh, heavens, how *could* she?

Phelix remembered that day they had walked down the mountain, and how Nathan would have taken her to lunch with the business people he was meeting. He had trusted her. *Had trusted her!* And—even after he had said that he loved her—her trust in him had not endured beyond that one won- derful night.

Phelix stopped hurting and started to fully trust the man she loved. She started to hope.

But she was the one in the wrong here. And if Nathan would ever speak to her again, it was up to her to put it right. Or at least to try. Nathan had his pride too—he would not be the one to contact her.

She recalled his mammoth pride when, facing ruin, he had refused to touch a penny of the Bradbury money—and she realised she would be fortunate if he did not tell her to go take a running jump.

Phelix looked at the phone on her desk. 'Learn to trust your instincts,' he had once told her. And it seemed to her then that, were she brave enough, there was only one thing that she could do.

She did not have his home number. But he could well be at his office, and she did know the name of his company. She looked it up in the telephone directory and, feeling on very shaky ground, took a deep breath—and dialled.

For the last time, though the ink was now dry on her resignation, she used what clout there was to be had in telling the receptionist, 'Phelix Bradbury of Edward Bradbury Systems. Mr Nathan Mallory, please.'

It worked in that in no time she was put through to his PA. But that was where, her insides so much of a mish-mash, disappointment awaited her.

'Mr Mallory is not in the building,' the PA informed her pleasantly. 'Can I help at all? He's not expected back.'

'That's very kind of you. But I need to speak with Nathan personally,' Phelix replied, having braved herself to make the call, not knowing if she was glad or sorry that he wasn't in. 'I'll try him in the morning,' she attempted, hoping to find the same courage by then that she had found so far.

'If you'd like to leave a message?' the PA offered,

adding, 'It's unlikely that he'll be available for the rest of this week.'

Bells rang, and Phelix realised she had been so caught up with matters personal that she had forgotten that anybody who was anybody in the scientific engineering world would be out of the country from tomorrow on.

'Switzerland,' she said without thinking.

'You know about it, of course.'

'I was there myself last week,' Phelix found she was volunteering. But, getting herself a little more together, 'Not to worry. I'll… It's not important,' she lied. Not important! It was just about the most important communication of her life!

Phelix left the Bradbury building, guessing that Nathan had either left his office to fly to Zurich or had gone home early prior to flying out—most likely with his father—the following morning. They would want to be there in good time for the round of talks that were to begin on Wednesday.

She returned to her hotel, but only to spend the next few hours with her thoughts constantly on Nathan and with such a yearning to see him in her heart that she did not know how to bear it.

She went to bed early and lay awake, sleepless, only to get up early on Tuesday with that ache for Nathan rising with her. She wondered when he would be coming home—and would she have the nerve to again ring his office?

In an attempt to fix her thoughts on something else, she left her hotel and headed for the estate agents. But with no idea what sort of accommodation she was looking for she just stood looking at the properties photographed in the estate agent's window—and was suddenly frustrated with the whole idea. She didn't know what she wanted…

Yes, she did! She wanted Nathan. She caught sight of her reflection in the window. Saw a dark-haired slender woman there—a woman Nathan had once called beautiful, a woman he had once said 'I love you' to—and all at once she knew she could not wait. And in that moment her mind was made up.

She could not go on like this. Not while there was a chance. Nathan trusted her; she would trust him. Her heart began to hammer. He had said he loved her. Loved *her*!

She would go to him. 'You must never do anything that doesn't feel one hundred percent right to you,' he had once said to her. But to go to him did seem right.

Phelix was on a plane winging its way to Zurich that afternoon when she started to wonder if she *was* doing the right thing. Pride and fear that Nathan might tell her *You must be joking* when she turned up at his hotel, attempted to steer her away from journeying on to Davos.

She pushed fear of rejection from her and made herself remember that he had told her he loved her. But—was she being very naïve? She did not want his telling her he loved her to be just a thing of the moment. Something meaningless that men said when in the throes of lovemaking.

Then she remembered Nathan's tender lovemaking, the way he had cradled her to him afterwards, gently stroking her hair, making sure everything was all right with her. He had called her 'sweet darling' afterwards, and gently kissed her, and held her as if he never wanted to let her go.

Her world had righted itself by the time Phelix had collected a car and had pointed it in the direction of Davos Platz.

But when, some hours later, she pulled up in the hotel car park, she was a total mass of nerves and was most reluctant to get out of the car.

She did not even know that Nathan was staying at this hotel, for goodness' sake! He could well have cancelled his booking and moved on elsewhere. And even if he was staying here he could well be out with his father somewhere, having dinner.

Oh, dear heaven, she felt close to tears. What if Nathan refused to see her? Refused to speak to her? She could hardly blame him—not after the way she had been to him on the phone.

Suddenly then Phelix had a moment of courage and, not wanting to be hampered with her luggage, she left the car and went as quickly as she could into the hotel.

Having thought until she could think no more, she took the lift up to the fifth floor, knowing that Nathan would know, since there was no good business reason why she was there, that she had journeyed to Switzerland solely to see him.

With nerves biting she knocked on the door that had used to be his and waited. She heard a sound inside and wanted to disappear. But, when she had never run after a man in her life, and would have said the chances of her doing so were ridiculous, she found she could not run away. She was paralysed.

Then the door opened, and as scarlet colour flooded her face she swallowed on a severely dry throat. The room had not been appointed to someone else. Tall, dark-haired, and with a wonderful mouth, Nathan stood there.

He stared at her with grey eyes that for a brief mistaken moment she thought lit up to see her. But in the next brief moment, as he coolly looked back at her, she had to accept that that was just so much wishful thinking on her part.

Though he did seem as speechless as her. But not for long. And when he did speak it was not, as she had feared, to tell her to get lost, but to state in a short, cold tone, his eyes steady on her nervous expression, 'You took your time!' But when she was starting to fear he might yet slam the door hard shut in her face, he opened it wider. 'You'd better come in,' he invited, but did not sound too welcoming!

CHAPTER NINE

PHELIX preceded Nathan along the short hall. The room was similar to the one she had used. A double bed tucked away in a large curtained-off alcove with a sitting room in front of it. She heard the door close quietly behind her and her mouth went dry.

Nathan had been expecting her? 'You took your time,' he had said. Had he been expecting her to make the journey from England to Switzerland?

She made it to the centre of the room, and turned around. Oh, how dear he was to her! 'You—knew I was on my way here?' she questioned, her voice husky with nerves. Except for telling her hotel in London that she was going away for a few days, she had notified no one else.

Nathan solemnly studied her. She hoped her colour had died down. 'I rang my PA after lunch. She told me you'd phoned yesterday—but that it wasn't important,' he informed her. He looked at her expectantly, but she couldn't speak. She had come all this way, and suddenly she had lost her voice. But Nathan was still looking at her intently. 'Was it important after all?' he asked. But still the words would not come. And Nathan, still waiting, watching and waiting, taking in the shadows beneath her eyes, leaned back against the wall, and went on thoughtfully, 'It seems to me, and I could well be mistaken here, that for you to have picked up your passport and come here to see me would make it very important to you, in some way.'

Phelix opened her mouth, but the words she wanted to say just would not come, no matter how much she urged them. And instead she found she was blurting out, 'I've resigned my job—with immediate effect.'

Nathan did not look too impressed. 'You're saying that since you had nothing better to do you thought you'd take a flight—?'

'No!' she protested. And, as realisation struck, 'You're not going to make this easy for me, are you?' He did not answer, and Phelix swallowed on a dry throat. Be brave, she instructed, but was not feeling very brave. Though she did find her voice to admit, 'You—are not mistaken. This—to see you—is important to me.'

Whether Nathan could see that she was under some kind of stress—all her life she had kept her feelings battened down—she did not know but, even though his tone was still cool, he unbent sufficiently to suggest, 'Why not take a seat and tell me about it?'

She was glad of the offer. She went and took a seat on the sofa, Nathan took the chair to the side of it. 'I—er...' she began, and could have wept that the words she needed seemed to be locked up in her throat.

But as she struggled, so Nathan seemed to relent a little. 'Tell me,' he prompted.

'I...' She tried, and then suddenly she felt stronger. 'I—wronged you. I—um—wanted to apologise.'

He stared at her, his expression unsmiling. 'That's a fair trip to say sorry,' he commented.

She looked at him. He looked tired—as if he, like her, had

spent a few sleepless nights. 'I've—had a few—er—trust issues,' she confessed.

Nathan nodded. 'Let me guess—your father put the boot in where I was concerned, and did it so successfully you didn't know where the hell you were?'

'That about sums it up,' she admitted.

'You know where you are now?'

She wished that he would hold her. Phelix felt she would be much better able to talk to him about things that were personal to her and to him if Nathan would just hold her. One arm around her shoulders would be enough. But, no, she had hurt him, and his pride, by refusing to trust him and, as she had thought, he was not going to make it easy for her.

Or… As she looked at him, something seemed to click. By telling her that he loved her, Nathan, much more sensitive than she had realised, had laid himself bare. She had, so to speak, thrown that love back at him, rendering *him*—vulnerable. And he, all male, did not like it.

But his expression was solemn still, giving no hint that he might care so much as a button for her. 'Yes, I know where I am now,' she agreed quietly, and, because she felt he needed to know, 'For years I have been put down by my father. He has attempted and very often succeeded in undermining my confidence.'

'With all you have going for you—your brain and your beauty—you are still short on confidence?'

Oh, Nathan—he thought she had beauty. Her heart melted. She was all his—couldn't he see that? But a dreadful thought suddenly struck her that perhaps, after the way she had seemingly rejected his love, she had killed any feelings he had for her!

But she didn't want to think like that. Would not think like that. She would trust. That was why she was here—because she trusted Nathan.

'My father is very clever; he can be subtle when he needs to be. But, sharp or mean, he never lets up chipping away at me.' She hated talking about her father this way. But Nathan was far more important to her than any totally undeserved loyalty to her father. 'I thought I had grown away from his power to get to me. And I was sure I had. Only—' Phelix broke off, the words to tell Nathan of her feelings for him wedged tightly in her throat.

'Only?' he prompted.

'Only…' she tried, and forged quickly ahead. 'Only I'd never—er—um—cared about any m-man the way I had feelings for… And—and, well, I expect, think, I must have left myself rather exposed.'

Phelix dared a look at Nathan then. She knew her colour was high, knew that he had observed it. But his expression did not change, was stern, if anything, when, as if intent on making her push through the barriers built up in her over the years of living with her unfeeling father, he asked, 'Am I to suppose, Phelix, that I am the man you care about?'

And that annoyed her. 'You can *ask*?' she challenged warmly. 'After what we…'

'There are more ways of saying you care for someone than by making love with them,' he replied bluntly.

And that was it as far as she was concerned. She got up from the sofa, and, as he stood up too, 'You're not going to forgive me, are you?' she asked, not needing an answer. 'There's nothing more to be said,' she stated proudly—and would have walked by him, heading for the door. But before she had gone two steps she felt Nathan's hand, firm on her arm, halting her, turning her round to face him.

'Oh, no,' he said shortly. 'You may be academically bright, but emotionally you're all at sea. But you've put me through hell, Phelix Bradbury, and you're not getting away with it that easily.'

She pulled to try and shake his hand from her arm. It did no good, but only made matters worse in that Nathan's other hand came up to her other arm to hold her still. But she was angry with him still—how much more of her pride did he expect her to ditch, for goodness' sake?

'You think you're the only one who's had sleepless nights?' she charged shortly. Love him to bits though she might, there *were* limits. Besides, what confidence she had found was already starting to crumble.

'Serves you right!' he answered toughly. But then, as he looked at her, suddenly his tone was changing. 'Oh, hell,' he groaned. 'I can't stay mad at you!' And it was less harshly that he said, 'We've come a long way these last eight days, Phelix. I've watched you blossom from a proud but cool woman, with a permanent touch-me-not air, to a warm, wonderful and responsive woman. I've watched and admired as you have pushed your way through your bottled up emotions, and I've—waited.'

'Waited?' she queried, needing her wits about her. But his hold on her, just his touch, was making a nonsense of her attempt at logical thinking.

Nathan looked deeply into her wide green eyes. 'You know how things are with me,' he said steadily. 'You've intimated you care for me. Have—?'

'Are th-things still the same with you?' she asked, suddenly feeling so nervous she didn't know if he realised that she was asking him if he still loved her.

He shook his head. And she nearly died in fear that she, by her lack of trust, had forfeited his love. But it was not that. 'You know,' he said, just that short sentence, and she realised then that, having declared he loved her, he was not going to repeat it while she was still holding back.

'I—trust you,' she responded.

'You're sure?'

She would have thought that the fact she was her in Davos with him proved that—but only then did she see the extent of the hurt she had caused him.

'I'm so sorry,' she apologised again, and, needing a clear head suddenly, made to move away from him. When he saw that she was making for the sofa, and not the door, he let her go. She re-took her seat and waited until he had resumed his seat in the chair he had vacated, then, trying to put events into some kind of sequence order, she began to explain. 'I was still in some kind of w-wonderland when my father charged into my bedroom on—er…'

'Sunday morning,' Nathan put in quietly.

She tried to smile her thanks but, remembering the horror of it, her smile did not quite make it. 'I've had years of my father shouting and bellowing about the place, but all that happening in my bedroom after—' She broke off to take a shaky breath. 'Anyway, my emotions were all churned up without me suddenly realising there was a thunderstorm going on. There were you, having eight years previously been done down by my father, now being screeched at by him for your trouble. There was him, his face contorted the way it was that night…that night…' She was choked suddenly.

But, as if all at once seeing that there was more trauma in her life than he had known about, as if her suddenly haunted expression was more than he could take, Nathan had quickly left his chair and was sitting next to her, his hands holding hers.

'That night?' he pressed quietly.

And she did trust him, and for the first time ever something unlocked in her and she found she was able to confide in this man she trusted. 'That night, the night my mother died, there was a terrible storm.' She paused, but, as if sensing that she needed to get this said and out of her system, out into the open, Nathan did not interrupt her. 'My parents had separate rooms—the thunder woke me,' she went on, her voice staccato. 'My mother didn't like storms either, so I went along to her room to check that she was all right.' Phelix took another shaky breath. 'She was not all right.' She relived the awful scene. 'Apart from the flashes of lightning, the room was in darkness. But my father was there. In the lightning his face was evil, enraged and evil…' Her voice petered out. Nathan's grip on her hands firmed, and she gained strength to whisper, 'He was assaulting her.'

'Oh, my darling!' All pretence at being aloof fell from Nathan as he gathered Phelix in his arms and held her.

'My mother was a gentle genteel person. She left home that night.' Phelix wanted it all said now. 'That is, my mother had always planned to leave my father, but he said she would have to leave me behind, and she couldn't face leaving me to be brought up alone and by him. But that night she couldn't take any more. I've since learned that she phoned Henry—he told me last Friday that he had always hoped to marry her— though my mother never knew. They were just very good friends then. She needed one, a friend. Anyhow, she could not take any more abuse after that, and rang Henry. She was out in the road when she was struck by a car.'

Tenderly Nathan kissed her brow. 'Go on,' he urged gently.

'That's about it, really, other than each time there's a violent thunderstorm I still see that scene, the evil in my father's face, my mother pleading with him.' She took a shaky breath, and, having released that awful memory for the first time, began again, 'So there we were last Sunday morning—strangely I wasn't aware of the storm going on until my father came in raging—and shame such as I'd never experienced swamped me.'

'Not shame because of what had taken place between us?'

'No!' she exclaimed. 'I was totally enchanted by what had

happened,' she confessed, without meaning to. Nathan's arms about her tightened, and she hurried on, wanting all the stomach-churning sickness of it said and finished with. 'I was embarrassed—mortified—for you! There you were on the receiving end of my father's rancour, there was my father spitting vitriol, and there was lightning and thunder crashing about reminding me of that other ghastly scene.'

'Sweet love,' Nathan murmured. And, having got everything out into the open, having wanted everything said and done, it seemed as if Nathan understood that she needed to be free of it all, understood that she needed to get this out of her system, because, 'Finish it, Phelix,' he bade her gently.

'There's not much more. I was being crucified on Sunday by thoughts of how awful it must be for you to be embroiled in such an ugly scene. I was drowning in the humiliation of being certain that, while it was not such a rare experience for me, such scenes had never taken place in your family home. I just wanted you to go. Did not want that you should be dragged into it, have to suffer and be part of it.'

'I wanted to take you with me,' Nathan owned.

'Did you?' Phelix asked, believing him, feeling choked.

'More than anything,' he admitted. 'But against that you were telling me to go. And while I was able to ignore your father, I could not ignore you, or the fact that from the way you were gripping on to that bedsheet—apart from my knowledge of your modesty—I knew there was no way you were going to get out of that bed with both me and your father standing there.'

Phelix went a shade pink. She had been naked apart from that sheet, and Nathan had known that. He must have recalled too how the night before she had needed the light out before she had been able to shed her clothes in front of him.

'You're probably right,' she had to agree. 'Though I wanted you to ask me to go with you.'

Gently Nathan placed his lips on hers. 'Dear Phelix,' he breathed. 'I came back for you when your father kept blocking my phone calls. I wasn't sure if I'd be making matters better or worse if I came up to the house, so stayed outside…'

'And then got my mobile number from Henry?'

'After a long wait.'

'I wasn't very nice to you—I'm sorry,' she apologised.

'I could have throttled you,' Nathan stated, but there was a warmth for her there in his eyes as he said it. 'I knew after that call that your father had got to you. I'd no idea what he told you, but how could you believe him—after what we had shared? I thought I had your trust. I—'

'I'm sorry,' Phelix burst in to apologise again. 'I really am. It's just that I have a bit of—um—difficulty getting close to someone, and—er…'

'And—er…?' Nathan prompted.

'I'm—learning.'

'I'll teach you,' he promised, with such a wonderful smile she just had to smile back.

'I went to see Henry—to hand in my resignation,' she added. 'I'd been in a bit of a stew,' she confessed. 'My father had done his work well. But then there was Henry, telling me more or less how he would trust you above my father—and I began to see everything from a different angle.

'You started to really trust that when I told you I loved you, I meant it?'

'Oh, Nathan!' she whispered, tears springing to her eyes.

'Don't you dare cry on me!' he instructed swiftly.

And she laughed. Oh, how she loved him. 'Are you going to forgive me?' she asked.

'For so cold-heartedly telling me goodbye after I'd declared my heart is yours?'

'I made you angry?'

'Livid,' he answered cheerfully. 'And I'll admit all over the place emotionally. I flew here yesterday to stop myself coming to look for you.'

'You would have tried to find me?'

'As I saw it, I had two options. Either I came looking for you—when from the way you'd ended my call you would probably slam the door in my face for my trouble. Or I could leave you to work things out in your own time and then, hopefully, if you loved me even half as much as I loved you, *you* would come looking for me.'

Phelix had to smile again, her heart full to bursting. She hadn't been able to tell Nathan that she loved him, but he knew. Apart from so willingly giving herself to him, the very fact that she was here in Switzerland—having come looking for him—told him that she loved him.

'I rang your PA…'

'That's when I started to hope I wouldn't have to come looking for you.'

'That I'd come to you?'

'I hoped you might ring my PA again. I instructed her in the event that you did to make sure she gave you my mobile number and my home number,' he revealed. 'I hadn't dared to hope you'd hop on a plane to come looking for me. But— here you are,' he said gladly, and pulled her up close and kissed her long and lingeringly, giving her a rueful look and putting some minute space between them. 'As tempting as you are, my lovely darling, I want every doubt you're ever had about me cleared away before—'

'I don't have any doubts,' Phelix answered, knowing now whom she should trust—and who she shouldn't.

'So what did Bradbury say to turn you against me?'

'He could never turn me against you,' she confessed shyly. 'It's just—it's all so new to me, I suppose. When I'm with you everything seems so right. It's just—when you're not there...'

Nathan gave her a loving smile. 'He took advantage of me not being there to defend myself to get to you.'

'He's good at it,' she owned, and, as she felt herself growing in confidence that Nathan did truly love her, she did not want any secrets from him. 'I'm afraid he started to first spoil my memories by saying how you'd set me up. And then, when I wouldn't believe that, he went on to say how you'd used me to get me on-side regarding this wretched JEPC Holdings contact...' She halted when Nathan stared at her in disbelief.

'The man's in a world of his own,' he commented. 'Beyond it being massive, nobody knows for sure exactly what the proposal is yet. And?' he pressed.

'And how you had deliberately targeted me.' Nathan looked interested. 'You don't want to hear the rest of it.' She shied away from telling him what her father had said about Nathan wanting to divorce her. It was a subject she did not want to bring up. She did not care what happened with her and Nathan in the future. It was enough to know that he loved her now.

'And?' Nathan pressed again, determined, it seemed, to have nothing hidden away in dark corners.

'And,' she went bravely on, 'how the only reason you'd come to that conference anyway was because you knew that I would be there. That you could—'

'It's the truth,' Nathan cut in. 'The *only* reason I came was because of you,' he said succinctly.

Her eyes went wide. He had said on the phone that she was very much part of the reason he had decided to attend. But, that speech he'd had to make aside, the *only* reason? For ageless moments she stared at him, but seconds later she had rallied. 'I trust you, Nathan,' she said.

He just had to kiss her. But pulled back to murmur ruefully, 'Let me continue before you cause me to forget everything. 'Over the years—slowly at first as he got to know me—Henry Scott has been feeding me various snippets about the woman I had married. How you were taking this exam or that exam, what a brilliant mind you had, how you were growing daily more and more beautiful. It was Henry, having told me you had an inner beauty as well as an outer beauty, who told me you'd be in Davos last week. By that time I was beginning to wonder if maybe I shouldn't perhaps arrange to see this star of the legal profession myself.'

'Henry…!'

'I've an idea he approves of me.' Nathan smiled. 'Anyhow, when my man had to pull out last week, although I'd already got a substitute lined up, I found myself hesitating.'

'I'm glad you came.'

'So am I!' Nathan answered warmly. 'I was aware of you from the moment you walked in. I knew Ross Dawson, of course, and I was acquainted with Duncan Ward and Chris Watson—the Bradbury team—but surely the absolutely stunning creature standing with them wasn't that bony little scrap Phelix Bradbury!'

'You wouldn't have recognised me if I hadn't been with them?'

'I knew as soon as I looked into your wonderfully gorgeous green eyes that it was you.'

'Oh, Nathan.'

'Dearest Phelix—I was instantly bewitched by you.'

'No?' She couldn't believe it, but recalled, 'We met in the park—that afternoon.'

'I was starting to discover what was to become a vital need to be anywhere where you were.'

Her eyes grew saucer-wide. 'Honestly?' But, thinking of

how they had frequently seemed to 'bump' into each other, she did not doubt him. 'Oh, Nathan,' she whispered again.

His mouth curved in the most wonderful smile. 'You were getting to me, my darling,' he said, laying a tender kiss on her mouth. 'Though I rather think you must have touched my heartstrings eight years ago when, while my every instinct was telling me to slam out of your home, I discovered that I just could not abandon you to your terror in that storm.'

Phelix looked at him and came close to telling him that she loved him. But something seemed to be holding her back. So—she kissed him.

'You're coming along very nicely,' Nathan said softly, appreciative of her initiative in kissing him. 'So there am I, my lovely darling, trying to deny what is happening to me…'

'You wanted to deny it?'

'It was turning me into someone I did not recognise,' Nathan replied. 'I was sure it was nothing to me that you were out dining with Dawson.'

'You barely acknowledged me,' Phelix recalled.

'Why would I? It was bad enough that you were with him, without you laughing with him and obviously enjoying his company.'

'You were—jealous?' she asked, astonished.

'You could say that,' he admitted.

'But—but we'd only met again that day!'

'That's what I told myself. What did I care?'

Phelix smiled this time. 'But—you did?'

'Enough to change my mind about returning to London as soon as I'd delivered that speech. Which, incidentally, you nearly messed up for me.'

Oh, she loved him so—loved this closeness, this freedom with each other. 'How?' she had to ask.

'As I was speaking I looked for you, found you—your

eyes met mine and my heart started to pound, and for a moment there didn't seem to be anyone else in that room except you and me. And for that split second I forgot every word of what I was talking about.'

'Ooh!' she sighed, and felt able to confide, 'I was going to leave too. As soon as I knew you were there at the conference I was going to catch the next plane.'

'I'm glad you stayed,' Nathan murmured. 'But not so glad last Friday when your father gleefully told me you'd gone home.'

'It was because of Henry.'

'I know that now, but back then, while I'd done my best to tread carefully with you, I was starting to panic that I had frightened you off the night before...'

'When you kissed me,' she supplied, and just had to kiss him again. 'Just in case you have any lingering doubts,' she explained, 'you didn't frighten me off.'

Nathan held her, and kissed her, not in the smallest hurry. But he again pulled firmly away. 'Life was dull, dull, dull without you,' he stated. 'How could you have left without a word?'

'I'm sorry,' she offered.

'I understand—now,' he said, but went on to reveal, 'Though at the time it hurt that you'd left without a word. I was in love and vulnerable,' he explained. 'We had seemed to be getting on so well, but had I read it wrong? Was it *not* just shyness that you hadn't left me a message? Was it that you just didn't care?'

'I didn't know,' she said huskily.

'Didn't know what you were doing to me?' He smiled then. 'So I followed you back to London, but was certain I wasn't going to contact you.'

'You soon made a date with someone else.'

'Oh, I do hope that's a bit of green-eye I hear in your voice,' Nathan offered delightedly.

Phelix looked at him, her heart full. 'True,' she admitted, unable to lie to him.

'With you on my mind the whole time, it wasn't much of a date.' He immediately salved her feelings. 'I was driving near your home when the storm that had been threatening suddenly erupted.'

'You remembered my fear of storms?'

Nathan nodded. 'And that if you were home you'd be in that mausoleum of a house all on your own.'

'I was so pleased to see you,' she admitted. 'And—' shyly '—that you stayed.'

Tenderly they kissed. And, as if they could no longer resist each other, they kissed and held, and kissed again.

'Trust me now?' he asked.

'Oh, I do,' she replied. 'When I think of how you have trusted me, I can't bear to think of how I doubted you.'

'You're forgiven,' Nathan said warmly.

'You'd have taken me with you to your business lunch that day. Do you remember—the day we walked down the mountain?'

'I would have,' he replied without hesitation. 'It was a defining moment.'

'Defining?'

'I knew then that I was sunk,' he confessed cheerfully. 'To have included you in that business meal would have been against everything I know. Yet I didn't want to part from you. I just wanted to be near you,' he said simply, and went on, 'Which is why I was so impossible when, looking forward to dinner with you on Thursday, you had the nerve to tell me you couldn't make it.'

'It was either that or have my father join us.'

'A fate worse than death.' Nathan grinned, and kissed her, and confessed, 'I was delighted when, unable to keep away from you, I tracked you to your dinner with your father—*and* Dawson,' he added heavily. 'But you forgave me my churlishness and even defied your father by agreeing to meet me later. It was then that I really began to hope that you might be starting to care a little for me.'

Again Phelix came near to revealing her true feelings for him. But she knew that he must know anyway. Though—perhaps not, she realised in wonder, because all at once Nathan was looking at her very seriously. And when he spoke she suddenly knew that the time had come when for him—for his love and his vulnerability and his pride that she had so badly bruised—she must push through that final barrier.

'Once, up on that mountain, I offered you my heart. I meant it then. I mean it now.' He paused, and then, never more serious, 'Will you now take it, Phelix?'

Her heart thundered. He had told her he loved her, and she believed him. Incredible as it still seemed, he loved her—and she believed him. And she knew what he was asking.

'If you will take mine,' she replied, her voice barely audible. She thought then that he might draw her close. But he did not.

'Why?' he asked, his eyes steady on hers. Just that *why*, and nothing more.

'Because...' Her voice was cracking. 'Because...' She took a deep and steadying breath, and, her trust in him absolute, 'Because—I—love you, Nathan,' she said at last.

'Darling!' he breathed, and did not wait to hear any more, but held her tight up to him, tight up to his heart.

For ageless minutes they just held each other. Phelix's heart was full to overflowing to be held by Nathan, her love, to be able to hold him, her love, with no barriers.

The ringing of the telephone startled them apart. 'Ah—my father!' Nathan exclaimed. 'I was supposed to be meeting him.' He, albeit reluctantly, let her go. 'I'll be right back,' he said, and went to the bedside telephone. 'I'm sorry,' she heard him apologise. 'I'll—we'll be down in a few minutes.' There was a pause where Phelix guessed his father was querying that 'we,' and then Nathan's voice, joyous, as he told his father, 'Phelix has arrived—she's come to put me out of my misery.' Another pause, then Nathan was saying, 'See you shortly,' and replacing the phone and turning to her.

By then Phelix was on her feet. 'I—er…' she mumbled, feeling suddenly nervous.

Nathan came over to her and took her in his arms. 'I—er—nothing,' he said, placing a light kiss on the tip of her nose. 'I've told my father all about you—he can't wait to meet you.'

'You've told him?' she gasped.

Nathan smiled. 'On the flight over. He could see I was abstracted; he wanted to know what was troubling me—I told him of this beautiful girl I'd married, and how—'

'You told him you were married!'

Nathan looked at her sharply. 'You sound as if you'd rather I hadn't?'

'It's not that,' Phelix said quickly. 'It's just—my father said you'd told him you were going for a divorce as soon as you could. I just thought…'

'Stop thinking and listen to me,' Nathan instructed.

'You didn't tell my father…?'

'I did,' he owned. 'My stars, did he do his work well!' Nathan exclaimed in disgust. 'Hear me out, my darling. Your father was cock-a-hoop when he told me how you'd taken the first plane you could back to London. I wasn't going to let him see how devastated that made me, so I told him what had been in my mind anyway—that I couldn't wait to divorce you.'

'You're going for a divorce?' she asked quietly.

'*Not now!*' Nathan stressed in no uncertain fashion. '*Then*

I was of the view that, with your father attempting to taint everything, I would end this marriage that had begun with him pulling the strings, and then I'd spend the following three months hopefully getting you to care enough for me, to marry me, *for me*—nothing to do with him.'

'You want to marry me?' Phelix asked, startled.

'That was before Saturday. That was before I made you mine, my darling. Ever since then I have regarded you as my wife, the other half of me. I can't divorce you now, Mrs Mallory,' he added softly. 'You are now a part of me,' he said tenderly, going on, 'What we can do, if you'd care to, is to renew our vows—with love.'

Phelix was feeling all choked-up and misty-eyed. 'You really want to stay married to me?' she whispered.

'There is no way you're getting away from me now, Phelix Mallory,' he answered firmly, but asked quickly, 'You don't want to, do you? Get away from me?'

'Never,' she replied.

'Will you, then, my darling, stay married to me, come live with me?' he asked.

Her heart was thundering. Never had she known such joy. 'Oh, yes, Nathan,' she answered. 'Oh, yes.'

'Sweet darling,' he exclaimed, overjoyed, but decreed, 'One kiss, then you must come with me and say hello to your father-in-law.'

'Oh, Nathan,' she sighed. 'I'd love to meet him.'

That one kiss became two, and Phelix's brain was away with the fairies when Nathan, with a most loving look to her flushed face, made a determined effort and, keeping one arm about her, turned her purposefully towards the door.

'Er—I'd better—um—think about doing something about getting a room,' she plucked out of somewhere as she sought to concentrate her mind on matters other than what Nathan could do to her and how he could make her feel. 'I—' She broke off as Nathan stood back and looked at her just a mite incredulously. 'What?' she asked.

'Hmm, at the risk of not sparing your blushes, dear Phelix, this is a double room,' he reminded her. And, if she had not quite caught on, 'That bed over there is more than big enough for two. And—' he smiled lovingly into her eyes '—we *are* married, my love.'

'Oh!' The wave of warm colour to her face was instant. And, remembering the raptures of Nathan's lovemaking, 'Oh,' she whispered softly, dreamily.

And Nathan, seeing her response, was delighted. 'Care to share?' he offered tenderly.

'Please,' she answered huskily. 'Yes, please.'

THE BROODING
FRENCHMAN'S
PROPOSAL

REBECCA WINTERS

To all you wonderful readers who've been so faithful
and have sent words of kindness and appreciation
through your letters and e-mails.
Every author should be so lucky.

CHAPTER ONE

TOWARD evening, Laura Aldridge, dressed in a cocktail dress of apricot-colored chiffon, stepped out onto the balcony of her bedroom at the Laroche villa. It overlooked the shimmering blue Mediterranean, and down a few steps lay a crescent-shaped swimming pool to complete the magical setting.

Located on Cap Ferrat, a small peninsula on the French Riviera, the villa, heavily guarded with security, formed part of the treasured real estate of the European aristocracy.

The balmy air of early July felt like the tropics. She lifted her fine-boned face to the gentle breeze filled with the scent of roses. It teased the ends of her pale-gold hair and caused the chiffon to flutter against her generously proportioned figure.

For the first time in six months Laura could breathe more easily knowing Ted didn't have a clue where she was. The men he'd hired to keep tabs on her, his way of reminding her she was his possession and he was going to get her back, wouldn't have been able to trace the helicopter that had whisked her here earlier today. To elude him for a few hours, let alone a day and a night, was so liberating she wished she could disappear from his radar forever.

Since her legal separation from Ted Stillman, Laura had been going by her maiden name of Aldridge while she fought for the divorce he'd vowed never to give her. He wasn't about to let her spoil his run for congress next year. By threatening to use the millions of dollars from his high-profile, politically ambitious family to keep their case tangled up in the courts, he hoped to bring her to her senses.

It would be to his detriment though, because she refused to go back to him and had no desire to ever get married again. She'd removed her rings. All she cared about now was never having to see him again. Being thousands of miles away from the Stillman political machine helped. Saint-Jean-Cap-Ferrat was the playground of princes, and not even Ted's family with all their influence and connections had an entrée to it—thank heaven.

By a stroke of fate she was the guest of Guy Laroche and his wife, Chantelle, whom she'd met eleven years earlier in California. The summer before starting college Laura had been a part-time lifeguard and baby-sitter at the five-star Manhattan Beach Resort Hotel catering to VIPs from all over the world. Her boss had assigned her to baby sit the Laroche child, impressing upon her that the Laroche name moved mountains in the financial world of the Côte d'Azur.

They'd brought their one-year-old son Paul with them, a little boy Laura absolutely adored. Over that ten-day period he went from clinging to chairs and tables, to taking a few steps on his own toward her. His endearing ways caught at her heart. And she had often dreamed that one day she would have a darling, dark-haired boy of her own just like him.

When the three of them had flown on to Hawaii, Laura had felt a wrench to see them go. In that short time Chantelle had almost become like an older sister to her, and Guy had been the most charming man Laura had ever met. The French couple had been so in love and so crazy about Paul, it had been a joy to get to know them.

They'd all become such good friends, and the Laroches had made Laura promise that if she were ever to travel to France, she could stay with them for as long as she wanted. In the beginning they had sent her post-cards from all their travels and pictures of Paul from Cap Ferrat where they lived, but in time they lost touch.

It wasn't until two days ago, while Laura was on a work assignment in Siena, Italy, for the Palio horse race, that she heard some tourists speaking French and remembered the French couple and their baby. Though she'd be flying home from Rome shortly, she decided to phone the Laroche company and see if she could reach them just to say hello.

When Guy had realized who was calling, he sounded overjoyed to hear from her. By an amazing coincidence he and Paul were joining old friends in Siena to watch the Palio, something they did every year, and Guy had insisted on meeting up with Laura there. She would sit at his table for dinner while they got reacquainted.

Laura wondered why he didn't mention Chantelle

coming with him, but since he didn't offer an explanation, she didn't ask.

Late yesterday afternoon she'd had her reunion with Guy and little Paul, who was now twelve and as handsome as she'd imagined. Though it was a heartwarming moment, she sensed right away that something was wrong.

Guy had changed from the fun-loving man she remembered into someone who looked older than his forty-four years. His dark-brown hair had traces of silver and his patrician features were more pronounced. He'd become so serious. Paul, too, seemed too sober and polite for a boy his age.

After seating Laura at his right, Guy made all the introductions, starting with his good friend Maurice Charrière and his wife Yvette. They'd brought their son Remy who was good friends with Paul. Once Laura had met everyone they began eating, but at one point Guy started to choke on his food.

Since Laura was sitting next to him, she didn't notice his distress at first. Neither did the party of intelligent, well-dressed people with him. When he tried to stand up, it became clear he was struggling. They all looked horrified and got to their feet, but no one knew exactly how to help him.

Being a part-time CPR instructor and lifeguard for over a decade, Laura immediately acted on instinct and jumped up from her chair to get his breathing passage cleared. Though she'd saved many lives from near drownings—including her husband Ted's—this was her first save on land with the Heimlich maneuver.

As soon as Guy had recovered enough to be comfortable again, he was embarrassingly grateful. In his beautiful English he thanked her profusely and made a huge fuss over her for saving his life. Laura assured him that anyone who had knowledge of the Heimlich could have done it and she'd just happened to be in the right spot at the right time. Everyone disagreed and Maurice claimed her to be a heroine.

Later that evening, after the riders had galloped by in all their fabulous trappings, Guy accompanied her to her hotel while Paul stayed behind with Remy and his parents. Before she went up to her room Guy begged her to change her flight until the day after and come to the villa in Cap Ferrat the next day. Chantelle wanted to see her.

Over dinner Guy had informed Laura that Chantelle had been hurt in a car accident three months ago. Though no bones had been broken, she'd been severely bruised on her legs. Now she was physically recovered and could walk the way she did before. However, she clung to her wheelchair like it was a security blanket and refused to get out of it and resume her life again.

Laura cringed to hear the awful news. It explained the dramatic change in him.

According to Guy, the psychological impairment had made her paranoid, unwilling to be with people, but Chantelle had insisted that he bring Laura home with him. Since Laura had finished her work and was ready to fly back to Los Angeles, she didn't have a reason why she couldn't accept their invitation. In the end she said she could put off her flight to the States for a day and then fly out on the next flight from nearby Nice.

The following morning Guy had her flown to Cap Ferrat in his helicopter. It landed on his property where a limo drove her the short distance to the entrance of his Mediterranean-style villa. She walked into a world of art treasures, murals, mirrors, Persian rugs and sumptuously appointed rooms decorated in silks and damasks. The classic furnishings mixed with some contemporary pieces made it a showplace and a haven.

After one of the maids had shown her to a dreamy guest suite of pale pink and cream where she'd be staying the night, Guy came for her and took her to see Chantelle who, at the age of forty-three, still looked like she could grace the cover of *Vogue* magazine in her stunning black-and-white cocktail dress.

When Laura had first met her in California, she'd thought Guy's beautiful brunette wife had that Audrey Hepburn look…small, graceful. But the thing that struck Laura now was the lack of vivaciousness that had been an integral part of her personality eleven years ago. Her sad brown eyes seemed to carry the grief of the world in them.

She seemed truly happy to see Laura again, and when Guy had told her about his choking experience, Chantelle had thanked her for saving her husband's life. She had told Laura that she wanted her to stay at their home for as long as she could, but no demonstrative hugs accompanied her offer. She certainly wasn't the gregarious person she used to be.

It was so unlike the old Chantelle that Laura wanted to cry her eyes out. Only now did she realize how difficult this change in his formerly, outgoing, loving wife must be for Guy. She could understand why he and

Paul were so subdued. According to them, Chantelle had become paralyzed with fear since the accident.

Laura was acquainted with fear and knew that it came in many forms. In the beginning of her marriage, she'd learned things about Ted that had caused her to fall out of love with him. However, fear of reprisal had prevented her from confronting him, let alone standing up to the powerful Stillman dynasty. If she'd had more courage, she would have left Ted within months of the ceremony.

Obviously Chantelle was suffering from a different kind of fear. The experience of being trapped in her car for four hours before someone had found her had scarred her psyche in some complicated way. Laura carried her own psychological scars and couldn't blame Chantelle for hers, but she understood Guy's anguish.

Laura thought back to the friendship she'd maintained with one of the people she'd once saved from drowning. The teenager was in his twenties now, but he was still terrified of the water. She suspected Chantelle refused to get out of the wheelchair because she was terrified people would think she was ready to resume life. But as Laura had discovered, you couldn't make a move until your mind gave you permission.

In sympathy with the Laroches' tragic situation, she left the veranda and went back in the room to put on some lotion before joining the party. While she was applying it, she heard a rap on the door to her luxurious suite.

She guessed it was one of the maids, but when she opened it she discovered Guy standing there, looking distinguished in a sport shirt and slacks in a linen color. Though he appeared too drawn and worried for someone in his prime, the rest of his body seemed fit enough and tanned.

"Do you mind if we talk for a minute?"

"You mean here?"

"Yes. I'd rather no one else overheard us."

"If that's what you wish. Please, come in."

The foyer led into a sitting room with a spacious bedroom and bathroom hidden beyond the French doors. He sat down on one of the upholstered Louis XV chairs. She took a seat on the Jacquard-print love seat facing him.

Leaning forward with his elbows resting on his knees he said, "Before you meet everyone, I was hoping we could talk seriously for a moment. Would your husband be disappointed if you didn't get back to California right away? I'm asking for a specific reason."

Up to now Laura had avoided talking about her past, but Guy seemed so intent she didn't hold back. "I've been legally separated from my husband for six months, Guy," she admitted. "My divorce can't come soon enough."

Lines bracketed his mouth. "I'm sorry you're in so much pain. I had no idea."

His compassion prompted her to tell him the truth. "Any pain I suffered happened during my two-year marriage, which turned out to be a profound mistake. I assure you the separation has been the cure. My husband is fighting the divorce and keeping tabs on me, hoping to get me to come back to him, but it won't happen. I plan to win my divorce in my next court appearance."

She could hear his mind working. "Forgive me for speaking frankly then, but is there someone else waiting for your return?"

"No," she answered quietly. Even if there were someone, her attorney had told her to stay clear of any man so Ted couldn't use it for fuel against her.

"What's wrong with the men in your country?"

"Not the men, Guy. Me. I made an error in judgment when I married my husband. Since the separation I've been too busy traveling with my job to think about anything or anyone else. Why do you want to know?"

A sigh escaped his lips. "You've met Françoise of course."

Laura nodded. She was the middle-aged woman who helped out with Paul and provided companionship for Chantelle during the day while Guy was at work.

"She's going on vacation for two weeks starting tomorrow. I've scheduled another woman to fill in, but I was hoping I could influence you to stay on while Françoise is gone, provided your work schedule could allow it."

"Guy—"

"Let me finish," he implored. "When Chantelle said you were welcome to stay and for as long as you wanted, I was overjoyed. Since the accident she hasn't shown an interest in anyone. But she trusts you. After the way you took care of Paul in California, she loved you. Since you two have a history together, it's obvious she doesn't feel like you'll ask more of her than she's willing to give."

The man was desperate.

"Much as I'd like to be of help, I'm not a doctor."

He shook his head. "She already has the best there is. I'm talking about her response to you. If you were to be around during the day, not every minute of course, I'm hoping that one of these mornings soon she'll start to confide in you like she once did. It's my opinion you could find a way to help her open up. I'd give everything I had for such a miracle."

Laura grew restless. "Today she responded to me, but you know as well as I do a short visit is a good one. I'm afraid that if I stayed, she'd grow to resent me being around and close up completely. I wouldn't want you to take the risk of that happening."

"There'd be no risk. You're a very peaceful person, and just what she needs. You handled Paul so beautifully she accepted you without question eleven years ago. That hasn't changed. It's why I feel you could be of help. If you would extend your time here a little longer, who knows what could happen."

"I don't know, Guy."

"Just promise me you'll think about it," he begged. "Naturally I would pay you a generous salary."

Laura drew in a sharp breath. "I'm flattered to think you feel my presence could benefit her, but I would never take your money." Laura managed just fine on the money she made earning her living, and she hated the idea of receiving money she hadn't earned herself through hard work, even if she were entitled to it. She hadn't touched the money the court had ordered Ted to pay her and was thinking of donating it to a charity.

Laura's experience with Ted had made her wary of

men with a lot of money and power. Too late she realized Ted had chosen her to be his trophy wife, not the love of his life. Like all the Stillman men, he had thought nothing of being with other women while hiding behind his marriage to Laura, but it appeared that Guy, who could buy the Stillmans' assets many times over, wasn't cut from the same kind of cloth.

"Does that mean you would consider staying here out of friendship then?" His eyes went suspiciously bright. "I might have died at dinner from lack of oxygen if you hadn't acted as fast as you did. I feel closer to you now than ever. That's why I'm going to tell you something very personal.

"Chantelle and I have both been given a second chance at life, a life she used to embrace, but since the accident things have changed. We have drifted apart and I feel a gaping hole opening between us. In the past we always attended the Palio with the Charrières. This year she told me to go without her. I only went with Paul because she got agitated when I told her I wouldn't leave her.

"Something is terribly wrong and holding her back. The psychiatrist working with her is frustrated there has been no breakthrough yet. She hasn't allowed me to make love to her since the accident. I love my wife, Laura. I'm willing to do anything to get her past that barrier she has erected, but I'm afraid something happened while she was waiting to be rescued that terrified her."

"Like what?"

"Maybe some monster came along and molested her

while she was trapped and she can't bring herself to tell me."

Laura shuddered at the thought. She had to agree it was possible, though she couldn't imagine it. "You don't think she would have told you?"

He jumped up from the chair. "I don't know. I don't know anything anymore." Guy was in pain. The way his voice throbbed revealed his agony.

Chantelle Laroche had to be one of the luckiest women alive to be truly loved by her husband. Not just on the surface, but deep down in his heart and soul where it counted.

She supposed Carl, her boss in L.A., might be willing to let her extend her time in Europe for another two weeks and call it her vacation. She could even make it a working holiday, which she knew would please him. She doubted she could make a real difference with Chantelle, though if Guy was this determined to get his wife back, Laura was willing to try to get on her old footing with Chantelle.

"Tell you what, Guy. My boss should be in his office right now. I'll phone him and if he says it's all right, I'll be happy to stay and see what I can do. Chantelle was so wonderful to me back then, and who wouldn't adore it here with all this beauty? You live in a paradise only a few people in the world are privileged to see."

The men Ted had hired to follow her every move would have to possess extra powers to know her location right now. Two weeks free of the Stillman net would be a bonus she hadn't counted on this trip to Europe. In her heart of hearts she had to admit that in wanting to keep her whereabouts a secret from Ted, Guy's proposal couldn't have come at a better time.

He moved closer to grasp her hands. "You are an angelic woman, Laura. I don't know what good I've done in this life for you to come into it again at the moment you did, but I will always be indebted to you. Whatever you need or want, it's yours."

"Thank you." She rose to her feet and accompanied him to the door. "I'll join you after I've made my phone call."

"I can't ask for more than that."

Raoul Laroche slipped into his brother's villa through a side entrance closest to his own smaller villa on the south of the family's private estate. He joined Maurice who stood just inside the French doors of the living room. *"Eh bien, Maurice. Qu'est-ce qui se passe?"*

His head turned. *"Bonsoir,* Raoul! I didn't know you were back from Switzerland already."

"I finished business faster than I thought and got home this afternoon," he muttered. "As Guy was leaving the office he told me he was giving a party, but he didn't tell me why. What's the occasion? Since the accident Chantelle has avoided company like the plague."

"This is different. He wanted everyone to meet Mrs. Aldridge, the American woman you're staring at."

Raoul realized he *was* staring. It irritated him that Maurice had noticed. "Who is she?"

"The woman who saved him from choking to death."

His black brows met. "Literally?"

After Chantelle's accident, the idea that his elder brother had experienced a close call like that wasn't exactly the best news in what had started out to be a hellish afternoon. He'd received another abusive phone call from his ex-wife, Danielle, swearing she would end her life if he didn't give their marriage another chance. Raoul had become weary of her attention-seeking tactics and had cut her off, but the distaste he had felt stayed with him.

"Quite literally." Maurice sounded shaken.

"When was this?"

"Last evening at the Palio in Siena. We were eating dinner with Luigi before the race started. I didn't realize Guy was even in trouble until she came flying to the rescue. She grabbed him and performed the Heimlich maneuver. Out came a piece of roll lodged in his throat and suddenly he could breathe again. It was over within minutes."

Raoul murmured *Grace à Dieu*. He was thankful his brother was all right, but continued to frown. Guy hadn't said anything to him about the incident while they had both been in the office earlier, and it was strange for him not to share something that had been a life-and-death situation. "What she's doing here in Cap Ferrat?"

"Guy wanted to do something to thank her and decided a party would be a good way to celebrate."

"And Chantelle agreed?" Considering the guilt Guy had suffered over feeling responsible for Chantelle's present condition, not to mention the fragile state of their marriage at this point, this piece of information was somewhat disturbing. The woman was a virtual stranger, even if she had saved him from choking.

"It would seem so. Mrs. Aldridge is extraordinary," Maurice exclaimed. The awe in his eyes and voice as his gaze wandered over her left little to the imagination. This woman might be at least fifteen years younger, but age didn't matter when she was built like a mermaid decorating the prow of an eighteenth-century ship.

Even from the distance separating them, she oozed more unconscious sensuality than should be let loose on humanity. Between her wide-set green eyes and a sculpted mouth, his brother's male guests could be forgiven for halting midconversation to drink in the sight before them. The female guests pretended without success not to notice the goddess floating about in Guy and Chantelle's house.

The scenario would be laughable if Raoul weren't one of the males affected by her femininity, which was even more provocative because she was modestly dressed in a summery outfit and seemed oblivious to the sensation she created. But he knew better. A woman who looked like her understood precisely the power she wielded.

Raoul had been targeted by such a woman in his early twenties and had come close to ruining his life because of her. Back then he'd become too physically enamored of her to read the signs, but fortunately he had discovered the truth behind her facade just in time. She'd lied about everything including her name, and had hoped to make Raoul husband number three and live the rest of her life in comfort.

Though it had come as a bitter blow to his pride, he'd survived and had finally gotten her out of his system.

When he had met Danielle he had been immediately attracted, and since she came from a good family with money and didn't need his, he was able to let his guard down and had proposed to her shortly after.

Another fatal mistake. In time his supposedly adoring wife had turned out to be a much worse liar. It had spelled the end of their marriage, and no amount of pleading could ever resurrect the feelings he'd once had for her.

One of the maids offered him a glass of wine. Raoul turned her down, needing something a lot stronger. "How long will she be here?"

"She's been working on assignment in Europe. I have no idea how soon she has to get back to her job."

But not to her husband? Raoul mused cynically. She stood five foot seven, maybe eight, a height he discovered held an appeal he hadn't consciously thought about until now. Again he chided himself for noticing something that shouldn't even have played in his mind.

"What does she do?" Besides save lives...

Maurice took another sip from his wineglass. "I wouldn't know. The choking incident took precedence over everything. Guy asked us to keep Paul occupied while he accompanied her to her hotel."

Ciel! Terrific marriage the woman had. What was Guy thinking? Through shuttered eyes he tracked her movements. "Where's she from?"

"Southern California."

The mold of her body ruled out her being a supermodel. She was probably a grade-B actress who didn't have to act to get a part. All she needed to do was walk and breathe.

His jaded gaze flicked to his sister-in-law who sat composed in the wheelchair drinking her wine, looking young and elegant. And untouchable...

When Raoul thought about the drastic change in her since the accident, his gut twisted. She didn't need any more trauma. What in the name of all that was holy was Guy doing bringing this woman into their home? The sooner Mrs. Aldridge boarded her flight and left, the better.

He was about to ask more details, but Guy had spotted him standing next to Maurice and escorted his esteemed guest toward him, cupping her elbow with a familiarity Raoul found disturbing, if not repellant.

"Raoul? I'd like you to meet Laura Aldridge. Laura? This is my younger brother, Raoul, the brains of the family. She's the woman who saved my life yesterday."

"So I heard," he murmured, striving to keep his voice steady when what he really wanted to do was take his brother aside and demand an honest explanation. He reached for Mrs. Aldridge's hand, noticing she didn't wear a wedding ring. *"Enchanté, Madame,"* he said on purpose.

Only a woman who was confident in herself would give him a substantial shake in return, yet her hand with its tapered fingers and manicured nails was soft and well shaped...like the rest of her. When Raoul realized where his thoughts had wandered, he cursed inwardly.

"How do you do, Mr. Laroche," she responded in a polite but dismissive voice, as if she knew he'd been assessing her and didn't like it.

That, plus the surprising intelligence coming from her eyes and expression put his teeth on edge. "It's fortunate for the Laroche family that you save lives in your spare time."

She smiled easily, but it was meant for Guy's benefit. "It's one of the things I do for a living."

Intrigued in spite of his growing frustration over his reaction to her he said, "You're an EMT then?"

Guy grew serious. "Laura is a part-time lifeguard at Manhattan Beach in California."

Like *Baywatch*, Raoul mused. He recalled the reruns from the famous American television show of the late eighties. He imagined most Frenchmen had derived pleasure from watching the female lifeguards plunge into the Southern Californian surf and come back out again. "I didn't realize the Heimlich maneuver was used in those kinds of saves."

Her body language didn't change, but her dark-fringed eyes turned a deeper green. "It isn't."

"Which makes me even more blessed," Guy murmured, his gaze focused on her in a kind of adoration Raoul hoped Chantelle couldn't see from where she was sitting. It seemed a great deal had gone on in his brother's world while Raoul had been away on business the last few days.

"It truly was miraculous," Maurice chimed in.

Guy nodded. "I want you to be the first to know that Laura has made arrangements to take some time off work, so she's going to be our house guest for a couple of weeks while Françoise is on vacation. I'm hoping her presence will be good for Chantelle."

Raoul needed a moment to recover from the stunning news. Something didn't add up here. Last evening was the first time Guy had met this woman. Raoul didn't buy it. What self-respecting stranger would accept an invitation like the one Guy had offered within a day of meeting each other?

Perhaps Mrs. Aldridge and Guy's relationship had begun before Chantelle's accident, and maybe Chantelle understood much more than anyone guessed. This would certainly explain the drastic change in her behavior. If so, his brother was playing a very dangerous game that was so unlike him, Raoul felt as if he'd just been kicked through a stone rampart.

His thoughts reeled. More than ever he was suspicious of the whole situation his brother had orchestrated with Mrs. Aldridge's blatant eagerness. While her lips curved in a faint smile at Guy's announcement, a tight band constricted Raoul's chest, but he couldn't afford to let his brother see he was affected by the unsettling events.

Was it possible his brother had been hiding an affair that had been going on for some time? Had she arranged to sit near him yesterday while he faked the choking incident, thus giving him an excuse to bring her into the home he'd made with Chantelle? It was as if they'd had a longtime association and only now had decided to make it public.

For years Raoul had considered that Chantelle and his brother had the perfect marriage, which included a wonderful son. He'd never known two happier people. His own travesty of a union brought on by his wife's lies only highlighted the difference between them, or so he'd thought. *Mon Dieu*—had Raoul been wrong and his brother had only been putting on an act for everyone?

"How nice you have the kind of job that allows you that kind of freedom."

The classic line of her jaw became more delineated, as if his comment had reached its intended target and had disturbed her. "I'm very lucky to have such an understanding boss."

Not luck. There wasn't a man alive she couldn't enamor to the point he'd give her whatever she wanted—even Guy, the man Raoul had always looked up to for many reasons, especially for his high principles.

Raoul needed that stiff drink now. Focusing his gaze on his brother he said, "If you'll excuse me, I'll say hello to Chantelle." Maybe the mention of his wife's name might shame Guy back into paying attention to the woman he'd married, but his brother had Mrs. Aldridge on his mind and Raoul's comment passed him by.

After a brief look at the woman who'd managed to get beneath his skin the way no woman had ever done before, Raoul headed for the bar in the study off the living room. Hopefully a scotch would dull his senses, which had come alive the second he'd laid eyes on her. With fortification he might just be able to face his sister-in-law and not give himself away before he knew all the facts. Raoul intended to have Mrs. Aldridge investigated, because blind or sighted, a man could be excused for succumbing to her, but what did Guy really know about her. With her particular talents, she'd already gotten him to move her into his house.

"Raoul?"

He tossed back his drink before turning to Maurice who'd followed him. *"Oui?"*

"Can we talk for a minute?"

"Bien sur. Let's go out by the pool." He opened the doors that led to the patio area where they could be strictly alone. "What's on your mind?"

"Your brother."

He was working up to something. It was possible that like Raoul, Maurice had come to the realization Guy had done something stupid and was going through a midlife crisis. Guy and Maurice had been friends for years. Maybe he could shed some light on his sudden, aberrant behavior.

Raoul eyed him for a moment. "I'm worried about him, too."

"He's so desperate at this point, I'm afraid he's grasping at straws."

Grasping at straws?

That wasn't exactly what he'd expected to hear from Maurice. Raoul rubbed the back of his neck in an effort to collect his thoughts.

Was Raoul the only one who could see what was going on here? If so it was because a woman had made a fool of him years ago and he'd learned his lesson.

There was no doubt the situation was desperate. A woman who looked like Mrs. Aldridge wasn't safe around any woman's husband. Another vision of her swam before his eyes.

"Yvette thinks there's too much of an age difference for this to work," Maurice explained. "I tend to agree with her."

Ah. Now he understood. Maurice had seen the writing on the wall. The clever man had used his wife and Chantelle's friend, Yvette, for the excuse to warn Raoul about this woman Guy had installed in the house. A younger woman who'd never be able to relate to Chantelle? But of course that wasn't what he'd really meant. Maurice was too discreet for that.

Suddenly Raoul felt a distaste for this conversation that bordered on gossip. "In the end it's Guy's call isn't it," he muttered, wanting to be loyal to the brother he loved. "Now I'm afraid you'll have to excuse me. After my trip, I need sleep."

He took off for his own villa one swift stride at a time.

CHAPTER TWO

ONCE Guy's brother had left the villa, Laura could breathe more easily and circulated among the guests. The second she'd sensed his piercing black gaze focused on her, she'd felt tension. No…it was more than that. He clearly didn't like her and she didn't know why.

It shouldn't have mattered one way or the other, yet across the crowded room she'd been perplexed by the hostility she'd felt coming from the brooding, olive-skinned male who stood an easy three inches taller than Guy. Certain body-type characteristics linked them as family, but not so their coloring. Instead of brown hair like Guy's, Raoul's longish, almost unruly black hair with dark whorls against his neck, framed brows of the exact color.

He wore the same expensive kind of clothes as his brother, but there the resemblance ended. It was her impression that beneath the silk material covering his chest breathed a physique containing a power barely leashed.

She wouldn't call him handsome. He was much

more than that, but on an entirely different level. Gallic to his aquiline facial features, he exuded an overwhelming male sensuality her body responded to in spite of her efforts to remain unaffected.

Thankful she was no longer the object of his intense male scrutiny, she finished talking to one of the guests and walked over to Chantelle, who was surrounded by several of her female friends including Yvette from the Palio. They chatted, trying to draw her in, but Chantelle remained completely uninvolved, almost as if the party was not happening.

Laura sat down in a nearby chair and massaged her temples where she could feel a headache coming on. To her surprise Chantelle said, "I have painkiller if you need some, Laura. Come with me."

Laura hadn't realized Chantelle had been watching her, and her offer was an unexpected glimpse of the woman she had once been. Whatever had prompted it, Laura jumped at the chance to get on the old footing with Chantelle if it was possible.

"I could use some relief. Thank you."

She followed Chantelle, whose surprised friends parted so she could move her wheelchair out of the salon. Guy caught Laura's glance and nodded as if to say he was pleased with this much progress.

Chantelle had mastered the art of maneuvering her wheelchair over the Turkish rug covering the marble floor. She fairly whizzed out of the salon and down the right wing of the villa to the apartment where she and Guy lived. Before Laura could open the doors, Chantelle had already done it herself and rolled through the lavishly appointed sitting room to a table where she kept a bottle of pills.

"Take this." She handed it to Laura. "I have more in my bedroom if you need them."

"Thanks so much."

"You're welcome." She flashed Laura a glance. "I saw Raoul talking to you earlier. He's been very protective of me since the accident and can be quite forbidding sometimes, but don't let him scare you off, Laura. Raoul has his own demons he needs to deal with. Guy brought you to our home at my request. Raoul has his own home. Your being here is none of his business. Good night. I hope you sleep well."

Laura had been warned and dismissed. "I'm sure I shall. I hope you do too. Good night."

All the way to her own suite, Laura rehearsed everything Chantelle had told her about Guy's brother. She hadn't worked out whether Chantelle liked Raoul or not, but several things had become perfectly clear.

Not only were Chantelle's mental faculties razor sharp, but this was a house full of secrets. Laura had the premonition that in accepting their invitation, she'd walked into the middle of a war zone where there were landmines ready to go off with one misstep. The trick was to survive for the next two weeks without getting blown up in the process.

She took two pills, intending to go to bed, but she was too worked up to go to sleep yet. A swim in the pool sounded the perfect antidote for insomnia.

After removing her clothes, she slipped on the one-piece white suit she always wore as a lifeguard. With a towel over one arm she walked down the stairs off the veranda to the patio. She put her towel on a lounger before jumping into the water. The tepid temperature delighted her, and with a sigh she lay back and kicked her feet. In this position she could look up at the blue canopy above with its thumbnail moon and twinkling stars. Sheer paradise.

When she reached the edge, she turned on her stomach to do laps, needing the exercise. Back and forth she went at full speed, feeling the tension leave her body, but near the other side she collided with a hard-muscled male body and felt strong arms go around her, pulling her against him.

A soft gasp escaped her throat. She lifted her head to discover Raoul's dark face just centimeters from hers.

"I…I didn't realize you were in the pool," she stammered like an idiot.

"My villa is on the other side of the hedge. I dived in before noticing you," came his deep, grating voice.

The brothers lived out of each other's pockets. More than ever she understood Chantelle's warning.

His black hair was sleeked away from his forehead, revealing the masculine beauty of his bone structure. The combination of scents from the soap he'd used earlier and the fragrance of her shampoo wafted in the air surrounding them.

Without being able to touch bottom, their bodies brushed against each other. As his powerful legs tangled with hers, she felt an unexpected quickening of desire so intense, she could hardly breathe. The flicker in his black eyes meant he'd registered her reaction. This close to him she couldn't hide the charge of electricity arcing through her. It didn't help that the dusting of black hair on his chest and legs reminded her just how male he was.

Her attraction to him was so potent, it was humiliating. She flung herself out of his arms and kept swimming until she reached the other end of the pool. When she raised her head, she discovered Raoul waiting for her, not in the least winded. He examined her through slumberous eyes. "Shall we race ten laps? The winner can choose the prize."

Laura was intelligent enough not to get into any kind of race with him because he'd win, and she wasn't up to handling the kind of prize she was sure he had in mind. "It has been a long day. I'm afraid I'm too tired to be at my best. Perhaps you should ask Paul. He sings your praises."

Not willing to prolong this conversation, she executed a backward somersault and swam to the other end of the pool. After climbing out to get her towel she didn't look back, but she still felt a pair of penetrating black eyes follow her progress back to her room.

A quick shower and shampoo did nothing to relieve her heightened senses. In his arms she'd come alive. It was shocking to realize she could respond like that when she thought those feelings were permanently dead. On his part he'd done nothing to make her aware of him. He didn't have to. Raoul Laroche was one of those men endowed with traits irresistible to women.

After washing out her suit, she got ready for bed. But when she climbed under the covers, she lay awake for a long time troubled by the sensations still passing through her body. Pure physical chemistry had a lot to answer for. It had little to do with liking or disliking him.

Her mind insisted on going over the interrogation Raoul had put her through earlier in the evening. Every comment or question had stretched the boundaries of civility, and Laura couldn't help but wonder if he was this unpleasant to every stranger he met or if she was the exception.

The two brothers were the pillars of the Laroche financial world. Maybe they were too closely connected and the lines between their professional and personal lives became blurred more often than was healthy.

Judging by Chantelle's remarks, Raoul had a history of issues. Though it might explain his acerbic disposition to a point, Laura was at a loss to understand the caustic edge that had been directed at her personally. She wasn't mistaken about that.

She wasn't mistaken about the fire he'd lit, either. He'd held on to her a little too long for someone who couldn't stand her. Of course, men had an easier time separating their rational thoughts from their physical drives, but Laura wished she could view that moment in the pool with the same sangfroid as Raoul.

He wouldn't have trouble going to sleep tonight. There'd been a number of beautiful women at Guy's party who could make any man's pulse race including his, but it wouldn't mean anything more to him than the pleasure of the fleeting moment.

She hadn't seen a wedding ring on his finger, which

meant Raoul was either a bachelor or divorced. Maybe even separated and waiting for his freedom like Laura. Depending on who asked for the divorce, he could be impatient to be let out of his prison, or dying inside because he was still in love with the woman he'd married.

If he was like Guy, it was probably the latter. That might account for his jaded, pointed remarks meant to inflict pain because he was hurting.

Troubled by Guy's dark, aloof brother, who unfortunately lived on the estate and shared the pool, Laura turned on her side, willing sleep to come. From now on she'd swim during the day to avoid another encounter like tonight. That way there'd be no accidental coming together in the pool, catching her totally off guard.

For one insane moment she'd thought he had been going to kiss her. What was more insane was that she wouldn't have stopped him. How bad was that? The temptation to taste his mouth had left her breathless.

Those feelings happened between near strangers all the time. It was called lust, a word she'd heard all her life, but had never experienced until tonight. Such feelings were wrong. Even though he'd been borderline cruel to her, somewhere deep inside she knew he would make a gratifying lover.

Ashamed of her thoughts, she turned on her stomach and pulled the pillow over the back of her head in the hope of warding them off.

Since the moment Laura had left the pool, Raoul had done twenty laps in order to exhaust himself before going to bed. He'd purposely run into her in order to provoke a response, yet it was Raoul who'd been the one affected.

His ploy to keep her in the pool longer had failed. Worse, the fact that Paul's name came so easily to her lips rankled. If this workout didn't help him sleep, then he'd have to resort to something medicinal.

As he heaved himself out of the water, he heard his brother say, "Raoul? What are you doing here?"

You mean what am I doing out here when I have my own pool?

That was a good question.

Of course, Raoul could have asked a few salient questions of Guy. What made the situation so precarious was the fact that there was only one reason his brother had sauntered out here in his swim trunks.

Like hungry sharks, two grown men were lurking in waters while they circled around a certain woman's bedroom. Viewed from a distance, the scene was appalling. Laura had made fools of them both.

"Paul asked me to swim with him earlier." It was only the truth. "But when I came out here to find him, he was gone. How did Chantelle handle the party?"

Guy walked over to him, his towel slung over one shoulder. "I don't know. She was asleep when I looked in on her. Did Laura swim with you?"

Was that jealousy Raoul detected?

Guy would be shocked if he knew what Raoul hadn't done with her but wanted to. *Ciel!*

The idea that his brother could be having an intimate relationship with her made Raoul see black. "She did a few laps and went in the house."

"So she didn't say anything about Chantelle?" Guy sounded worried. He should be. In fact he ought to be petrified!

"Why would she?"

Guy ran a hand through his hair. "During the party they left the salon together. I was wondering what they talked about."

Raoul shrugged. "I guess you'll have to ask her in the morning," he said pointedly. "That *is* the reason you invited her here, to be a companion to Chantelle, *n'est-ce pas?*"

His brother nodded.

About now a confession was called for. A little sign of remorse for what he was doing to his wife, not even behind her *back* at this point! But no such words passed his lips. Instead, much to Raoul's chagrin, the disappointed look on his face betrayed his true agenda.

Guy had no shame, yet with Raoul watching, his brother couldn't very well walk up the veranda steps to Laura's bedroom. For Chantelle's sake the knowledge that Guy couldn't be with Laura tonight filled Raoul with relief. On a purely personal note it pleased him no end.

"It looks like you won't be needing this." Raoul reached for his brother's towel. Taking his time, he began to dry himself off. No way did he intend to leave the patio until Guy had gone. Tonight's assignation had been foiled. Raoul had zero sympathy for his brother.

"I may be late going into the office in the morning," Guy muttered, showing strains of being beaten. There was no 'may' about it. With Laura living on the premises, it was doubtful the company would see him for the next two weeks.

"I'm afraid I won't be there either. Jean-Luc wants me to look over that complex in Antibes. Why don't you go with me? We'll decide if we want to buy it. With Laura keeping Chantelle company, you can get away for a little while without worrying."

Maybe on the drive he could get his brother to break down and tell him what was going on. They'd never kept secrets from each other in their lives.

Guy shook his head. "Not this time. You go ahead." In the next breath he left the patio, his mind and thoughts elsewhere.

Raoul stayed where he was. Part of him was torn up inside to see the change in Guy. The other part felt disgust over his possible romantic involvement with the woman Raoul couldn't get out of his mind. Laura Aldridge was almost fifteen years younger than Guy. On the loose in Europe, he wondered how many other men she'd ensnared before targeting his brother.

As Raoul had learned, a woman like that didn't have to earn a living. He doubted Laura even had a real job. That business about getting her boss's permission was a con if he'd ever heard one. She lived off her victims. When she'd had enough and was bored, she moved on to the next poor devil whose bank account held a twelve-figure balance. Why couldn't Guy see this?

Tomorrow he'd phone his attorney. It wouldn't hurt to run a check on the American woman. She might not be who she said she was. She might even have a police record on both sides of the Atlantic.

After their parents had died years ago, Guy had always looked after Raoul. Now it was Raoul's turn to protect his brother from a possible predator who had the kind of face and body to tempt every strata of saint down to sinner.

The next morning one of the maids led Laura to a patio off the dining room, where Chantelle was seated. It overlooked a fabulous, multicolored rose garden. She'd smelled their fragrance last evening and couldn't get enough of it.

"*Bonjour,* Laura."

"*Bonjour,* Chantelle." she said back, trying to imitate the sounds. More than ever she marveled at this family. They all spoke English so well. She couldn't imagine learning French with the same fluency.

Her hostess had already wheeled herself to the rectangular glass table supported by ornate wrought iron legs. Laura put her sketchpad down against one of them and took a seat across from her while another maid served them breakfast. The patio having a western exposure, they were shaded from the hot sun.

"How did you sleep?"

"Once the pills worked, I passed out. Thank you for giving them to me. I need to go to a pharmacy and get some of my own."

"Anything you need, all you have to do is ask."

"That's very kind of you."

Like Laura, Chantelle had dressed in a white knit top and matching shorts. She looked cool and perfectly beautiful. Laura's heart felt a wrench to realize that beneath her facade lived an emotionally frozen woman.

"These croissants melt in your mouth."

Chantelle flashed her an unexpected smile. "I'll tell the chef."

Laura chuckled. "To be honest, I feel like I'm in fantasyland."

"I've been there."

"I know. I tended little Paul while you and Raoul walked around Disneyland. You have no idea how much I envied you your wonderful husband and son. Yours was the kind of marriage I wanted one day."

When Chantelle didn't respond to her remarks Laura said, "Actually I'm talking about a completely different place. Your home is a fantasyland—out of this world. Those rose beds are so perfect. You must have the best gardeners on the Côte d'Azur."

"Before my accident, I did all the weeding myself. Now I have to tell them how to do their job. They miss too many."

"Let me do it while I'm here—" she blurted.

Chantelle cocked her dark head. "You like gardening?"

"I remember talking to you about the grandmother who raised me, but I probably didn't mention that we lived in a little forties bungalow in Manhattan Beach. She loved flowers and had me out working alongside her when I was just a girl. It was the one job I loved most, probably because it was outside."

"Is she still alive?"

"No. She died eight years ago. I kept up the yard until I got married. My husband convinced me to sell it. I haven't done any gardening since."

Laura wouldn't have listened to Ted except that a developer was planning to buy the whole strip of houses around there and build a mall. The price being offered was better than what an individual buyer might pay for it. That had been Ted's reasoning at the time.

After she had reluctantly sold it, the project had fallen through, but she had a feeling Ted had known it would. He just didn't want her holding on to her memories. Everything to do with him had been a mistake.

Not liking the direction of her thoughts, she munched on the chilled honeydew melon, her favorite.

Chantelle eyed her over the rim of her coffee. "If you're serious about the weeding, be my guest."

"I already am." They both smiled at the same time. "It would make me very happy to get out there so I can feel useful. My hands are itching to dig into the soil."

"I know the feeling."

How sad that Chantelle could admit to such a thing, yet she refused to act on it.

"Tomorrow I'll ask the gardener to bring you some gloves and the things you'll need."

"Thank you."

"I believe there's an artist in anyone who loves gardening. After you've finished eating, may I see what you've been sketching?"

Guy had hoped Laura would draw his wife out, but so far Chantelle was the one forcing Laura to open up.

"I'll show you now." She reached for the pad and handed it to her.

After Chantelle flipped the cover over, a soft gasp escaped her lips. She studied the top page, then began thumbing through the others. Finally she raised her head. Her eyes were shining. For just a moment, she was like the old Chantelle.

"You've captured the whole Palio—the people…the costumes…the horses…the city— You're a genius!"

"No—"

"Indeed you are. What medium do you work with when you make these life-size? Oil? Watercolor?"

"Neither. I studied graphic design in college. After I graduated, I went to work for a video game company in California. My job is to provide interesting backgrounds for games which other people in the company develop."

"Video games? Like the ones my son plays, much to my disgust?"

"I'm afraid so," Laura admitted. "The technology is so advanced, the industry has taken off. With my pencil I create backgrounds for all ages. This one on the Palio will be used as a horse race obviously. Each horse and rider runs through a separate part of the town with many obstacles to overcome. My job is to find unusual places that suggest games to me."

"Where else have you been?" Chantelle actually sounded interested and Laura could glimpse shades of her former self.

"Two months ago I spent a week in Hamlin, Germany, to create a background for a children's game. It's an adorable town with a lot of carvings. My grandmother read me all the fairy tales. One of my favorites was 'The Pied Piper.' I came up with the idea of him leading all the children out of the town and the player has to prevent them from following him by using various methods that take a certain amount of skill.

"After leaving there I went to Holland for a week to sketch the windmills and old gabled houses for another game about stopping the holes in the dikes."

Chantelle shook her head. "But this is remarkable! *You* are remarkable!"

"No, but I must admit it's a lot of fun to get paid a commission for doing something I love. In between times, I still work part-time as a lifeguard at the beach. As you can imagine, I've done the sketches for an underwater video game for children. It involves a merman." An image of Raoul in the pool suddenly flashed into her mind, causing her to take an extra breath.

"When do you have time to see your husband?"

At the mention of Ted, Laura shuddered. "My two-year marriage failed almost from the start, Chantelle. He's an attorney from a political family, but he assured me he wasn't interested in politics. I told him I didn't want to be married to a politician and put him off for a long time until I was convinced he meant it.

"A few months into our marriage I learned he'd always planned to run for Congress. Everything had been a lie. He didn't love me, all he wanted was to parade me in front of people, something I abhor.

"Six months ago, after I learned he'd been with other women, I found the strength to leave him and file for divorce. He's refusing to give me one, but in time I'll get it and he won't have a choice."

"Bravo!" Chantelle exclaimed. "Once a liar, always a liar." She said it with such vehemence, Laura had the idea Chantelle was speaking from personal experience. But surely it wasn't anything to do with Guy....

"In Ted's case it's true." Her gaze flicked to her hostess. "He's nothing like your husband, who absolutely adores you."

The second the words left her lips, the atmosphere changed. Chantelle handed her back the sketchpad.

Laura couldn't bear the thought that Guy might have lied about something that could have hurt his wife so profoundly. In fact she refused to believe it. "Has he left for his office, or will he be joining you?"

"He's in his study on a conference call."

"Lucky you to have him at home." Whether it irked Chantelle or not, Laura had said it. "What are your plans today?"

"I'm having my massage in a half hour, then my hair done. Later I plan to do some reading out here."

"Mind if I sketch while you read? The rose garden, in fact your whole villa with that maze around the back, has given me an idea for a children's game, but only with your permission of course."

"What's it about?" Chantelle sounded pleased by the idea.

"It's not fully formed in my mind yet. Maybe later you can help me brainstorm."

"You wouldn't mind?"

"Mind what?"

The interjection of a silky male voice sent a small shiver through Laura. She didn't have to turn her head to know who'd come out on the patio.

"Bonjour, Raoul. What's going on around here?

Doesn't anyone have to go to work anymore? After being in Switzerland, I would have thought you'd be in your office at the crack of dawn. Instead here you are and Guy's still on the phone in the den."

Laura watched him move around the table to kiss his sister-in-law's cheek. Dressed in a black silk shirt and gray trousers that molded his powerful legs, he looked incredible. "I'm on my way to Antibes on business and thought maybe you and Laura might like to go with me. You could do a little shopping. We'll pack your wheelchair."

"Not today. I have other plans, but I'm sure Laura would enjoy getting out."

Laura's heartbeat sped up at the mere idea of being alone with him. "That's very thoughtful of you, Chantelle, but I'm perfectly happy here." Guy was counting on her.

"Nonsense. You won't be gone all day, will you, Raoul?"

"That depends."

Laura had a feeling he'd said that just to get under her skin. Nothing had changed since last night. She could still feel his antipathy.

"Go with him, Laura. The drive might give you more ideas. Paul and his friends will be around. I'll be busy keeping an eye on them."

For some reason Chantelle wanted to be left alone and she didn't care if she pushed Laura on to her complicated brother-in-law. Maybe Laura had offended her by saying what she had about Guy. It probably felt like she was pressuring her.

If any progress was going to be made with his wife,

she needed to refrain from talking about her husband in front of her. No matter how anxious Guy was to bring his wife around to her normal self, Laura's grandmother would remind her of the old adage about eating an elephant one bite at a time.

"By your silence, one would assume you're afraid to go with me," Raoul mocked before devouring a croissant. "I promise not to drive off into the sunset with you, Mrs. Aldridge. Whatever would Mr. Aldridge say."

"*Assez,* Raoul! If you keep this up, she'll get the wrong impression."

"What impression?" His hooded gaze swerved to Laura. "Is that true?" After asking the question, he proceeded to eat a small bunch of purple grapes.

For some perverse reason he enjoyed needling her. Unfortunately, Chantelle wasn't being any help. Laura had the distinct feeling she enjoyed the repartee. The two of them shared a unique relationship she couldn't begin to understand.

Making a decision not to be a part of it, she stood up from the chair and reached for her sketchpad. "How soon did you want to leave?"

From the gleam in his dark eyes, her question had pleased him. "Right now."

"Then give me a minute to change."

His gaze traveled over her in lazy appraisal. "You look fine as you are."

"Thank you, but if I'm going to do any shopping, I'd feel more comfortable in a skirt. Where shall I meet you?"

"I'll bring my car around the front of the villa."

"Give me five minutes." She looked at Chantelle. "While I'm out, is there something I can pick up for you? A book you've been wanting to read?"

"Nothing for me."

"A special treat then?"

Chantelle flashed her a smile. "That's very sweet. Thank you for offering, but *non merci.*"

Laura planned to bring her back something anyway. Her gaze flicked to Raoul who was eyeing her strangely. "I won't be long."

His lips twisted. "Did you hear that, Chantelle?"

She chided him without rancor, "Not all women are as impossible as you choose to believe. A woman as lovely as Laura doesn't need to primp."

Not wanting to hear any more, Laura left the patio to change into her wraparound skirt in a taupe color with white trim. Before coming to breakfast she'd caught her hair back in a ponytail with a white scarf. Because she thought she'd be in the house with Chantelle all day, she hadn't bothered with makeup.

She wouldn't bother now. Raoul Laroche would have to take her as she was. Hopefully her demeanor didn't reveal her highly emotional state. It wouldn't do for Raoul to know how much his nearness affected her.

After filling her tote bag with supplies, she made her way to the front of the house before the five minutes were up. No sooner had she closed the door behind her than she saw a white cabriolet Porsche wheel around the drive.

A cry of alarm escaped her lips. How had Ted found her? How did he get past the security guard? For a moment she felt sick to her stomach.

CHAPTER THREE

RAOUL was surprised to discover Laura waiting for him.
To find a woman ready on time had to be a first. He
coasted to a stop.

However, the sight of her champagne hair and unmistakable figure made him slow to realize she had a
pallor that hadn't been there when she'd left the table.
He had a suspicion she'd seen Guy on her way out and
they'd had words. To learn Laura was leaving the villa
with Chantelle's blessing in order to go with Raoul
must have upset his brother.

Pleased to have foiled another attempt for Guy to be
alone with her, Raoul reached across the seat to open
the passenger door for her. She looked good. Most
women past their teens couldn't get away without
wearing makeup, but she carried it off perfectly.

Beneath the attractive skirt, her gorgeous long legs
were bare. Much to his chagrin he could find nothing
artificial about her. The more she underplayed her
looks, the more she stood out like a fresh peach
warming in the sun, all pink and golden.

Her arm brushed against his as she fastened her seat

belt. His body quickened at the contact. The recurring sensation wasn't supposed to happen. Once she closed the door, he put the car in gear and took off without saying anything. He followed the winding drive flanked by cypress trees until they passed the guardhouse and came out on the coast road.

After a few minutes he said, "If Chantelle had come with us, I would have brought the sedan. Do you mind the top down? I can always put it up."

"That's up to you. Frankly I like being able to see all around," she responded without looking at him.

The women he knew didn't want to be blown about, but as he was finding out with Laura, she wasn't your typical female. She didn't talk incessantly, a quality that should have pleased him since they were going to be together for as long as he felt like keeping her away from Guy. Yet the fact that she appeared so relaxed with him actually irritated him.

"This area isn't that much different from your coast in Southern California."

"It's completely different," she countered. "The ocean and the sea can't be compared." Having been to California on several occasions, he privately agreed with her. "All those ancient little villages I saw from the helicopter tucked away high in the Maritime Alps create a charm like no place else on earth."

He hadn't realized Guy had flown her here in the helicopter. That was an unprecedented move on his part. His brother was in deep.

She recrossed her legs, probably on purpose. Among other things it drew his attention to the bone-colored leather sandals encasing her feet. No toenail polish. Everything *au naturel.* So far he couldn't see anything he didn't like and he'd been trying!

"You've traveled in Europe before?"

"Some, but not along the Riviera. It's breathtaking."

Raoul hated to admit *she* was too. The truth of it shook him almost as much as the fact that she didn't give anything away she didn't want him to know.

He came to the turn for Cros de Cagnes and veered left to follow the coast road. "What is it you do for a living…besides rescue drowning victims?"

She put on a pair of sunglasses. "I draw landscapes to create backgrounds for video games."

Video games? Raoul had to admit that was one answer he would never have expected. "What genre?" She was an artiste all right, but the kind she was alluding to came as a revelation, if it were true.

"Mostly for children and young adults."

"No war games?"

"If you mean the kind guys from eighteen to thirty play all day and all night long, then no."

Whether she was conning him or not, he couldn't help but chuckle because what she'd said was so true. After she gave him some examples, he was prompted to ask the name of the company she worked for.

"Other World Video Games. You've probably never heard of it."

"I can't say I have." So far she'd picked something so safe, he couldn't accuse her of lying until he'd researched it. "How long have you been doing that kind of work?"

"Since college."

"Did you get a degree?"

She nodded. "Graphic design."

While his mind did the math he remembered something. "At breakfast I saw you with a sketchpad."

"Yes. It's filled with drawings of Siena and the Palio. I was working on a scene when your brother started to choke. Chantelle wanted to see it."

To his dismay, every time he asked her a question, she answered it without hesitation. If she had things to hide, he wouldn't know it from her seemingly forthright manner. So far she hadn't asked anything of him. The idea that she was merely tolerating him didn't sit well.

Raoul kept telling himself he was doing this for Guy's sake, but a part of him knew that wasn't totally true. Laura Aldridge had captured his attention in too many ways to lie to himself.

Earlier this morning he'd phoned his attorney and asked him to run a background check on her. Louis promised to get back to him when he had any solid information. In the meantime it was up to Raoul to learn what he could from the woman herself. If he asked more personal questions, maybe he could get her to squirm. That's what he was looking for, to catch her in something that would give away her agenda.

"How do you balance your work and marriage?"

After a quiet interval, she said, "I don't."

That's right. She only had time to concentrate on ruining someone else's. Her refusal to play his game had just raised the stakes. He took the next right that brought them into Juan-les-Pins, an extension of Antibes.

"I'm going to check out a complex of buildings in

the yachting district that our company might purchase for our export line. It won't take me long. Afterward I'll drive us through Vence to one of those little villages you referred to. We'll have a late lunch and do whatever we feel like."

She nodded as if amenable, but he felt her tension because she'd only been putting up with him until they returned to the villa. He could tell by the rigidity of her body that her patience was wearing thin. That was the crack in the veneer he'd been waiting for.

"Would you like me to stop and get you a drink first?"

"No, thank you. I have a bottle of water in my bag if I get thirsty."

Still no eye contact. To travel around Europe alone picking up vulnerable men, she'd learned to be independent. It was part of her mystique, another intriguing trait he hated to acknowledge.

A few minutes later he pulled up to the entry of an empty warehouse and parked the car alongside a bank of palm trees. They'd shield her from the sun while he was inside. Jean-Luc, their company's real estate agent, was already in front of the doors waiting for him.

As soon as he saw them, the older man headed for the Porsche. One look at Laura and he started salivating. It put Raoul in mind of Guy, who would have had the same reaction when he'd seen Laura for the first time. The identical thing had happened to Raoul, causing his own desire and anger to flare.

On impulse and something else he couldn't put a name to yet, he leaned across the seat and kissed her full on her unsuspecting mouth. It happened so naturally she didn't have time to resist.

That was the idea. Jean-Luc was bearing down on them. A picture was worth a thousand words, so they said. He was the biggest gossip on the Côte d'Azur. He had to be to stay in business. By tomorrow word would have reached Guy's ears that his brother was involved with a blond bombshell, and Guy's hands would be tied.

If he confronted Raoul, Guy would be admitting his own guilt. Though he'd be furious with him at first, it would expose Laura for the opportunist she was. One day Guy would thank him.

But Raoul's thoughts faded as the taste of her was all he'd imagined and more, prompting him to take his time until she tore her lips from his. "How dare you," she cried in a low tone.

Her outrage sounded genuine enough, but it came an instant too late because she'd started to respond to him before catching herself. It wasn't something you could hide. If she was supposed to be involved with Guy, what did her reaction to Raoul mean?

To his dismay another part of him didn't want to know the answer because for an insane moment he was enjoying himself too much. Raoul couldn't abide the thought of her responding to him and his brother, too. Yet that was why he'd done this experiment, to find out what kind of woman she really was.

He smiled. "Come on, Laura. After what almost happened in the swimming pool last night, we both know you didn't mind it all that much." Satisfied to see the rush of hot color sweep into her cheeks, he left her to her own devices while he levered himself from the car to intercept Jean-Luc.

Denied an introduction, his curious friend would be even more eager to know the identity of the new mystery woman in Raoul's life.

"Oh-la-la—" Jean-Luc clapped him on the shoulder as they walked toward the doors. "When your ex finds out about that one, she'll want to scratch her eyes out."

Raoul grinned despite his torment. "She can try..."

The other man's laughter rang in the air.

What Jean-Luc didn't know was that Danielle was no match for the woman whose lips were as soft and lush as the rest of her. In trying to protect Chantelle, it was guaranteed Raoul had opened himself up to an infinite number of sleepless nights and cold showers.

Laura couldn't stop the trembling. Though secretly thrilled to realize the desire she'd felt last night wasn't all on her side, she was also terrified. What if one of Ted's undercover agents had discovered where she was staying and had followed the Porsche to Antibes.

With a telephoto lens they could've taken pictures of Raoul kissing her. That kind of evidence could influence a judge into siding with Ted's attorney to hold up the case. Who knew how long it would take before she obtained her divorce? Laura didn't dare entertain a relationship with Raoul that could jeopardize everything she'd been working so hard for.

She reached in her bag and drained her bottle of water in an effort to rid herself of the imprint of Raoul's hard mouth. Those male lips that could twist with mocking cruelty had covered hers with enough coaxing pressure to draw a spontaneous response she'd had no power to stop. Knowing that he had a distinct dislike for her made her physical reaction to him even more unacceptable.

Though their kiss had been real enough, she sensed he'd done it for the other man's benefit. To what end she didn't know. If Raoul was trying to frighten her off, he didn't have to wait until they had an audience. Things were more of a mystery than ever unless Chantelle was somehow behind all this.

It pained Laura to think that Chantelle might have asked her brother-in-law to find a way to get Laura to leave the villa without involving Guy. If she truly didn't want her husband's attentions, then of course she'd resent his bringing Laura into their home to try to help. Thinking back to this morning, Chantelle had been adamant that Laura go on the drive without her.

Laura could leave France tonight of course and probably ought to, but she owed Guy a truthful explanation. No matter what, her loyalty was to him. Yet to tell him what had happened today could also hurt him deeply if he didn't know his brother was working against him to get rid of Laura.

She couldn't figure it out. The two men's relationship had to be somewhat normal, didn't it? Otherwise Raoul wouldn't have been at the party. Surely if there was real animosity between them, the brothers wouldn't work together or live in such close proximity to each other.

Stymied by so many unanswered questions and the

kiss that still haunted her, she came to the conclusion that all she could do was bluff her way through the next two weeks and avoid Raoul as much as possible. He liked making trouble, but she could give it back if she had to.

If things became impossible, she'd go to Guy and tell him she'd changed her mind about staying. To make a good case she'd tell him she didn't want his family involved in the event Ted found out where she was staying. Surely he'd understand that. Who knew what complications might arise that could upset Chantelle unnecessarily.

Laura was so deep in thought she didn't realize Raoul had returned until she heard the door open. In that brief moment she glanced around and their eyes met.

"You surprise me," he said after starting the car.

"What? That I didn't run away from you?" She sighed. "I've been kissed before by men I didn't know, even when I wasn't saving their lives." Enjoying turning this back on him she added, "If you were that anxious, you should have taken advantage while we were in the pool last night, but then I suppose you stopped short because you were afraid someone might be watching."

The car leaped ahead. His eyes burned like black fires. "Were you disappointed?"

"I think so."

"Only think?" he challenged.

For a moment he sounded playful rather than serious, catching her off guard. She couldn't help smiling.

If this was part of his game, he was good at it. He was gorgeous, too. The most beautiful man she'd ever met in her life. Southern California was full of them.

Her husband, Ted, had stood out, but no one came close to the gut-wrenching sensuality of Raoul Laroche.

Then his eyes narrowed on her mouth before his expression hardened, causing lines to darken his features. He turned his attention back to the road leading out of the marina area and in a flash, when she'd felt buoyant for no reason, the moment disappeared as if it had never been.

Instead of the interrogation he'd subjected her to on the way to Antibes, he remained silent during the picturesque drive into the colorful hills with their patches of tuberose and jasmine. The tension between them was almost palpable, but until he explained himself, Laura had nothing to say.

Though she was tempted to ask him to take her home, her pride had gotten in the way. She didn't want him to think his tactics back there had succeeded in destroying her confidence.

The scent of flowers grew more intoxicating the higher they climbed to the craggy summits. His Porsche was made for these hairpin turns on narrow roads. He handled his car like a Formula 1 driver, removing the worry she wasn't safe. Any fear she harbored came from her own susceptibility to his potent charisma. Just watching the way the steering wheel responded beneath his strong hands, the fluid motion of his powerful body when he moved, brought her pleasure.

Before long they entered a quaint medieval village perched on a spur of land with a stream running through the rocky gorge below. The sign said Tourettes Sur Loup. She loved the unique names.

He pulled into a parking lot full of other cars and

turned off the motor. "I'm confident the artist in you will find something to purchase once we've eaten. The village is full of local artisan crafts."

She listened for that dreaded trace of mockery but didn't hear it. Relieved he'd decided not to hound her for the moment, she alighted from the car before he could help her. Laura would be all right if he didn't touch her. If someone was photographing them from a distance, she wouldn't provide them another opportunity to catch her in an intimate moment with Raoul.

They entered beneath an arched porte with a tall clock tower and followed the main street through the oldest part of the town filled with tourists. "The village was fortified in the Middle Ages," Raoul explained. "These are the only walls remaining."

"It's unreal," she cried softly, her gaze traveling down a sunken, stone-paved path centuries old.

He led them to a little café where they ate *steak aux frites* and topped it off with a *tarte à l'orange,* a village specialty. Replete after the delicious meal, they explored the myriad of shops displaying local crafts. Laura wanted to buy everything, but in the end she purchased nothing except an oval-shaped, locally woven basket full of violets that grew in the region. Their deep-purple color thrilled her.

"I'm paying for these," she announced, putting some Euros in the woman's hand before Raoul could pull the necessary bills from his wallet.

He eyed her skeptically. "You're sure this is all you want? You can't take flowers back to Los Angeles with you." Oh how politely he'd said the words, like he was speaking to a child. She got the impression he couldn't wait for her to announce her departure plans.

For a little while she'd forgotten that Raoul was her enemy, and with that reminder the enjoyment of the last hour vanished.

"They're for Chantelle." A thank-you gift for allowing her to stay in their home. "She misses puttering in her garden. I thought she might enjoy these." Laura buried her nose in the petals to inhale their sweet perfume.

When she lifted her head, she caught a look of something she couldn't decipher in those black depths before he took the basket from her. A small shiver ran through her as they retraced their steps to the car parked beyond the walled town.

After she climbed in, he placed the basket on the floor behind her seat where the flowers would be protected. This time she was careful not to look at him. That way she wouldn't be subjected to any more fiery darts of accusation.

Once again they were traveling along the back roads of Provence that were more alive and colorful than any painting she could ever create. They eventually passed through another charming town whose name she couldn't pronounce.

"This was the home of Marcel Pagnol," he informed her in a gravelly voice. "In case you don't know wh—"

"I know," she cut him off. "Hollywood made his novels world famous. I've been seeing *Jean de la Florette* around every farmhouse and fountain."

By the shifting of gears she realized she'd irritated

him. "You could have played the part of Manon. She was a child of nature, too."

"You mean the girl who had every man in the village lusting after her?" she inquired. She shook her head despairingly. "You might have spared me that."

Through the grimace he said, "You're the one who chose to read something negative into my remark. In my own apparently obtuse way I was attempting to pay you a compliment."

"You mean to make up for your uninvited advance in front of the real estate agent?"

His lips thinned in response. "I preferred Jean-Luc to think I was having an affair with you."

"Nice," she bit out. "There's nothing a woman loves more than to be considered a man's girl-toy. Yet I have to admit I'm surprised that a Frenchman like you who knows he's attractive and can obviously have his pick on a whim has to prove anything."

She smiled in satisfaction to see the way his fingers tightened on the wheel. Unable to resist she said, "Evidently your agent is a member of the good-old-boy's network. Every society in the world has them, especially among the exceptionally rich and famous.

"Are you hoping word of me will get back to your latest girlfriend? Or your wife? Or possibly your ex? Or maybe your almost ex? Now I have to ask myself if you're praying she'll finally leave you alone, or maybe this woman is another man's wife and you're counting on her jealousy to bring her to heel."

She heard a volley of French invective that needed no translation. "That's quite a tongue you've acquired."

"It's been sharpened on wealthy men like you who collect women like some people collect shells." The Stillman men led the pack.

"How many have there been?" he ground out.

"Thousands! However, I dare say that's not as many as your fertile imagination suspects." Laura laughed in pain. "Me thinks I'd better get myself away to a nunnery quick before you become my next victim. Heaven forbid, eh?"

"Heaven forbid," he muttered so morosely, she felt it to her bones. Ridiculous as it was, his repudiation stung.

They'd reached Nice and were following the signs for Cap Ferrat.

"Now that we've gotten all that out of the way, Raoul, maybe we can both enjoy the rest of the short drive back to the villa. The next time you decide to invite me anywhere, better not obey the urge or I'll know you're only lusting after me. For your information, that's the biggest turn-off to a woman there is."

He turned his head in her direction. "Then how do you explain your response when I kissed you?" came the slithering taunt.

The man was a devil. "Chemical reaction." Knowing what question he would ask next, she answered it. "And yes, it happens every time. It's my nature. You already called it and you'd be right because clearly you're a very intelligent man, so consider yourself warned."

She was sure he drove them above the speed limit to reach the villa. The second he pulled to a screeching halt, she got out of the car and reached for the basket of flowers. As she turned around Guy came down the steps to greet her. He waved to his brother.

The sight of him was like a balm to her soul and she flew toward him. He put his arm around her, flowers and all and smiled warmly at her. "How was your day?"

"I discovered it's true. Provence *is* God's garden. These are for Chantelle."

As he took the basket from her, his eyes misted. "Let's take them in to her. She'll love them."

Without a backward glance Laura walked into the foyer with him. The click of the door coincided with the squeal of tires out on the gravel.

Guy looked askance. "Did Raoul tear around with you the whole day like that?

Now would be the perfect time to confide in him about his brother, but she couldn't do it. Whatever rush he got out of insulting her, it would grow old with time. She could outlast him.

"Of course not. I think he was anxious to get back to his villa for an important phone call with the agent." Even if it was a lie, it was an innocent one. "Let me freshen up, then I'll join you and Chantelle."

"What did he think of the property?"

She averted her eyes. "I'm not sure. He didn't really say. See you two in a few minutes."

Once in the guest suite, Laura decided to phone her best friend in California, who lived in the apartment across the hall from her. Cindy, who'd been divorced for a year, was keeping an eye on her place and gathered the mail for her from the box downstairs. In case there was a bill she hadn't taken care of, she needed to know about it and get it paid. Laura did the same thing for Cindy when she flew to Georgia to visit her family, and the two women had formed a close friendship. If Ted ever came to the apartment when Laura was out, Cindy documented the time so Laura could give the information to her attorney. There was a restraining order on him, but Ted chose to ignore it whenever he felt like it.

When she and Cindy played tennis or saw a film, they commiserated about the men in their lives and talked about the ideal man who would one day sweep them off their feet. One of these days Laura would confide in Cindy about Raoul, but she knew he was far from her ideal man. He was arrogant, frustrating and it was all right for him to make insinuations and ask all the impertinent questions he wanted, but she noticed he never did tell her one thing about himself. The very thought of him triggered a fresh spurt of adrenaline.

Restless as a caged animal, Raoul paced the rooms of his villa, but the bars were invisible. He could step outside anytime he wanted—beyond the flowering hedge if he so desired—in order to have access to her.

He desired all right.

During their outing she'd been playing him with a master hand. The lines were so blurred at this point he didn't know what was truth and what was the lie. When she had rushed toward Guy like that, all the breath had left his lungs. His brother in turn had showed her the kind of tenderness he felt for someone he truly cared about, loved even.

Was that the result of her saving his life? Could the answer be as simple and as complicated as that?

In desperation he phoned Louis, but his attorney had left his office for the day. If he'd found the information Raoul had requested on her, he would have phoned him back by now anyway. It appeared he would have to wait a little longer.

An hour later, after a shower and shave, Raoul decided to go over to Guy's and take him aside, lay it all out. He couldn't go on like this another twenty-four hours.

Laura had said she'd been in Europe before. If his brother had been having a long-term affair with her, then Raoul needed to convince him to give her up for all the obvious reasons. Chantelle would never get better if she thought she'd lost Guy.

His sister-in-law had guts and courage to welcome Laura into their home at her husband's request. But when she must surely be bleeding inside, how long could she keep up her convincing front?

More to the point, how long could Laura stay under that roof knowing her presence had to be crucifying Chantelle? He raked his hands through his hair, trying to fit all the pieces together, but that was the problem. Just when he thought one would go into place, he discovered it was the wrong piece or the wrong place.

Earlier when Laura had told him she was buying the violets for Chantelle, he could have sworn she'd done it out of kindness, nothing more. At one point the jabs and arrows had seemed to change to gentle teasing. Their conversation had slid in and out of context until he didn't know where he was with her.

Prepared for the fight Guy would put up, he left the house for his brother's. Raoul found the family eating dinner on the patio. The basket of violets served as the centerpiece. There was no sign of Laura.

"Hey, Uncle Raoul."

"Hey, yourself, Paul."

Chantelle looked up. "There you are. If you want to join us, I'll tell cook."

"I'm not hungry, *merci.*"

His brother, acting as if nothing was wrong, motioned for him to sit down. "How did it go with Jean-Luc? Was he right about the complex? You think it's worth purchasing?"

What a cool customer his brother was. Raoul could only marvel. "I want a few days to think about it."

Guy nodded. "Thanks for taking Laura with you today. When I told her how much you dislike playing tour guide, she said she was doubly grateful for the way you put yourself out."

If that was a direct quote, and it sounded like it was, Raoul had reason to believe Laura had told Guy the truth, that his younger brother had trespassed on his private territory earlier today. That changed the timing of Raoul's agenda. He would wait and see what his brother did with the information when they were alone.

In case it brought Guy to his senses before things went any further, then it would have been worth it...even if Raoul would always be haunted by the memory of her mouth moving beneath his.

Chantelle swallowed the last of her tea. "Laura assured me she would treasure the memory of your trip to Tourettes. She's truly *une enfant de la nature* to bring me these violets."

At the reminder of their conversation about Manon, the hand in Raoul's pocket formed a fist. Incredibly it seemed Laura had won Chantelle's acceptance. Or had she? Was it all pretense?

He gazed around their little *tableau à trois*. While Paul ate his dinner oblivious to the tension, Guy sat there with no intention of giving anything away in front of Chantelle. She'd probably known about his extra-marital affair for a long time. It was understandable why Laura hadn't yet made up the fourth to this *spectacle à Laroche*.

Getting to his feet he announced, "I'm going for a dip in the pool." Maybe Guy would follow him and demand an explanation. If not now, later.

At some point Laura had to make an appearance. Raoul had nothing to do but wait for everything to play out. He walked through the villa to the patio where he stripped down to his swim trunks and dived in. A good workout was what he needed to release his pent-up negative energy.

Ten minutes later he was finishing his laps when Paul made an appearance from around the side of the house.

Raoul smiled at him from the other end. *"Salut, mon gars."*

"Hi." His nephew, still dressed in shorts and a T-shirt, sat down on the edge and dangled his strong legs in the water.

"Did you have a good time at Claude's today?"

"It was okay. How long ago did she leave?"

Not sure he'd heard Paul correctly, Raoul swam across to him. "Did who leave? Your *maman* was sitting at the dinner table ten minutes ago."

"I meant Laura."

"I wasn't aware she'd gone anywhere." He hoped she was in her bedroom nursing a migraine over her guilt.

"She was going to start teaching me CPR, but I guess she forgot. The maid said Laura asked Pierre to drive her someplace in the limo so papa wouldn't have to leave *maman*."

That bit of news sent a shockwave through Raoul's body. What destination did Laura have in mind tonight? Had she planned to be with another man she'd met before? Nothing about her added up. There was only one way to find out the truth. He picked up his clothes and started for his house.

"Do you want to stay and swim with me?"

"I'm afraid I can't right now. I have plans, but we'll do some laps tomorrow."

"Okay."

"*À toute à l'heure.*"

"*Ciao.*"

Once he reached the house Raoul pulled out his cell phone and dialed the limo driver. Pierre picked up on the third ring. "*Oui, Monsieur Raoul?*"

"Where are you now?"

"Villefranche."

"*Et Mme Aldridge?*"

"She's walking the grounds of the Villa Leopolda."

"How much longer do you expect she'll be?"

"Since she just got started, I would imagine a half hour anyway. Is there an emergency?"

"*Non.* This can wait. *Merci,* Pierre." He clicked off.

CHAPTER FOUR

LAURA was making her way back from the Villa
Leopolda estate when she discovered the limo was
gone. In its place an unfamiliar black Mercedes sedan
stood parked, but a dangerously familiar Frenchman in
cream trousers and a soft yellow crew neck lounged
against the front fender watching her progress.

After their wild skirmish that had raised more questions than it had answered during the day, there was no
escaping Raoul. As a matter of fact, she did wonder if
he might come looking for her because he was a man
who couldn't tolerate unfinished business. She had
thought she'd figured out why he didn't like her, and
under the circumstances she had made up her mind to
be nicer to him.

Guy's family was very close-knit. While they were
going through this terrible period with Chantelle, Raoul
obviously resented any outsider coming in. Laura could
understand that. With tensions running high it was
always harder to behave normally around a stranger.
Raoul wasn't used to anyone else being there. Perhaps

he was even a little jealous that he didn't have Chantelle's full attention when he did drop in.

Because Laura had half expected to see him before the night was over, her footsteps didn't falter as she made her way toward him. It was only 9:20 p.m., that magic time of night between darkness and light.

He waited with his powerful arms folded. Though a modern man in contemporary clothes, he had the look of a dark, forbidding prince who might have had the estate behind her built for his own private pleasure.

A strange half smile lifted one corner of his compelling mouth. "If you're in the market for a piece of property, the villa can be purchased if you make an offer over 500 million American dollars."

She stopped three feet from him. "That's what the pilot told me when he flew me over it when I arrived here. I'm afraid I don't earn that kind of money."

"A woman like you doesn't have to."

Another glove slapped against her cheek. And here she'd been feeling more charitable toward him.

"You mean all I have to do is ask *you* to buy it for me and *voilà*—it's mine?"

He straightened to his imposing height, reminding her how incredibly appealing he was. "It might be…for a price."

She nodded. "That's fair. I doubt even King Leopold's first mistress knew he only planned to install her here for a season. She was a fool…like all the others that followed her. What *is* yours? Price, I mean." It gave her a secret thrill to bait him.

His expression hardened, filling her with satisfaction

that he couldn't have it all his own way every second. "It might be too high."

"You mean for a woman like me," she mimicked him. "You've made your point and are probably right."

"Stop the pretense, Laura."

She'd had it with him. "What have I done wrong now, Raoul?"

A bleak expression entered his eyes, almost human. She didn't know he could look like that, and it softened her to discover he might have feelings. "According to Pierre, you've been out here two hours. That's a long time when you can't even tour the rooms."

"I wasn't interested in the interior."

"Somehow that doesn't surprise me."

"Since you've already decided what kind of woman I am, I guess it wouldn't."

He sucked in his breath. "What's your real reason for being here?"

She laughed. "My real reason? What's yours?"

His black brows formed a bar above his eyes. "Paul hoped you'd be back so you'd teach him CPR."

"Paul was very endearing when he said he'd like to learn, but I couldn't pin him down to a time. We decided to play it by ear."

"Are you certified?"

"Yes. Since you're such a protective uncle, I'll have you know I've taught hundreds of people."

"Even adult males?"

She cocked her head. "Are you needing a lesson?"

"And if I were?" he mocked.

She eyed him frankly. "I don't know. Can you afford

me? But maybe the better question to ask would be, can your reputation stand being in the company of a married woman like me?"

A little nerve hammered at his temple. "*How* married are you?" he demanded.

If she wasn't mistaken, the subject had him all worked up. This was getting fascinating. "You either are, or you aren't. Which are you, by the way, Raoul?"

"Don't change the subject."

"It's the same subject, as far as I can tell, Raoul. Why don't you want to talk about yourself? What are you afraid of?" she teased with a smile. "Has your wife hired a private detective to follow your every move so he can show her pictures of the latest woman in your life? I'm told blackmail is still big business in France. Especially when you're talking the Laroche fortune. Come on and tell me the truth. Who has more? You or Guy?"

His chest rose and fell visibly. "Does he know what you've been doing out here alone?"

Laura couldn't keep up with his thought processes. He was all over the place. She felt like she was on the witness stand. "Of course. He's the one who suggested I ask Pierre to drive me."

The glitter coming from those dark eyes jolted her. "Guy would do anything for you wouldn't he."

"Well...I did save his life."

"Can you prove it?" he bit out.

"No, but I imagine if you ask any of his friends who were there like Maurice or Luigi, they would be able to tell you. Luigi was exceptionally grateful to me too. In fact, he asked me if I'd like to spend the night at his villa in Rome, but Guy got to me first."

Raoul shifted his weight restlessly before staring into her eyes. "I'll concede I've been a little rough on you. For the last time, why did you come out here to this villa?"

"So if I tell you now, you'll believe me?"

"Let me hear it first," he murmured, though it seemed to cost him to allow even that much latitude.

"I wanted to do some sketches of the estate while there weren't too many people around." I wanted to get away from you. "During the day visitors often stop to talk or ask questions and it interrupts my concentration. Does that satisfy you?"

"No." He almost hissed the word.

The white-hot heat of anger ran up her body to her face. "That's because you hoped to catch me with a man so you could tell your brother to throw the scheming opportunist out of his house. Before you do that, you'd better be able to explain how I had time to do *this!*"

She opened her tote bag and thrust the sketchpad at him. "Go on. Look inside. I dare you," she whispered because if she said it in any louder, she'd rouse the security people stationed around the villa.

In an economy of movement he turned back the cover. It was a new sketchpad, the one she'd put in her purse before they left for Antibes. The first three pages were drawings she'd done down on the marina while she had been waiting for him. However, the next twenty contained her series of the Villa Leopolda.

Not even Raoul could argue that she'd had time for a secret tryst and still complete that many detailed drawings in a two-hour time limit. This was the first time he'd seen any of her artwork. He studied each one for an indefinite period. She experienced immense delight watching him eat crow.

Eventually he closed it and handed it back to her. His eyes were mere black slits. "You're very gifted," his voice grated.

"But you still dislike me. I can live with that as long as you stay out of my way until the two weeks are up. So far you've had trouble in that department." His lips thinned at that remark. She couldn't be happier. "As you can see from your own experience, men have a hard time leaving me alone, whatever their private reasons. It gets tiring and I'm tired. May I have a ride home, please?"

After a thorough study of her features, he opened the front passenger door for her. She moved past him and got in, thankful she'd worn pants with her striped top. Every time his searching gaze wandered over her, she felt exposed and vulnerable.

Once he closed the door and went around to the driver's side, she slipped the sketchpad into her purse, but when she started to fasten her seat belt he forestalled her and drew her into his arms. The action brought her cheek against his freshly shaved jaw, causing her hair to flounce like gold silk. Sensing he was going to kiss her, she hid her face in his neck.

He bit her earlobe gently. "You know we've both been wanting this since we met. Why so coy, Laura?"

She admitted it, but he'd chosen the wrong word. It

had a connotation that meant she was playing a game, pretending to be shy while at the same time being intentionally flirtatious and silly. Though he hadn't meant to, he'd brought her back to reality in a hurry.

She moved her head so she could see into his eyes. "That's right," she mocked. "From a woman like me you want brazen. I'm afraid I'm all out of that flavor today."

His face darkened with lines. "Let's find out, shall we?" He crushed her mouth with his own. Slowly he began devouring her, giving her little chance to breathe with her gathered so closely against him. The primitive nature of the kiss rocked her to the core, calling out her natural desire.

With no other people around, Laura had the sense they were far away from civilization. Alone with this man, she was spinning out of control. It frightened her she could feel this way so fast and she started to pull away.

"I'd say that was an interesting experiment," he murmured against her lips before allowing her to move away from his arms. "It leaves me to wonder if you respond the same way to other men...to my brother for instance."

Her head jerked around. Shock set her back so it was difficult to find the words. Her veins had turned to ice water.

"I knew you had your suspicions about me, Raoul, but do you mean to tell me you've been kissing me, holding me, and all this time you've believed that Guy and I are lovers?"

His features remained impassive. "You have no idea how much I haven't wanted it to be true."

"But there's a part of you that still believes it?"

"Laura—"

"You *do!*"

He shook his head. "I know Guy wants you for comfort. I've seen it with my own eyes."

"Comfort is a far cry from a sexual relationship!"

His eyes had a desolate cast. "They can be two sides of the same coin."

"That's true if you're in love. Guy's in love with Chantelle!"

"She doesn't want him anymore."

"So you assume he's turned to me?" Right now she was so hurt she wanted to die. "I want to go back to the villa. Would that be too much to ask, or shall I just jump out and walk home?"

The tension vibrated between them before he started the motor and pulled out of the parking area onto the main road. He worked with calm precision. His movements automatic. Poetry in motion, but it had the effect of infuriating her more.

The silence on the drive back to Cap Ferrat was louder than any more questions he could throw at her. All the time he'd been vetting her, he refused to satisfy her curiosity about him on a solitary thing.

As he pulled up to the front of the darkened villa she tried to get out, but he'd set the lock. When she glanced over at him, he lay back against the seat seemingly relaxed for the moment, but she wasn't fooled. He could pounce at the slightest provocation.

"Perhaps now that we've both had a chance to cool off," he drawled, "you'll tell me the real reason you accepted my brother's invitation to stay with them."

She bowed her head. "Since you've already been told the first version, perhaps you should be asking your nephew. He was at the Palio and heard Guy ask me to come."

"Paul doesn't have a clue about a woman like you."

"*Merci.*"

His muffled French curse rent the air inside the car. "You know what I was implying."

"I'm not sure I ever know what you really mean and I'm too exhausted to undergo another interrogation."

"That's too bad because I want an answer. Even you have to agree that after one meeting in Siena while you're supposedly working, it was highly irregular for you to come into his home the very next morning and end up being his wife's companion for the next two weeks."

She flung herself around so she was facing him. "You obviously meant 'highly suspect.' I suppose it is…coming from a paranoid, bitterly jaded, twisted mind like yours. It's evident someone scarred you for life, Raoul, that's why I have no intention of answering any more of your questions. It would be pointless. Let me out of the car."

"I'm not through with you yet," he countered, making no move to undo the lock button at the side.

Laura had reached the limits of her tolerance. "Then let it be on your head." Without thought for the consequences, she reached over with the intention of pressing on the horn so security would come running, but Raoul was too fast for her and caught her in his grasp.

"Let's finish what we started a few minutes ago, shall we? Nighttime means we don't have an audience, so you don't need to worry that I have any other interest than enjoying myself with you."

Once more his mouth descended on hers, stifling any sound of protest she made. With an urgency that seemed part of the need that was driving both of them, he coaxed her lips apart again, provoking a kiss from her she couldn't hold back. Like a match to kindling, the pressure of his mouth, the feel of his hands running up and down her arms set her on fire.

Raoul's sensuality made her feel things she'd never felt in her life. How could she be doing this after only a couple of days of knowing him? This had to stop, but when she tried to ease away from him, he pulled her closer against him and this time the horn did sound loud and long.

The shrill din brought Guy out the front door where the lights from the foyer of the villa illuminated the interior of the Mercedes. Paul was right behind him. On a groan she moved back to her side of the car, but Raoul held on to her wrist and her action wasn't fast enough to escape him. They'd been well and truly caught.

Guy came down the steps to open the door for her, but of course it didn't give. Laura struggled in vain to pull her hand out of Raoul's grasp. To her chagrin he used the button from the control panel to lower her window.

With her left hand still trapped in his, he leaned across her body. The action caused his shoulder to brush against her chest. "Sorry for the noise, Guy. It was an accident. I hope it didn't upset Chantelle."

After a slight pause, "No one was in bed yet. What happened to Pierre?"

"I caught up with him at the Villa Leopolda and told him I'd bring Laura home."

Guy studied Raoul thoughtfully before glancing at Laura. "Were you able to do some drawings?"

"Yes. The light was perfect."

"*Maman* wants to see them. The Villa Leopolda is one of her favorite places. Can I take them to her?" Paul asked.

"Of course. Here." She reached in her bag for the sketchpad and handed it to him. "Let her keep it tonight. I'll get it back from her in the morning."

"I'd like to see them first if you don't mind, Paul." Guy started looking through it. He kept shaking his head before staring at her. "You're not only an angel, you have genius."

His kindness after Raoul's cross-examination brought tears to her eyes. "It's not true, but thank you."

In the awkward silence that followed, Laura was tempted to expose Raoul to his brother, but at the last second she couldn't do it, not in front of Paul. In truth this fight was between the two of them and no one else.

Since Raoul still had hold of her, there was only one thing to do. Let Guy think what he was already thinking, that she and Raoul had been kissing and somehow in the enclosed space they'd honked the horn by accident.

"Paul? I understand you wanted me to start teaching you CPR tonight. Sorry I wasn't around. You name the time and we'll do it."

"Okay. Can my friends learn it, too?"

"Of course."

"Thanks."

Guy smiled at her. "Don't worry about locking up when you come in, Laura. I'll still be awake and will take care of it."

Raoul's hand tightened just enough to prevent her from getting out of the car to join him.

"All right. See you two in the morning."

With sketchpad in hand, Guy followed his son into the house. As soon as he shut the door, Raoul said, "The fact that you didn't say anything to Guy about me means you're willing to put up with almost anything in order to remain here the full two weeks. I'm giving you warning I'll be watching every move you make."

She smiled so he could see it. "Like I said, men have a habit of hanging around me whether their company is welcome or not."

His eyes glittered. "It's that chemical reaction they're after."

"Et tu, Brute?"

"I'd be a liar if I didn't admit it." He kissed the palm of her hand before letting it go. Thanks to Raoul, she discovered her palm was as sensitive to his touch as the rest of her. She heard the click of the lock. Now that he was tired of torturing her, she was free to go, for the moment.

Raoul watched her get out and hurry inside the house before he took off for his own villa. Guy was good at disguising his true feelings, but one thing was clear,

Laura was playing at something by not running after Guy to tell him every monstrous thing Raoul had done.

He was guilty of a lot. The more appealing she was to him, the more aggressive he'd become. He wasn't proud of his behavior. He'd never treated a woman this way in his life, not even Danielle at her worst. Something about Laura Adridge had permeated deep into his psyche.

If she really had only met Guy for the first time at the Palio, he could understand the pull on his brother. But he still couldn't fathom the act of bringing her into his home…unless he was trying to make Chantelle jealous so she'd fight for him.

Was that what Guy was doing? With Laura's knowing or unwitting cooperation? Yet he couldn't imagine it because Paul wouldn't understand. No, Raoul could scratch the jealousy theory and was back to square one where he had no answers except one. She hadn't lied about her artwork. Her talent left him speechless.

He let himself in the house and headed for the bathroom where he kept painkiller. He'd developed a headache that throbbed more violently when he thought of what was going on at Guy's.

Chantelle's feelings aside, Raoul hadn't missed the look that had passed between Laura and his brother after he'd complimented her. Those tears shimmering like green gems had brought Guy to his knees. She had him so sewn up, it wouldn't surprise him if he ended up divorcing Chantelle.

Raoul was aghast that he had allowed his own thoughts

to get that far. Whatever, he had to believe this problem with Chantelle was temporary. He would never have guessed anything could rock the solidity of their marriage.

Then again, Raoul couldn't have imagined that a woman like Laura existed, let alone that she would show up in Guy's world. She was so beautiful Jean-Luc had gone into ecstatic raves over her. "She's the embodiment of my every fantasy, Raoul. You lucky dog you."

During his walk with her through Tourettes, he'd pretended he didn't mind that every red-blooded male within sight was instantly in love and followed her with his eyes. Men dreamed, but only occasionally did they see a female in the flesh who surpassed those dreams.

A woman like her—maybe married several times and apparently still attached to her latest because she needed money—wouldn't know what it was to be faithful, but enough money might keep her around for a long time. Guy's assets would entice her indefinitely.

With Chantelle constantly keeping him at a distance, his brother was ripe to make a mistake that would tear the entire family apart. Maybe Guy and Laura weren't lovers yet, but Raoul couldn't stand by and watch to see it eventually happen.

And you know why, don't you, Laroche. Because you want her yourself. He grimaced at his own weakness before getting ready for bed. Just as he was about to climb in, his cell phone rang. He reached across the covers to pick it up. When he discovered who it was, he answered the call.

"*Eh bien,* Louis. Tell me what you've got."

"Not much yet, but I did find out one important thing. Her passport lists her name as Laurel Aldridge Stillman."

Stillman!

So she had lied about her name.

"She's twenty-nine. Address is 302 Fair Oaks Drive, Santa Barbara, California. I'll call you if I learn anything else."

"*Merci,* Louis. You do excellent work. *Bon nuit.*"

For Laura to be living in Guy's home as Laura Aldridge, it was evident her marriage was in trouble. Lies had destroyed Raoul's own union. What part did they play in the disintegration of hers?

After hanging up, Raoul leaped off the bed and went into his study. Before he started making phone calls, he'd do a little research first and see if anything came up on the Internet.

He put in her full name. Almost instantly whole pages of Web addresses appeared. He scanned the listings. One stood out—theodorestillman.com.

Raoul clicked to it. There she was, bigger than life and utterly breathtaking, sitting in a raft near a typically blond American male. The article beneath the photo read:

Mr. Theodore M. Stillman, known as Ted to his older brothers in the law firm of Stillman, Stillman and Stillman, of Santa Barbara, sons of Former Congressman William Stillman of Santa Barbara, and the late Governor Richard Stillman of the great State of California, is seen here with his beautiful wife Laurel Aldridge Stillman, formerly of Manhattan Beach, California, as they take time out from their busy schedule to float down the Colorado River. Ted is planning to run for the congressional seat next year once occupied by his father. Donations to his campaign can be made by clicking here.

Adrenaline filled Raoul's system as he looked for a date when the picture had been taken. When he couldn't find it, he clicked to the other sites. For the most part she was shown in a photograph at a lunch or a gala looking more subdued than her husband who was always smiling—like the kind of slick car salesmen Raoul couldn't abide.

One site put up by the Manhattan Beach Police Department drew his interest. It was a picture of her in a simple summer dress standing next to the police chief. Raoul studied her exquisite features. She was beaming. The article read:

Chief Jose Garcia presents the Meritorious Service Award to head lifeguard Laura Aldridge for her constant devotion to duty. She holds the record for the most saves in Manhattan Beach in ten years—467 people can be grateful she was on duty the day they found themselves in trouble.

Raoul could hear himself taunting her, "Can you prove it?"

Two mornings later Laura was pulling weeds around the side of the villa when her cell phone rang. Only two people had her new number, her attorney and Cindy.

She checked her watch while pulling off her gardening gloves. Eight-thirty in the morning in Cap Ferrat meant 11:30 p.m. in California. For either of them to phone her this late their time meant something was wrong. She couldn't handle any bad news where Ted was concerned. Please be Cindy, she murmured to herself as she slid the phone from her blouse pocket.

When she saw her friend's name on the caller ID she expelled a sigh of relief and clicked on.

"Hey, Cindy. What's going on?"

"Plenty. Guess who just got the landlord to let him into your apartment?"

For once her body didn't break out in a cold sweat. In fact, Laura could jump for joy. "You've just made my day, Cindy."

"You mean you're not upset?"

"I reached that stage months ago. Don't you see? This means Ted's minions lost track of me the day Guy flew me here in his helicopter. I can guarantee he thought my boss was lying to him when he told him I was still in Europe, so he decided to break into my apartment and try and catch me at home."

"Why doesn't he just give up?"

"His pride. No other Stillman has had a divorce. He wants to use me, but it'll never happen. My attorney's going to love hearing this. Ted has ignored the court order. Unless the Stillmans own the judge, Ted's in big trouble."

"I'm glad."

"So am I."

"How's it going with Chantelle? Are you making any progress?"

"I've gotten her to come outside in her wheelchair while I weed. We talk about the history of Provence. She's very knowledgeable. I've learned tons, but I don't see her warming to her husband yet. It kills me because he's always so sweet to her. Today I'm going to ask her if she'll go to lunch with me somewhere exciting, but I'm not holding my breath."

"All things taken into account, you sound happier than I've ever known you to be."

Laura turned on her stomach and stretched out on the grass lining the flowerbed. "Oddly enough, I am. Guy's villa is a Garden of Eden. I'm sitting in the middle of the most gorgeous arrangement of rose beds you've ever seen. Beyond them is the Mediterranean. This morning it's a dazzling blue dotted with sailboats. The air is so fragrant a good perfumer should market it."

"It sounds divine, and no serpents in sight."

"I didn't say that, Guy has a brother."

"Older or younger?"

"Younger. The dynamo at the Laroche Corporation."

"Handsome?"

Laura closed her eyes, pressing her hot cheek against her arm. "Find a picture of Adonis and add ten years to him. Even then you won't do him justice."

"Good grief—"

"You can say that again."

"Laura—"

"Yes. I'm in lust with him."

Cindy burst into laughter. "How wonderful!"

"It's what I call pleasure-pain. I still haven't found out his marital status and he believes I'm Mata Hari. When we *are* together, it's like a duel. He has a rapier tongue that can slice you into pieces faster than Zorro."

"What?"

"It's a long story. Do you have time?"

"All night."

She rolled back over to feel the full rays of the sun on her face and legs. With her eyes still closed, she told her about the outing to Tourettes Sur Loup and ended with the other night when she'd discovered him waiting for her outside the Villa Leopolda. She hadn't seen him since and had missed their lethal skirmishes a lot more than she was willing to admit.

After she'd told Cindy all her theories about why Raoul had been so cruel, her friend said, "Maybe he's in a bad marriage like you and is frustrated to be attracted to you when he's not free. Since he hasn't chosen to tell you his marital status, why don't you ask Chantelle?"

Laura expelled the breath she'd been holding. "I could, but I don't want her to think I'm here for any reason but to be her friend for a while. She has to learn to trust all over again. If she thinks I have another agenda, it could ruin any ground I've made with her."

"I see your point, so why don't you ask Guy?"

"I don't dare talk to him about his brother for the very same reason. The truth is, he hasn't offered any information. They're a very closemouthed family—aristocratic, if you know what I mean. I've been learning things on a need-to-know basis only."

"Wouldn't Guy's son be all right to ask?"

"No. He's good friends with his uncle. They share everything. I have no doubt Raoul vets Paul about me. I don't want to give him anything he can use against me. The other night Paul told him I'd gone out in the limo and the next thing I knew, Raoul came to find me."

"Sounds thrilling to me."

"It would have been if I thought Raoul didn't have another agenda, but he does. That's why if I were to ask Paul any questions that didn't have to do with him, it would stir things up. I'm trying to stay out of trouble and mind my own business."

"Your life story is better than the latest vampire novel I'm reading."

At that remark Laura laughed. When it subsided she said, "Raoul would make a gorgeous vampire."

"According to your description, he'd make a gorgeous—"

"Don't say it," Laura broke in. "I can't afford to think it."

"But you have thought it. I can hear it in your voice."

"It's this place, Cindy, it's out of this world."

"Then what are you going to do about Raoul?"

She moved her arm in front of her eyes. "Nothing."

"You mean you're going to let nature take its course."

"That's the way it has to be. Now I've kept you up too late and you need your beauty sleep. I'll be seeing you in about ten days, but I'll call you before then. Take care."

"You, too."

Laura rang off, thinking about everything they'd discussed. As she lay there soaking up the sun, she felt a cloud pass over. That was odd. She hadn't seen any clouds on the horizon this morning. She removed her arm to look up at the sky and let out a slight gasp.

It was Raoul blocking the sun's rays. He was supposed to be at work! Had he heard any of her conversation with Cindy before he'd moved right in front of her? She found herself the object of his piercing black scrutiny. It took her breath.

He looked impossibly striking in a light-gray business suit that molded his hard-muscled body to perfection. After two days' deprivation, to have this kind of reaction to him alarmed her.

She sat up and got to her feet. Her sleeveless pink blouse and white shorts covered her adequately, but when his gaze roved over her she trembled for no reason. "I take it you were looking for me."

"Chantelle said you were out here somewhere. Next time I can't find you, I'd better look under a few plants. What has you so fascinated?"

"While I've been gardening I found something interesting. I planned to show it to Chantelle, but she was on the phone. Then I had to take a call and forgot about it until just now."

"Your boss?" Raoul was always quick to make assumptions.

"No, my best friend, Cindy. We live in an eight-plex across the hall from each other. She watches my apartment for me while I'm away on business." Laura knew what he was thinking and decided to satisfy that insatiable curiosity of his. "It's big enough to fit into my closet in the guest bedroom."

His lips twisted into a smile. "But it's yours."

"Exactly."

"Where is this thing you found?"

"Oh—it's here! I took it in the house and washed it." She picked it up off the grass and handed it to him. "I think it must have been a pin. There's a little boy's face on it. So precious." Laura suddenly felt a pain as she thought about having a real little boy of her own. He would have Raoul's arresting features. She shook her thoughts away, reminding herself that it was foolish to think such things.

He studied her for an overly long moment before giving it his attention. "Where exactly did you find it?"

"Around the east side of the house near the sundial."

"I'll have to call the university about this. You've just found a Gallo-Romain artifact. Most of them have been discovered on Mont Leuze not far from here. If you found this on the property, there are probably more."

As he lifted his dark head, his eyes shot to hers. "Lifeguard, artist…now archaeologist. There's no end to your talents, is there?" He handed it back to her.

Was that a trace of levity she heard coming out of his all-male mouth? Too late if it wasn't because he had her smiling. "Did you have breakfast with Chantelle?"

He slid one hand in his jacket pocket. "No. I've just come from an early business meeting. Why do you ask?"

She moistened her lips that had gone dry in the heat. His eyes followed the movement. "I was hoping she'd had a good night. Maybe I can get her to go out to lunch with me today."

"Chantelle won't do that for anyone," he said in a withering tone, "not even for you."

Laura frowned. "I appreciate the encouragement."

He cocked his dark head. "Once again I try to pay you a compliment, but it's always misconstrued. I was attempting to tell you that she likes you. If anyone could get her to step foot off the estate, it would be you." A thread of sincerity ran through his words.

"Thank you for that," she whispered.

"When I asked her if she'd like to get out today, she told me she had a headache. Since I can't prove she doesn't, I have to leave well enough alone."

She smoothed some loose strands from her brow. "If it's this hard on you, imagine how Guy must feel."

His lips tightened to a narrow line. "A wife who no longer desires her husband is the kiss of death to a marriage."

There was such a deep kernel of suffering she heard in his voice just now, Laura felt a wrench for him. He'd been severely wounded by a woman. She was at a loss what to say to comfort him. It was crazy to think that after the hurtful way he'd treated her, she still wanted to.

"Was there a reason you wanted to talk to me?"

"Yes. The son of a close friend of mine is a competitor in the Tour de France this year. I promised I'd watch for him in the stage coming up tomorrow. Since it looks like the American team is going to win the whole thing, I thought you might like to come with me and we'll cheer our countries on."

He had an ulterior reason for inviting her, but she couldn't prevent the burst of excitement spreading through her body. She longed to spend the day with him, doing something with him that was unrelated to the problems at the Laroche villa. Perhaps she would see a more relaxed Raoul, she might even be able to get him to open up about himself some more. And she had always wanted to see the Tour in person.

"We'll leave midafternoon and fly to Alpe d'Huez in the helicopter. It's a little mountain town. I've booked rooms there. Tomorrow we'll be at the summit to see who goes over first, then we'll fly to Bourg d'Oisons at the bottom to watch the winner cross the finish line. If it's possible, I'll introduce you to Alain Garonne."

Those were names associated with cycling she'd heard of for years. "I…I'll have to check with Guy," she stammered, so thrilled at the prospect of going with him her legs shook.

"If you insist," he muttered, his eyes shuttered.

"Since he asked me to be a friend to Chantelle, I don't want him to think I'm taking advantage of his hospitality."

"No. I'm sure you wouldn't want him to think that." Was he being sarcastic again? She couldn't bear it. "He's at the breakfast table with Chantelle if you want to ask him now."

She nodded. Leaving her things where they were, she followed Raoul around the side of the villa. His long strides mesmerized her as much as the male symmetry of his body. When they reached the patio she saw that Paul had also joined his parents.

Raoul reached for some toast, leaving it to Laura to broach the subject. The moment she did his nephew said, "Can I come, too?"

"You have your dental check up this afternoon, Paul," his mother reminded him. She turned her head in Laura's direction. "The Tour de France used to be one of Raoul's passions. I have no doubt he'll bore you with statistics, but if you're a fan, too, then it should be an exciting experience."

Guy nodded his assent, but he seemed dispirited and preoccupied.

Raoul's gaze swerved to hers. "I'll come for you at three o'clock. Pack a jacket. The mountains cool off in the evening."

She couldn't understand the almost triumphant gleam in his eyes before he disappeared.

CHAPTER FIVE

THE girl from downstairs shot Laura an unfriendly glance. She probably wasn't a day over twenty-two. "You lock it from this side. Or not," she added pointedly before her gaze swerved to Raoul once more and remained riveted.

Had Laura ever acted as desperate over an attractive man at that age? She surely hoped not.

Ever since they'd flown to Alpe d'Huez in the French Alps and had arrived at the Auberge Hôtel where the rooms were upstairs in the loft, the girl at the front desk had fallen all over herself to attract Raoul's attention. The village was packed with tourists from many countries gathered for tomorrow's race. An electric excitement filled the air.

Everywhere she and Raoul walked after leaving the helicopter, some female smiled at him, inviting him verbally and with a sultry look to come and party with her and her friends. Though they could see Laura was with him, they considered this event a free-for-all.

Once the girl had left them alone, Raoul carried her overnight bag into her room and set it down on a chair.

"As soon as you're ready, we'll find a restaurant and eat."

"Five minutes is all I need."

His veiled eyes took in the pleated tan pants and white cotton sweater she was wearing before they lifted to her face. When he looked at her like that through his sooty lashes, she felt her insides melt. "I'll meet you downstairs in the lobby."

With a nod Laura shut the door behind him, but she had to cling to the handle for support. He didn't have any idea what his physical presence did to her. Was there ever a more gorgeous man born than Raoul? She was certain he'd intended to bring someone else, but that was before Laura had become a guest in his brother's home. Since then, all plans had changed.

Laura decided he saw her as a freeloader who was taking advantage of Guy, something Raoul couldn't forgive her for, so he'd brought her here with him. Anything to get her out of the villa where she'd made herself at home after saving his brother's life. He probably worried she would try to find a way to stay on longer. Even if she denied it, he wouldn't listen.

Clearly it irritated him that she felt comfortable enough to work in the garden as if she was the chatelaine and Chantelle the guest. He mocked everything she did. Once in a while he let up on his baiting for a moment, but she was under no illusion that his opinion of her would ever soften.

Since she couldn't do anything about his mindset where she was concerned, she decided to enjoy this unexpected trip and not let his jibes ruin the pleasure of this experience. Too soon she would have to go back to California. When she returned she would demand the earliest court date possible to be legally free of Ted.

Hopefully he'd done his worst by defying the court and breaking into her apartment. Laura had a witness on this one. Not even his brothers with all their political clout could block the divorce much longer.

Before coming to Europe she hadn't thought beyond simply getting away where she wasn't forced to think about Ted's next ploy to get her to come back to him. However, everything had changed since the Palio. Being Guy's guest had meant she'd dropped from the radar screen, forcing Ted's hand.

It felt so wonderful to be free for a little, but she realized she wanted to be divorced as soon as possible, whatever it took. Though she could lie to herself all she wanted, one truth stood out from all the rest. Meeting Raoul had made her want to speed up the timetable.

Not because she had hopes of any kind of relationship with him. It wasn't possible because, for one thing, he wasn't free. Laura didn't know the specifics, but some woman had a hold on him that had darkened his pysche, blighted his world.

Chantelle had said as much, although she hadn't used those exact words. Since her brother-in-law definitely didn't approve of Laura, her warning hadn't come any too soon. There were times when she felt he despised her. But then there were other times…

The fact that she could respond so strongly to him in a man-woman way in spite of his enmity had taught her there could be a life out there for her. Laura just had to find the right man and she was sure that good men existed. Look at Guy!

There wasn't a finer husband in the world or one more devoted to his wife. First, however, Laura had to be officially divorced, something she intended would take place as soon as she returned to Manhattan Beach.

Pulling the band off her ponytail, she went into the bathroom to brush her hair and arrange it in a loose knot on top of her head. A fresh application of peach-frost lipstick felt good after working in the sun over the past few days. That much exposure had brought out her California tan, something inevitable because of her life-guarding duties.

A few new lines around her eyes reminded her she wasn't getting any younger. One day in the near future she wouldn't have the stamina for that kind of work anymore. Life was passing. She'd be thirty next month. If she didn't hurry and do something about it, she could miss out on the best part—like a loving husband and a family, a child to call her own. But whenever she thought about the few years left to try to have a baby, she got too emotional. She wouldn't think about that tonight.

Right now a man who had ambivalent feelings toward her was downstairs where more devastating salvos awaited her. She was ready. She had put on her female armor and was prepared for the next skirmish with the enemy, a man she physically desired to the boiling point. Laura hadn't been kidding when she'd admitted the truth to Cindy.

It was the farthest thing from love; in order for that

to occur you had to like each other first. You had to develop a relationship based on trust and mutual understanding. There had to be respect and unselfishness. Admiration for the other's accomplishments. Patience for the other's imperfections. Without those qualities, the most torrid affair would burn up in the oxygen with no ashes to prove anything had ever taken place.

Laura went back into the room. Maybe she'd want a wrap later, but the upstairs was still warm from the day's heat. She'd rather not be bothered with anything but her tote bag. After locking the adjoining door and the door into the hall, she headed for the stairway. On the way down, she saw a dark-blond guy coming up with a Team America logo on his pullover. He bore a superficial likeness to Ted.

The color in his cheeks plus the glaze filming his eyes indicated he'd been partying for a while. She'd seen that look at the beach too many times to mistake it for anything else. And of course he just had to put his hand against the wall so she couldn't proceed.

"Hello, hello…" He smiled at her as if he'd just won the lottery. "Am I hallucinating or are you the most beautiful female I ever saw in my life, sweetheart?" He looked her over, not hiding anything he was thinking. She was used to it.

She had two choices. Use a maneuver that would cause him to fall down the stairs, or she could go back to the room until the drunken oaf was no longer in the hall.

Then to her surprise she didn't have to make either choice because Raoul had come up behind him and put him in an arm lock with a mastery that made her shiver.

"Go on down to the foyer, Laura. I'll join you in a minute."

Laura didn't stay to hear any more. The guy was big, but he was no match for Raoul. She'd barely made it to the front desk when he joined her.

"Are you all right?"

She laughed gently, unable to suppress it, now that the irony of the situation had struck her. This was the first time he'd ever shown true concern for her welfare, but he couldn't know that the only moments she'd felt threatened in Europe had been with him.

By his frown he was waiting impatiently for an explanation.

Her eyes searched his. "If you could have seen the look of fury on his face when you pulled a half nelson on him, you'd understand why I found it so amusing. Thank you."

He didn't smile. "How many times a day does this happen to you?"

Not that again— "Dozens! But as you can see, I've survived so far."

"If I didn't know better," he said in a thick tone, "I'd think you were hiding out at Guy's for protection."

She looked away. Her only purpose for being there was because of Guy's invitation, not to elude Ted, that had just been an added advantage. But this conversation was getting too close to certain truths. Though she and Guy had an understanding that she would try to help Chantelle open up and face her fear, he wasn't forcing Laura to stay.

Naturally she could leave anytime she wanted, but then she'd miss out on these infuriating little moments with his brother that thrilled and tantalized her, forcing her to come back for more. Better to let him go on thinking the worst about her. "Can you offer a better place?"

"Let's eat and we'll talk about it."

That sounded vaguely ominous. Maybe he was on an errand for Chantelle and had brought Laura to Alpe d'Huez to tell her she wasn't wanted at Guy's. Perhaps Chantelle hoped she'd be gone by tomorrow and had been the one to suggest Raoul bring her to see the Tour de France, making it sound as if it were his idea.

It hurt to think Chantelle might have been the reason behind this whole outing. She'd always loved her and wanted more than anything to help her overcome her problem since the accident.

Was everyone in the Laroche household playing a part, even Guy, who'd known from the beginning this experiment would never work and was in denial? She didn't include Paul. He was too young and innocent.

When they stepped outside the hotel, she realized night came early to the mountains, yet everywhere she looked people were milling around. Lots of partying was going on. She saw lovers with their arms flung around each other.

It was the kind of summer ambience that brought back a rush of nostalgia for something she couldn't name. Dreams still not fulfilled? The hope of youth long since past? Whatever it was, she felt an ache made worse because of the aloof male whose very existence filled her body with a painful hunger. Not that she could do anything about those feelings.

She didn't like Raoul, either. Most of the time he infuriated her. It was very unfortunate that although he resented and insulted her, he was able to ignite her senses at the same time.

He turned his dark head toward her. In jeans and a light-gray Polo shirt, he looked sensational. "What do you feel like?"

In case he thought she expected dinner at a five star restaurant while she sponged off him, she glanced at the café across the street. "Coke and pizza?"

"You can have that anytime."

"After the crab salad I had for lunch, I'm not that hungry, but we can go wherever you want."

He gave an unconscious shrug of his broad shoulders. "Pizza's fine."

The place was filled with a noisy crowd and people dancing. They had to wait for a bistro table. To converse was almost impossible with the loud music. It wasn't bad pizza but they served the Pepsi without ice and it tasted awful. All in all she'd made the wrong choice.

When she happened to look at him, his mouth broke into a white smile that transformed him, causing her heart to skip a beat.

"You *knew* how bad this would be!" She tossed a wadded paper napkin at him. To her amazement he caught it. "I only picked this place bec—"

"Because you were trying to prove you're someone other than who you are," he cut her off smoothly.

With a few hurtful words he'd destroyed a golden moment. The demons Chantelle had talked about were too much for Laura. "I'm glad you know me so well.

Under the circumstances you won't mind if I leave you to pay the bill."

She stood up to get away from him, but he prevented her from leaving. "Where do you think you're going?" His dark gaze challenged her. "I happen to know you deserve better than this place or the Auberge."

Laura felt as if she'd suddenly been caught after being pushed off a high castle wall. She simply didn't understand him. He blew hot and cold so fast she couldn't keep up with him.

"We haven't danced since the pool," he reminded her. "You have to admit it didn't last long enough." His thumb caressed her palm, causing her body to go weak. Her heart pounded too hard to be good for her.

"I admit it," she whispered. When Raoul was like this, Laura couldn't think why she should be keeping him at a distance. For once she didn't feel like fighting him. She couldn't, not when he'd just pulled her into his strong arms. "I haven't danced for so long, I've forgotten how."

"Then we'll do what everyone else is doing and simply move in time to the music," he murmured against her lips.

With their bodies so entwined there was no air between them. His mouth was a temptation she couldn't resist and didn't want to. They slowly began savoring each other while they swayed to the music. Their bodies fit perfectly together. She felt as though they were one throbbing entity floating above the world. As the songs changed, so did the intensity of each kiss.

"Raoul," she gasped softly, from needs that caused her to ache.

"Deny it all you want, but it's been like this with us from the start," came his husky response against her neck.

While she clung to him in the middle of the chaos going on around them, she heard some American say, "It looks like those two need a room."

Quick to respond, Raoul whispered against her ear, "Aren't we fortunate it's only across the street. Come on. Let's get out of here."

He put some bills on their table and guided them out of the bar. It had grown more crowded since they'd come in, but she hadn't noticed. At the moment Raoul was her whole world. Laura couldn't get alone with him fast enough.

She held on to him as they made their way back to the Auberge. The depth of her euphoria had caused her to be careless. Ted's minions could be taking pictures, but suddenly it didn't matter to her. Raoul, too, seemed heedless of those things that had been haunting him, making him so cruel to her earlier. Now all that had gone. Nothing registered except this sweet, unexplored heat building between them.

Once Raoul had let them into his room, he picked her up and carried her to the bed. She pulled him down beside her. In the dim light of one small lamp, his hair and skin, his features took on the cast of a dark prince whose black eyes burned with desire for her.

Before she gave in to the clamoring of her senses, she needed an answer to one question. "I haven't asked

before now because I didn't think you and I would—"
She hesitated, then started again. "I didn't think we'd—"

"—become lovers?" He finished the thought in a silken voice.

Her face went hot. "Yes. I know so little about you. Are you single? Divorced? You've never said."

He followed the line of her eyebrow with his thumb. "You really don't know? Even after living in Guy's home?"

"No," she answered honestly. "The subject has never come up."

"Why didn't you ask me if I was married?"

She groaned inwardly. "I didn't think it was necessary."

"Why?"

"Because I don't believe you would be here with me like this if you were married. Despite the way you've treated me at times, my instincts tell me you're an honorable man."

His eyes grew veiled. "I've been divorced from my wife, Danielle, for a year, if that's what you mean, but it doesn't necessarily prove me to be honorable. Otherwise I wouldn't be on the verge of making love to Mrs. Theodore Stillman would I?"

The enchantment of the night splintered into a thousand pieces.

Laura could move fast when she had to. Her job at the beach demanded it. She rolled off the other side of the bed and flew out his door with her tote bag. Within seconds she'd locked herself in the adjoining room. It didn't take him long to knock on the door separating them.

"Open up, Laura," sounded his deep voice. "It's time for us to have a serious talk, I think."

At this point she felt sick to her stomach and was so upset she was shaking. How long had he known her real name?

"Why didn't you say you'd been in contact with my husband?"

"Not contact. I had you investigated."

She threw her head back, absolutely stunned. "Why?"

"To protect my family."

Her body shuddered. All along he'd seen her as a threat. "Finally some honesty from you Raoul. My father-in-law already had me thoroughly investigated before he allowed his son to marry me. You and he have a lot in common. I guess that's what comes from having money and power for so many generations you've forgotten the human element.

"If you love Guy, I advise you not to tell him what you've done because in the end, it might come back to hurt you. He's the kindest, most wonderful human being I know and in case you haven't realized it yet, he loves you dearly. Good night, Raoul."

Raoul passed a hand over his face. Was every woman a liar?

For the past little while he could have sworn the two of them were feeling something deep and real between them. Yet all Laura Stillman could think about was Guy.

His poor, beguiled brother was in love with a very

married woman who had a wife's access to her
husband's fortune. Louis had done his homework. That
Fair Oaks address had the same kind of exclusivity as
many of the places near Cap Ferrat.

What was she doing in Europe picking up rich men
using her maiden name? She had a successful million-
aire husband of her own in tow with looks like a
younger Robert Redford. The woman obviously had
no shame.

While he stood there trying to blot pictures of Laura
and her husband making love from his mind, the hotel
phone rang. Raoul grimaced. After being found out, she
was too petrified to face him, so she'd resorted to the
phone.

With his emotions exploding all over the place he
walked to the bedside table and grabbed the receiver.
Fighting for calm he answered, "Laura?"

"Who's Laura?"

Danielle—

Another one of her desperate, attention-seeking
phone calls. Perfect timing.

"Don't hang up on me yet, *mon amour.* I remember
a passionate night we once spent at the Citadel in Alpe
d'Huez during the Tour de France. I thought you might
be there for this year's race. When they said you weren't
registered, I called several other places.

"What are you doing at the Auberge? Slumming with
the riffraff doesn't sound like you. Do you have any idea
how much I miss you? I know I was wrong for what I
did, but how can you throw away what we once had?"

"It's too late, Danielle."

"Of course it isn't. Oh, Raoul, I love you still so much." She pleaded. "Please let me show you how it can be again. Give us a second chance—"

For a moment he heard the old Danielle in her voice, but her repentant plea still didn't move him. Five days ago something had happened to Raoul that had turned him into a different man. Someone new had entered the picture....

He glanced at the door to the adjoining room, his pulse pounding while he waited for Laura to make a move.

"It's too late." Far too late. "*Adieu,* Danielle," he murmured.

Raoul put the phone back on the hook, smothering her angry shout. Before she could call him again, he turned off the ringer.

He could go down to the bar, but no amount of alcohol would wipe out the sting of Laura's lie. Even though her betrayal was against her husband and his brother, Raoul was the one reeling.

Laura cried so hard all night that when morning came, her eyes were swollen shut. When she left the room at 7:30 a.m. with her overnight bag, she was forced to cover them with her sunglasses.

She hadn't seen or talked to Raoul since he'd dropped his bombshell outside the door last night. Because he'd brought her here to suit his no-longer-secret agenda, she didn't feel obligated to discuss anything more with him. She'd see the day through and tough it out, but that was it. When they returned to Cap

Ferrat, she'd stay out of Raoul's way until she returned to the States.

The Auberge served a continental breakfast in the dining area off the foyer. Only a few people were eating. The rest had left to line the road while they waited for the bikers making the ascent. After choosing a baguette and some juice, she sat down at a table. Though she had no appetite, she knew she'd better eat something.

While she munched on the bread without enthusiasm, Raoul entered the dining room wearing his jeans and a navy sport shirt, unbuttoned at the neck where she could see a smattering of dark hair. She closed her eyes tightly to shut off the view, but it was too late to stop the warm rush that permeated her weakened body.

He reached for her bag and took both of them to the counter in the lobby to be held until later. Afterward he wandered over to the side bar for a cup of coffee and a baguette. When he returned, he took the seat opposite her and dunked his bread in the hot liquid before eating it with obvious enjoyment. There was clearly no problem with his appetite.

"When you're ready, we'll walk over to the road and watch what we came to see." His voice sounded half an octave lower this morning. Even after everything that had transpired, she still ached for him.

There was a tiny cut at the side of his jaw where he must have hurt himself shaving. It was the only thing she could find that might indicate he wasn't in total control. Somehow the thought was reassuring.

As she was finishing the last of her juice, he lifted her sunglasses from her face. His knuckle brushed the end of her nose. "I thought so," he muttered before setting them back in place.

She froze. "You're a true Frenchman all right. When you butcher your animal, you don't leave any parts."

A faint white line of anger circled his mouth. Good.

He got up from the table at the same time she did. Like a couple who'd lived too long together and didn't find pleasure in each other's company, they left the hotel with several feet between them and made their way down the side street to the main road packed with fans. It was tragic, really, that she couldn't enjoy the glorious view from this famous spot, but she was too numb.

Raoul found a place where they could stand and see everything. She people watched in order not to stare at him. They were probably the only two fans on the mountain who weren't chatting excitedly. After twenty minutes the first cars riding ahead of the bikers came in sight. The crowd grew noisier. Pretty soon there was an explosion of sound because the first five racers had been spotted.

They looked hot and miserable. Deep lines around their mouths reflected the strain on their bodies. Everyone passed them cups of water. Sometimes the passage became so narrow she was afraid a tourist would ruin the race for them. Finally they cycled in front of her and Raoul. None of the five were on the French or American teams.

A few minutes after they started down the other side of the summit, up came the peloton. For a second she spotted the biker in the yellow jersey. The whole scene looked chaotic when you were seeing it in person rather than on TV. The cyclists rode past, their legs moving like pistons. Several of them fell back, their bikes moving wobbly, as if the racers were on the verge of collapse.

All this effort to see them go by. Now it was over.

She glanced at Raoul through her sunglasses. "I'm going to walk to the helipad."

He nodded. "I'll be there as soon as I collect our luggage."

Without watching him, she took off down the mountain at a brisk pace. It felt good to expend some energy. This was one time when she wished she could plunge in the surf and swim way out to catch a wave.

Amazing that by the time she reached the helicopter, Raoul had somehow caught up to her and showed no signs of being winded. She greeted the pilot, then climbed in the back and strapped herself in.

Raoul stowed their bags, then took his place in the copilot's seat. He spoke in rapid French to the pilot before the blades began to rotate. Once they were whipping the air, the helicopter lifted off, leaving her stomach behind.

The scene out the window could only be described as spectacular. She could see the zigzag road beneath them, but there was no sign of the cyclists because the helicopter was headed in the opposite direction from Bourg d'Oisons, the end of the day's eighth stage.

She didn't need to ask Raoul anything. He'd accomplished what he had come here to do, but since she hadn't given him the satisfaction of an explanation, he was taking her home, thank heaven.

While Raoul and the pilot talked quietly together, the uneventful flight back to Cap Ferrat allowed her to sleep. When she woke up, she was surprised to discover they'd landed on the estate.

Raoul had already climbed out of the helicopter and had put her bag in the limo. "Pierre will take you to the villa."

She said a collective thank-you to him and the pilot before getting in the car. Raoul shut the door as if he couldn't wait to see her gone from here. Nothing could hurt more than the memory of last night when she'd thought Raoul had truly started to care for her. To think all along he'd been waiting for the perfect moment to expose her. The pain of it was excruciating.

After reaching the villa, Pierre got out and handed her the overnight bag. She thanked him before hurrying inside the house. She almost ran into Guy, who must have heard the helicopter and was coming out to greet her.

He gave her a hug before looking at her. "What's wrong?" he asked immediately. "You look pale. Did the helicopter make you ill?"

"Oh, no. I'm a little tired." She put her bag down.

"You're back sooner than I would have expected."

"As it turned out, Raoul didn't want to see the end of the stage because his team wasn't winning." A white lie, but it was the best she could come up with at the moment. He smiled. "My brother always was a terrible loser. Now you've seen him at his worst."

Guy could have no idea…. "How's Chantelle?"

A shadow crossed over his features. "She went down for a nap a little while ago."

"And Paul?"

"With a friend. They've gone bike riding."

"Guy—" She took a huge breath. "Could we talk in private?"

"Bien sur."

"But if you were working—"

"It's nothing I can't do later. Let's go to your sitting room. No one will disturb us there." That's right. It was the one room in the villa off-limits to Raoul.

He carried her bag down the hall for her. She went inside the suite first. After he followed her in, she shut the door and they both sat down on the chairs placed around the coffee table.

"Guy—there's something vitally important I have to tell you."

"I already know."

She blinked. "Know what?"

"About you and Raoul."

Laura started to feel sick again. "There is no me and Raoul, Guy." Her heart was thudding too fast for it to be healthy.

"Jean-Luc seems to think so. He called me this morning. He doesn't want to lose out on this latest sale in Antibes. Since Raoul won't commit yet, he's been trying to convince me the property is worth buying. That's when it all came out. He saw you in front of the warehouse with my brother."

Laura sat forward in a panic, her thoughts reeling. "If you're talking about that kiss, Raoul did it as a joke. Chantelle told me he has his little demons. I think one came out that day."

Guy chuckled. "My brother has been full of surprises lately."

"He's very amusing. I know it didn't mean anything. He said the real estate agent was a huge gossip, and he wagered you'd hear about it within twenty-four hours. Looks like he was right.

"Seriously though, you've all been terrific to me including Raoul, who's been kind enough to show me around. He made it possible for me to see a stage of the Tour de France. I was thrilled."

He nodded. "I'm glad you're having a good time."

She eyed him soulfully. "I am, but we both know that's not why I'm here. I wish I could say I was having a lot of success with Chantelle."

"While you've been here, I've seen a change in her. You've brought new life into the house. Don't give up on her."

"Of course I won't, but there's one more thing I'm worried about. My husband has the resources to try to find me while I'm here. I just want you to be aware of it. You need to know his name is Theodore Stillman. He's an attorney from Santa Barbara, California, with enough backing from his family to cause trouble if he wants. If there's the slightest problem that could upset Chantelle, I'll leave here."

Guy's mouth firmed before he stood up. "Don't you worry. I have my own attorneys who can deal with anything the Stillman attorneys might concoct."

Laura didn't doubt it.

"Do you want cook to fix you a late lunch?"

"No, thank you. I think I'll rest for an hour. Maybe

by then Chantelle will be up and I'll tell her about the race."

"She'll love that. See you later."

As he leaned forward to give her a kiss on both cheeks, she heard Raoul's rasping voice in the periphery. "The maid said I'd find you in here, *mon frère.*" He moved deeper into the sitting room. His glittery gaze fell on Laura.

"I did knock, but you didn't hear me. Sorry to disturb, but Paul has had a mishap on his bike coming home from his friend's. An ambulance took him to the hospital to check him out. The E.R. called to say he's fine. They're ready to release him to his parents."

"He's all right?" Guy looked visibly shaken. Raoul nodded. *"Grâce a ciel!"*

"Do you want me to get him?" Raoul asked. "If he's here before Chantelle wakes up, then she won't be as disturbed when he tells her what happened."

"Let's both go, Raoul." He turned to Laura. "Will you stay here? If Chantelle wakes up before we're back, tell her we went on an errand."

"I will, but, Guy? Maybe she should be told. Paul's her son, too. She adores him. If she thought he needed her, she might forget herself for a little while and go with you. You never know."

His eyes grew suspiciously bright. "Why didn't I think of that? *Dieu merci* you're here, Laura! I'm going to wake her up right now. Things couldn't be any worse than they have been. Why not act on your suggestion and see what happens?" He kissed her cheek again before dashing out of the suite.

CHAPTER SIX

LAURA stood there trembling. "If you don't mind, I'd like to be alone."

"What if I *do* mind?" Raoul challenged. His brother had gone. "Did you tell him I had you investigated?"

Her eyes looked wounded. "I don't know why you bother to ask me, when we both know you don't believe a word that comes out of my mouth."

He raked a hand through his hair. "That's not true, Laura."

"I thought you would want to go with your brother. He needs you."

"I think I'll wait a few minutes. You gave him an idea. Coupled with his guilt over the accident, he might achieve a little success with Chantelle."

When she bit her lip like that, her whole persona changed from the confident woman of the world to someone sweet and vulnerable. Which one was she, or was she an amalgamation of both?

"Once before, you mentioned Guy's guilt about the accident. Why should he feel any blame?"

Raoul rubbed his chest absently. "Apparently they'd

had an argument that day, one of the few in their marriage. Chantelle was all set to visit a good friend of hers who lives in Monaco. Guy is superstitious about certain things and he told Chantelle he didn't want her to drive the Monaco road, because it was too dangerous. Princess Grace died on that road.

"She refused to listen to him on that subject. On that particular day he forbade her to go, but she went anyway and ended up having the accident. Not on that road, as it happens, not even in Monaco. It took place in Nice. She was driving her sports car too fast. It shimmied on a bridge. She lost control and it rolled into some heavy shrubbery where the car lay hidden for four hours."

Laura sank down on the nearest chair. "How ghastly."

"It was, for a lot of reasons. Guy took it all on, saying it was his fault he'd upset her, thus the reason she'd gone over the side. When the doctor told her she was fully recovered and could stop using the wheelchair, she reverted to the way she is today.

"At first Guy thought she was teasing to get back at him, but after twelve hours it became apparent something much more serious was preventing her from returning to normal. Needless to say, he's been going downhill ever since, as has their marriage."

A gasp escaped her throat. "All they need is this bad news about Paul." She covered her eyes with her hand. "How serious are his injuries?" she whispered.

"A gash on the side of his left thigh. It took ten stitches."

"Ouch."

"He'll be fine."

"Was it his fault?"

"No. A truck passed another car and drifted into the bike lane, sending Paul flying."

"That must have been so frightening for him." She jumped back up from the chair, obviously too restless to sit. "Your family can't take much more."

Raoul studied her well-shaped head, marveling at the color of her pale-blond hair. It had an ethereal quality, all the more stunning on such a striking woman. Today she wore it loose from a side part. Of all the styles, he liked it the best.

"I couldn't agree more." He moved closer to her. "My brother is more fragile than you know. Whatever goes on between you and your husband is your own business, but if it could hurt Guy, then it becomes *mine*. Why are you afraid to talk about your husband?" he asked her in a voice she had never heard from him before: soft, gentle.

A nervous hand went to her throat. "Why haven't you ever talked about your wife?"

Her response exasperated him. "Because this is about Chantelle and Guy, not me. Are you in some kind of trouble?"

"That depends on your definition of the word."

"You mean Guy's going to help you."

She flashed him a warning glance. "I'm afraid that's none of *your* business. Unlike you, I meant no offense. In case you didn't notice, I don't ask you personal questions."

"I've noticed," he said sharply, growing more frustrated every second. "What would you like to know?"

He watched her swallow, another telltale sign she was growing more and more uncomfortable. "Nothing."

Such an innocuous word said so innocuously. "Surely you've wondered why I don't seem to have a household of my own."

"Not really."

"That's a lie."

She folded her arms against her shapely waist. "Since you're now reverting to your baser instincts, I guess that's my cue to ask the ten-million-dollar question."

He smiled wickedly and her insides lit. "It's nice to know you put that high a price on the answer."

She tossed her head, causing her hair to float above her shoulders. "All right, I give up. Why did you and your wife divorce?"

"She lied to me about something I can never forgive her for. All the time we were married I thought she wanted children as much as I did. We planned to have a family, but she never had any intention of getting pregnant."

Something flickered in the depths of those green orbs. "She did a very cruel thing to you. I'm sorry."

"Aren't you going to ask me anything else?" he prodded.

"I don't need to. A lie says it all, don't you think?"

If he didn't miss his guess, that was pain he heard in her voice. "Not all. The follow-up might be. Am I sad about my marriage being over? Am I happy it came to an end?"

Her expression closed. "If you're sad, then it's a tragedy. If you're happy, then it speaks for itself."

"What about *your* marriage?" he drilled her, ready to erupt if she didn't tell him something he could understand.

"You mean am I in a state of bliss, or someplace lower?"

A tight band constricted his breathing. "I think the fact that you're living under Guy's roof says a lot."

"There you go, then." She smiled. "You have your answer."

His hands shot to her shoulders. He shook her almost roughly. "Don't do this, Laura. I'm not asking you these questions out of some twisted desire to torment you. Has your husband been abusive to you?"

She averted her eyes. "Not physically."

"But there are other ways."

"That's true, but I don't wish to discuss it, Raoul." Her breathing had grown shallow. "How long have you known my married name was Stillman?"

"Not long."

Her eyes filled. "Then why didn't you confront me immediately instead of plunging in the dagger last night?"

He'd only meant to get the truth about her feelings for her husband out in the open, but things were fast escalating out of control. He found himself kneading her upper arms not covered by her blouse. His thumbs smoothed her skin with its golden glow. Her body was warm and fluid. Fragrant.

"Last night still haunts me, so I'll ask it another way. Is fear of your husband the reason you've sought Guy's help?"

Her lips were only inches apart from his. "After the history between us, why would it possibly matter to you?"

"Because you're a married woman, and I need to kiss you again or go slowly out of my mind."

She quivered against him. He felt her warm, sweet breath on his lips as she said, "You've already done that on several occasions."

"Not like this…"

With his conscience nowhere in sight, he covered her mouth hungrily. She'd been a temptation since he'd first seen her in Guy's living room enamoring all his male guests.

"We mustn't—" she cried, refusing him entry. Not to be defeated, he kissed his way around her lips, finding every line and curve, lingering on the fuller parts. That brought another small gasp, giving him the entrée he craved. He slid his hands over her back and pulled her into him so he could drink deeply.

She was ready for him, just like last night. Her little moans closed any escape hatch he should have been looking for. Slowly covering every inch of skin, his mouth moved to her throat where the pulse at the base throbbed wildly.

Raoul thought he'd known rapture before, but never like this. "You're so beautiful, Laura. I ache whenever I think about you, let alone look. I want you."

She reached up to cup his face before pressing a lingering kiss to his lips. "There's nothing like it, is there? A fire that burns so hotly you think you can't live without it." Her eyes burned with that fire. "But somehow we do." One more short kiss and she eased out of his arms.

"*We* don't have to live without it," he murmured huskily.

"Yes *we* do." She'd already backed away emotionally from him. "Our lives were going in two different directions when we collided. The chemistry's real, Raoul, but that's all. I'm still Mrs. Stillman, and I'm here at Guy's request to try to help Chantelle."

He felt as if his air supply had just been caught off. "Have you considered that Chantelle might see you as a threat?"

The way she looked at him, he might as well have slapped her. She studied him for a long time. "Your divorce has given you such a cynical view of life, you don't know what's real anymore. It's sad because you're truly a wonderful person in so many ways.

"Over the last few days there've been slices of moments of sheer pleasure with you. I thank you for those, but Chantelle gave me some good advice on my first day here and I quote, 'Don't let him scare you off, Laura. Raoul has his own demons he needs to deal with. Guy brought you to our home at my request. Raoul has his own home. Your being here is none of his business.'"

She walked to the door of the suite. "You look exhausted. You'd better go home and get some sleep, otherwise someone else I know is going to end up in the hospital before the day is out. I'll phone you if there's any kind of development."

His eyes probed hers. "I could use a few hours, but I'll be back. Care to join me?" he asked, smiling wickedly.

Her heart thudded in her chest. "If that's a proposition, it's not a flattering one. You're half-dead."

"You want me fully alive, is that what you're saying?"

Her breath caught. He might be exhausted, but the wicked smile was in evidence. "I'm saying the timing is wrong, even for chemistry. You know the expression 'There's a time to weep and a time to laugh…a time to mourn and a time to dance'?"

"And now isn't the right time for us?" he murmured. Laura nodded. "It's your loss, Laura. I think there is more than just chemistry between us."

Laura couldn't take any more. Since he made no move to leave she said, "You're welcome to stay in here and sleep. I'm going to find out whether Guy was successful in getting Chantelle to go to the hospital with him. When Paul comes home, I'll send the maid to let you know."

Raoul felt like he'd just awakened to a nightmare.

The sound of a car in the drive had Laura putting down her sketchpad to dash to the front door. When she opened it, the sight of three people getting out of the limo brought tears to her throat. Chantelle had gone to the hospital with Guy to bring their son home. Another big step for her.

Dear Guy. He had double duty. After he and Pierre lifted Chantelle and her wheelchair to the top step of the porch, he rushed back to help Paul with his crutches. One pant leg had been rolled up high enough to expose a patch of gauze and a bandage covering his wound.

Knowing Chantelle wouldn't want Laura to say anything about this minor miracle of her going to the hospital, she focused on her son.

"Hey, Paul, maybe we should have taken you with us to see the Tour after all," she called out.

He looked up at her with a wan smile. "How was it?"

"Not nearly as hair raising as what happened to you. Is your bike ruined?"

"Yeah."

"I'm sorry. A bike can be replaced, but there's only one Paul Laroche."

"Will you be my nurse?"

Laura smiled and gave him a kiss on the cheek. "I insist on it." Her gaze switched to Guy, who winked at her. He looked happier than she'd seen him since her arrival in Cap Ferrat. Today had been a milestone, not only for Chantelle.

She wheeled through the foyer. "We're very thankful to bring you home in one piece, *mon fils*. Let's get you to your room."

"Do I have to go to bed, *Maman?* I want to lie on the lounger out on the patio."

"You're sure it's not too hot for you?"

"I'll arrange the umbrella for him," Laura offered.

Everyone moved through the house to the patio off the dining room. "Has the medicine made you sick?" his mother asked.

"No. I'm hungry."

Chantelle looked at him with loving eyes. "You've a cast-iron stomach just like your uncle."

"Did I hear my name taken in vain?"

Raoul's head and shoulders had emerged from the pool. He must have slipped out the front door after Laura had left the guest suite. Had he gotten any sleep?

With enviable male grace he levered himself out of the water and onto the tile. In a few strides he reached his nephew and laid the crutches at the side of the lounger so Paul could settle back. Then he tousled his hair. "It looks like you're going to live. Just don't do that again."

Laura's eyes closed. She was still throbbing from the touch of Raoul's hands moving over her back and arms earlier with an urgency that had left her breathless.

"It was the truck driver's fault."

Guy came out with a glass of lemonade for him.

"Merci, Papa."

"I'm going into the house to talk to cook," Chantelle said. "Giles called and wants to know how you are."

"I'll call him later. He was ahead of me and luckily didn't get hit."

Laura hunkered down at his side. "He was lucky, but you carry the mark of bravery."

A smile broke out on his attractive face. One day he was going to be a heart breaker like the rest of the men in the Laroche family. "Yeah."

"Yeah."

"Who won the race?"

"The Dutchman came in first," Raoul informed him. "Places two and three went to the Spanish," he added while he and Guy pulled up chairs next to him. "Not a Frenchman among them."

Paul frowned. *"Zut alors!"*

"Not an American, either," Laura interjected, having pulled up another chair. Paul hooted.

For the next half hour she listened as Raoul gave them details of what they'd seen earlier in the day. Part was in English for her benefit, but a lot of it was in French. She knew he was knowledgeable, but she had no idea he could rattle off names and statistics like a pro announcer, let alone recall everything while she'd been standing there in monstrous pain.

If ever she needed proof that a man could compartmentalize his interests from his emotions, this was it.

Late afternoon turned into evening. Chantelle put a puzzle together with Laura while Paul introduced her to some of his favorite teen rock music. Raoul and Guy discussed a little business. After dinner he convinced his son to go to bed. Tomorrow he could have his friends over.

When Raoul said good-night to everyone and took himself off to his villa, Laura felt a loss she could hardly bear. As upset as she'd been over his admission that he'd had her investigated, his concern that Ted had abused her took away a lot of her pain.

She'd give anything to follow him so they could talk more. So far she hadn't been inside his villa, nor was she likely to be invited. If he'd lived there throughout his marriage she would have no idea, but she felt a deep curiosity over what he did away from his family.

A man like Raoul wouldn't have been celibate since his divorce. If he had a lover, he'd been sandwiching her in since he'd taken it upon himself to keep an eye on Laura. Last night at the Auberge she'd come close to giving him everything. *Oh, Raoul.*

After a sleepless night, Raoul pulled on his swimming trunks. He had a plan in mind to get Laura to himself. That meant spending a little time with Paul at the pool.

Sure enough his nephew dressed in shorts and a T-shirt was already stretched out on a lounger. His leg had been propped. Raoul dived in the water. When he came out the other end, Paul smiled at him. *"Bonjour, mon oncle."*

"Bonjour, mon gamin. Have you had breakfast yet?"

"Yes. I ate out here with Laura."

They'd been up early. "Where's your nurse now?"

"She's bringing me some things from my bedroom."

"Have you made plans with your friends yet?"

"Nope."

"How would you and Giles like to go boating with me and Laura today?"

"Cool!" he cried. "She didn't tell me."

"It's my surprise."

"Hey, Laura," he called to her as she walked out on the patio carrying some things in her arms. Dressed in her white swimsuit with a French braid fastened to the top of her blond head and those long legs going on forever, she looked so beautiful Raoul almost fell back in the pool. "Uncle Raoul is going to take us out on the cruiser! He said Giles could come with us!"

Other than her eyes turning a more brilliant shade of green, she didn't react or make up some excuse why they couldn't go. "As long as it's okay with your parents, I don't see why you shouldn't enjoy a lovely day like this on the water."

She bent over him. "Here's your Ipod, your Game Boy, some sunscreen and the album."

"Thanks."

"You're welcome."

"How about something for me?" Raoul asked, drawing her attention.

"Breakfast coming right up." She disappeared before he could stop her.

Paul started poring over a picture album. "Hey, Uncle Raoul? Do you want to see something cool?"

He pulled a chair up by the lounger. "What is it?"

"Some pictures of me and Laura."

"Bien sur." Giles must have taken them.

"Maman found them for me last night before I went to bed."

Found them?

Paul handed over the album. He had it opened to a page with a dozen small photos. They were snapshots, the kind printed years ago. Consumed by curiosity, he studied them.

To his shock he saw Laura in a swimsuit much like the one she was wearing now, but she was a teenager! His mind reeled. The little dark-haired boy she was holding was Paul! In another picture she was dressed in shorts and a blouse while she helped him walk. Still others showed them with Guy and Chantelle on the surf or around a pool.

The blood hammered at his temples. Absolutely stunned, he lifted his head. "Where were these taken, Paul?"

"At the Manhattan Beach Resort Hotel in California," Laura answered for him. She put the breakfast tray on the little table next to Raoul. "The last summer before I started university, I was a part-time lifeguard and babysitter there." Her gaze flicked to Paul.

"The manager asked me if I would do a special favor and become the Laroches' nanny for the ten days they were there at the beach. I took one look at little Paulie as I called you, and my heart melted on the spot."

"You called me Paulie?" He laughed.

For a moment her gaze met Raoul's. "I did. You had the most gorgeous brown hair and eyes for a one-year-old. Such smooth olive skin. Chantelle kept you dressed in the cutest little white sunsuits, and you were such a good boy, always smiling. There wasn't a child around to compare to you. Of course, that's because your parents are beautiful people inside and out.

"I thought Guy was more handsome than that French movie star Louis Jourdan and your mom was even more stunning than Audrey Hepburn. When you all had to leave for Hawaii, I cried my eyes out."

Paul smiled up at her. "You did?"

"Yes. For ten days I'd had the time of my life. Your parents begged me to go with all of you. You know how generous your dad is. He said he'd pay for everything, and your mom insisted you wouldn't be happy without me. They made me feel wonderful, but I couldn't go. It was time for my classes to start."

"I wish I could remember."

She patted his shoulder. "That's why pictures are so important. Do you know when we went to Disneyland, I pretended you were my little boy? Of course with my coloring no one would believe it, but I always said that when I grew up, I would want a little Paulie of my own. No one else would do." Her gaze met Raoul's as her words sank in.

Raoul wondered why she hadn't had children with her husband and sensed that there was more to her marriage to Theodore Stillman than she was letting on.

"Don't tell Giles you used to call me Paulie. He'll tell everybody."

She kissed his cheek. "Don't worry. It'll be our secret."

Paul looked at Raoul. "Promise you won't tell, either?"

He had to clear the lump in his throat before he could talk. "I swear."

"Good." He reached for his Ipod and began listening to his music while he played with his game.

Raoul ate his breakfast and looked through the album, always coming back to the page that revealed a history he'd known nothing about. Laura waited until he'd finished his last roll, then she took his tray to the house. When she returned, he was waiting for her.

"Why didn't you tell me?" he ground out.

Her delicately arched brows met in a frown. "I assumed you knew. Don't you remember the time they went on that long trip?"

"Yes, but I never connected their activities with you."

"I guess it didn't occur to them to remind you of it. Even so, what difference does it make?"

He shot out of the chair. "You know damn well it makes every difference. I thought you were a total stranger!"

"It's been eleven years. For all intents and purposes, I *am*. You have every right to want to protect your loved ones, Raoul. Did you tell Chantelle and Guy you had suspicions about me?"

"No." Raoul had kept his feelings to himself and allowed them to blind his opinions toward Laura.

"That's too bad. You could have saved yourself some initial grief."

"Laura," His voice grated. He'd said unconscionable things to her. "I already told Paul I was taking the two of you out on the boat with me today. Giles can come, too, if he wants." He took a deep breath. "I'd like us to start over again."

Out of wooden lips she said, "You mean no pistols at dawn?"

"None. No swords, slings or arrows. I'll come unarmed."

One brow lifted. "Raoul Laroche, unarmed?"

He lifted his hands.

A faint smile curved one corner of her pliant mouth. "You look about as innocent as Vercingetorix before he swept down on Gergovia, but it might be worth my trouble."

Raoul burst into laughter. "I had no idea you were so knowledgeable about Gallic history."

"Chantelle is a fan of one of the most famous French warriors in history."

His heart rate sped up. "If you have any other conditions, I'll do my utmost to grant them."

Their gazes fused. "For one day I'd like you to show up without your glasses."

"I don't wear any. My eyesight is 20/20."

"I'm talking about those lenses you look through from the inside. You might like what you see without them."

If he liked what he saw any more than what was in front of him right now, he was in danger of being consumed by her fire.

A few hours later Laura came up from the galley of the cruiser with two orange drinks for the boys. She arranged the large umbrella so Paul stayed out of the hot, late-afternoon sun.

"Will you two be all right if Raoul and I take a swim? We'll stay near the boat of course." She made sure his sore leg was elevated.

Paul nodded. Both of them were too involved in their electronic games to talk.

"Then we'll see you in a little while."

"Ciao," they both said at the same time.

She walked to the rear of the big cruiser where Raoul was waiting by the ladder. In black trunks his powerful, tanned body took her breath. Laura felt his black eyes roam over her as she removed her beach coat.

He'd been the perfect host so far, but this would be the first time they had been alone since taking the boat out.

"I swear the Italians invented the greatest word in the world."

"You mean *ciao*," he surmised correctly.

Laura nodded. "You can have a whole conversation with it. Hi—goodbye—and in English it sounds like 'chow,' meaning food."

He chuckled. "Lunch was delicious by the way."

"You liked my hamburgers and chips? You weren't faking it?"

His expression remained benign. "Would I do that?"

She started to say yes, then remembered their pact. "I'm glad, then."

Recognizing she'd practiced self-control, his eyes smiled, filling her with warmth. "Are you ready for our swim?"

They were anchored a couple of miles off the point of Cap Ferrat in a calm, pale-blue sea. Conditions were ideal.

"I've wanted to do this since the day I arrived." So saying she climbed up on the side and dived straight in.

"How is it?" he asked as her head bobbed up.

She treaded water. "Fantastic. It has to be close to eighty out here, a good twelve to fifteen degrees higher than the ocean off Manhattan Beach. Come on in."

He dived off the top of the ladder, reaching her in a few swift kicks. She loved the way he looked when his black hair was plastered to his head, almost as though the water brought out the primitive in him.

Pretending he was after her, she did the back stroke around the cruiser so she could watch him. Maybe he could read her mind because he stayed a body's length away while he did the front crawl, as if he were toying with her before he seized his prey. Each time his head lifted above the water, their gazes connected, making it a little more difficult for her to breathe.

She swam full circle. When she was almost to the ladder, Raoul galvanized into action. He snaked an arm around her waist and towed her with him the short distance to the bottom rung. By now her heart was fluttering like a hummingbird's.

Their mouths gravitated to each other in a long, drawn-out, saltwater kiss that shook her to the foundations. He'd locked his legs around hers, making escape impossible, but she didn't want to escape—far from it. Being with him like this had transformed her. She felt alive and treasured for herself. Odd how she'd never felt beautiful before.

His breathing sounded shallow once he'd allowed her up for air. "Let's go below deck," he murmured in a thick toned voice against her nape. "I can't begin to do what I want with you out here."

She clung to him. "We can't anyway. There's a pair of chaperones on board."

"Let's take them home. I'm going to fix you dinner at my villa where no one will be around to disturb us."

Laura kissed his jaw. "I understand you have a pool."

"I do. It's shaped like a full moon."

"Do you ever swim in it?"

"Not for years."

"Why?"

"Have you ever noticed how lonely a pool can feel when you're the only one in it?"

She rubbed her cheek against his. "Yes. Did you live there with your wife?"

"No. Danielle's from Vence. When we married, she wanted to continue living there. It's only twenty minutes from my work, so we bought a home there."

"I remember it. You drove us through the main street after we left Tourettes. It's a charming town."

"I agree. Her parents still live there."

It was heaven to be able to talk to him like this. "How long were you married?"

His eyes played over her features. "Five years."

More than double the length of Laura's fiasco of a marriage. "Does she still live there?"

"Yes."

"Do you ever—" She looked away. "I mean, do yo—"

"No." He read her mind. "My feelings for her died long ago. Naturally I have memories of us falling in love, but not the emotions that once accompanied them."

Laura nodded. "I know what you mean."

"Then why are we wasting our time talking about the past?"

Laura didn't want to think about it, either. "Can we swim in your pool tonight?" she asked in an aching voice.

He pressed an urgent kiss to her mouth. "I'm living for a moon bath, as long as you take it with me."

As a shiver of delight ran through her body, she heard a familiar voice call out. "Uncle Raoul? When are you coming back?"

That slight tinge of anxiety was the only power that could have wrenched her from his embrace.

CHAPTER SEVEN

BEFORE Raoul pulled into the boat slip, he saw Guy waving to him from outside the limo. Surprised to have a welcoming committee, he shut off the motor and reached for the ropes to secure the cruiser.

His brother came onboard to help Paul back to shore using his crutches. "Did you have a good time?"

The boys nodded. "We had hamburgers for lunch!"

Guy winked at Laura. "I'm partial to those myself. Come on. Your *maman* is missing you."

Laura followed them to the car with an armload of items. Raoul started to catch up with her to help, but Guy held him back.

"You have a visitor waiting for you outside your villa."

It could only be one person. "Danielle."

He nodded. "She influenced the guard to let her through the gate. She called me and said she planned to wait for you no matter how long it took."

A full-blown bash to the gut would have been more welcome. Once again Danielle's timing was unbelievable, particularly in view of his conversation with Laura earlier.

"It's all right. I'll take care of it." She'd wanted a showdown for a long time. He'd give her one, but not in his house. Their confrontation would be short and sweet, then he'd go for Laura and take her back home with him.

"One more thing," Guy said. "Have you made a decision on the warehouse at the marina?"

"I have, and I don't think it's worth it."

"Have you told Jean-Luc yet?"

"No."

"Then do it tonight. While you're at it, tell him you want all gossip stopped and stamped out immediately about the woman he saw you kissing last week or we're taking him off the payroll."

"You're referring to Laura of course."

"You know I am." Guy sounded angry. Possibly angrier than Raoul had ever heard him before.

"I'll do it right now if you wish. May I ask why?"

"No. My reasons are personal."

The heat of anger flared up in him. "What exactly did she tell you?"

"It's what Jean-Luc told me! Why else would Danielle show up on the estate and force her way in? She's out to cause trouble, and I won't have Laura dragged into the mess. She saved my life, *mon frère*. Do you have any comprehension of what that means to me?" His voice literally shook.

If Raoul didn't know before, he did now. He couldn't remember the last time Guy had pulled the older-brother routine on him.

"Laura has influenced Chantelle to do things I wouldn't have imagined. I don't know what we'd do without her and I don't want to find out. I trust you to deal with the situation, Raoul."

After he walked back to the limo and it disappeared around the incline, Raoul got Jean-Luc on the line. It was too late for damage control, but an edict from Guy would ensure the agent's cooperation from here on out.

With that taken care of, he called Danielle on his cell phone. The second she picked up he said, "I'm down at the dock. If you want to talk, it will have to be here. Otherwise you'll be waiting there indefinitely."

"I just want to know one thing. Are you involved with that American woman living with Guy and Chantelle?"

Jean-Luc hadn't wasted any time. Raoul had no one but himself to blame and instantly regretted his impulsive actions from that day. Guy was right, it wasn't fair to drag Laura into this mess. "We've been divorced a year, Danielle. My business is my own."

"You *are* involved!" she cried emotionally. "How much does she mean to you, Raoul?"

That was a question Raoul didn't even want to think about, because he knew that the answer would disturb him. "I'm hanging up now, Danielle."

"You can't marry her, Raoul! You can't, I won't let you!"

He clicked off, then phoned security and told them to escort his ex-wife off the estate. Danielle needed help, and he'd begged her to get it when they were married, had offered to pay for it, but she had always refused.

Ironically, though, she'd just hit on the truth. Laura was still Ted Stillman's wife and out of bounds. But Raoul was determined to find out why she was still married to the man, because he knew she couldn't be in love with him anymore.

After he reached his villa he received another call, this time from the deputy minister of finance in Paris. The other man was calling an emergency meeting of the economic committee first thing in the morning. Raoul needed to bring all the latest banking figures with him.

He groaned. To get all that together would take him till midnight. This was one meeting he couldn't get out of. The night he'd anticipated with Laura would have to be put off. He was beginning to believe the last few hours had been nothing more than an unattainable dream.

When he tried to reach her to explain, Guy said she was in with Paul. Totally frustrated, he told his brother he had to fly to Paris and would get in touch with Laura later. Guy said he'd tell her, but he sounded more preoccupied than usual. After they hung up, he headed for his bedroom and started throwing things in his suitcase.

The maid knocked on Laura's door the next morning and brought her a breakfast tray. On her way out she asked Laura if she needed anything washed. She did actually. It forced her to get up and face the day. After the heavenly afternoon she'd spent with Raoul, her disappointment over not being with him last night had just about killed her.

Once dressed in shorts and a T-shirt, she put her hair in a ponytail and went in search of Chantelle, who would have had breakfast by now. Another maid informed her Guy had left to take Paul to Remy's house, but he'd be back shortly. In an aside she mentioned that Chantelle was having a bad morning. When Laura asked if she was ill, the maid shook her head. Guy's wife had been crying and wouldn't stop.

There could be many reasons for her tears. Laura vacillated between doing a little gardening or going to check on her. In the end she walked down the other hall to the master suite. The minute she put her ear to the door, she heard heartwrenching sobs coming out of Chantelle, the kind that couldn't be dismissed.

Deciding to take the chance she might get told to leave the villa and never come back, Laura opened the door and tiptoed inside. Beyond their sitting room was the master bedroom, but her sobs came from an adjoining room. Evidently she and Guy lived in separate rooms.

The door to Chantelle's room stood ajar. Laura looked in. Chantelle sat on an upholstered bench in front of her dressing table with her head buried in her hands. The wheelchair was pushed away. She wore a lovely lemon-colored nightgown. It looked like she'd been brushing her dark chestnut hair. Such a beautiful woman. No wonder Guy was beside himself.

Taking a deep breath she said, "Chantelle?"

She lifted her head to reveal a glistening wet face. "Please leave me alone."

Laura was prepared for that. "I can't. It's because I see myself in you. No one sobs the way you're doing unless you've reached the breaking point. I reached mine six months ago. If my best friend hadn't intervened and helped me to leave Ted, I don't know what I would have done.

"I didn't come in here for Guy's sake. He's gone with Paul. I came for me because I can't bear to see you in this kind of pain." She moved closer and hunkered down next to her. Looking into her eyes she said, "You've got to talk to someone. Let me be a sounding board. Please."

In the quiet, a gold and crystal clock with angels moving their parts chimed ten o'clock. Laura waited, holding her breath.

"I'm dying, Laura," Chantelle said in a dull voice. "I have a brain tumour and I am going to die."

She didn't say it hysterically. It came out as a statement of fact.

Laura fought her own hysteria.

"When did you find out?"

"Right after the accident when they did a CAT scan and an MRI. They found it and said it was inoperable. If I hadn't had the car accident, I wouldn't have known until the symptoms began to appear. They said I would start to show signs within three to four months and be dead within a year."

"Obviously, Guy doesn't know anything about this."

"No. He'll find out soon enough."

"That's why you've been pushing him away?"

"Yes. I know my husband. We love and need each other too much. I decided to distance myself so that when things get difficult, it won't be such a shock to him. He and Paul have each other."

Laura groaned inwardly at Chantelle's desperate situation. "Have the symptoms started?"

"Two migraines."

What Chantelle was doing was more painful for Guy than the death sentence, but in Chantelle's mind she'd chosen to handle it this way. Laura wouldn't be able to talk her out of it. Without hesitation she wrapped her arms around her and rocked her for a long time.

"You can never tell him, Laura."

"No. I won't. But this is affecting everyone, Chantelle. Not just Guy but Paul, too. It's even been hard on Raoul. He loves you and has resented me for being here to try to help when he can't."

"I know. I purposely didn't tell him we knew you previously."

"Why?" Laura couldn't believe what she was hearing.

"The more he's distracted, the more he leaves me alone. He was born with extra radar. He's not like Guy. Since his divorce and my accident, he's over here constantly, always trying to get me to do things, hoping I'll turn back into the old Chantelle. I can't bear his scrutiny."

Laura could relate to that, too. "That's because he loves you so much."

"I love Raoul, too. He is a wonderful brother to me. That's what has made this so much harder."

She bit her lip. "How can I help you, Chantelle?"

"I want you to stay with us to the end. Paul would be thrilled, and he'll need you when the time comes. Would it be possible, Laura?"

"I...I don't know." There was too much to process at once.

Chantelle stared at her through drenched eyes. "When Guy said you were calling from Italy, I couldn't have been happier and told him to invite you to the house. It's like my prayers had been answered. Little did I know you would save his life that night! I love you, Laura, my family loves you. We need you now."

Laura took a fortifying breath. "I'm going to have to speak to my boss again."

"You'll be safe with us. I'd like to see that husband of yours try to bother you here. Guy wouldn't stand for it."

Right now Laura's thoughts weren't on Ted. She was envisioning everyone's pain and trauma over the next few months when Chantelle started degenerating. The thought of it was unbearable.

"Guy's going to be back soon. Let's go out to the rose garden so he won't know you've been crying."

"I'll get dressed."

They hugged for another long moment before Laura left the room.

She wished she could wave a magic wand and restore Chantelle to the happiness of her life before the accident. To think she'd been living all these months knowing she had an inoperable brain tumor…

For herself, Laura wished she could run into one pair of arms for comfort and know she would always be welcome there. While Raoul was still in Paris, the only panacea for her pain was work, whether it be helping with Paul, doing some gardening or keeping Chantelle company.

By the next evening she was ready to make that important phone call to her boss. While she was at it, she wanted to send him her latest artwork. In order to do it, she needed access to a scanner.

Laura glanced at Paul, who'd used his crutches to walk her over to Raoul's villa from Guy's. His leg was healing so well he really didn't need crutches anymore. She couldn't get over how agile he was again.

"Are you sure your uncle won't mind?"

"Nope. I use his stuff whenever I need it for school. *Maman* gave you her permission. He won't be home until tomorrow night. She said that conference in Paris ran over another day. Come on in."

Raoul's home was more contemporarily furnished, but equally elegant. "This is a beautiful place."

"My grandparents used to live here, but I don't remember them. Papa said they died in a plane accident." She'd wondered about Raoul's parents, yet another scar to add to his damaged heart. "Sit over here and I'll show you how his scanner works."

Laura had brought all three sketchpads she'd filled so far this trip. She needed to download everything she scanned and e-mail it. Depending on what her boss thought of her work, she'd broach the subject of staying in France for an indefinite period. As much as she wanted a divorce from Ted, Chantelle had become her top priority.

It would mean taking a leave of absence from her lifeguard job. Plus she'd have to discuss the whole situation of her apartment with Cindy.

After a few run-throughs with Paul on Raoul's state-of-the-art equipment, she felt she could take it from here. "You're a whiz, *mon ami.*" He'd been teaching her some basic phrases. "I think I'm ready, thanks to you. Why don't you go now. Giles is waiting for you."

"Call the house if you have problems."

"I don't plan to have any."

He grinned. *"Ciao."*

"Ciao."

Once she got the knack of it, the scanning went fast. Before long she'd done the downloading. A press of the button and they were sent. Before she left to go back to the other villa she phoned her boss. He'd be in his office by now. It was after 9:00 a.m. his time.

"Other World Video Games."

'Hi, Sandra. It's Laura. Can I speak to Carl?"

"Sure. Just a moment."

While she waited, she studied a grouping of small-framed pictures on the shelf above his desk. She reached for one of them. Raoul and Guy were just young boys surrounded by family. Laura loved them so much she wanted to steal them.

"Laura? How are you?"

"I'm fine, Carl. And you?"

"Swamped as usual. What's going on?"

"I wanted you to know I just sent you a file of all my sketches."

"Terrific! Let me take a look while you're on the line."

While they were busy chatting about business, she heard an ear-piercing whistle. "These are fabulous, Laura! I mean really fabulous!"

"Oh, good. I'm glad you like them."

"Like—the guys in the backroom are going to go crazy! Don't you ever leave me, honey."

Carl was the only man she didn't mind calling her that. "Actually, that's what I'm calling about."

"No. I'm not going to listen."

She laughed. "I have to be serious for a moment." In the next breath she explained her dilemma and ended up in tears.

When she'd finished he said, "Let me sleep on it and we'll talk tomorrow at the same time."

"Thanks, Carl."

"Thank *you*. By the way, Sandra's been documenting the number of calls your husband has made to the office. She has the telephone company printouts. The pile is growing."

"It's *his* funeral, but I'm sorry you've been bothered. Tell her I owe her."

"No problem. Talk to you tomorrow."

"Tomorrow." She clicked off.

"What's so important about tomorrow?"

Laura spun around in the swivel chair. "Raoul—"

He wasn't supposed to be home until tomorrow night. She shivered to think that if he'd come in a few minutes sooner, he would have heard her telling Carl about Chantelle's condition. The little picture she was holding fell on the area rug. "Oh, I'm sorry." She rushed to pick it up and dropped her cell phone.

Raoul was there so fast their hands brushed. He was still in his gray business suit. When he lifted his dark head, their faces were level. Mere centimeters apart. It only took a little tug to pull her down on the floor next to him.

"On the flight home I wondered how I was going to get you alone before the evening was out."

She'd made up her mind they couldn't do this until she was free from Ted, but her puny efforts to resist were no match for his hard-muscled strength. He stretched out on his back and pulled her on top of him. Taking his time he threaded his fingers through the fine-spun gold of her hair.

"Umm…you've been out in the sun this afternoon." He kissed every feature of her face. "Much as I like the taste of your lipstick, I like the taste of the strawberries you had for dinner. They're sweet like your mouth. You'd have to be a man to know what it does to me."

With one hand at the back of her waist, the other spanning her neck, he gathered her tightly against him, searching for her mouth until they clung in a wine-dark rapture.

One kiss. That was all. It started out slow, then began building, shooting fire through her body until she felt an ecstasy almost beyond bearing. Somewhere outside the euphoric haze holding her in its thrall she heard the phone ringing.

"Raoul—" she moaned helplessly, but he wasn't listening. In a dizzying motion she was turned on her back, her face cupped between his hands. He lowered his mouth to her eyelids and earlobes.

"You're gorgeous," he whispered in an aching voice. "I can't get enough. Three days away from you have been an eternity." His lips swept over her cheeks and throat before coming back to her mouth over and over again in a rhythm so intoxicating, he might as well be putting her under a spell.

He was the vortex drawing her in with a hold so strong she had no concept of time or knew where she was.

"Laura?" She heard Paul on the voice message. "*Maman* said to call and tell you Uncle Raoul is home so you won't be surprised."

"I should call him back," she said, trying to roll away from him.

"He doesn't expect a response."

Raoul slid his hands to her shoulders from behind. The second he touched her, she felt like she was undergoing a meltdown. He removed the picture she was holding in her hand. "I like this one, too," he murmured into her hair. "I'm eight here. Guy's fourteen. Give me some time and I'll show you *my* baby pictures."

She'd love to see them, but her heartache over Chantelle was too great to get back to the happiness she'd experienced a few days ago out on the cruiser. Slowly she moved away from him and started gathering up her sketches.

He put the picture back on the shelf while his gaze remained riveted on her. "What's wrong? Where have you gone since I left?"

She could try to keep her heart from hammering, but when she was anywhere near Raoul, her body reacted with a will that knew no master. This time, however, it was vital she deflect his radar, a precarious assignment under any circumstances, but especially now.

"While you've been in Paris, there's been a development."

Over the past seventy-two hours she'd been forced

to come to grips with the knowledge that Chantelle's days were numbered. There'd been more nights when Laura had cried herself to sleep because she'd had to bear the burden of it alone. Now there were two inconsolable women in the villa.

His body tensed. She could see it in the rigidity of his jaw. "Go on."

"Chantelle has asked me to stay on longer than the two weeks."

Raoul shrugged out of his suit jacket and tossed it over a chair back. Rolling up his shirtsleeves he said, "I don't understand why that's so upsetting to you when it's clear the family adores you. Did you say yes?"

She rubbed her temples. "Not yet."

Through slumberous eyes he examined her face and figure. "Come into the kitchen with me and you can tell me why. The heat in Paris was stifling. I need something cold to drink."

Whether she should or not, she followed him through his beautiful home to the immaculate kitchen. He opened the fridge and pulled out a bottled water. "Would you like one, too? I don't have anything else to offer. I haven't entertained since my divorce. I'm afraid my cupboards are embarrassingly empty."

"Please." After removing the lid, he put the cold bottle against her hot cheek for a minute. She could almost hear it sizzle before he placed it in her hand. She took a long gulp while he began drinking his. At one point their gazes collided. Her hand tightened on the bottleneck in reaction to that penetrating look. "If you came to my apartment in Manhattan Beach, I couldn't even offer you water."

He drained the rest and put the empty bottle on the counter. "Does that mean you're inviting me?" The depth of his tone traveled to her insides, causing her to grow weak with the longing to experience more of his passion. He was like a drug her system recognized and wanted above everything else.

"I wish I could," her voice shook.

Shadows marred his handsome features. "What's the hold your husband has on you?"

It was time for the truth. "I fell out of love with Ted soon after we were married. I'm trying to divorce him, but he's giving me trouble."

There was a moment of quiet before he said, "How long were you married before you filed?"

She took a fortifying breath. "Two years."

"How did you meet him?"

"He was out on the family yacht with a group of friends. They'd come down the coast from Santa Barbara. It was a beautiful day, but there was some wind that had kicked up moderate swells. Four of them decided to swim in the ocean for a little while. I was on lifeguard duty.

"I'm always looking through my binoculars for signs of trouble. You can usually tell when a person is starting to drown because their hands go up and their head goes back. While I was spotting different people, I saw this swimmer struggling and raced out."

"Ted, obviously."

She nodded. "When I brought him in to shore, he was in serious trouble. It took a long time to revive him. The paramedics arrived and took over, but they didn't give him much of a chance to survive. A week later I had a phone call from my supervisor telling me that Congressman Stillman wanted to meet me."

"I think I can write the script from here."

"It's transparent." She laughed sadly. "One thing led to another and I met the older man and his son, Ted. They wanted to thank me for saving Ted's life. In fact they were so grateful they couldn't do enough for me. Flowers, dinner at their home."

Raoul's brow lowered. "Sounds like Guy and Chantelle."

"But there's one huge difference," she declared. "Guy hoped I might be able to help Chantelle. Ted pursued me relentlessly. I was attracted and fell hard for him. He decided he would marry me. I became his trophy wife."

The use of that word made his lips thin.

"He never shared his dream with me about going into politics. I was a naive fool to think we could have a normal life. He insisted I be in all his photo shoots."

"I saw one of you on the Colorado River."

She bowed her head. "That was a nightmare trip. They all were. We were never home to make a home. Ted demanded I give up both my jobs and be available to him for his campaign. He liked the idea of being a young, hip congressman with a wife he could show off.

"Too late I realized he had no depth and was just using me. In fact Ted could only love himself. I saved his life and he mistook it for love. So did I. His father encouraged our union because to quote him, 'I looked good in print.'"

"You can't blame him for that," he said under his breath, but she heard him.

"Toward the end of our marriage, I refused to go on any more trips with him. His mother begged me to work things out with him one more time. So I showed up at his hotel one night and discovered him with another woman."

Raoul bit out an epithet.

"One of his ex-security men told me it was the usual pattern with the Stillman men. I went back home. On the advice of my friend, Cindy, I found an attorney who wouldn't be intimidated by the Stillmans and I filed for divorce."

"When was that?"

"Six months ago. Ted's been fighting it ever since. He's afraid a divorce will finish him in politics. The Stillman family has never had a divorce. Their record is clean, so to speak, so he has refused to give me one.

"When I return to Manhattan Beach I'll take him to court. With the documentation I've accrued, the judge will have to grant it unless he's in their pocket, but I have to be careful."

He squinted at her. "Why?"

"As I told Guy, Ted's been having me followed in the hope than he can get something on me to hold up the divorce. My attorney told me to stay out of the limelight. I'm still a married woman so I have to be careful not to give him an opportunity to get a photo of me with a man that could be misconstrued in any way."

He gave her a brooding stare "You mean like a picture of me kissing you down by the marina that day."

She nodded.

"I'm sorry," his voice grated.

"It doesn't matter. I'm just glad Jean-Luc wasn't working for Ted. I don't want anything to hold up my divorce, but now that Chantelle has asked me stay longer, it puts a court date off that much further." She stared at him. "Did your wife fight your divorce?"

His chest rose and fell sharply. "Yes, but I had the resources to end it quickly. Is lack of money the only problem holding you up?"

She nodded. "I earn enough from both jobs to pay my attorney in increments. He's willing to carry the loan for as many years as it takes me. My problem is, if I stay here, I can't work so I can't build up my savings."

"You know Guy would give you any amount you need."

"I believe he would, but I'd never take it. The Stillmans use their money to buy people and favors. Being married to Ted sickened me on the subject."

"Certain marriages have a way of doing that," he muttered.

It was time to get off the subject that had brought deep pain to both of them.

"Raoul…Chantelle said I could use your scanner, but I still want to thank you. I decided to send my latest sketches to my boss. It was a good time to ask him if he thought he could give me a leave of absence so I'll have a job to return to after Chantelle…no longer needs me."

He moved closer. "So you've decided you'll stay?"

"Yes. In fact, I'd like to get back to the villa and tell her before she goes to bed."

"Then don't let me stop you."

Somehow she hadn't expected he would allow things to end this way. She'd thought he would pull her into his arms and beg her not to go, but obviously he was still battling some dark places in his psyche, left over from his divorce.

CHAPTER EIGHT

WITH her phone in hand, Laura paced the floor of her bedroom. "You're sure you don't mind, Cindy?"

"What else do I have to do? Bringing in the mail and letting the cleaning crew in once a week is nothing! I haven't seen your husband since last time. Is that good or bad?"

"I don't know, but I can't thank you enough. I'll make it up to you."

"You already have by letting me drive your car when I need one."

"It has to be driven once in a while."

"Agreed. Now tell me about Raoul."

"I haven't seen him for close to a week. He left for Switzerland again, and now I've learned he's been in Lyon."

"I bet you're dying."

"I am." Laura didn't know if these trips were partially because he was in some kind of pain he still couldn't bring himself to share with her.

"How long a sabbatical has Carl given you?" Cindy asked, tactfully changing the subject.

"We worked out two and a half more months. More than that and he'll have to hire someone else."

"But Chantelle might live another year. No one ever really knows about these things."

"I know. I'd give anything to talk to her doctor, but of course I can't."

"What about Raoul, do you think you can tell him?"

"I don't know, Cindy. They are such a close family, it is surely going to destroy them. I don't know how I am going to go on keeping this secret to myself for much longer, but I don't want to break Chantelle's trust in me."

Cindy paused before answering. "I think you know Raoul better than most people, and it seems to me that he is the one you should trust with this. Think about it, Laura, it might help them more than they know right now."

"You're right, Cindy, I'll think about what you said. Anyway, enough of that. I won't keep you any longer. Call me anytime."

Laura hung up the phone feeling guilty their conversations always kept Cindy up past midnight. But her friend insisted it was the best time. Thank heaven for her; she provided a much-needed outlet. They both did for each other.

She moved off the bed and went into the bathroom to brush her hair. By now Chantelle would be ready for a morning swim. Laura changed out of her nightgown to her swimsuit and left the bedroom for the patio.

Normally Chantelle was already sitting there eating toast and drinking her coffee. Laura sat down to breakfast without her. She'd be along, but when it got to be

10:00 a.m. and there was still no sign of her, Laura began to get nervous. Maybe she was having one of her crying spells.

After checking with the maid, who hadn't seen her, Laura decided to go to her bedroom as she'd done once before. This time when she walked in, she found Chantelle in her swimsuit and beach robe, but she was lying across the bed, white-faced.

Alarmed, Laura leaned over her. "Chantelle? Are you having another migraine?"

"Yes. I've taken my prescription for it. Give me another half hour and it will pass."

A cold hand squeezed her heart. This was the second attack since Laura had been in Cap Ferrat. "Can I get you an ice pack?"

"It doesn't help. All I need is quiet and no light."

"Then I'll go." Laura felt horrible she'd disturbed her.

Guy phoned. He always did this time of day to see if his wife needed anything. When Laura picked up and told him about her headache, he said he was coming home from the office. The poor thing couldn't get any work done while Chantelle was like this.

By the time he arrived, Laura had showered and dressed for the day in a plum colored skirt with a matching print top. She'd arranged her hair in a French twist at the back of her head secured with a tortoiseshell comb.

Since Guy had come home, she told him she would ask Pierre to drive her into Nice to pick up some of

Chantelle's favorite chocolate truffles. His wife loved one in the afternoon with a cup of coffee.

Guy told her to take as long as she wanted. He wasn't going anywhere. Raoul had returned from Switzerland and would be handling everything at the office until further notice.

Her pulse raced just hearing that unexpected news. Without wasting any time, she left the villa. Pierre knew exactly where to go in Nice. Within a half hour she'd made her purchase, but when he asked her if she was ready to return to the villa, she said no. In the next breath she told him to drive her to Laroche headquarters and asked if he would wait for her.

After Pierre pulled up in front, she climbed out and rushed inside the luxurious office building located outside the old part of the city. The security guard near the elevators told her she wouldn't be able to see Monsieur Laroche without an appointment.

"Please ring and tell him it's Mrs. Aldridge on an urgent matter."

He did her bidding, then told her to wait. After he'd made the call, his attitude changed. Suddenly he apologized all over the place, offering her his seat and a drink if she'd like one. She shook her head.

Whatever Raoul had said had lit a fire under him. It had the effect of a soothing balm because she hadn't known what kind of reception she would get. Raoul ran hot and cold depending on his mood and the situation at the moment. Evidently, he didn't want her going up to his office suite, so she had no choice but to wait.

"Laura?" sounded that deep husky voice she'd missed so horribly. She whirled around to discover Raoul striding up to her dressed in a midnight-blue suit and dazzling white shirt with a monogrammed tie. He was too attractive. She could hardly breathe.

He'd come down a private elevator further along the hall. She could tell because there weren't any buttons. You had to use a specially coded card key made for a select few.

His eyes played everywhere, setting her on fire. She could hear it crackling, could feel the tremendous rise in temperature heating her body.

"I…I hope you don't mind me bothering you here at work, especially when Guy said you just flew in, but this is vital."

Something in her demeanor must have told him she wasn't kidding because his expression grew solemn. "How did you get here?"

"With Pierre. He's out in front."

She heard his sharp intake of breath. "Let's go."

He didn't touch her, but she sensed he wanted to. Whatever black mood he'd been in a week ago seemed to have dissipated. With the sparks they were setting off right now, the slightest provocation made them combustible.

She noticed he sat opposite her once they were enclosed inside the limo, as if he didn't trust himself to be next to her. It was just as well since she didn't trust herself. He signaled to Pierre to take them home, but she shook her head.

"I have to talk to you first. Ask him to wait."

"What's this all about? I thought you made a commitment to Chantelle to stay."

Where had that come from? A fierce look had taken hold of his features. Could she hope that she'd grown on him enough that he couldn't tolerate the idea of her leaving?

She wasn't talking about their physical chemistry, which was so powerful she quaked with yearning if she allowed herself to remember that night at his villa. She was thinking of emotions that drove two people together and kept them that way for a lifetime because they didn't need anyone else to complete them.

Guy and Chantelle were the perfect example of what she was talking about. On a moment's notice he'd left work to be at her side, even if she pretended she didn't want him there, because he loved her. It was because of that love Laura couldn't live with her secret any longer.

She'd promised Chantelle she wouldn't tell anyone, but she had wrestled with her conscience long enough and had to break her silence, for everyone's sake.

"This isn't about me. Chantelle's home with a migraine."

A bleakness entered his eyes. "I know. Guy said he was going home to be there for her. She gets them on occasion."

Laura had never prayed harder in her life that she was doing the right thing. "I know why she gets them, Raoul. I know everything."

A stillness invaded the car's interior. A grim expression crossed over his striking features. "You know the reason for her behavior since the accident?" he whispered in shock.

Laura nodded. "Last week I found her sobbing. She lay across her bed like a forlorn little doll, white as her sheets. She told me to leave, but I insisted on staying until she admitted what was going on. That's when it all came out.

"After she was taken to the hospital following her car accident, she found out she had an inoperable brain tumor and was given less than a year to live."

"What?" Raoul looked as if he'd just heard that life as they knew it was about to be obliterated.

She swallowed hard. "It's taken me time to comprehend what she told me, so I can only imagine what you're feeling right now. It isn't fair what's happened to her, but then life really isn't fair." Her voice shook.

"Start from the beginning," he demanded through lips that looked as chiseled as the rest of his features.

"Though she didn't tell me, she must have sworn the doctors to secrecy. After being utterly devastated by the news, she came up with the idea to push Guy—all of you—away, in order to prepare you for her death.

"Her migraines are purely stress related because of the secret she's been holding back." For the next few minutes Laura told him everything she knew and remembered of their conversation.

When she'd finished, Raoul's mouth had gone white around the edges. His black eyes impaled her. "It's been a whole week. You should have come to me the moment you knew."

"She swore me to secrecy, Raoul, and she trusts me. If you only knew how I've been struggling ever since. You know how deeply I care for her. I couldn't stand it if I lost the trust she has in me. But in the end I couldn't keep it in. That's why I finally came to you."

"To lie to this degree…" He bit out and shook his dark head. "Chantelle couldn't possibly love Guy the way I thought she did—the way *he* thought she did.

"For over three months she's caused excruciating pain to her own husband, to her son. To me," he said scathingly. "This news will destroy my brother. What kind of woman does that to a man?"

"Don't," Laura begged him. "You couldn't begin to know what frame of mind she was in after the accident. She was still in shock when they told her." Laura leaned across to put a hand on his forearm It was hard as steel. There was no give, even with her entreating him.

"Raoul," she said softly. Seeing him in so much pain was devastating.

He ignored her entreaty and pulled out his phone. After he told the driver to take them home, he lay back against the seat with his eyes closed, his pallor unmistakable. They didn't talk the rest of the way.

The minute Pierre stopped the limo, Raoul hurried inside the villa with her. Laura didn't know how he was going to broach the subject to his brother, but she was terrified.

Her heart sank when one of the maids saw them in the foyer and came over to Raoul. She explained that

Guy had taken Madame to the hospital because the pain had gotten worse. Paul was at Giles's house.

"You go," Laura cried as he turned to her. "She needs her family." What if the end was coming sooner than the doctor thought? "If Paul should phone, I'll tell him."

He nodded grim-faced and rushed out of the villa.

"Guy?" Raoul whispered. "While Chantelle's still asleep, we need to talk. Come out in the hall with me."

He shook his head. "I don't want to leave her."

Since the conversation in the limo with Laura, Raoul was alive with grief and rage. The morphine cocktail drip helping Chantelle to recover from this latest migraine brought home the reality of her true condition. Seeing her stretched out on the examining table, helpless, was killing him.

In the two hours he'd been at the hospital with his brother, the color had returned to her cheeks. Both he and Guy breathed easier because of it, but Raoul didn't want to wait any longer to tell him the brutal truth.

With reluctance Guy got up from the chair and followed Raoul to the reception area outside the E.R. where half a dozen people were sitting around waiting. Raoul purposely walked him down a corridor. When he found an empty examining room, he pulled him inside and shut the door.

"Sit down, Guy. I have something to tell you."

"I can't sit."

He eyed his brother soulfully. "You're going to need to."

Guy's face went ashen before he did Raoul's bidding.

"I know the reason for the drastic change in Chantelle."

His eyes widened. "She told Laura?" Lines of exhaustion from worry made him seem older.

This was the hardest thing Raoul had ever had to do in his life. "Yes. I just came from talking to her. There's no easy way to say this, so I'm just going to go ahead. Chantelle is dying of an inoperable brain tumor."

By now Raoul would have told Guy the heartbreaking news. Since Laura couldn't do anything for anyone, she decided to fly to Marseille and take a tourist boat out from the port to the Château d'If a mile away. This was one time when she needed to get away from the villa. Guy had told Laura to use the helicopter anytime she wanted. It was at her disposal.

Armed with a couple of new sketchpads and pencils, she embarked on her journey. She needed to immerse herself in work for a few hours to deal with the pain.

Dumas had made the fortress famous in his novel of *The Count of Monte Cristo,* which Laura had read years earlier. According to Chantelle, it was a square, three-story castle built by François I in the early 1500s. The perfect kind of setting for a videogame.

Her drawing ended up taking the whole afternoon. There was one more level of the castle to go before she went back to the mainland.

Despite the tourists milling around, Laura had managed to fill a sketchpad already. The guide at the château had explained that the former prisoners were treated differently depending on their wealth and social class. Edmond Dantes, the prisoner in Dumas's novel, had been incarcerated at the bottom of the dungeon below the waterline. No windows, no amenities.

Wealthier inmates, on the second level, had their own private cells. Each level was different enough to make up a unique game. The top of the castle had been built for prisoners who had outside help to pay for the privilege. There were windows, a fireplace and a garde-robe. The whole château was a natural. Once a player mastered the dungeon level, he could move on up to the second level and then the third.

Deep in concentration on the last page of her drawings, she was scarcely aware of the activity going on around her. "Didn't you hear the guide?" a man said near her ear. "They're closing for the day."

The sound of his voice was so familiar to her, it caused her to drop her sketchpad. Raoul picked it up before she could and looked through it. "The same quality, the same verve," he muttered.

"Thank you." The words came out close to a whisper because she was so amazed to see him here. He'd been on her mind continually. If he'd already told Guy, she couldn't tell. In the dim light his eyes had never looked so jet-black.

"The pilot's waiting to fly us back. Let's go."

She put her sketchpad in her tote bag and followed him down the ancient stone stairs to the entrance. They took the tender back to the mainland. Within a half hour they'd landed on the estate, where the limo was waiting. Raoul told the driver to drop them off at his villa.

All the while she'd had to contain her misery while she waited to hear the worst. When he ushered her inside his living room, she couldn't stand it any longer and wheeled around. "If you don't tell me what's happened, I don't think I can stand it."

He removed his suit jacket and tie before standing in front of her. "As we speak, Guy, Chantelle and Paul are at the hospital in a private room while she's still re- covering from her migraine."

The tears she'd been fighting gushed down her cheeks. "It must be so awful, I can't bear it."

"You could say Guy came close to losing it when he demanded to meet with all her doctors. Then a strange thing happened." He cocked his head. "They all denied she had a brain tumor. To prove it, they did another MRI on her. It only took ten minutes. They found nothing on her brain of any kind."

"What did you say?" Laura cried.

"When Chantelle awakened from the medication, they asked where she had got the idea she was dying. She told them exactly what she told you. So they called in the attending E.R. physician who was on call the day of her accident. It appears that while she was lying there, she overheard him talking to another doctor about another patient who'd been brought in."

"You mean Chantelle's not dying?" Her voice sound more like a shriek.

He shook his head. "She's in perfect health."

"Oh, Raoul, thank God!" She flew toward him and threw her arms around him, sobbing. She must have hugged him for ten minutes.

"Thank God," he eventually said in a gravelly voice, but something was missing. Where was his joy?

She didn't understand and eased out of his arms to look at him.

What she saw in his expression alarmed her. She knew he was exhausted from his business trip. Coupled with his agony over Chantelle, he looked dissipated, though she knew he wasn't. Even in this state he was devastatingly attractive, but he was definitely behaving strangely.

Her anxiety was at a pitch. She searched for a reason. "Can't Guy forgive her?" she cried.

Raoul stood planted there as still as a piece of driftwood left high and dry on a lonely beach.

"I have absolutely no idea, but I do know this. If Chantelle were my wife, I couldn't forgive her." Suddenly his eyes pierced hers like lasers. "I'm convinced there's no such thing as an honest woman."

His words sounded the death knell to their tender relationship.

Raoul couldn't forgive Laura for keeping Chantelle's secret from everyone for a whole week. He might as well have said, "Get out of my sight and never come back."

Her body shrank from the knowledge. She turned away from him and ran out of the villa. As soon as she could pack her things, Raoul would get his wish.

CHAPTER NINE

THE judge adjusted his bifocals. This was it. Laura held her breath while her attorney squeezed her arm to give her courage. He read:

> "In the matter of *Stillman v. Stillman,* the case brought before the Court of Santa Barbara in the County of Santa Barbara, California, the Court has read the petition for divorce on the grounds of incompatibility and finds all documentation in order. Therefore a decree of divorce between Laurel Aldridge and Theodore Stillman has been granted on this fifteenth day of August.

"Counselors will get together on your own time to agree on disbursement of monies and property." He pounded his gavel. "Court adjourned." The judge stood up and left the room.

Laura swung around and hugged her attorney. "Thank you. You'll never know how I've longed for this day."

He smiled. "By keeping a low profile all these

months, there was nothing your ex could find on you to try and prolong your case. Without children involved, I was able to get the earliest court date for you."

"I'm aware of all you've done for me and can never thank you enough."

"Do you know what I admire about you most, Laura? Besides refusing all money or property, you refused to charge him with adultery. One day when he's a congressman, he'll thank you for not dragging his name through the mud. His public record will remain clean. The man's luckier than he knows."

"He doesn't believe that, but whatever he thinks, it doesn't matter. It's over. Thank you again for helping me believe this day was going to come."

"It's been my pleasure. Come on. I'll walk you out."

She held on to his arm, leaving Ted and his brothers glaring at her from the other side of the aisle. She couldn't figure out why. He was free to find a new trophy wife. One who wanted it all, too.

Cindy stood waiting outside the doors of the courtroom. The minute Laura saw her she hugged her for a long time. "I'm finally free." The tears rolled down her cheeks.

"Where do you want to celebrate before I have to get back to work? Name it. It's my treat today."

Laura eased away from her and wiped her eyes. "Thanks, Cindy. How about we meet for a hamburger at the Z-Top."

"You're on, let's go."

It didn't take long to reach their rendezvous point. Once they were served, Cindy smiled at her. "Are you officially Ms. Aldridge again?"

Laura nodded. "That was part of what was included in the decree. My whole life's going to change, not having to answer to Mrs. Stillman anymore."

"Today you're no longer a celebrity."

"Nope. Just me, thank heaven. For the last year I've envied you being free. Now I don't have to look over my shoulder every minute. I can't believe that when I go home, I don't have to worry about Ted barging in on me or phoning me at odd hours. I'm my own person, just like I used to be."

"Not quite your own person," Cindy said cryptically.

She stopped munching. "What do you mean?"

Cindy gave her that knowing look. "Raoul, of course. Ever since you flew home from Cap Ferrat you haven't been yourself. Knowing you as I do, I'd say you're emotionally drained. You've lost weight you know."

"After living at Guy's house with that cook of theirs, I needed to shed five pounds."

"Lie to anyone else, but not me. I feel responsible for having given you the wrong advice."

"But you didn't!" Laura assured her. "You posed a question I had to answer to my own satisfaction. How could you possibly be blamed for that? If I'd never phoned you, I still would have done exactly what I did. When you make a promise to someone as serious as the one I made to Chantelle, you don't break it without a darn good reason. I needed that week Raoul was gone to be certain."

"That's what makes you my best friend."

"Thanks for that, Cindy." She smoothed the hair away from her temple. "Raoul despised me for not telling him everything the second Chantelle broke down and revealed what was really going on.

"You know that old adage about the third time being the charm. Raoul's wife lied to him, couple that with the information I held back from him. Add to that Chantelle's betrayal. It was the last straw for a man whose psyche is already very dark and complicated.

"During the time I was there we'd talk for a little bit, then he'd close up. It was inch by inch all the time. I still don't know that much about him. A man who can't communicate his deepest feelings isn't capable of having a relationship, sustained or otherwise. Raoul's one man who travels alone. That much I learned." As she spoke Laura felt a sharp pain deep in her heart at the thought of what might have been.

"I'm sorry," her friend whispered.

"So am I, but there's not a thing I can do about it. When I was at his villa, I saw these pictures of him and Guy when they were little. They both looked so happy. It's terrible to think a bad marriage can change a person that drastically.

"Once in a while I saw glimpses of another Raoul with no shadows. The only time we really communicated—" She got the pain in her chest again and couldn't go on. "You know."

"Yup. When it was good, it was very good," Cindy murmured. "That's the part I'm waiting for with Sam." Sam was Cindy's new love interest, and it had taken a while for the woman to move on after her bitter divorce, but it seemed things were finally looking up for her. Laura was delighted.

"At least you two are really talking now. Sharing. I'm envious." When it got bad with Raoul, it was the end of Laura's world. She shook her head. "I've got to stop this."

"Want to go to a film tonight? Eight o'clockish?"

"I was just going to suggest it. Tomorrow my life-guarding won't start till noon so I can sleep in."

"Lucky you."

"Speaking of luck, Carl said my sketches of the Chateau d'If won me a week's vacation even though I already took extra time off in Cap Ferrat. Want to fly down to Mexico with me in September? I'm going to do some sketches of pyramids and temples while I'm there."

"Ohh. I'd love to see them. Let me talk dates with my boss and I'll get back to you."

"Good. We'll get one of those inexpensive package that won't set us back too much." She checked her watch. "I've got to get going."

"So do I."

Laura started to put some money down, but Cindy stopped her. "I'm paying this time, remember? How often does a red-letter day like this come along?"

Hopefully never, since it implied having lived through another ghastly marriage. Laura had no intention of making that mistake again. The only man she wanted had a view on marriage that guaranteed he'd never repeat the experience, either.

With another merger successfully pulled off, Raoul left the Credit Suisse Banque and told the limo driver to take him to his apartment on the Boulevard General Guisan in Lausanne. He pealed off his suit jacket and tie. By the time he'd taken the private elevator to his penthouse overlooking Lake Geneva, he'd broken out in a cold sweat. It had soaked most of his shirt. He began unbuttoning it.

There was no point in lying to himself. He was in a depression nothing pulled him out of anymore. Since his marriage to Danielle had fallen apart, work had been his savior. Now not even another business transaction guaranteeing the Laroche Corporation would remain in the black for years to come brought him any pleasure. The realization that nothing seemed to matter disturbed him to a frightening level.

He needed a shower and a drink, not necessarily in that order. Tossing his clothes on the nearest chair, he headed for the liquor cabinet and almost stumbled over the pile of unread newspapers that had fallen out of the basket.

"*Bonsoir,* Raoul."

His head reared back before he came to a standstill. Chantelle—

She was sitting in the middle of his couch looking better than he'd ever seen her, wearing an all-black cocktail dress with spaghetti straps. When she dressed for the kill, no one did it with more elegance. Her arms were outstretched on the back of the couch. She'd crossed her legs and was swinging one foot up and down, drawing his attention to her black high heels. She'd cut her hair in a short, becoming style that framed her face.

"Guy and Paul are meeting us here in fifteen minutes for dinner, so you and I don't have a lot of time."

"For what? I didn't invite you here."

She looked around. "The place is a mess. Marie told

me you let her go until further notice. That didn't sound good." Her gaze came back to him. She stared without blinking. "Go ahead and get it off your chest. Tell me I'm the most evil, vile creature who ever climbed out from under a rock. Say it! 'You're less than a human being, Chantelle! You're not fit to breathe the same air as your husband and son!'

"I disagree of course. You can take it up with the Almighty when you get there. From the looks of the way your suit hangs on you, you're fading fast and it won't be long.

"One of your problems is, you never knew a love like mine and Guy's. He understood the second I told him. He forgave me because that's what real love is all about. After we made love, he admitted he would have done the same thing I did if our positions had been reversed. Remember something else. I never pushed our son away.

"Hearing that I was going to die—that I would be leaving Guy—was like a knife cutting the heart out of my body. It was either lie to him or ruin every day of his life sobbing in his arms. I could be much braver at a distance.

"I don't expect you to understand me. I don't expect you to like me, even if I adore you. What I do expect is that you come home. Of course, if there's a reason you can't because you're dying from some incurable disease you picked up rather recently and are too terrified to talk about, then who better than me to use for a sounding board. I've been there.

"Laura forgave me and wished me happiness. Before

she went back to California, she left me a letter with a box of my favorite truffles. It said that after seeing Guy and me together, she realized a great love like ours only comes along once in life and she understood why I tried to make my passing easier on my loved ones.

"I sent her a letter back telling her I forgave her for breaking her promise. I should have known she was so crazy in love with you she couldn't keep anything from you. Guy has always called her an angel. I believe she is. There's no guile in Laura. Beneath that gorgeous exterior, she's good clear through."

Raoul heard a sound behind him. When he jerked his head around, Guy was walking toward him with Paul. They'd never looked happier in their lives.

His nephew eyed him up and down. "I hate to say it Uncle Raoul, but *Maman* was right. You need help."

Guy smiled. "You do."

Laura put on some more sunscreen. She'd been sitting on the tower for the last hour. Four in the afternoon was the hottest time and the busiest. The last week of August was the best season of the year for tourists and locals to hit the beach.

From her perch she saw every sight imaginable. Lots of couples, some holding hands, others playing around throwing each other in the surf. Kids buried up to their necks in sand. Runners splashing in the water, teens playing volley ball. Life.

Her body gave a little heave of longing. To ward off the ache, she lifted the binoculars to her eyes. In her view she counted eighteen swimmers in the water. The surf was crumbly and didn't hang well. Not much wave to catch at the moment.

Five surfers eventually made their way back in on their boards and didn't go out again. Three kids on tubes moved further down the beach to the jurisdiction of the next lifeguard. Four guys in black wetsuits body surfed for ten minutes, then came in to play with a Frisbee. That left six people in the water. Two people wore life preservers. The other four were waiting to catch a big wave. They would have to be patient.

Finally one started to form way out. She could hear their shouts as they got ready to ride it. At first she counted four heads being swept in, coming closer, then there were three. The other swimmer had gotten pulled under. She waited for him to pop up again. When he did, she sensed he was in trouble. His head was back and his arms lifted in the air.

She removed her binoculars, jumped down from the tower and raced into the water at full speed, passing the other swimmers like a torpedo. If he'd taken in too much water, she'd have him back to shore and resuscitated before he suffocated.

When she was within five feet of him, he slid beneath the water. She immediately did a somersault that propelled her under him so she could get the hold on him to bring him up.

He was a strong, hard-muscled male with a powerful physique, reminding her of Raoul. With his black hair, he could almost be the man whose memory had tortured her day and night.

When they broke water, she began the side crawl

to bring him in, but he fought her. Sometimes a drowning victim panicked and didn't understand they needed to cooperate.

"Lie still and let me help you," she called out, but he struggled harder than anyone she'd ever saved. She feared she might not be able to do this alone. Frantic at this point, she kicked harder, trying to build momentum until he stopped resisting her. Hopefully someone on the beach realized what was happening and would bring help.

"Come on—let me do all the work," she cried in desperation. They were only halfway to shore now. Though it was a short distance, it seemed like miles. Then everything changed. Suddenly the man escaped her hold and she became his victim. With tremendous energy, he got her in the same grip she'd put on him and they headed full force for shore.

In the next breath he carried her to the beach and sank to his knees before laying her down. She felt his hands cup her face. She knew those hands and that body. Opening her eyes, she was met by a pair of piercing black ones.

"Raoul—"

"Don't talk, Laura," he whispered. "I'm about to give you the kiss of life. If you fight me, everyone on the beach will know it."

In her whole life, she'd never had to be saved, but if she *had* been drowning, her shock wouldn't have been as great as it was now.

He covered her mouth in an all-encompassing kiss that went on and on. For propriety's sake he couldn't touch her. His mouth had to make all the contact. Her senses responded, screaming for satisfaction only he could give.

When she didn't think she could stand it any longer if he didn't crush her beneath him, he relinquished her mouth with reluctance and sat back. "How are you feeling now?" he asked in a husky voice.

She was too dazed, and he was too gorgeous. A crowd had gathered round. She would have to tough her way out of this one.

Flashing everyone a smile, she rolled onto her side and got up, wiping the sand off her thighs. "Everything's under control," she told them. By now a leaner Raoul than she remembered had gotten to his feet, all six foot three of him. "Go on, everyone. Do what you were doing."

With smiles, the group dispersed little by little.

Raoul stared at her. "I for one intend to go on doing what I was doing with you. But not here. I arranged for another lifeguard to relieve you."

She looked over at the tower. Sure enough Mike Segal was there with a grin on his bronzed face. He waved and tossed her the beach bag that held all her essentials. Raoul caught it.

"My car's out in the parking lot by yours," he murmured. "Shall we leave yours here, or do you think you're recovered enough from your near drowning to drive and I'll follow you to your apartment."

She stared boldly at him. "It's the kiss of life that's made me so unstable."

"Let's go home and talk about it."

Laura started to tremble. "I don't want to talk. We always get in a fight."

His expression grew solemn. "I swear I won't let that happen."

"Raoul—" She couldn't take it again if they had words and he walked away.

"I came as soon as I could. You probably need your sandals." He handed her the bag.

She took it from him and pulled them out, but her gestures were all done in slow motion. This really wasn't happening. Raoul wasn't really here. She'd gotten too much sun and was hallucinating.

As she bent over, she reeled. He caught her against him and braced her body until she'd put them on. His lips brushed against her neck. "You feel so good I don't think I can walk, either."

"We have to!"

"Shall I carry you?"

"No!"

"We'll help each other."

Instead of two people who didn't like each other anymore, they put their arms around each other and slowly walked to the parking lot behind the palm trees bordering the sand.

He opened her car door and helped her in. "Please don't kiss me," she cried.

Without saying anything, he closed the door. She didn't mean it. The lazy smile he gave her let her know she didn't.

Still in a daze she watched him walk over to his rental car. He must have hidden the keys beneath the front mat. Still trembling, she rummaged for her keys and started the car.

Her apartment was only a mile and a half away. She pulled into her stall, then got out with her bag and signaled for him to park in the guest stall. With a suitcase in hand, he strode toward her. With every step her heart hammered harder.

He followed her inside the hallway. As soon as she opened her door, she said, "Make yourself at home. You can have the shower first. The bathroom is the first door on the left down the hall past the living room."

Afraid to look at him, she took off for the other part of the building. She needed time to absorb the fact that he'd flown to California to see her. After their last parting in his living room when she'd rushed toward Guy's villa, she was positive she would never see him again.

Laura gave him ten minutes before she returned and found him in the living room on the couch, looking at one of her video game magazines. He'd dressed in tan trousers and a coffee-colored silk shirt. Everything he wore looked fabulous because he was such a striking man.

"I'll be with you in a few minutes."

He lifted his head and eyed her thoroughly. "Take your time. I'm not going anywhere."

Laura showered in record time, then put on a pale-orange sundress with a little white jacket trimmed in orange plaid. She'd washed her hair. After blow-drying it, she fastened it back in a French twist. Slipping into white sandals, she made her way to the kitchen.

"What can I get you?" she called to him.

"Water will do."

"One water coming up."

She grabbed two of them and walked into the other room. Afraid to get close to him, she placed his water on the coffee table before subsiding into one of the chairs opposite him.

Their eyes met. "You realize I'm never going to live this down with my colleagues."

He leaned forward to get his bottle. "It's past time someone did a favor for the lifeguard who has done at least five hundred saves by now."

"You read about that, too?" She unscrewed the lid of her bottle and took a long swig.

"Since Guy invited a Mrs. Aldridge into his home, I haven't been able to satisfy my curiosity enough about her."

"Is that why you're here?"

"No. I've come for an entirely different reason."

She pressed her lips together. "How's your family?"

He cocked his dark head. "Happier than I've seen them in years. Because of you, Guy and Chantelle are on a second honeymoon in Turkey with Paul."

Tears sprang to her eyes. "That's the best news I could ever hear. Though I realize what it has cost you to let me know, I thank you."

An odd sound came from his throat. "If you hadn't found the courage to force Chantelle to tell you why she was crying that day, we might all still be in the dark and suffering."

She swallowed hard. "You didn't feel that way about me the last time we were together. I realize that in keeping the truth from you about Chantelle as long as I did, it was the coup de grâce for you."

"My behavior was inhuman," he exclaimed in a voice of self-abnegation. "You have every right to tell me to get out and never come back. Why do you think I pretended to be drowning? It was the only method I could think of that might give me the upper hand long enough to beg your forgiveness."

"That was very clever of you, but then I'd expect nothing less from Raoul Laroche. You make a powerful lifeguard yourself. Anytime you want a job, I'll put in a good word for you with my boss."

"What do I have to do to get in good with you?" The velvety question resonated to her bones. When she looked in his eyes, they looked suspiciously moist.

She fidgeted on the chair. "Since you continually find another reason to see me as the enemy, I don't know what to say. Do you realize we've never lasted more than a couple of hours without you throwing your darts at me?"

His expression grew bleak. "It began with Danielle. I've already told you a little about her, but not nearly enough. When I married her it was with the idea that we'd start a family right away. She *knew* how much I wanted to have children. After Paul was born, Chantelle couldn't conceive again because she went through early menopause."

"The poor thing," Laura moaned. "I've often wondered why they never had another baby when Paul is so wonderful. It's sad."

Raoul got to his feet with restless energy. "After two

years of marriage without results we consulted Danielle's OB. He said to keep trying because he could find nothing wrong with either of us. If she didn't conceive within six months, he'd refer us to the fertility clinic.

"After four years I was ready to try in vitro, but Danielle fought me. At first I couldn't believe it. When I talked to Chantelle about it, she said she had the strongest suspicion my wife had been lying to me about wanting children.

"Once that seed was sown in my mind, I confronted Danielle. It was a nightmarish scene I wouldn't have an enemy live through. The moment she cowered from me, I *knew*. When she realized she was caught, it all came out. She'd been on the pill long before our marriage took place and had never stopped taking them."

Laura shook her head. "Why?"

"She said we had the perfect marriage without children. She had friends whose marriages had failed because of children. Danielle didn't want that to happen to us."

A cry escaped Laura's throat. "I don't know how a woman could be that cruel. A lie like that would have turned me inside out, too, Raoul. I'm so sorry." It explained why he'd been so horrified over Chantelle's lie. "She had no right to do what she did."

"Danielle was too narcissistic to think beyond her own view of life."

"No wonder you lost your trust. Four years wasted when you could have divorced and married someone else who wanted children."

He rubbed the back of his neck absently. "At least when you went into your marriage, you and your husband both knew that you didn't want children."

Laura jumped out of the chair. "You're mistaken about that, Raoul," she cried. "I've always wanted children. Little Paulie made me want them more than ever. But soon after I married Ted, I fell out of love with him. There was no way I would bring a baby into a loveless marriage. It deserves the love of two parents who are madly in love with each other, like Chantelle and Guy."

Raoul looked stunned. "Is Ted still fighting your divorce?" he asked with new urgency.

"No. I won my divorce decree last week, August 15 to be exact."

A noticeable pallor appeared. "You mean you're free and clear of him?"

"Yes. I even had my name legally changed back to Aldridge. After Guy asked me if I would try to befriend Chantelle, it turned out to be an added blessing for me because Ted didn't know where I was.

"He broke into this apartment while I was away, and my friend Cindy across the hall documented it for me so I could take it to court. Because he ignored the restraining order and harassed me at my jobs, the judge granted the divorce without a problem." Her voice shook. "It was nice to know not everyone was in lockstep with the Stillmans."

"Laura—"

"Yes?" Her pulse was skidding off the charts.

"Do you want to have a baby with me?"

"Yes." She didn't have to think.

He blinked. "You just said yes."

She nodded. "I'm in love with you."

"That's what Chantelle said, but you couldn't be—"

"You mean after all the terrible things you've said and done to me?"

"I treated you so abominably, you have every right to throw me out."

"True, you have, but when you love someone the way I love you, you can forgive them anything."

"*When* did you know?" Now he was the one trembling.

"Well, it was lust at first sight in Guy's living room the night of his party and went downhill from there. I saw Mr. Adonis staring daggers at me. He was standing there with Maurice. I said to myself, 'I don't know how I'm going to do it, but I want to belong to that man forever.' And that was before I even knew if you were available or not."

He moved closer. His incredible black eyes were smiling. She'd only seen them do that a couple of times.

"It's your turn to tell me what I'm dying to hear." She smiled back at him. "But I'll let you off the hook. I don't think you can even say the words yet. It doesn't matter. I know what I feel. Anytime you want to get married, just tell me. I've been practicing writing my name in my sketchpad like all silly girls in love."

She walked over to the desk where it was lying and handed it to him. "Here. Take a look."

His breathing shallow, Raoul lifted the cover. She'd filled the first page with twenty lines of script. All said something different. "Madame Raoul Laroche." "Madame Laurel Aldridge Laroche." "Monsieur et Madame Laroche." "Madelaine Laroche."

He darted her a glance. "Madelaine? That was my maternal grandmother's name."

"Chantelle told me. That's if we have a girl. If we have a boy first, then we need to think of something very special because he'll have such a special father."

Raoul put the pad down before pulling her into his arms. He rocked her for a long time. In his arms she felt she'd come home at last.

"I've been staying at my apartment in Switzerland since the day you flew here. Day before yesterday I walked in after work and realized that a life without you wasn't a life at all. I no longer cared if you didn't want children. As long as you loved me and only me, I'd deal with it.

"Make no mistake, Laura. I'm in love with you. You have to marry me soon. We're so good together."

"And so bad apart," she whispered against his lips before devouring them.

"You're so good." He ran his hands up and down her arms. "Guy saw the sweetness in you before he ever brought you into his home. The whole family loves you. I adore you." He kissed her fingertips.

"I love them." She slid her arms around his neck. "Kiss me, darling," her green eyes implored him. "Bring me back to life again."

Raoul needed no urging because she *was* his life.

COMING SOON!

LET'S TALK
Romance

For exclusive extracts, competitions
and special offers, find us online:

f facebook.com/millsandboon

◎ @millsandboonuk

🐦 @millsandboon

Or get in touch on 0844 844 1351*

For all the latest titles coming soon, visit
millsandboon.co.uk/nextmonth